I0779134

KREVAX

THE NOSTALIEM TRILOGY

THE NOSTALIEM TRILOGY

In reading order:

Krevax

Dust

(Coming: July 2026)

KREVAX
THE NOSTALIEM TRILOGY

L. C. WALTERS

WICKED INK
PUBLISHING

Krevax (The Nostaliem Trilogy) : Book 1
Copyright © 2025 by L.C. Walters

Published by Wicked Ink Publishing Ltd.
www.wickedinkpublishing.com

Cover and book design © 2025 by Wicked Ink Publishing Ltd.
Editors: Raymond Griffiths & Adam Bamford

First Edition: July 2025
Printed in Canada

Library and Archives Canada Cataloguing in Publication

Title: Krevax / L.C. Walters.
Names: Walters, L. C., author.
Description: Series statement: The nostaliem trilogy ; 1
Identifiers: Canadiana (print) 20250221276
Canadiana (ebook) 2025022688X
ISBN 9781998278114 (softcover)
ISBN 9781998278121 (EPUB)
Subjects: LCGFT: Science fiction. | LCGFT: Dystopian fiction. | LCGFT: Novels.
Classification: LCC PS8645.A492 K74 2025 | DDC C813/.6—dc23

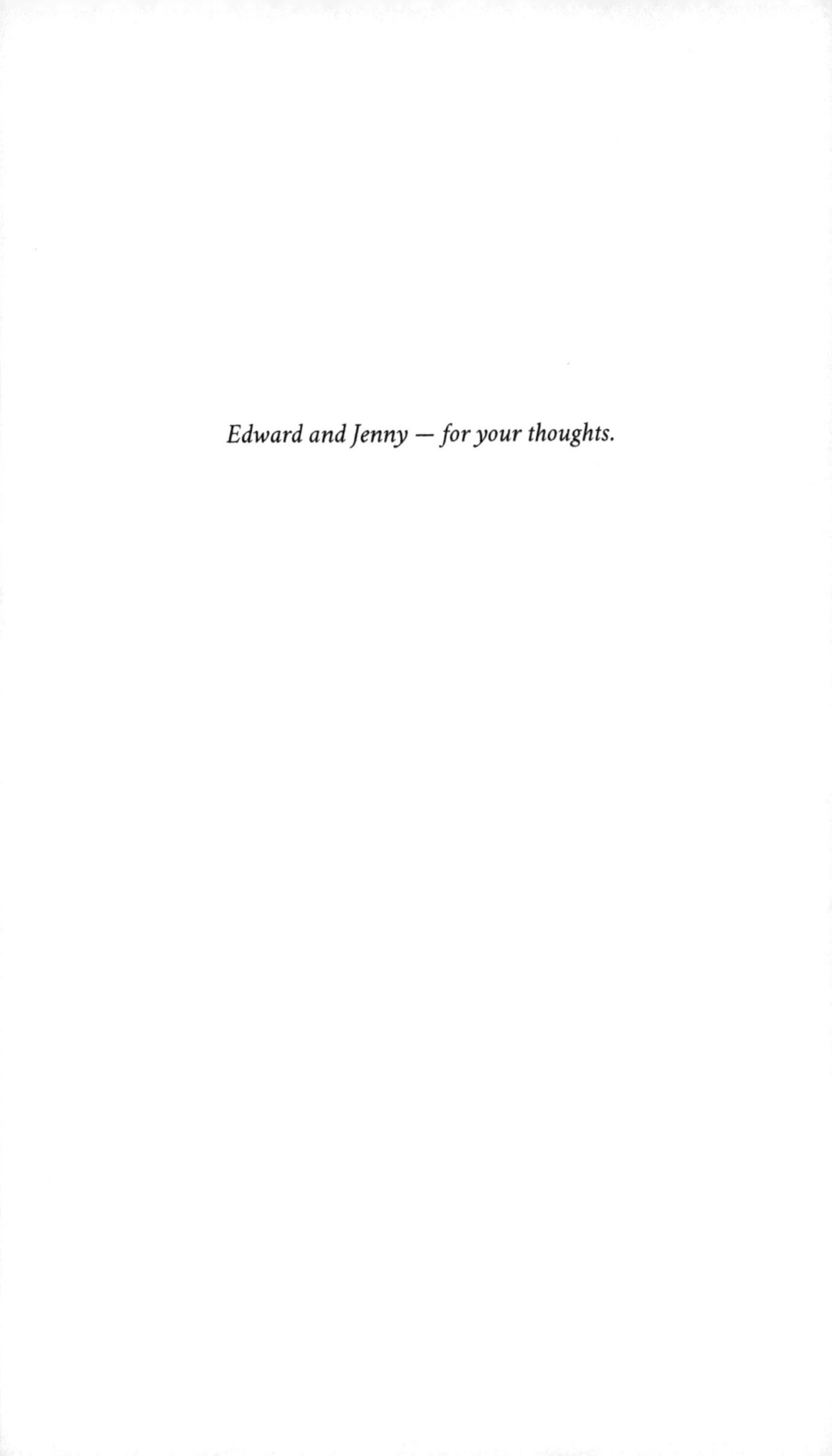

Edward and Jenny — for your thoughts.

Where dreams come at a price,
and every step is a fight for freedom.

KREVAX

THE NOSTALIEM TRILOGY

01 | NIGHTMARES
BLACKWELL

Despite the hour, the constant roar of the Manufacturing District pours into Charlie Blackwell's apartment. Inside, the empty white walls stand as shrines to his unspoken loneliness, offering no comfort as he once again suffered through an endless bout of insomnia.

On one side, a single mattress sits with a matching sheet, on the other an open closet with seven black and red striped uniforms. The clock above his bed ticks 3:27 AM. He glances up at it with angry, hooded eyes. *Shit.*

Blood courses through his sinewy muscles as he forces himself to do one more push up. With each exhale, the weight of the day lessens, but it's never enough. Shaking his head of black curls, exhausted, he feels the sweat drip down his forehead.

Lying on the cold concrete floor, he slows his breath. For a moment he imagines it stopping all together. *I wish I could float away from this place, be nothing, unaware, unburdened, dead.*

The chemical and smoke-laden air stings his throat, forcing him back into his body. He looks up through the large window, above at the thousands of glowing advertisements which flood in and illuminate his bronze-brown skin.

Waiting for the switch, he stares for a moment, his expression stained by sadness.

Click.

The advertisements switch for the upcoming day, and he zooms through the new images. A moment of satisfaction and then he slips back into his discontent. The looming black-windowed Watchtower in the centre of the district catches his glance. I'm sure no one's watching. He looks away. It's rude to stare at another red stripe in his home.

Looking again back out the window, he observes how the tiger gargoyles glint in the light of the advertisements. Their claws seem to rip out from the turrets, with the flashing from the ceiling dancing on the metal.

A figure in a window seems to move, but it's more neon light playing tricks. Staring at the black glass, he imagines the bored faces of the red stripes behind them. All these power-hungry men with rotten cores, hoping for rebirth. He chuckles at this thought and then feels bitter. Fools.

Why would anyone want to come back here? I wonder if you can actually escape by taking nostaliem? No. I don't believe it. There's nothing left outside this soulless city.

With heavy limbs, he stomps towards his bed and takes off his shorts and tank top. Lying down, the cold presses into his bones. Pulling up the scratchy plastic-based sheet, he resists the urge to itch, instead staying wrapped in its illusion of warmth.

Neon blue light pulses through the window. He glances up at the advertisements, but even when he looks away, he can still feel the light flashing on his skin.

Try the improved Very Berry Blueberry Blast! Extra sweet with a zing of sour!

Closing his eyes, he turns further away from the advertisements, sighing. Very berry blueberry blast. Very berry blueberry blast. Very berry blueberry blast.

Hoping to rid himself of the message, he looks up again, reading an advertisement about *Rufold's Classic Sweet and Salty Potato Paste.*

Stop it. Sleep.

Shutting his eyes with exerted effort, he tries to focus on the darkness. Very Berry Blueberry. No. Inhale. Exhale. Inhale. Exhale. Very berry, very cherry, very strawberry, very raspberry, very berry blueberry.

Stop it! Shut the fuck up. Blast. Blast. Stop thinking. You're pathetic. You're too afraid to recycle yourself and you're too afraid to sleep. Maybe you should take nostaliem, then insanity would free you.

Sleep. Sleep. Very berry blueberry blast.

Charlie, sweet Charlie, wake up, young Charlie, have you considered Offspring?

The bright pink ad behind Very Berry Blueberry Blast whispers. Opening his eyes, he sees a pretty generator smiling with a sleeping newborn baby in her arms. Blackwell closes his eyes again, hoping to shut out the bombardment. The generator's question rings in his head. Have you considered offspring?

An uncomfortable pang hits him. No, I could never have offspring. I would never… in this place.

Closing his eyes harder, he focuses on his breath slowing and his muscles relaxing. Sleep feels so close, if only for a second. Then angry hands grab him, tearing him away as a desperate voice cries out. The screaming fills his head, high-pitched and terrified. Little hands reach out towards a face surrounded by dark red curls. He sits up hyperventilating, his nostrils flaring with each breath. No.

Despite his tired muscles, he climbs out of bed and

returns to his push ups. I won't sleep. The neon advertisements outside his apartment grow brighter, and finally the tracker in his wrist beeps.

Too exhausted to shower, Blackwell dresses in one of his black and red uniforms. Painfully aware of the day ahead of him, he makes his way down 16 floors and out into the unrecycled air of the tenth district.

The smell hits him first, garbage mixed with fuel, piss and chemicals. Crinkling his broad nose, he tries to expel the odour. A yawn makes it halfway out of his mouth before he retches at the taste of rust in the air.

His boots stick to the soiled ground as he weaves through the heaps of discarded items to reach his bike. He swipes his wrist to start the engine. Holding onto the cold metal bars, he shoots off down the road.

As the wind created from the speed tingles his face, he closes his eyes for a moment. What would it be like to have been born on the surface?

To see the sun, feel the rain, and breathe the air, instead of rotting in Krevax. He looks up at the fluorescent advertisements, feeling at first disgusted and then apathetic.

What if I went to the recycling facility instead? He sighs to himself, disappointed, knowing he won't go today. I'll go tomorrow.

A 10-foot hologram follows him as he moves through the streets.

"You are a great people, Krevaxers. Descended from warriors who survived the great famine," the Tzar of Krevax says, grinning with perfect teeth.

"Men who continue to fight for the strength of our industries, from farming the food we eat, to extracting essential minerals and fuels, to manufacturing our essential products. Krevax is full of powerful men who get their way, even when things get tough. Today we celebrate Krevax's

75th birthday!" Seventy-five candles pop up in the background, making the Tzar's hazel eyes twinkle.

"We celebrate its power, its strength, its boldness, we celebrate its men. We celebrate you!" Shaking his head, he attempts to dislodge the Tzar's fake cheerfulness.

The advertisement finally dissipates, and he watches the calm street of the Entertainment District go by. Drunks with their vodka sit hunched on the sides of society in decrepit attire, vomit-spewed garbage around them. He looks away.

Holograms of doxies sparkle above each brothel, slender spires pointing up like arrows at the dancing bodies. They're still quiet, but in the afternoon men would crowd in to drink, smoke, and fuck.

On the walls, tall screens of doxies in metal costumes dance in unison, blowing kisses at the empty street. Out of the edge of his view, a flash of three men standing in an alley, wearing red plastic masks on the lower half of their faces.

Pressing harder on the gas pedal, he ignores the Zorax gang members behind the brothel. Nothing matters. Whether it be gang violence or red stripe corruption, it's all the same. The buzzing neon green, highlighter pink, and bright yellow holograms recede in his mirrors as he continues up the spiralling highway.

As he enters the Generation District, more men have crowded out of their apartment buildings and the traffic slows. Concrete walls topped with razor wire stand on each side of the roadway. Above the traffic, glass bridges reveal generators in various states of pregnancy, labour, and infant care.

An ad for doxies irritates him as its flashing distracts him from the road. *Ruby Rose Brothel has the highest rated redheads in Krevax!* He turns his head away and re-focuses on steering his bike. Doxies–diseased, all of them.

Tapping on the gas pedal to stay pace with the traffic, he

steers his bike along the curved road. Up ahead, one of the district's entrances is being guarded by red stripes. He nods at his fellow law-enforcers as he passes their small plastic-sealed station.

The traffic continues to build as the road inclines into the Education District, where the energy and delight of the youthful had yet to be dismantled. Small smiling younkins throw garbage at each other, as sour-faced older boys crowd around the entrance ways smoking brightly coloured plastic cigarettes.

An alarm sounds, signalling the start of classes and the younkins run out of the streets and into windowless concrete buildings. Staring at the motorbike in front of him, he lets the commotion of the boys blur into the background.

The buildings turn into sleek black bulletproof glass as he arrives in the Enforcement District. Here the air felt cleaner and the bitterness of the chemicals left no taste of rust on his tongue.

Veering off the main road, he scans his tracker to open the divider arm and drives past the guard station. Blackwell descends into the pristine parking lot connected to Gromwell Station and parks his bike. At the nearest vending machine, he scans his wrist on the sensor.

"Charlie Blackwell, age 27, credits available - 1,159," an automated feminine voice says through the intercom.

Green bulbs light up all the options in the machine. He picks a tube of black coffee at the bottom, and ignoring the grumbles of hunger in his empty belly, drinks it in one gulp. Before walking away, he notices his sad reflection in the glass and stares at it for a minute.

A hum of electricity envelopes him as he walks into the Watchtower, where a large circle of dozens of high-speed black elevators greet him. Low-ranking red stripes climb into elevators, headed to their surveillance floor to relieve the night shift. A quarter around the circle, a metal door with an engraving of a roaring tiger leads to Gromwell Station.

He scans the sensor and walks into the cube filled with hundreds of small white plastic desks. Fluorescent panels light up the walls, ceiling, and floor with irritating pulsing light that make him woozy. Three elevators in the centre of the room move between the six floors, each with matching rows of shiny white plastic seats.

Blackwell climbs into the elevator with a group of red stripes and one black stripe. Empty-headed, mindless followers. Staring at the black stripe, a feeling of disgust and shame hits him all at once, but he doesn't understand why.

Leaving his feelings behind in the elevator, he exited onto the third floor. Staring through the clear plastic flooring below, he gazed at the men sitting in neat rows stacked like dominoes. Above him the pattern repeats through the clear plastic ceiling.

Making his way through the maze, he walks with his head down to a desk where a large stack of corpse-filled manila folders were waiting for him. Sitting down, he hunches over the small table, his legs bunched up under the seat. Without looking at it, he opens the first folder.

He's too tired to read through it, and instead lets his eyes glaze over, pretending to be productive.

The noise of detectives breathing, yawning, talking, coughing, walking, and shouting fills the surrounding station; not to be outdone by the constant clicking of keyboards, squeaking of chairs, beeping of trackers, and pounding from inside his own skull.

The mid-morning meeting bell rings out, making his head spin. Following a hoard of men into the elevators, he waits at the back as they move up to the top floor. The conference room condenses with bodies and hums with anticipation.

Captain Lewis, a stocky man with short straight black hair, is waiting for them at the front of the room; his red and black uniform ironed and pressed.

"Nostaliem," he yells in a gruff voice, waving a tawny-toned hand.

"What is it?" He narrows his angular eyes, staring at the crowd in front of him.

"An incredible dream-like drug that lets you see the surface?" He switches to a lower volume as the men watch.

"We've all heard the rumours." Blackwell shuffles through the crowd, making his way over to his two partners, Remi and Pratt, who he can see talking out of the sightline of Lewis.

Between Remi's deep brown complexion and Pratt's pale pink skin, the two are easy to spot together.

The captain yells again for effect.

"Bullshit! Nostaliem is poison, nostaliem is war, good men versus bad men! We must destroy it, before it destroys us..." He pounds his chest with a fist.

Blackwell clenches his jaw, feeling the breath in his chest tighten.

"We've all seen the dead bodies," Lewis says, staring at the men with a piercing look. "Men in their prime are overdosing on this toxic black powder. I need the gangs responsible for this stopped. Their men shot, their backs broken, their trucks burned, their stock locked away in evidence bags. The Zorax gang is our primary target! But anyone affiliated with gang activity is in our scope. No more overdoses, no more gangs, no more of this shit!"

"Is this about what happened to that judge in the Government District, captain?" Remi asks, glaring with wrinkled eyes.

Lewis stares back at him. Remi scratches his black and grey-streaked beard, almost concealing a smirk.

"Shut the fuck up," Lewis says. "This is about the future of Krevax and every citizen in it!"

Remi shrugs his shoulders and points his square jaw up, always ready for a fight. Lewis looks away and continues his speech.

"Right…" Remi whispers to Pratt. "That's why we're having this meeting now and not three weeks ago, back when the first body and bag of nostaliem were found in the Recycling District."

Blackwell dips his head in greeting, but his partners don't seem to notice him towering over them. Looking down at the ground, he feels defeated.

Pratt nods agreeably. "No one gives a shit about recyclers." His boozy breath makes Blackwell take a step back.

"I arrested a high-up Zorax member only two weeks ago, but the captain didn't let me question him, just sent him straight for recycling," Remi says.

"Ridiculous," Pratt says, his blond hair fluttering, as he shakes his round head.

"Well, they're easy enough to find," Blackwell interjects with an awkward laugh, trying to join the discussion. "Red masks aren't exactly inconspicuous."

The two men look at him and the conversation ends. With his stomach knotted, Blackwell looks up at the captain, pretending to be engrossed in his words. I should've kept my mouth shut.

"Alright, men," the captain says. "You know what you need to do. Squad A hit the streets, kill these dealers and get nostaliem out of Krevax. Squad B, reach out to your informants. We need to find out where this shit is being made."

Lewis picks up a pair of spectacles and puts them on, signalling he's done speaking.

The meeting ends and the men scatter back to their desks. Blackwell sits down in his plastic seat and reads through the files, all describing violent deaths. A high-pitched voice screams while hands reach for him, dragging him away, small and helpless.

Waking with a start, his breath fast-paced and shallow, he wipes sweat off his brow. *I fell asleep.* He closes his eyes to shut out the fluorescent lights in the station, but there's no escaping. The screaming nightmare is still there, waiting for him, torture on either side, asleep or awake.

Beep, beep, beep.

He slides his hand across his tracker, turning off the notification. Glancing down at the small projection screen above his wrist, he registers it as an alert for a removed tracker in the Entertainment District. Exhaling, he holds his head in his hands for a moment and then stands.

"Move it, Blackwell!" Remi yells from across the room. "Someone removed a doxy's tracker."

02 | CAGED BIRD

KALIANN

BLINKING OPEN HER EYES, KALIANN FEELS AGGRAVATED BY THE neon flashing on her mat. Frozen for a moment, a nervous energy builds, making pins and needles spread on her umber brown skin. She slumps forward and stares out the window, thick dark red curls glowing in the light of the advertisements. *The highest-rated doxies use Whippy Ribbons in their hair!* The words cause her to roll her eyes and she turns away.

Men don't care about ribbons, the highest-rated doxies have the prettiest faces. Ten other figures stretch and yawn on the concrete floor around her. Pushing aside a sheet, she stands, shivering as the cold in the brothel crawls over her.

With little awareness, she wanders over to a cubby labelled with the letter K, the last in the row being used. Letters A through J stand near their own cubbies, grabbing hair brushes, chewing dental gum, and sanitizing their faces with wipes.

Feeling wretched, Kaliann peered down the row of redheads–their defining feature. Nothing but bodies, empty vessels for angry men, beautiful animals, soulless, mindless, weak, pathetic. That's what everyone says. Doxies are objects; dolls in costume for patrons to undress. Feeling the cruel weight of her new awareness, she exhales slowly. That's what they say.

What's more important than beauty and youth when you're an object? She pinches the skin on her inner arm. I'm human, aren't I?

Tiptoeing over to the cracked mirror that spans a wall, she sits and brushes her curls in slow, methodical lines. She ties braids running from the base of her neck to the edges of her hairline, pulling the loose ends forward until it looks like a lion's mane.

In a burst of rage, she grins at the strange figure in the mirror. Now I see the object, with its shiny edges and soft curves. I see the beautiful animal that everyone wants to stare at, to touch. Men. They're animals as much as we are, with their sweat and their breath. They lie to themselves, imagining they're something above the needs of the body, unconnected to the rest of us.

The doxy in the mirror stares back at her, a reflection both uncomfortable and familiar. Fine. I will be an animal, a wild animal with teeth and claws. The desire to bare her teeth overcomes her, and she contorts her face into a rabid expression, imagining ripping into a body as it screams in terror. A smile creeps onto her face at the violent thought, and then it passes.

She grabs two ribbons from cubby 'k' and walks back behind the line of redheads to her spot. Crossing her legs, she puts the ribbons in her lap and chooses an indigo one. With expert precision, she pulls the ribbon through her braids, leaving large loops in between each neat weaving, which stick out all around her head. Another minute of twisting and tying, and a royal purple ribbon is also folded in.

After securing both ribbons with pins, she twists the remaining loose ends into small buns inside each of the ribbon loops. The perfect object. With a crack of a lid, the chemical-laden smell of black eyeliner fills the air. She applies the makeup to her eyelids and extends the lines down the sides of her nose, looping it under her cheekbones. The line ends towards a triangle point on her chin, completing the expected design. Kaliann inhales, but this time she can't catch her breath. The black liner feels heavy on her skin, despite its weightlessness.

"I expect you to bring back at least five clients each. We're low on credits this week," Brixton, the brothel director, barks into the room. "If you want to eat, you'll have to fuck."

Kaliann clips on the metal plates over her lavender underwear, ignoring the surrounding noise. She pulls the connected metal chains over her naked chest and ties them around her neck in a knot. I will cut it out of my flesh and run through the city like a wild animal, hungry for blood.

At her cubby, she touches a small piece of plastic with printed text hidden in the ribbons. Without taking the plastic out of the box, she discreetly reads the text.

Nostaliem. Open the eye. On the back is an address, an area of Krevax she had never seen before, except for in advertisements. Now that I opened the eye, I can't close it. Images of dark waves splash in her mind. On a summer's day, I swam in an ocean. She smiles at the strange experience that had recently consumed her thoughts.

The heat of the sun replays with phantom tingles on her cheeks. I've seen the sun, the actual sun in a blue sky. With nostaliem I can do it again and finally live in a world with nature. She pushes the plastic message into the ribbons and steps out of the sleeping quarters. I can escape and get enough nostaliem to leave Krevax forever. Walking through sheets of black hanging curtains, she takes a plain paste tube from a plastic basket at the front entrance.

Brixton smiles at her. "I like the purple on you."

"Thanks Brixton," she says with a fake giggle. *Fuck you.* An image of his face breathing over her flashes in her mind.

He reaches out and touches her waist with his hand. "After work tonight, come to my room."

"Of course." She kisses his cheek and walks out to the street. Anger is coursing through her and she can't relax her jaw, as she takes her place under a giant glowing red-haired hologram.

Around her, the other doxies dance and make pouty faces at the men. With a sharp inhale, she watches the passing faces in the street of the Entertainment District. As she waits for her chance to escape, she touches her numb fingertips together impatiently. *Breathe, it will all be over soon, just a few more minutes.*

A man walks over to her and sticks his hand into the side of her underwear. Feeling around her folds, he pushes two fingers into her body. She smiles, hiding the overwhelming feeling of disgust from him completely. After a minute, he removes his fingers and grabs Kaliann's waist, leading her into the brothel.

Brixton grins, exposing smoke-stained teeth. "Doesn't she look stunning in purple?!"

"Yes," the man says indifferently.

"It's sixteen credits."

"Fine."

"As always, a tip is customary if you like the service." Brixton leads them to a circular bed in the back corner.

The smell of stale sweat soaks her nostrils as they enter the black-curtained room. Plastic sparkling red lights hang on the ceiling in interlacing rows. Kaliann takes off her uniform and lies on the mattress. The man gets undressed and sits beside her. He doesn't look her in the eyes as he climbs on top of her. Pushing himself into her, he thrusts back and forth, his breath on her ear. Staring at the red twinkling lights on the ceiling, she makes the lights go bright, then dim, then bright again with her eyes.

Rolling off of her, he leans down to grab his clothes, as she watches frozen from the bed, covered in his sweat. After dressing, he drops a credit as a tip and leaves without a word. With the decorative metal, underwear and credit clutched in her hands, she pokes her head out of the curtain and runs down the hallway.

In the sleeping area, she tosses her costume on the ground and anxiously rummages through her ribbon box. She glances back at the brothel. Brixton is nowhere to be seen. She feels the raised text on her fingertips and pulls out the slip of plastic. Taking a deep breath, she bolts back through the brothel and up a staircase on the opposite side of the room. Semen drips down her leg and onto the steps.

In Brixton's apartment, she grabs a white suit and green sequinned shirt out of the closet. Once dressed, she pulls the ribbons out of her hair and rushes into the attached bathroom, grabbing a razor. The blades buzz alive and her hands shake as she shaves her head. She feels the red curls fall around her feet.

"I'm not staying in this cage anymore," she grins psychotically. "I'm a wild animal."

With the last strand on the ground, she touches the stubble of her bald head. She laughs unexpectedly and then cries, mourning her hair. Get it together.

Breaking the plastic cover that holds the metal in place, she pulls out a single blade. Tensing her left arm, she clenches her fist in anticipation of the pain to surge from the cut. She places the cold metal against the outline of the tracker. Dizziness fills her head as her heart pounds in her chest. One slice and it will be done. *Do it. Do it now.*

The room pulses as she pushes the corner of the blade into her wrist and slices lengthwise. Panic fills her at the sight of red dripping down her hand. Despite her attempts to dig in with her fingers, it's not deep enough.

Fighting the urge to vomit, she shuts her eyes for nearly a minute. *Again. You can't stop.* Opening her eyes, she slices the razor deeper than before. This time, she can hear the metal scraping against the tracker. She grabs the edge with her bloody fingernails and pulls out a thin metal disk, dropping it. *I did it.* Without warning, she pukes sour-bile paste onto the marble counter. Silence. She stares helplessly, terrified, waiting for the inevitable noise. The alarm on the tracker blares with high-pitched beeps. *Oh no. The credits!*

Racing out of the bathroom, she opens Brixton's drawers and dumps the contents on the ground. She doesn't find the credits, so crouches down and looks under the bed. Anxiety builds, making her chest constrict as she feels the edges of the mattress. The credits are nowhere and her heart is in her ears, shouting out the passing seconds.

Careening around the room, she tosses religious books, magazines, knickknacks, and financial notes from every surface, leaving behind random drops of blood. *Where are they? I know he has them.* In the closet, she rips the contents off their hangers, throwing them behind her. With trembling hands, she feels through the items scattered on the floor.

What if they're not here!?

Somehow, the alarm seems to be even louder than it was before. A tiny figure in a white mask stands at the door. Kaliann looks up in fear at Mary, Brixton's peon, who is staring down at her. The mask conceals her expression, but her eyes are wide.

"Please!" Kaliann whispers, as her legs give out from

stress. The peon runs over and leans down, ripping apart socks as fast as she can. Kaliann picks up the closest pair and rips them apart as well. Rolled up in a pair of socks, Mary finds the small bag of credits. She presses them into her palm for a second before passing them to Kaliann.

"Thank you," Kaliann says, her face flushed red and covered in bits of loose hair. She hands Mary the single credit and runs down the staircase. At the bottom, she can see Brixton leading another client to a bed. Walking with a false sense of calm, she heads towards the exit as the room flashes with her rapid breath.

Outside, she keeps her head down, not wanting to be recognized by the other doxies. The feeling of cold ground on her bare feet steadies her as she steps lightly to avoid shards of glass. She stares at the blood on the sleeve of the white suit, willing no one to notice.

Above her, the Watchtower's spotlight points at the brothel. Fear causes her to close her eyes, but she continues walking out of the circle of light. *I'm nobody. I can disappear into the crowd and no one will notice me.*

Wiping blood from her wrist, she holds her arm to her waist to stem the flow. Sirens move closer and red stripes fill the street. Nausea makes her feel like she's about to puke again, but she keeps moving forward. A shoulder collides with her head, causing her to fall back.

Glancing up, she sees a man glaring down at her with an expression of hatred. Cold sweat moves up her neck as she realizes it's a red stripe standing over her, his fists balled in anger.

03 | SCARED EYES

BLACKWELL

Blackwell's gaze fixes on the pitiful figure splayed on the ground. The blood-spattered man stares back with a look of uncontained terror. Rubbing his pulsing shoulder, his thoughts fill with disdain for the foolish younkin in the garish white suit.

"Drunk idiot! I'm not here to arrest you, you're just a maggot in my paste. A disgusting clump of squirming flesh that I pretend not to feel going down my throat." His attention shifts and he scans the faces in the crowd, and then jumps forward, cutting through the mass of bodies.

He speeds through rows of black curtains, following the arrows on his tracker to a set of stairs. Now he's so close he can hear the alarm from the tracker blaring above him. Running up the staircase, he enters the room with his gun drawn. The tracker lies in a puddle of blood in the bathroom.

"Come out, now!" he shouts, kicking a closet door open.

He peers underneath the bed for someone hiding, then jogs to the bloody bathroom, finding the apartment empty. Pressing on his tracker, he sends out the signal to deactivate the alarm. Taking a breath in the silence, he returns his gun to its holster and walks back to the entrance. Looking over the railing, he watches red stripes searching the rows of beds among the chaos of patrons.

"Hey!" a man yells, as a red stripe pulls back a black curtain, unveiling his naked body.

Turning away, Blackwell walks back into the bedroom, putting on a pair of blue plastic gloves. In the bathroom, he crouches down to pick up the tracker, but stops mid-reach, distracted by strands of dark red curls. Picking up a clump of hair from the puddle, he watches as blood drips from the ends. Did she shave her head?

The image of the drunk figure flashes in his mind, causing stress to bubble in his chest. That man had a shaved head and blood on his suit. Pushing down the worry, he tells himself it's a ridiculous thought. No, it can't be.

A doxy would never shave her own head. Someone must have forced her and then disguised her as a man. They would've dragged her out of here against her will. No doxy would run away from a brothel, it's their natural setting. Like a tick on an unwilling host, drinking its blood meal, they feed on the weaknesses of men. How would a doxy eat outside a brothel?

He pulls a plastic bag out of his tactical belt and collects the hair. Staring at the bag of red locks, something strikes him, but he doesn't know what it is, it's a feeling he doesn't remember having before, and so has no name for it.

The entrance to the bedroom is quiet, so he latches his finger around the edge of a glove and takes it off. Opening the bag, the feeling expands in his chest like the light from a warm candle and he touches the hair, before choking back the emotion in his throat. A strange and dark thought of recognition courses through his mind.

Shakily closing the bag, he stuffs it into a pouch in his belt, without labelling it. What am I doing?

Grabbing another plastic bag, he places the tracker in it and labels that one: **Case** #162300-BX; **Item**: Tracker; **Date**: 12, 31, 181 A.W.; **Test**: Blood DNA + Location Data analysis two weeks prior.

"What's this?" a man asks, walking into the ransacked bedroom, his arms wide as he stares at the destruction.

"Are you the director?" Blackwell turns to face him, pushing away the peculiar feeling.

"Yes, Brixton."

"I'm afraid someone has robbed you," he says, holding up the tracker.

"What?" Brixton looks confused. "Someone stole one of our doxies?" He kicks the wall, leaving a scuff mark from his boot.

Blackwell clicks on his wrist and scans the metal. "According to the tracker, number Delta, 432-99-77, Alpha." He glances up at the director. "I believe you registered her under the name..." He scrolls down.

"Kaliann." A full-body picture of the doxy floats above his tracker. Blackwell exhales slowly, staring at it. It wasn't her. That man looked completely different.

"Kaliann," Brixton says, shaking his head. "They stole Kaliann. Shit! The owner just finished paying her off." He pulls on his shirt collar.

"We were about to get a Lisa. A setback like this...." He trails off, lost in thought.

"I'm sorry. I know they're expensive."

"Yeah, they are." Brixton picks up a pair of socks. "What about my credits? Did they steal those too?" he shouts, ripping the socks apart like a petulant child.

"It would be best if nothing was touched," Blackwell says. "We will dust for prints." Brixton nods, staring down at the pile of his stuff, looking morose.

Waiting for the man to compose himself, Blackwell let his thoughts return to the red hair.

"Will you catch who did this?" Brixton asks.

"When did you last see Kaliann?"

"She just had a client. I led them to a bed and then left," he says. "That's what I always do."

"Do you have the client's information?"

"Yes, of course." Clicking on his wrist, Brixton swipes through a list of receipts.

"This one," he says, pressing and holding on the file to transmit it.

The file pops up on Blackwell's tracker and he approves it, and then reads over the details, tapping on the name Markum Hew. This opens to a file with the man's personal details and photo, which shows he's nearly 55 and set to be recycled at the end of the week. Lucky bastard. With nothing to lose, he could have stolen the doxy. Blackwell scrolls down to the bottom of the file and clicks on the button, 'Alert Notification.'

"Wanted for questioning." The words type on the page in **bold** text as he says them, and then confirming they're correct, he clicks send.

"Can you tell me, is there anyone who has a special interest in the doxy?"

"You mean like a regular client? She had at least a couple of men who would ask for her."

"What are their names?" Blackwell asks, nervously tapping his foot on the ground.

Why am I still feeling uneasy about the man with the shaved head? It wasn't the doxy.

"Um," Brixton mumbles, as he clicks on his tracker. Images of all eleven doxies pop up on a small projected screen above his wrist and he taps on Kaliann's picture, opening the page to her economic stats.

"These are the repeat clients," Brixton says, as he transmits the files. Blackwell opens the four files and repeats the alerts.

"I need the receipts from all of your clients today."

"Yes, sir." Brixton sends him the receipt list and stands silently. Blackwell opens a tab, labels it **Case** #162300-BX and adds the files he's collected.

"Can you tell me anything else about the missing doxy?"

"I honestly don't know?" Brixton says, shaking his head. "A doxy is a doxy, what is there to know about them, other than bra size and hair colour? I believe you already have that information in your file, though."

"Okay, our men will keep you posted." He gestures for Brixton to leave. The man nods slowly, turns and heads huffily down the stairs. Blackwell holds his wrist to his mouth. "Contact precinct." The screen goes yellow.

"Connecting," the automated feminine voice responds, and then the screen turns green.

"Captain Lewis, here."

"Blackwell here, sir. Someone has stolen a doxy, removed her tracker, and taken her from Foxe Brothel. We need a dusting kit, DNA swabs, and the lab crew to test the director's room."

"Green. I'll send them now. Did you check the log for trackers at the brothel today?"

"No, I'll do that and add it to the official case file." The call ends.

Blackwell opens the pouch and stares at the bag of hair. Despite knowing he should label and submit it as evidence, something holds him back.

Confused, he closes the pouch and clicks on his tracker, navigating to the button labelled *Red Stripe Services*. Opening it, he scrolls down the alphabetical list and chooses *Tracker Location Data*.

A schematic map of Krevax opens, and he clicks on the Entertainment District and zooms in on Foxe Brothel. Saving the tracker data from the last two hours, he adds it to the file and closes out of the tab.

"Connect with partners."

"Connecting," the cheerful feminine voice says, as the screen flashes from yellow to green.

"What's up?" Pratt asks, a slight slur in his voice.

"Remi here," Remi says with a brusqueness that suggests he's the boss, regardless of who's on the other side of the call.

"Blackwell here. I've taken the owner's statement. Any sign of the doxy?"

"No."

"None."

"I'm going to follow up on the last client seen with the doxy. I sent a list of the regulars, so we can break up the work. Add any statements you take to case number 162-300, Bravo X-ray."

"Green," both men say in unison, Remi's voice louder than Pratt's.

"I'll take Gamble and King," Remi says first, and then immediately hangs up.

"Sure thing, that leaves me Lake and Haliwell," Pratt says, a strained cheerfulness to his voice.

Blackwell nods and ends the call with a flick of his finger. The page closes, returning to the files the director sent him. Clicking on Hew's location data, a map expands out, which shows an orange dot in the Government District.

Fucking Government District. He shakes his head. Rich assholes think they own everything. Leaving the room, he watches as a peon stares at him from the top of the staircase. Blackwell looks away, ignoring her, and makes his way halfway down the stairs.

"You there," he shouts at a random red stripe, walking past the bottom of the steps.

This man's uniform has thin red stripes, instead of the thick red bars on Blackwell's uniform, showing he is of lower ranking. The man jogs up the stairs, and stands in front of Blackwell, two steps below him.

"Yes, sir?"

"I need you outside that room," he says, pointing up at the entrance. "Make sure no one enters until the crew arrives."

The man runs up the rest of the staircase and stands at the door. Blackwell looks around at the other red stripes taking statements from the men. *Everything's in order, we'll have the doxy back by the morning.* Leaving the brothel at a quick pace, he goes back to his motorbike.

He revs the engine and kicks forward on the ground, balancing as the bike takes off down the road. The image of the man spattered in blood reflects in every face he passes.

Why am I looking for him? He doesn't matter. He's no one, another drunk in the Entertainment District with nothing better to do but get himself beaten up.

A horn beeps at him and he swerves to avoid another motorbike, nearly causing an accident. *Shit.* Glancing up, he's surprised to see the mirrored glass of the Government District already on the horizon. *Pay attention! You're driving, you idiot.*

Despite his intentions, the man's face creeps back into his mind. Those scared eyes. Blackwell can't shake them.

04 | NOSTALIEM

KALIANN

AFTER YEARS OF LIVING IN THE SAME GRIND, DAY IN AND DAY out, this moment was visceral; scenes jumped forward, stopped in violent flashes, just to jump forward again. Kaliann watches the bridges of the Generation District flickering past her like spokes on a wheel. It was fantastical and terrifying. I've been ripped out of reality. Floating in a world without brothels, without doxies, without gravity to hold me down.

Awestruck, she stares up at the generators round bellies. She had never seen one before, not even in an advertisement. For a moment she wondered how they got that way, but then she remembers. Sterilization was presented as an award, part of a coming of age ceremony for a doxy. The memory stings her now, distorted from its original state. Why is it like this?

The motorcycle hums up the highway, unconcerned with her thoughts, oscillating between the generators' pregnant bellies and her own fears.

What happens if I get there, and it's deserted? Don't think that.

She sees a generator breastfeeding a pink-wrapped baby and looks away. The scene was too raw, like a lion ripping into a hyena, the true nature of their bodies on full display. Whoever's waiting at the end of this trip, they'll have nostaliem.

The concrete buildings of the Education District span out in front of her, revealing another alien world. Choking back tears, she watches younkins move haphazardly around the road, their cheerful voices calling to each other over the noise of the traffic.

Something about the scene feels like a memory, although distant and fuzzy on the edges. *I've never been here, have I?* She ponders this feeling of familiarity, but no answer comes to mind and then her thoughts return to nostaliem. What if I don't have enough credits...it won't matter, there are other things to sell. She watches the blood expand on the sleeve of the white jacket, wanting to lose herself in the abstract red line.

As her fingers grow numb from the cold, the concrete gives way to the black glass of the Enforcement District. Looking up, she scans the black towers for anything recognizable and then spots the Watchtower, which strangely comforts her. The normally terrifying faces of the gargoyles suddenly seemed kind, like they were watching over, instead of imprisoning with their constant gaze.

As the motorcycle turns away from the Watchtower, she fixates on the ceiling, noticing there's not one advertisement for doxies; no ribbons, metal plates, colourful underwear, or makeup. Rather, the ads comprise flavoured alcohols, cigarettes, weapons, and motorbikes. How odd to see someone's else's advertisements. Green glass pyramids sit on the horizon, their tips high above the surrounding buildings. She stares at them, as they unfold in the distance.

"What are those?" she blurts out, pointing at the closest one.

"You don't know?" the driver asks. "It's the Natatoriums. Haven't you been to service?"

"Oh! Of course, it's just been a long time," Kaliann says, her voice squeaking.

So, that's where Brixton goes to service every morning. As they enter the Devotion District, she can see the details of the first pyramid. It has a gold statue of a winged man above the entrance, his toned muscles shining in the light of the advertisements.

Inside there's a large circular bath with another gold statue, this one of a generator with a protruding belly. She stares at the belly, disturbed by its size. On the sides of the road, men cloaked in green velvet, wearing emerald crowns and golden rings on every finger, walk with lime green plastic bound books in their arms. Kaliann recognizes it as the *Book of Infinitum*, from Brixton's weekly sermons.

The streets here are clean and the air has a faint smell of chlorine. She takes a deep breath. *If I was a man, I would come here as much as possible.*

The motorbike winds with increasing speed up the highway, weaving through slower moving drivers. Ahead, the biggest pyramid yet, it's so tall it could hold three of the other Natatoriums stacked on top of each other. The walls of this one have reflective green glass, preventing outsiders from seeing the pool. *I wonder what happens there?*

On the other side of the pyramid, they enter the University District, where marble towers with small triangle-shaped windows stand regally above the main throughway. Men in black robes walk with heads held high through the triangular shapes left between the buildings. The chlorine smell of the Devotion District has disappeared, leaving behind nothing but filtered air. Sniffing, she was surprised to find there is no chemical smell, no usual taste of rust. Why can't the air be like this in the Entertainment District?

A bell chimes out in the distance making her jump in her seat and bringing awareness back to her stiff legs, but shifting her weight doesn't help the growing numbness.

"Are we almost there?"

"We have to go through the News District." the driver says.

Gripping the handles tighter, she tries to keep herself balanced. As the last marble university recedes, buildings made of endless screens replace them. Their labyrinthine structures twist in snake-like spirals around the highway, with every screen playing the same segment:

"Krevax is a thriving city! Can you say technology!" the pale, blonde newscaster says, grinning. "Men who lived on the surface may have had the sun, but they didn't have trackers accounting for their every need. The information at our fingertips would shock our ancestors." Kaliann stares up at the screens, feeling sick.

What information? The only thing on my tracker was hair and make-up tutorials.

The message continues as they drive through a tunnel, which expands out into one large screen, leaving the newscaster's face horrifyingly huge.

"Vending Machines! In Krevax, you don't have to waste your time searching for food or cooking. You put in a couple credits and get any flavour you could want from one of our millions of vending machines across the city." Nausea fills her stomach as she watches the newscaster's teeth open and close above her head.

"Talk about convenience! Talk about choices! Krevax simplifies human lives." The tunnel ends, and they are thrust back out into the sea of small screens. Exhaling slowly, she focuses on staying upright.

"Temperature Control! In the past, humans had to worry about getting too cold or too hot. This could even result in death! Now that we live underground, we set the temperature to a perfect 18 degrees Celsius. No need to worry about preparing for the weather." For a moment her hands clasp over her ears, desperate to stop the noise, but then she falls forward from losing balance and has to grab hold of the handlebars again.

"You get dressed and go, no special outerwear required. Our ancestors had to worry about precipitation! Could you imagine water or ice falling from the sky? Neither can we." Water falling from the sky? She shuts her eyes to escape the dancing visuals of raindrops.

"Recycling! By getting recycled, you will keep Krevax at the ideal population. The Recycling Program also prevents frivolous ageing, which would burden our system. Once your economic contributions are over, we celebrate your life in a special ceremony! If there was no recycling, you would need to rely on others for help as you became weak and decrepit. It's hard to even think about something that shameful!" The newscaster shakes his head.

Kaliann stares at her knees, and then at the wheels spinning below her, feeling shaky. We must be close now. You can do this. You are doing this.

"Num.." The voice trails off as they turn onto a quieter road. Thank Mary! They continue down the side road for the next 20 minutes. Barely holding onto the bike, she can no longer feel her feet or her fingers.

They cross into the Technology District, where thin towers climb 300 floors, connecting to the base of the Government District. But she doesn't notice the steel structures, or the flashing holograms fighting for her attention. All she can think about now is her goal to get nostaliem.

The driver heads toward an outer wall, where the towers give way to expensive cube homes, stacked like toy blocks, each adorned with their own rock garden and small fountain. The bike climbs a ramp twelve floors up and finally stops in front of one of the tiny cubes.

Kaliann tumbles to the ground, landing roughly on her elbows and knees. The driver looks down at her, confused. "That's three credits," he says

Standing with weak legs, she looks up at the driver. "I'm only stopping for a minute." He nods that this is fine and gazes up at the advertisements, uninterested. With quick steps, she heads up to the door and knocks twice. A peon appears wearing a copper lace and diamond adorned mask, showing extreme wealth.

"May I help you?" she says in a defensive tone. Kaliann takes the piece of plastic out of her pocket and hands it to the peon.

The peon reads it and then looks up at Kaliann, studying her for a moment. "I'm sorry, you have the wrong address."

"The address is right there!" Pointing, she gestures with her finger at the text as she jumps from foot to foot.

The peon goes to close the door, but a man sticks his hand in the way, swinging the door wide, revealing slats of wood on the inside walls. Gasping, she wants to move closer and touch the thing that had once been a tree. A rich, earthy, almost sweet scent fills her nostrils, like nothing she had ever come across before. That's what wood smells like!

"Then you must have stolen that!" the man says, staring at her with furrowed eyebrows.

Pulling her in by the shirt collar, he moves to shut the door, but then sees the taxi driver waiting.

"I didn't steal it," she says. "I can pay for the nostaliem!" He stares at her a moment, his expression cold.

"Listen, I can provide you with nostaliem this one time, but you're never to come here again, or mention this address to anyone." He snaps his fingers at the peon, and she disappears into an unseen room.

The peon hands Kaliann a small metal box engraved with an eye.

"For your silence," she says.

The man shoves her outside and slams the door. Grabbing the handrail to steady herself, she sprints down the steps two at a time, still holding the metal box.

With shaky hands, she stuffs the box inside the pocket with the credits. The credits! They didn't take them. Her heart is still racing from adrenalin as she climbs onto the bike.

"Where to?"

"The closest motel." The driver pulls away from the cube and heads back towards the News District.

Not five minutes later, they stop outside Sweet Dreams Motel, a seventeen-story building positioned between the two districts.

The driver holds out his scanner to take her payment. Staring at the numbers on the screen, she pulls out a small pile of quarter-point credits from the bag in her pocket and shows them to the driver.

With a grumpy face he holds out his hands. "It's five."

Nodding, she counts out 20 quarter-point credits and drops them into his hands. She stumbles away from the bike and walks up to the service desk.

Dumping the remaining credits on the counter, she rings the bell and waits. The attendant pops his head around the corner and lumbers over, as though awakened from a nap.

"How many nights will this get me?" she asks. He peers at

the pile of quarter-point credits in annoyance and then counts them one by one.

"Twenty-nine, twenty-nine and a quarter, twenty-nine and a half, twenty-nine and three quarters, thirty. That'll get you three nights."

"Fine."

"Room 12, on the fifth floor," he says as he slides over a plastic card. Snatching the card off the counter, she holds it to her chest like a prized possession.

The attendant watches her with a confused expression as she sprints over to the elevator. She pushes the button and stares at the doors, willing them to open quicker, and as they finally open, leaps inside. When they close behind her, she jumps at her reflection, startled by her bald head in the mirror.

Laughing out loud to herself, she touches the stubble with her palms. She exits on the fifth floor and tiptoes down an emerald green carpet. Outside room 12, she touches the card to the sensor and grins when it turns green. The door creaks when she opens it.

The room is small, with the only light from a triangular window on one wall. I have my own room, with a lock, and a bed, and a bathroom, and everything! Locking the door behind her, she takes off the stolen clothes, feeling relieved to have found sanctuary.

With itchy skin from bits of loose hair, she stares at the shower wishing she had enough credits to pay for extra water. She tries to wipe away the hair, but it's stuck to her. Oh well, I'll rinse off in the morning, like the men.

Lying down on the mattress, she rubs the rocks and dirt off of her feet. The cut on her wrist has stopped bleeding, but it looks like it will leave a nasty scar.

She pulls the metal box out of the jacket pocket and examines the contents. Inside are five small bags of black powder, a metal razor and a straw. A straw? You snort the powder! She shakes her head at herself. I can't believe I poured the powder into a gel hydration tube.

Exhaling, she puts the box down beside the mattress and rolls into an exhausted ball. The mattress has an intricate pattern of triangles spiralling in all directions. She traces the pattern with her finger before finally falling into an uncomfortable sleep.

After a few hours, she wakes up with a burst of energy, too excited to sleep. Leaning over, she opens the box and stares at the bags of powder.

Curiosity makes her pull out one bag of nostaliem and drop the contents onto the floor. Her hands are shaking with anticipation, as the razor cuts the powder into lines. Exhaling slowly to steady herself, she picks up the straw and snorts the first line.

Kaliann lies back on the mattress, staring dreamily, as she feels the drug take effect. The world around her fades, and then she's no longer in the motel room. She's somewhere else.

Wrapped in pink inside a clear plastic box at the other side of the room, dark red puffs of hair frame her sweet face. I can't look away.

"Please, can I hold her?" I ask, tears streaming down my face.

"No," a man in a white coat says, picking up the newborn. "It's against the rules."

"Please," I beg.

Without another glance, he leaves the room holding my daughter. I stare exhausted out into the hallway, too weak to stand. I wanted to hold you, to smell your hair, to care for you, to be with you. I'm so sorry. Another man walks in, holding a different newborn, this one wrapped in blue. He places the thing in my arms and leaves.

I stare down at the baby that isn't mine, but looks so much the same. I kiss this sleeping baby's forehead and smell this baby's hair. It's kind of sweet, kind of earthy, with a faint smell of milk. This baby cries and I rock him and then help him latch. I hope my baby is safe. I hope my sons are safe. I continue to cry, this time thinking of all my stolen children.

Kaliann opens her eyes and weeps. That generator was my mother! She grabs her head and shakes it, covering her eyes. When she swallowed the nostaliem, she was only an observer, but this was different. Not only could she feel everything her mother felt, she could also hear her thoughts.

At that moment, she knew everything about her, and essentially was her. How can I know she was my mother? I don't know, but I know she was. I had a mother. She was real. What were her memories?

She saw the sun and sky, she couldn't have been born in Krevax. What happened to her?

She quickly snorts a second line of powder, hoping to see her mother again. As the nostaliem seeps into her mind, the room melts away.

Behind me I hear the door open, but I don't look. I continue to watch the soft orange light pulsing in the windowless room. I wish to disappear into it. To burn up in its heat. I reach forward to touch the warmth, but the plastic is cold. Everything is cold in Krevax.

"They told me you were pregnant," he says.

"Yes." I turn to face him.

"I thought you would be happy?" He stares at me, his expression almost angry.

"I am." I give a small smile, but I know it isn't convincing. I could never be happy having a child in Krevax. I'll never be happy again.

"This will be our last meeting." He walks the last few feet towards me, holding out a metal box for me to take. "I bought you something." Exhaling slowly, I take the gift and open it. Inside is a necklace with a small copper sun.

"It's lovely, thank you."

"Can I help you put it on?" I turn around to let him put the chain around my neck. He pushes my dark red curls forward and latches it. "It's supposed to make the baby male."

"My first two were boys," I whisper, not wanting to remember their faces. It was too painful to think about them.

"That's a good sign," he says, smiling. "If this one's a boy, he'll go to the Government District." The Government District. What does it matter? He'll still just be an animal in a cage. I nod and then turn back towards the orange light.

Kaliann's eyes open and she finds herself back on the mattress, sobbing. Was that my father? I don't understand.

Her mind scatters through a million thoughts and she suddenly feels angrier than she had ever been. All the new and shocking information overwhelms her, leaving her shaking. Digging her fingernails into her thighs, she feels only anguish. I'll never be free. I'll never know my mother.

Falling on the mattress, crying, she buries her face into the sheets. I don't want to be here anymore. Screaming, she punches the wall, leaving her hands bruised. What is this place?

She rolls herself into a ball and rocks herself back and forth. We killed the sky. Tears pour down her cheeks and she can barely breathe through the panic.

"We killed the sky," she whispers.

She rocks back and forth, back and forth, back and forth. We killed the sky. We killed the sky. We killed the sky. Pausing, she drops her hands into her lap and stares through the window at the ceiling made of advertisements. We killed the sky.

Picking up the razor, she pushes the blade deep against her wrist and slides it lengthwise up her arm, this time deep enough to hit the artery. Blood pours down her hand and onto the floor, in a river of red.

Leaning over, she snorts the remaining lines of nostaliem with the straw. Pushing herself back on the mattress, she stares vacantly at the ceiling with her wrist hanging off the side, half closing her eyes as the drug trickles into her mind. The cold room disappears, and she finds herself somewhere warm.

Walking along a row of bright green peas, I listen to the sounds of the robins calling from the sky. Looking up, I watch the clouds move with the Autumn wind, beams of sunlight flashing on my face as I move through the stalks, my scalp tingling from the heat.

Reaching out, I touch the vines with my fingers. Pausing, I pick a slightly translucent pod and crunch through its shell to the fruit. I watch with fascination as my red tulip-patterned shoes crunch the flattened stalks.

"Lucy," my brother calls from the back of an old house, paint peeling off the wood slats, "Ma says it's time for dinner. Where are you?"

Giggling, I crouch down into the stalks, hiding from my brother's view. With a smile, he sighs, and walks to the edge of the porch, and then leaps into a run and disappears. I crawl through the stalks to confuse him, but he's too quick, and he picks me up with a gleeful yell, spinning me around.

The green stalks turn to eerie neon, the robins' chatter becomes screeching cries, and the sky morphs into swirling smoke. My heart is pounding and the whole place is swirling, darker and darker. The now black smoke swirls faster until it stops frozen, and pales.

With a shallow breath, the motel room takes shape again. Alone, Kaliann cries, away from any person who may have cared that her heart was slowing in her chest. In a final convulsing slouch, her body stiffens, and her heartbeat stops.

After a couple of hours, her face has twisted into a grimace as rigour mortis sets in. Outside the motel, the advertisements remain unchanged, dimming as time passes.

Hours tick by, but there is still no sunlight or moonlight,

only advertisements. Back in the room, Kaliann's head, neck, abdomen and shoulders turn a discoloured green, as her eyes and tongue protrude.

Blisters now cover her marbled complexion, as fluid oozes from her eyes, nose, and mouth, and her insides liquefy.

05 | GRACE
PRATT

"I can't believe we didn't find the doxy," Remi says, running his knuckles along the edge of the vending machine. The coil in the machine spirals until a tube of paste falls to the drawer below.

"Right," Pratt says. "It's strange no one saw her."

"Someone must have knocked her out and stuffed her in a bag, and now he has her locked up." Remi grins, his eyes bright with delight, as he grabs the tube of pepperoni paste.

"Maybe," Pratt says. "What are you doing after work today? I was thinking of heading to the Entertainment District?"

Scanning his tracker on the sensor, Pratt looks through the snack items and then chooses a hash brown paste.

"I can't tonight," Remi says, through a bite of his pepperoni. "Have a shot for me though."

"Of course," Pratt says, as he tears open the paste. "If I go."

Remi shakes his head. "Trevor."

Ignoring this judgement, Pratt returns to his desk, eating the mushy grease-soaked snack in two bites. He reads through the witness reports from the brothel again.

Despite over three dozen transcribed conversations, there's not one useful bit of information. Without another report to distract him, his shaking hands and throbbing head become unbearable. *I need a drink.*

Standing with an unbalanced swing back, he makes his way through the row of desks and out of the station. It always felt too risky to have vodka hidden at his desk. His small eyes dart at the faces in the street, as he walks a block away and gets in line at the hot coffee station.

The bright green sign reads, *Coffee! Coffee! Coffee! 100% artificial, but with more caffeine than the original'*

"What can I get you?" says a man in an oversized, navy blue apron, his face contorted with an expression of annoyance that seemed to protest his lowly position in life.

Glancing up at the menu, he reads through the items, despite having been here hundreds of times before. "I'll have the brown sugar and butter coffee."

"Name?"

"Pratt."

"That's three credits." He lifts his wrist, and the man scans away three credits.

With one last look at the line of men staring down at their trackers, or up at the menu, he heads to the bathroom. Unscrewing the sanitizer dispenser with three spins of each bolt, he reaches into a hidden hole and grabs two triple-ounce bottles of vodka; twisting open the plastic caps, he drinks them in a couple gulps.

After a moment of the alcohol warming his chest, he throws out the bottles and screws the dispenser back in place. Swinging open the door, he saunters back to the counter and watches the coffees being poured.

"Rat!" a man in another navy blue apron calls from behind the counter.

Shaking his head at the man, he steps forward. "It's Pa-ratt."

"Oh." The server hands the coffee over, impervious to anger. He throws open the door, sipping his coffee as he walks back to the station.

Sitting at his uncomfortable plastic desk he watches the seconds count down on his computer screen. Only an hour until I can escape these fluorescent lights. Still, it feels good to take the sharpness away from reality. Smiling to himself, he sighs, letting the piercing lights wash over him, his headache melted away by the alcohol.

"Pratt." Captain Lewis storms towards him. "What happened yesterday?"

"Um, I don't know," Pratt says, jumping in his seat. "We searched the brothel and the surrounding area."

"I already know that. I spoke with Blackwell and Remi. I'm here for your exact statement. Where were you? What did you see?" Sniffing the air, Lewis leans closer, examining Pratt's flushed cheeks.

"Well, after the notification went off, I headed straight for my bike." Pratt mumbles, gripping the edge of his desk with his hands. "Across the street from the brothel, I parked and ordered the lower-ranking red stripes to search the crowd. All three doxies I saw in the street had intact trackers. I also scanned all the doxies at Foxe Brothel. I believe Blackwell was inside the brothel, and Remi was scanning trackers outside the Pink Lace Brothel across the street. After about 20 minutes of scanning trackers, we sent some of the lower ranks to continue the search in a wider perimeter, and others took statements from clients who were there during the theft. Lastly, I went and interviewed two of the doxy's regulars."

"Are you done with this?" Lewis asks, picking up the

empty coffee cup, he smells it, his eyes narrowed judgementally.

"Ye.. yes," Pratt stammers, his cheeks blushing.

"Is that butter flavoured?"

"And brown sugar," Pratt says, smiling uncomfortably, not wanting to displease his boss.

"Rat?"

His cheeks flush even redder, to a bright crimson. "They got my name wrong." Scanning the faces along the row of desks, he hopes no one is paying attention.

Detective Croft, who sits a few desks away, is staring at them with a smile exuding unfiltered schadenfreude. When Pratt meets his eyes, Croft snaps his head down, looking back at the stack of papers on his desk. Bloody eavesdropping, boot licking…

"Pratt, are you listening?" Lewis glances in the direction he's staring, but misses Croft's prying, and looking back down at Pratt's red eyes, his expression is a mix of pity and annoyance.

"Yes, sir!" Great, I must seem like a drunken fool to him, gawking around like some dim-witted younkin. Wanting to run and push Croft out of his desk for this embarrassment, he holds his breath, fighting to force down his anger.

"Who spoke with the brothel director?"

"Blackwell."

"Is there anything useful in the statements you took?"

"No, nothing."

"Fine." Lewis walks away, leaving the coffee cup on the edge of the desk.

Pratt glares back in Croft's direction, but he never looks up from his work, steadfast in his performance of the dedicated worker. With a final angry grunt, he gives up, and looks back down at his own stack of files. Dammit. Lewis knows I've been drinking.

Wringing his hands, he exhales, wanting to imagine a world where he's considered a success and not a drunk. Unless he catches me with vodka at my desk, he won't say anything.

Thankfully, the last 50 minutes of work go by without incident. Pratt gets on his motorbike and heads to the Entertainment District. Wasting no time, he buys a large bottle of plain vodka, and twisting the cap open, immediately drinks a quarter of it. He enters Thieves Haven Pub, choosing a seat at the bar.

"What can I get you?" A brown-haired doxy leans over the sticky counter, revealing her cleavage, a fake smile plastered on her tired face.

"Do you want to take a shot of pineapple vodka with me?"

"Sure," the doxy says, smiling, and then pours two shots of neon yellow vodka and they clink them together.

"Lucky lottery," they say in unison and then throw them back, the tangy pineapple tingling their tongues.

"Another," he says, grinning.

She pours another two shots. "Lucky lottery!" This time louder. The sugar makes Pratt feel light-headed, but he ignores it.

"Oh, and one for my friend Remi." He laughs, gesturing to the empty seat beside him.

She nods and pours a final shot. Pratt tries to drink it, but has to swish it around his mouth before he can manage it, leaving the sugar-coating on his teeth.

"That's eight credits," she says, pulling out the reader before another drink can be ordered.

He holds out his wrist to be scanned and then tips her an extra two credits, feeling invigorated by their conversation.

"Thank you," she says, beaming.

With a final dip of her head, he watches her walk away with the empty glasses. Alone again. Around him the bar fills with men who've also left work. Sitting there awkwardly watching the joyful chatter, he feels keenly aware of his lack of friends. I hope she'll come back and talk to me.

As the doxy pours drinks for the other men in the bar, he wonders if she's avoiding him. Finally, he stands and wanders back into the street where the loud pumping music makes him feel off balance. Pratt careens through a group of drunk men singing

"Reach for the Orbs," the latest pop song to top the charts.

Laughing to himself he shuffles forward behind the crowd of singers. Idiots. They actually think they can win the lottery. No one wins. Taking another large gulp of vodka from his nearly empty bottle, vodka drips down his chin.

"We're all losers!" he yells to no one in particular.

His head spins and he leans against a concrete wall, watching passersby pretend not to see him.

"You look like you could use something to eat." Pratt turns to see a skinny younkin in a light pink dress.

"What would you know about it?"

"We have deep fried paste baskets at Crystal Faeries Brothel," she says.

"I'm not here for that." He waves the small female away.

She smiles, leaps to the side, and goes up to the next man standing aimlessly in the road. Looking directly up, the spinning slows, allowing him to balance his weight and stand up straight.

An ad for artificial licorice-flavoured candy dances and sparkles above him. I should eat something. Analyzing the road, he finally sets his sights on Kings Pub, knocking into strangers with each shaky step towards the entrance.

"Get off!" An angry-looking man wearing an expensive green and silver jacket slams him into the ground, indifferent to his red stripes.

"I'll arrest you," Pratt slurs back, but the man has already disappeared. With a sway backwards, and a step forward, he stood and hobbled into the pub.

"What can I get you, sir?" A doxy locks her arm around his hanging elbow, helping him to a seat at the empty bar.

Looking up at the menu, his eyes bounce slowly along the words. "Deep-fried french fry paste, and… the deep-fried pickle paste."

"Sure," she says and disappears behind the bar, pressing buttons on a small screen to complete the order.

Resting his head in his hands, he closes his heavy eyelids and takes another swig of vodka.

The doxy slides the order of food beside him and then picks up a cloth and wipes the counter. Glancing up at her, he stares at her large round eyes captivated by her appearance.

"What's your name?" he asks.

He knows it's not her, she's much too young, but despite that, he can't help but ask, because part of him wants to hold on to this false hope.

"Mandy," she says with a smile. "I'll be at Nubian Nights Brothel tomorrow."

Of course it's not her, but she has the same smile, or has my memory of her morphed?

"Did you know a doxy named Grace?"

"Um, maybe. I've known a couple. What brothel?"

"It doesn't exist anymore, but it was called Black Spice."

"I'm sorry, I've never heard of it," she says, giving him a thoughtful smile, and then greets the next customer, leaving him to stew in his sorrow.

Exhaling slowly, Pratt takes a small bite of the fried paste, which stings his pineapple burnt tongue with salt. She's dead, you idiot. She's been dead for years. Recycled. He tries to remember the details of her, but everything feels blurry; the noise of the bar fades out around him, leaving only his thoughts.

Slipping into a dream, he walks around the Technology District as a younkin. The advertisements follow him like mosquitos, swarming as he moves through the street.

"Trevor! Have you considered joining the Mighty Younkins?" An ad with a pale, raven-haired doxy tosses him a digital ball. "The City Champion wins a night with any doxy!"

Feeling uncomfortable at the offer for sex, he quickly looks away.

"Have you prayed today? The womb of Mary is here to guide you," a Shaxocs Caller says, staring at him suspiciously.

"Wash your sinful thoughts away at the Natatorium by bathing in the womb of Mary." Pratt pivots the corner to escape the Shaxocs Caller's stare, but as soon as he's taken a breath, another advertisement is injecting its venom.

"You need to toughen up, boy!" A large man in red workout gear jumps out at him from an ad in the alley. "My program will help you gain 50 pounds of muscle in just six weeks."

Kissing his biceps, he gazed up with a mirthful smirk.

"Vote, do your diligence and vote in every election." On the large screens, a man with a book and glasses follows him like a scurrying mouse.

"Every three months we vote in Krevax, to ensure that democracy is serving the people. The next election is in 22 days. Are you informed on the current candidates? There are 12 men to choose from: Lawrence Radcliff, Sean Rockwell, Tobias Freeman, Luke ..." Pratt turns into a new road, evading the election notification.

"A vote for Sean Rockwell is a vote for productivity!" A tall, chubby man thrusts his chin up. "I know how to get things done! Vote for me to fix Krevax's economy. Say no to bill 361-B, and yes to bill 523-F."

"Hi Trevor!" Grace says and blows him a kiss. "Come visit me in the Entertainment District."

"Are you hungry?" An image of paste tubes dancing in a circle flashes above him. He looks again for Grace, but she's gone.

"Try the new hamburger-flavoured paste, with natural and artificial flavours!" Pratt turns again, but this time he feels dizzy. Running faster, he tries to outrun the noise of the advertisements.

"Buy a new faster motorcycle from..."

"Take Abalix for a better night's sleep..." His head spinning, he turns down a new street, ads screaming at him from every direction.

"Are you feeling anxious? You may have a mental illness..." He closes his eyes.

"Scan your body for cancer..." He falls to the ground.

"Cotton Candy paste with a crunchy sour spoon, eat the paste, eat the spoon!" He opens his eyes and immediately pukes fried paste on the bar. A stout man grabs him by the shoulders, painfully pinching his skin.

"It's time for you to leave," he says, shoving Pratt out into the road. Stumbling forward, he walks towards a ditch and slumps over onto the garbage; with a last gulp of vodka out of the bottle, he washes away the taste of puke. I'm such a loser. Why do I still love you? Who loves a doxy? A dead doxy.

Around him the garbage shifts underneath his weight, making space for his head to lean against a pile of used food containers. With the empty bottle cradled in his arms, he falls back asleep.

Grace smiles kindly at him. "Back again, Trevor? You've been here seven days in a row."

Leading the way to a small room in the middle of the brothel, she pulls closed the black velvet drapes behind them.

"I know!" Pratt says, reaching out to hold her delicate hand, his heart pounding in his chest at the sight of her.

Grace flinches away and sits down on the bed. "Why did you do that?"

"I don't know. Can I though?" he asks and sits down beside her, reaching his hand out again, hoping to be close to her, wanting to call her his own.

"I guess, if that's what you want?"

"It is, yes," he says, and holds her hand. She glances over at him, with something sad in her expression, but says nothing.

Pratt rests his head on her shoulder, closes his eyes in the dream, and falls into a peaceful sleep.

06 | WINDOW WASHER

VIOLET

Footsteps shuffled through the hallway outside the white-walled, one-bedroom apartment. Violet flashes a nervous glance at the door as she wipes the window with a rag.

Listening intently, she hears a creaking sound and then it's quiet again. She breathes a shallow sigh of relief, nevertheless, behind the mask, her angular eyes are fearful. Looking slowly around, she examines the pristine apartment, where there isn't one speck of dust or item out of place.

A small table with two matching chairs sit near the entrance, their plastic washed to a clean shine. A carefully vacuumed couch, where she slept, took up one side. Above are plastic cupboards filled with alphabetically organized plastic tubes, cleaning supplies, and her small pile of belongings. In front of the couch is the wall screen, sprayed and dusted, which separates the two living spaces.

The window where she stood every evening runs along the entire apartment on one side, it's glass polished from top to bottom. Spraying the glass unnecessarily, she wipes the cleaner away with a skittish twitch. Hours pass in silence, but Violet doesn't leave the window.

She stands watching the entrance door over her shoulder, like a mouse trapped inside an owl's roost. When there's any noise in the hallway, she frantically sprays the glass again and wipes it with the rag. After another threat has ended, it takes several minutes for her to compose herself. Please. Let it be over.

The time on her tracker flashes 7:32 P.M. in lime green cursive. Shuffling her sore feet, she leans against the glass, but does not dare sit down. The hallway is dead silent.

Staring out the window, she glares at the same spot, an advertisement showing the power of *Klipper's Cleaning Supplies*.

The bright blue image flashes between a peon mopping a concrete floor, then it shows her dancing with the mop, and finally a smiling man patting her on the back. It says, *Make your Man Happy with Klippers Improved Formula!* Make your man happy? The words make no sense. No one has a man. The men are the ones who have peons.

Closing her eyes for what feels like a second, her alarm announces it's 10:30 P.M, jolting her awake. She stares at the apartment door. Everything is still untouched and clean.

With shaky hands, she sprays the window and wipes away an ear print. She puts the cleaning supplies in the cabinet above the couch and walks over to the entrance-way closet. Undressing quickly, she tosses her clothes in a bucket and wraps herself in a worn towel.

With trembling hands she opens the door an inch, looking through the crack of light. Peons have filled the hallway, their chatter echoing off the walls. Throwing open the door, she scrambles into the crowd of other females and gets in line for the bathroom. Her eyes dart at the faces in the hall as she reaches the stall.

Once inside, she locks the handle, exhaling a held breath. Sitting down, she reaches into her body, and pulls out a small cup. Examining it for a moment, she re-inserts the cup, feeling disappointed. Still no blood?

A shallow breath constricted her lungs, and she has to close her eyes to recover from the growing feeling of faintness. She sprays her hands with sanitizer and turns, opening the door an eye length.

Another peon is staring at her impatiently, her foot tapping in quick succession on the carpet. She swings open the door and walks past her, making her way down to the showers in the basement. Four other peons in various states of undress stand in Section Two, Violet the shortest among them.

Unlike the others, she leaves on her mask. The cold water turns on and she stands under it shivering, quickly soaping her brown skin with olive undertones. Holding her mask slightly away from her face, she scrubs, before letting the mask snap back once the soap bubbles have stopped stinging her eyes.

Steam fills the room as the other peons enjoy the hot water, for the price of five credits a head. Springing out of the cold, she wraps her underfed frame in the towel and puts her head down, rushing to the elevator.

Pressing the button for the top floor with a numb finger, she stares at her reflection in the mirrored walls. At the top of the apartment building, the door to the elevator opens, but she doesn't move, rather she continues to stare at herself.

Despite her efforts, she cannot stifle a sob and holds the towel up to her mask to muffle the noise. She stands there continuing to sob, black straight hair dripping, chest heaving. You're so weak. Worthless.

"Beep"

The elevator is called back to the waiting horde in the

basement. Taking a deep breath to gather herself, she presses the button for two. The elevator opens on the second floor and she tiptoes back to the apartment. As she reaches the door she doesn't open it, but presses her ear against it, listening. Grabbing the doorknob, fear courses through her like electricity as she twists it and pushes into the apartment.

Slowly opening the door wide enough to slide through, she steps inside, her shoulder against the frame to close it as quietly as possible behind her.

"Click"

Everything is the same. Gliding silently through the room, she opens the door at the end of the couch. She breathes a sigh of relief when she sees the bedroom is empty. I'm alone.

Walking back to the entrance, she hangs her towel in the closet and dresses in another light grey peon uniform. The noise of peons returning from the showers fills the hallway, causing her to dash to the couch.

Everything's okay, it's just the others coming up from their showers. Under the cushions, she pulls out a folded sheet and wraps it tightly around her body. Pulling her knees up to her chest, she leaves nothing but her mask exposed and watches the room through the slits. She holds onto her knees even tighter as fear climbs up her spine.

The ceiling of advertisements calls down to her. *Can't sleep? Try Auloren for a restful night.* The soft purple ad shows a smiling man with his head resting on a pillow. She stares at the pulsing light until her eyelids feel heavy and finally close.

A group of young girls sit in a circle around a box of three items; a mask, a ribbon, and a link of copper chain. Violet reaches out her hand and picks up the mask. The other girls stand and begin running chaotically all around her.

One of them kicks her in the head as she runs by and yells, "put it on."

She lifts the mask to her face. Sharp teeth fill the once smooth plastic. As she tries to push the mask away, it only digs deeper into her flesh.

Screaming in pain, she feels the plastic eating her skin away as she claws helplessly. Violet wakes with a start to a shuffling sound outside the door. The sheet is wet from her sweat, but she's too afraid to move. She stares at the metal groove lines on the doorknob, holding her breath. Rigid.

With the sound dissipating, the room returns to silence and she exhales. I wish I was anyone else. She closes her eyes and an uneasy sleep follows.

Violet jolts awake when the alarms blare for the men to shower. He didn't come home. Maybe he's dead? She shakes her head. No, he'll be back tonight, it was just another night in the Entertainment District.

Folding the sheet, she puts it under the couch cushion and wipes away the dents in the fabric. Looking through the cleaning supplies, she makes a checklist on her tracker of things she needs to buy; rags, sanitizer, screen cleaner. Then she looks through the vase of plastic tubes on the dining room table. I'll get a couple more flavours. Turning back towards the couch, she walks past it and into the bedroom, where a large king-sized bed takes up most of the room.

In the closet there are six red-stripe uniforms and a wall of cubbies filled with clothes, books, and bottles of booze. Violet looks through the multi-coloured bottles of liquor, noting the blueberry vodka, which sits more than half empty.

Opening the bottle, she takes several gulps until her breathing slows, and then returns the bottle to the shelf. She walks back through the apartment and out the front door. In the elevator, a peon from the third floor tilts her head to her in greeting. Violet tilts her head back.

"You're the one who always takes the cold showers, aren't you?"

"Um, yeah," Violet says.

"Why?"

"Um." Violet looks down at her feet. "It's expensive."

"Oh, it's not that expensive! I would never shower in cold water. It's the only time of the day I don't feel frozen. Aren't you cold?" She moves closer to feel Violet's arm.

"A bit, I guess," Violet says, stepping back, as she wraps her arms around her chest. The elevator doors open.

"Well, have a good day."

"Thanks," she says, watching her walk away.

Oh no. I didn't tell her to have a good day. What's wrong with me?

As the elevator doors close, she also realizes this is where she's going too, and grabs the metal door, so she can scoot through. Walking out into the Enforcement District, black glass towers over her as the Watchtower looms in the distance.

Wandering through the streets, she stops to touch cracks on the concrete ground, watching how the neon ceiling above burns shadows below her feet. In an alleyway ahead, small shops press together between the towers.

The first shop was filled with ornate, brightly painted plastic flowers. When she touches one of the fake rose petals, the feeling of the felt material almost makes her sneeze.

Across the street, she can see the small decrepit concrete building where she buys her cleaning supplies. She steps inside and slowly winds through the overstocked aisles, collecting a bag of rags, sanitizer spray, and a small bottle of screen cleaner.

In the last aisle, a small blue bottle labelled *Ocean Spirits* catches her eye, and she picks it up and opens it, smelling it deeply. It smells sweet. I wonder if the ocean actually smelled like that?

Continuing through the aisle, she touches the other

pretty rainbow-coloured bottles on the shelf, before going up to the cashier to pay.

"That's one and a quarter credits," the attendant says as he places the items in a plastic bag.

Nodding, she holds up her wrist and he scans it. With a quick step out into the alley, she leaves the shop and stops at a vending machine: "Violet, Peon, 17, credits available - 89."

After choosing two pastes from the machine, one Very Berry Blueberry Blast, and one French Fry flavoured, plus two tubes of hydration gel, she looks around to make sure no one is observing her too closely.

When she is sure it's safe, she squishes between the wall and the vending machine, and sits out of sight from the crowd. Opening the cap on the hydration gel, she drinks a sip before setting it aside, then opens the Very Berry Blueberry Blast, taking a small bite. It's sweet and sour.

Breathing a heavy sigh, she eats the paste as people shuffle past her, unaware she is watching. Violet studies how they all have different ways of walking, how some people talk loudly with their hands, and how others make themselves so small they almost seem invisible. Tracing a scratched line in the concrete beside her, she wonders how long she could stay hidden.

After a couple of hours, she stands and slides back out into the open space. Wrapping her arms tight around her waist she moves through the crowd in a large loop back towards the apartment. Traffic filled with the noise of men on bikes, in large trucks, and behind wheels of two-doored cars, move thoughtlessly through the streets.

Red stripes walk confidently into the black buildings around her. I forgot the blueberry vodka! She shakes her head. It's okay, now I have something to do tomorrow. She looks up at the advertisements and closes her eyes. They say the sun feels warm. I hope that's true. That way, when I get to the Orbs, I'll never be cold again.

Up ahead, she can see the dark grey apartment building and dread fills her stomach.

"Hey!" It's the peon from the third floor again. "It's you, right?"

"Yes, still me."

"Good, come to the nail salon with me. A few of us from the building are going," she says, her eyes smiling behind the mask. "I'm Nancy, by the way."

"I have too much to do today."

"Oh, that's okay, maybe next time." Nancy turns on her heel and walks away.

"It's Violet," she says impulsively, making her stomach turn. Why did I do that?

"Nice to meet you, Violet," Nancy says, calling back.

Feeling her cheeks flush, she snaps her gaze down and stares at the ground. With an awkward jog, she hurries back to the tower and pushes the button to call the elevator.

In the elevator, she stares at her reflection in the mirror, lifting the bottom edge of the mask slightly up, and then letting it snap back. The doors open on the second floor and she shuffles back into the empty apartment, her mind lost in sorrowful thoughts.

She puts the tubes of paste and cleaning supplies away. In the bedroom, she pours plain vodka into the blueberry vodka bottle until they're both about half full and then takes another swig of the diluted blueberry booze.

Grabbing a laundered rag and a half-empty bottle of glass cleaner, she stands in her usual spot in front of the window.

07 | A DESOLATE SHADOW

BLACKWELL

BLACKWELL, REMI AND PRATT STAND IN A SEMI-CIRCLE, WHITE masks on their faces.

"What happened to its hair?" comes a muffled bark from Remi.

"Maybe the motel attendant shaved it?" Pratt says. "I've seen hair for sale in the lower districts."

Blackwell's face is emotionless, but the feeling of sudden panic makes his hands numb as he stares at the doxy's rotted face. The drunk man. It's him. Or… her. Sick balloons in his stomach and he has to force it down.

Two images flip in his mind, the drunk man and the bag of red hair, toggling like a deck of cards with only two numbers, the joker and the queen.

"Maybe the spider who stole her took it as a souvenir," Remi says and then laughs.

Blackwell shakily leans over and picks up the white suit and shimmering green shirt. Will they see in the footage that I let her get away? What does it matter?

If they fire me, I'll finally have a good enough reason to recycle myself. The deck in his mind slows and then stops on the red hair, making the strange feeling return. What does this mean?

"What would he do with it?" Pratt asks.

"Who knows?" Remi clicks on his wrist. "I'll ask him." He taps on the Sweet Dreams Motel in a map of the district.

"Whoa, no recent trackers of men in this room, except the attendant who called us in." He holds his wrist up to his mouth and says, "call precinct."

"Connecting."

Moving awkwardly to the other side of the mattress, Blackwell leans down, picks up a metal box with one blue plastic gloved hand and opens the lid. Inside are four small, clear plastic bags of black powder. Was she taking nostaliem?

"Captain Lewis, here."

"Remi here, the doxy is dead, and the man who did this has no tracking data…" Remi trails off, as Blackwell holds up the metal box for him to see.

"Nostaliem," Blackwell says.

"Okay, we have nostaliem on the scene as well," Remi says.

"Nostaliem? With the dead doxy. I'm sending a lab crew up there now." The call disconnects.

"Nostaliem," Remi says. "This stuff is everywhere now."

Blackwell nods and pulls out an evidence bag from his belt. Was she taking nostaliem before she ran?

He labels the metal box: **Case** #162300-BX; **Item**: Drug Paraphernalia; **Date**: 13, 02, 181 A.W.; **Test**: Blood DNA + fingerprints + Substance Analysis.

"If there's nostaliem," Pratt says. "Do you think she did *that* to herself then?"

"No way." Remi shakes his head. "I'm sure the sick fuck who kidnapped her, took it himself, and then killed her."

"So when you take nostaliem you can either do *that* to yourself, or to someone else," Pratt says.

"Exactly," Remi says, nodding. "Must be some high."

With forced calm, Blackwell grabs plastic tags from his belt and clips them to the white suit and green sequined top, mislabelling them **Case** #126300-BX. Next, he correctly labels the details: **Item**: clothing (3 pieces); **Date**: 13, 02, 181 A.W.; **Test**: Blood DNA + Fibres.

If they track them down, they will explain it away as a simple accident. Even better, they'll just get lost in the system, no suit, no DNA swabs showing I was in contact with her.

It was also crowded, so maybe they won't have a good camera angle of me running into her? Why am I thinking about this?

It doesn't matter. None of this matters. Still, just in case I don't go to the recycling facility tomorrow. Once marked, he leaves the room and walks a few steps into the hallway, away from Remi and Pratt. Why did she want to leave?

Pulling off his blue gloves, he brushes the inside of his wrist, making the projected screen light up above his tracker.

"Connect to Red Stripe Database," he whispers. The screen flashes yellow, then after a moment turns green.

"Connected," the screen says in a syrupy feminine voice.

"Send all the files on females with removed trackers," Blackwell says.

Maybe females run away?

His arm lights up purple and he quickly scrolls through the hundreds of thousands of files, randomly clicking on one. The file describes the kidnapping of a young generator by members of the Prekap gang. Swiping them to the left, he deletes the list.

"Send unsolved files on females whose trackers were removed." This list is smaller, but still in the tens of thousands.

If a female actually ran away, maybe they would have no suspects? Another swipe to the left.

"Send files on females whose trackers were found cut out, but no suspects were found."

Two files load onto the screen, he clicks on the first one, Designation: Generator, Number: M-730-83-00H, Name: Zoe, Age: 35, Date: Month - 09, Day - 01, Year - 177.

The file describes an escape from the recycling facility. There are always runners from the Recycling District, impressive she actually got away.

He clicks on the second file, Designation: Generator, Number: K-729-01-74D, Name: Rose, Age: 23, Missing: Month - 06, Day - 22, Year - 180. Hmm, both generators.

Blackwell clicks on Rose's photo, which opens to a form that is empty except for one line: *footage shows the generator stealing an infant.*

A generator stealing an infant? I've never heard of that happening before?

With a press and hold on the screen, he saves the files in his personal folder, then clicks on the current case file and types "deceased" below Kaliann's photo. With an uneasy exhale, he walks back into the room to finish collecting evidence.

"I once got malicadihea from a doxy..." Pratt blurts drunkenly and then blushes a deep red, his voice trailing off as he pulls out a sharp surgical blade from a black case.

"That's nothing! I've had them all at least once, and some of them twice," Remi says, boasting.

"You would," Pratt says, laughing as he makes a cut below the rib cage and inserts a glass thermometer into the nick. With a slow step, Blackwell searches the rest of the room for evidence.

"Well, there's no exact timeline." Pratt holds up the thermometer.

"This body is 18 degrees Celsius, the same temperature as the city." He shakes the thermometer. "Based on the condition of it, I'd say it's been between 28 and 32 hours."

"Mm," Remi says. "The official time of death is…" He pauses as he fills out the form on his wrist. "13, 01, 181." And then looks up.

"Pratt, are you good to stay here until the lab crew arrives?" Pratt nods as he wraps the thermometer back in the foam and closes the protective covering.

Unzipping a larger black case, he pulls out a camera and begins taking photos of the body. Remi follows Blackwell out of the room.

"You know, I don't understand why anyone would try this shit," Remi says.

Blackwell continues to walk down the hallway in silence. Why would a doxy run away from her brothel? Why would a generator steal an infant?

Remi sharply pokes Blackwell's right shoulder in response to the silence. "You don't agree?" They stare off momentarily.

"Nostaliem, you're right, of course," Blackwell says.

Remi looks annoyed, but doesn't push the conversation further. Blackwell turns away from him and they stand, waiting for the elevator in silence. The metal doors open as Remi looks suspiciously at Blackwell, but neither speak as they climb in.

As they move down the side of the metal building, they watch the city swallow them. Vast towers stand like statues of gods, nearly touching the ceiling of advertisements above them. The elevator doors open and the men walk out into Krevax, the last city on Earth, 120 million hearts beating in a cold concrete cage.

They walk through the parking lot towards a row of bikes. Blackwell shifts to balance the weight of the metal underneath him. Revving his bike forward, he heads toward the highway, watching the Technology District stream by. Men in muted suits of navy, grey and forest green move through the bright streets, their noses practically touching their handheld screens. The holograms and loud advertisements of the district whirl by, making his head throb.

As he crosses into the News District, he focuses on the feeling of his cold handlebars, shutting out the aggressive propaganda permeating every wall. Most importantly, he keeps his eyes down to avoid the gaze of any newsmen, as they were always looking for a story. Hell, they'd recycle their peons just to hear a new one, from the next peon in line.

Blackwell looks up enviously, as the marble towers of the University District come into view. If I was smarter, maybe I could have been a political scientist. The scent of tobacco in the air leaves him imagining himself smoking in one of the secret speakeasies behind a wall of old books. Perhaps in the next life. I could start it tomorrow, if I was brave enough.

The road curves lower and they enter the Devotion District. The scent of chlorine makes his nose crinkle in disgust. Fuck the Shaxocs Callers. Anxiously, he stares ahead, wanting to leave the holy district as quickly as possible. Sirens pierce the quiet at the border as he crosses into the Enforcement District and can finally breathe easily.

As he moves through the black towers, he veers to the right, towards the entrance to the station, descending past the security booth and into the parking lot below.

At the bottom, he parks his bike in its designated spot and stands, stretching out his legs. She must have known she was going to die. There would be no coming back from shaving her head—hair is a key part of a doxy's identity. I guess she's braver than me.

Drifting past the circle of elevators, he uses his tracker to access Gromwell and makes his way silently to his desk. An uncomfortable pit grows in his stomach and he vibrates his knee against the wall.

If she's braver than me, how can she be an animal? Are doxies really animals, or are they like us?

He inhales sharply, as Kaliann's red hair once again flashes in his mind. She shaved her head and cut out her tracker, so she could escape to try nostaliem. A pang of sadness hits him. She made all those choices. It doesn't matter anymore, she's dead.

But why did I take her hair? For what feels like an hour, he sits staring at the wall, trying to understand, but he can't make sense of it.

Pulling his chair closer to the desk, he grabs a file and begins reading through the report. The file describes a nostaliem addict's deceased body, this one, a young man, discovered a few days prior.

Flipping the page, he stares at photos of the naked body with slit wrists. He grabs the next in line, the description of another nostaliem addict follows, this time a man in his late 40s was pictured on a mattress in an empty room. Blood pools around the body from where he has shot himself in the head.

Looking at the dozens of files containing bodies of dead men, he thinks about the thousands of other cases that had already been filed away.

Why are there so many bodies?

You can get recycled if you're tired of living, but now… suddenly all these men are choosing to die at their own hand, and leaving their bodies on display. Even Kaliann shaved her head and left her body to rot?

We have half of the Enforcement District investigating nostaliem and we don't even know what it is. Maybe, I should take nostaliem, then I could definitely kill myself. The violent self-inflicted deaths stream through his mind and he shakes his head. *I don't want it to be like that.*

By now it's late and Blackwell can't ignore his stomach any longer, so he finally heads out of the station. The road is dead, except for bored men out looking for violence. The bike hums through the darkened streets as he makes his way back to his apartment. Blackwell parks and walks towards a fluorescent vending machine, scanning his tracker on one light. Pain pulses near his temples from the flashing neon.

"Charlie Blackwell, age 27, credits available - 1,156," an automated feminine voice speaks through the intercom.

Green bulbs light up behind all the items. Wasting no time looking through the assortment of ever changing artificially flavoured pastes, he immediately chooses the plain variety in the top corner, along with two hydration gel tubes.

After tapping on the screen, the tubes worth one credit each fall into the drawer. He pushes on the bottom of the tube and eats the entire thing in three bites. Twisting the cap off of a gel tube, he drinks it and throws the empty plastics on an already overflowing garbage pile, pocketing the second hydration gel for later.

He walks past his bike towards a grungy-looking building and scans his wrist, making the door swing open. In front of him the out-of-order sign dangles over the elevator and he turns towards the stairs, swiftly making his way up 16 floors.

In the hallway he hears his neighbour yelling profanities at his peon, but ignores this and continues to his apartment. The door shuts behind him, trapping him once again in isolation.

Removing his clothes until he's just in his boxers, he pulls out the bag of red curls from underneath his mattress and lies down, staring at it. The strange feeling returns, something about it is comforting, but also sad and slightly unnerving. He buries his face into his elbow to block out the advertisements, but sleep doesn't come.

After hours of tossing and turning, the morning alarms blare over the intercoms, relieving him from his torture. Standing up, dishevelled, he returns the bag of hair to its spot under his mattress and walks over to the closet. He grabs his towel and leaves for the basement.

Men filter into the shower stalls around him, as he waits under his spout in section 16, holding a bar of soap. The angry man from across the hall stands under a spout a few feet from Blackwell, his expression a permanent scowl. The alarm bell goes off for the showers and the icy cold water turns on.

Scanning his wrist to pay four credits for hot water, he turns it to the highest temperature possible and stands under the stream, scalding his skin. For one perfect moment warmth envelops him as he scrubs away the dirt and dust of yesterday, then the alarm bells signal the end of the water and cold air climbs over him again.

Wrapping his waist with the towel, he heads towards the exit, following a line of men climbing up the stairs.

Back in his apartment, he dresses in another black and red-lined uniform and grabs a pack of dental chewing paste. He spits the paste into the wrapper and leaves, heading for one of the communal bathroom stalls on his floor. In the bathroom, he throws out the wrapper, pees and wipes his hands in sanitizer.

A line has formed and he side steps past the men in matching grey uniforms, as they stare up at him disapprovingly. He knows no Manufacturer wants to share living space with a red stripe, but can't imagine leaving his younkin district.

A stabbing ache fills his chest as he continues on towards

the stairway. The lights outside shine at full capacity and the advertisements above him glare.

Ignoring his hunger, he heads past the vending machine and climbs onto his bike, making his way through traffic up to the Enforcement District. At the security booth, he nods at the guard, and continues down into the parking lot. Walking past the Watchtower elevators and through the tiger-engraved door, he enters Gromwell Station.

He steps into the first open elevator and leans his head against the wall, wishing he'd been brave enough to get recycled. The doors slide open and he heads towards his desk, avoiding his coworkers as he passes by them. He sees an unmarked white envelope sitting on top of the stack of folders. Picking up the envelope, he turns it over a few times, before pulling out a typed letter.

Charlie Blackwell, Vice Detective at Gromwell Station - 6:00pm tonight - 2961-43rd Block, Recycling District. I have an opportunity you are looking for.

Blackwell shakes his head. An opportunity I am looking for?

The only thing I'm looking for is death. He tosses it onto his desk, but continues staring at it.

Could this have anything to do with Kaliann?

He picks up the letter again. No. This must be something else. No one cares about a dead doxy. He re-reads the words. Whatever this is, it could be a good way to die.

08 | WAITING
VIOLET

VIOLET STARES OUT THE WINDOW, WHERE AN AD WITH A shimmering rainbow catches her attention.

Dancing hands in tiny aprons, salsa their way across purple, blue, green, yellow, orange and red rings, each one with a different colour nail polish. *Looking Your Best Makes Cleaning Fun! Rainbow's Nail Service!*

Looking down, she stares at her own colourless nails, flaking from chemicals. Footsteps move in the hallway behind her, causing her shoulders to tense in fear. The door across the hall opens with a loud creak.

"Hi Sally," the man says to his peon, a smile in his voice.

"How was your day, sir?" Sally asks cheerfully.

"Busy, but good, I..." His voice disappears as the door shuts.

Pain swells in Violet's chest. According to the *laws of Shaxoism* in the *Book of Infinitum*, those who have been weak will receive punishment in their future lives. I am being tested for being weak in my last life and it is vital I prove myself in this one. If I fully embrace this punishment and show strength, I will be reborn into better circumstances.

Heavy footsteps enter the hallway, and she holds her breath. Please don't let it be him. Let him be dead in the Entertainment District; killed in a bar fight. The door clicks open, making her jaw lock, and she sprays the cleaner, glancing back nervously. No. It's him. He's home.

"Get over here, now," Remi says, pointing at the ground as he sits down at the plastic table. "Take off my shoes."

Violet drops the spray bottle and rag in fear. You can get through this. Just do exactly what he says and it will be fine.

"Yes, sir!" Scurrying over, she kneels on the ground in front of him and unlaces the first black boot, sliding it off his foot.

"This table feels sticky." Remi wipes the table with his palm. "What do you do here all day?"

"I'll clean it!" Violet stands to go grab the cleaner, but Remi pushes her back to the ground.

"Later," he says. Staring at the boot still in her hands, fear pulses through her, making the triangle pattern of the fabric on the laces jump out at her with each beat of her heart. Everything's okay. You're okay.

He smacks her across the cheek. "Pay attention. Are you going to let me sit here all night with one boot?"

"No, sir." She grabs the other boot and unlaces it.

With her ear still ringing from the slap, she watches him open a tube of pizza paste and lean back into the chair. Taking off his socks, she rolls them in a ball, grabs the boots, and places the items in the closet. Hiding her look of anguish behind her mask, she returns to his feet and rubs them.

"I saw a dead doxy today," he says, chuckling. "Even rotting, she had a prettier face than you."

Violet closes her eyes and continues rubbing his feet. Just breathe. It will be over soon.

"Someone kidnapped and killed her, slit her arm wide open," he says, as he grabs her left arm and holds it up.

"Right here." Grinning, he traces down her arm from her wrist to her elbow. Staring hard at his bare feet, she's too afraid to look up.

"Are you listening?" he asks.

"Ye…yes," she stammers, trapped with her arm in the air. He shoves her away.

"Bring me a drink."

"Yes, sir." Disappearing into the bedroom, she screams silently behind her mask, her hands in tight fists.

Stop it. This is temporary. When you have saved enough money, you can buy into the lottery. Grabbing a plastic cup from above the liquor bottles, she unsteadily holds it as she pours some of the diluted blueberry vodka in. She opens a second bottle and pours in a splash of pineapple vodka to cover the dilution.

The room pulses around her and she can barely see, causing her to fall to the ground, vodka splashing on her arm. Get up.

With the smell of alcohol in her nostrils, she wipes her arm on her apron and walks back into the kitchen. After placing the cup on the table in front of Remi, she nervously waits for his reaction. While reaching for the cup, he glances down and stares at the wet mark on her apron.

"That better not be vodka," he says, leaving the cup untouched.

"I don't think it is," Violet whispers, trying not to cry. He rips it off of her and smells it.

"This is expensive." He throws the apron at her head. "You fucking useless bitch!"

"I'm sorry," Violet says and falls into a ball at his feet. Leaping out of his chair, he grabs a handful of her hair and pushes her head into the ground.

"I should break your neck." Remi's hot breath hits her ear. "One day I will, just you wait."

"Please," Violet says.

After a minute, he lets go of her and sits back down. Frozen, she doesn't move, but listens to him take a sip of the vodka. Warm liquid spreads down her legs. No. Please don't.

"Disgusting animal," Remi says. "You better clean that up." Standing, he steps around her and walks to the couch. The screen switches on and the sound of race cars going around a track roars out.

"And that's lap number 100, only 50 more to go," an announcer says. *"Fendley and Jabbar are fighting for the lead now. Vuniz looks to be making..."*

Violet tunes out the noise and rolls over onto her back, staring out at nothing. Get up. Clean up. Get up now. Still, she can't move. Minutes tick by, but still she is lying in her pee. I'm disgusting. An ugly, disgusting animal. She digs her nails into her wet knees. I deserve this.

After an hour, the screen turns off and Remi shuts the door to the bedroom. Sitting up, she looks around the dark room, the neon lights from the advertisements making the shadows shift around her.

She stands and heads towards the cabinet with the cleaning supplies above the couch. Collecting a rag, an empty bucket, and an all-purpose spray, she wipes her legs, then soaks up the pee on the ground, squishing the liquid into the bucket. Once the floor is dry, she sprays the cleaner and returns to the cupboard, where she takes a dollop of sanitizer and rubs the gel on her hands and legs. Grabbing a fresh cloth, she wipes the floor until it's clean.

She pulls herself up beside the table and feels the entire surface. It isn't sticky. It's not fucking sticky. You're sticky. She wipes it anyway and then returns the spray to the cupboard.

At the entrance of the apartment, she undresses and wraps herself in a towel from the closet. Stepping out into the empty hallway with the bucket on one arm and the laundry held in the other, she tiptoes to the bathroom.

Once hidden behind the door, she pours the pee down the drain and wipes the bucket with a sanitizing cloth. She drops the dirty clothes back in the bucket. Holding her breath, she cracks open the door to look out into the hallway. Remi is standing there blocking her way, smiling hatefully, making all the hair on her body stand on end.

"Take off your mask," Remi says.

Violet wants to run, but there is nowhere to go. Pulling the mask off and up over her head, she watches the plastic shimmering slightly in the light, pretending nothing else exists.

A man from the apartment across the hall opens his door. Staring at him silently, Violet pleads for help with desperate eyes. Walking past them, he averts his gaze, and closes the door to a stall at the end. Remi grabs the mask out of her hands and pushes her into the bathroom. Her whole body shakes uncontrollably with fear. Please. Don't. Please.

"Let me go," she cries. "I need to shower."

"Stop talking." Remi holds her neck, forcing her to look at her unmasked face in the mirror.

"Look," he says, laughing. "Can't you see your garbage? Not even pretty enough to be a doxy. No one cares if you live or die."

Violet looks at the terrified face and doesn't recognize herself. She sees pieces of a body where nothing seems to fit. It isn't me. It isn't anything. He pulls the towel she is clinging to away from her body, dropping it on the ground. She hears him unzip his pants. Terror stops her from screaming or pushing him away.

She stares at the drain. It isn't my body. The metal reflecting bits of the surrounding room. It isn't anything. The pattern of the scratches criss-crossing over each other.

Garbage. Nothing but garbage. Drops of saltwater rolling down.

I wonder if the Orbs have oceans? I bet they do. When I get there, that's the first place I'll go. Another tear hits the metal and slowly makes its way to the sewers below. He pushes her head into the mirror. Violet closes her eyes. It isn't me.

When I live in the Orbs, I'll swim in the Ocean every day, and the sun will keep me warm. I bet they have real fruit up there. None of the artificial pastes. I wonder if blueberries are actually blue? I bet they are. Bright blue, just like the sky. They probably grow on trees, like the ones in the lottery advertisements. Tall trees. Taller than the tallest towers in Krevax. Each one with thousands of blueberries.

Finally, he lets go of her head and she stands there paralyzed. Pulling his pants up, he opens the door and leaves without a word. Violet slumps to the ground feeling faint.

Weakly, she puts on the mask, wraps herself in the towel and grabs the bucket. Numb. She can't seem to feel any part of her body. It's not my body. It's not me.

Listlessly, she walks through the hallway, past the apartment, to the elevator. In the empty basement she lies down on the ground, waiting for the water.

09 | SECRET ASSIGNMENT

BLACKWELL

THE STATION FILLS WITH THE CACOPHONY OF RED STRIPES, BUT for once Blackwell doesn't notice. *An opportunity I am looking for?*

He mumbles the obscuring phrase to himself repeatedly until it seems to lose meaning. *What if it's actually something interesting…* He shakes his head. *Nothing here is interesting.*

Looking at the rows of working men below him, he feels dissociated. *This endless work, just cogs, pre-built and defined, my body could go on without me, like a train bolted to a track. Whatever is at the end of this letter, it will be better than this.*

Walking purposefully out of Gromwell Station, his lips curve upward in a slight smile. *At the very least, it will be a better death than the recycling facility.* Climbing onto his bike, he rushes through the Education, Generation, Entertainment, and Manufacturing Districts, as they are as familiar to him as the taste of plain paste.

As he enters the Purification District, the stronger taste of chemicals hits him in the back of the throat and the smell is nearly intolerable. *It stinks in a way that multiple showers* could not fix. Trying not to breathe, he drives past the open pits of sewage, watching them spin down into the lines of white pipes.

Men in overalls work with the fast-moving wastewater, walking angrily around with clipboards, checking off tasks and inspecting machinery. At the center of the district, he looks up at the crowded apartment blocks surrounding the Watchtower. Jolting away from a sudden burst of fiery sparks beside him, white spots blind his retinas for the next minute. A loud buzzer, signalling the next batch of wastewater to be filtered, makes him grind his jaw.

Up ahead, he can see yellow-stained smoke stacks from the Power District. As he crosses over the border, the air tastes bitter and grimy on his tongue, leaving grit on his teeth. Looking around at the emptiness of the district, Blackwell feels the hairs on his arms stand on end.

More than half of the population was gone in monthly rotations, drilling for oil, fracking for liquid gas, mining for various minerals, and monitoring nuclear facilities.

On the side of the highway, the bag of a peon splits open, leaving plastic paste tubes scattered on the road. Pushing on the brake, he watches her lean down and pick up the items. I can't stop! What am I doing? He speeds up again, but he can see her clearly as he passes. Her hair has gone entirely grey.

Grey hair? I've never seen a peon with grey hair. I guess they don't have a recycling date like the rest of us, and they're not cheap to buy, especially not in the Power District. Flashing a curious glance back at her, he slows down again.

Maybe I should talk to her? Stopping on the side of the highway, he goes to turn around, but pauses, he had never attempted to speak with a female before.

Instead, he watches her mask disappear into a crowd of men as she wanders through an alleyway of small shops, and then revs his bike forward again. I wouldn't know what to ask her. Besides, she wouldn't have known Kaliann. He shakes his head. None of that matters now.

As he moves deeper into the lower districts, the air is so thick it hits his lungs like a coating of paint. He stifles a cough. Even the advertisements seem to have lost their neon, as the dust muted all colour. With eyes stinging from the chemicals, he wraps a black bandana around his face to muffle the smell of rotten eggs.

The bike weaves dangerously through overloaded 18-wheelers, past dust-covered apartment buildings and around smoke-stained transport stations, where trucks loaded fuels, minerals, and metals to be sent up to the Manufacturing District.

At last, the radiant UV lights of the Farming District come into view. Hydroponic potato fields, 10 stacks tall, tower over him, their green leaves entwined with wire mesh, roots hanging free of soil. Pickers standing on tall ladders fill large baskets on their backs. The dust is gone, and he removes the bandana, breathing deeply. It almost smells green underneath the rot of distant garbage.

He looks up at the long rows of lights and untrimmed plants that block half the screens. Closing his eyes momentarily, he feels a slight tingling sensation touching his cheeks, almost like warmth. I would like the sun. Refocusing on the road, he can see the white towers that mark the border into the Recycling District. Crossing over, he enters an eerie darkness, where the advertisements have been hit by one too many rocks.

He drives past the long line of people waiting to be processed at the recycling facility, watching as some wail in grief. My death will be a good one, a man's death, not a task on some recycler's to do list.

On the other side of the marble building, heaps of garbage piled high in every direction, made of objects in every colour, muddle together into strange shapes with the dust. The smell of burnt human hair punches his nostrils. On the edges of the unmaintained road, recyclers move through the rubbish in hodgepodge outfits, piling metals, plastics, hair, and fabrics onto their backs.

He glances up, expecting highrises, but only finds strange half-built homes, some piled on top of each other, four floors high. The energy, which pinpricks his skin, feels tense with potential violence.

He drives through the debris at a rapid pace, indifferent to crashing, but too afraid to force the wheel. Ahead is the address he's seeking, a decrepit shack with broken windows and spray-painted outer walls. Coming to an abrupt stop, he climbs off the bike and looks around to make sure the street is empty.

The area seems abandoned, which makes sense given the potent addition of an unknown smell. Making his way to the front door, he knocks four times. After a minute there's still no movement.

Pushing on the handle, he finds it unlocked and the floor inside dusty, as though no one had walked on it for many years. After searching the entire place and finding nothing useful, he exits, closing the door behind him.

Driving up a few blocks, he hides his bike behind a smashed vending machine. Running back to the house, he crouches behind a small heap of garbage and shook his wrist twice. The time displays: 5:12 P.M.

Above, the lights from the remaining advertisements were dimming. Each breath in, he imagines another layer of polluted dust building up, slowly blackening his lungs and killing him.

Forty-five minutes pass quietly as he sits impatiently fidgeting with a hangnail on his thumb. A limo pulls up and stops in front of the shack. A side door swings open and four men climb out, three in all black with oversized guns, and one in a tailored blue suit.

The Tzar of Krevax is standing just feet away, his angular face familiar from the many advertisements the man appears in, talking about the benefits of recycling and the lottery.

He strides into the house, grinning widely and speaking exuberantly to the men. Watching from the other side of the road, Blackwell can't make out the words.

What does the Tzar want with me? I'm nobody. Maybe this is actually something... After a minute of contemplation, he steps up to the door and knocks once. The door swings open and a bodyguard points a gun at his head.

"State your name."

"Blackwell," he says eagerly, excited by the possibility of a man's death.

The guard lowers the weapon.

"Downstairs," he says, motioning towards the stairwell.

At the bottom, the Tzar is standing in the center of an empty room waiting for him. It takes a moment for his eyes to adjust to the dark, and at first it's hard to make any distinct features out, as dancing multi-coloured light from the advertisements distorts the Tzar's face.

"Charlie," the Tzar says, smiling. "It's good to meet you."

Why is he calling me Charlie? I don't know you. No one calls me that name. Glancing up at the man, he can see he is easily half a foot taller than him, a perspective he rarely experiences.

"I've asked you here to discuss an important matter, but we need to keep this brief. I've chosen this location because the surveillance of the Recycling District is less than thorough and I don't want anyone knowing we've met. Can you keep our meeting private?" He stares intensely. Blackwell nods.

"Good. I have a job for you."

He wants to give me a job?

"The importance of Krevax cannot be overstated. The very survival of our species depends on the success of this…" He glances up.

"Underground city. And this success requires a strict balance, one that has recently been disrupted. It's clear to me you are a resourceful individual, an intelligent man, which is why I want you to find the source of nostaliem. I need someone I can trust, and I believe you to be that person."

The Tzar pulls out a folder from the inside of his suit jacket.

"Nostaliem is coming from somewhere," he says, handing the folder to Blackwell.

"I need you to infiltrate the Zorax gang and get the exact location of their lab."

He stares at Blackwell's face for a moment and then adds, "This assignment must remain a secret."

"You want me to go undercover?" Blackwell asks, his eyebrows raised. If I take this job, I'll probably be dead by the end of the week.

"You will be taking a personal risk, but if you succeed, you can leave behind this hole in the ground and join the Orbs." The Tzar lifts a hand to shake.

"Agreed?" Blackwell stares at him, something stirring in his mind—a flicker of doubt.

"Agreed." Blackwell shakes his hand, gripping the folder. Better this than the recycling facility. He grins to himself. I won't make it to the Orbs, but I'll still get where I want to go.

The Tzar leans in and hugs him, and Blackwell stiffens, his body rebelling against the unexpected contact.

What is wrong with him? He suppresses the urge to shove him away. The Tzar steps back and reaches into the other side of his jacket, as Blackwell stares up at him angrily.

"I'll transfer some extra funds into your account," he says, as he pulls out a pen.

"This is a video camera." He holds it out for Blackwell to take.

"Anything you record by holding the cap down will immediately upload to my personal drive. Ensure you're providing weekly progress reports." Blackwell takes the pen.

The Tzar turns towards the stairs. "Goodluck, Charlie."

Blackwell watches him walk up the stairs. That was weird. With the folder clutched in his hand and the pen in his pocket, he listens to the sound of the limo's engine sputter on.

What was that?

It doesn't matter. I finally have a plan I can stick with. Shuffling through the papers, his heart beats fast with adrenalin. The folder contains information about a Zorax drop for a shipment of nostaliem tomorrow night. He sprints up the stairs and out of the abandoned shack.

Blackwell tucks the folder into the compartment under his seat and speeds home. Parking his bike, he stops at the vending machine, scanning his I.D. on the sensor.

"Charlie Blackwell, 27, credits available - 2,153." He closes his eyes.

Why does the Tzar care about nostaliem? And why me?

Choosing his usual paste at the top of the machine, he watches it drop into the drawer. If I find out, I find out, what matters most is that I finally get to die.

With that thought, relief floods through him and he grabs the plain paste. The 16th floor is thankfully quiet. Scattering the papers over his mattress, he reads them again.

10 | DARK ZONE
TINIK

Bones pressing through her shirt, Tinik leans against the wall, her deep obsidian skin bright against the concrete behind her. She shifts her sore feet.

I'm not standing in this shit alley. I'm not even here. Instead, my body is in the recycling facility, reliving this very moment in my mind as the poison releases. I know all the things to come and I am completely prepared.

This moment isn't scary, it's familiar, like reading an old book. I already know that I'm going to find you. Right now I'm moving towards you, one step closer every day. Shut up, Tinik. Shut up! Pay attention.

Pulling a hand-rolled cigarette from behind her ear, she holds it between her teeth, before reaching for the matchbox in her red pants pocket. Fumbling to remove a match, she scrapes it against the side of the box and holds the flame to the end of the cigarette.

Breathing in deeply until smoke fills her lungs, she exhales, thankful for the brief respite from hunger. Neon advertisements light the alleyway from above, flashing on her shaved head.

An ad for doxies catches her large, round eyes with its bright purple twinkling. *Find the sexiest doxies at Exotica!* In it, a nearly naked doxy with long black hair hangs off of a bed, her eyes are closed and her mouth hangs slightly open. Tinik takes another slow drag of the cigarette, an expression of pity on her face.

Bad luck being a doxy, I'd rather be a peon.

Repositioning her shoulder against the wall to stop the tingling in her left hand, she jumps when a moving ad pops up on the ground beneath her. It covers the entire width of the alley and extends six feet on either side of her position. In it, a red stripe arrests a man for drug use, then in the next frame, the same man is at a graduation ceremony to become a lawyer. At the end it spouts the phrase, *"Say no to Nostaliem."* Or say yes.

She balls her hands into fists and continues down the alley to a spot with static ads. Sighing nervously, she picks at the frayed strings on her green shirtsleeve.

She looks up as the sound of an engine grows closer. A bike turns into the alley and screeches to a stop in front of her. Exhaust fills the air in a thick plume of smoke, making her cough. Tinik stares at the man and he stares back at her.

"Passphrase?" he says gruffly.

"A wet doxy in a jar of jelly," she says, her heart pounding in her ears.

Months ago she had perfected her voice to sound masculine, but it still made her nervous. The man gets off the running bike and carelessly drops it to the ground, he then hands Tinik a rolled-up piece of plastic and walks down the alley alone. She stares in the man's direction until she can no longer hear his footsteps and then unrolls the message. The instructions make her breath quick.

After reading them a second time she lights another match, burning the words. Dropping the burnt message and cigarette butt on the ground, she heaves the bike up and climbs onto the seat.

Taking a deep breath, she twists hard on the almost out-of-reach handlebars and rockets forward. Zipping through the city streets, she spirals lower into the Earth, her heart thumping in her ears.

Continuing down the highway as fast as the bike will go, air whips at her face as the neon lights stream past her. She's blinded for a moment as the advertisements end at the edge of the Recycling District. In the darkness, the bright spots in her eyes fade and she sees several tunnels up ahead. She stops a moment, unsure of where to go next. In the distance, bobbing closer, a younkin moved erratically on a rusty bike. Could he be another recruit?

The heavily tattooed younkin stops and scans his wrist, opening a map of Krevax. Tinik can see an orange dot, showing a destination outside the city's borders. He swipes the map away and moves forward into one tunnel. She revs on the gas and follows him.

As the sewers open in front of her, connecting to the wastelands of the Dark Zone, she can hear other engines in the distance. They drive deep into the black, far from the light of the advertisements. Finally, they stop and wait at the edge of an expansive cavern. The one Tinik followed gives her a suspicious look, and she stares back indifferently.

What'cha gonna do? Nothing.

They sit waiting as more recruits slowly arrive until a dozen or so have joined the group. Some of them spot Tinik and laugh, their voices echoing cruelly in the cavern. Aware she is the smallest and with the darkest skin tone, she stares back angrily, but says nothing. Fuck off.

Admittedly, her green and red clothes stood out, even among these younkins. Other than that, they all had a strikingly similar appearance, all too thin, too young, and with shaved heads. A man wearing all black with a tattoo of a cockroach on his face pulls up behind them. The recruits turn towards him eager for him to speak.

"This is a test for new recruits to join Zorax," he shouts. "The 14 of you are here because you've been the most successful at selling nostaliem in your district. There is a drop off of nostaliem in the Dark Zone tonight. It's your job to help the crew bring the drugs back to base. If you accomplish this task, you will move on to the next phase." At the end of his speech the man turns his bike around and rides away.

"There!" the largest boy yells.

Tinik looks up and sure enough, a large metal container is being lowered into a chute through a crack in the rock. The younkins race to chase after it.

As they get closer, thick chains lower the container to the ground. A loud bang is heard above them and the black is lit up with orange and yellow. Shots pour down on the small group, causing panicked chaos.

Staring in shock, she watches as some younkins jump off their bikes and attempt to run into the sewers. Others head further down the highway, trying to escape there. Red stripes seem to come from every direction, their sirens screaming as they approach. Shit.

Her bike flips as a bullet hits her front wheel. Rolling down the side of the highway, she falls into a trench. She stares up at the rock ceiling, catching her breath. The chute has broken, and the crew above appears to be engulfed in flames.

Crawling back up the rocks, she looks over the edge and sees one recruit, dead with a bullet in his skull and half his face scraped off by the pavement. In the distance, the red stripes have surrounded the container of nostaliem. Blood is dripping from scratches on Tinik's shoulders and back.

Crouching, she bolts across the road and down the opposite rock wall. At the bottom, she slides through a metal pipe and runs towards the Recycling District. You're alive. At least you're alive.

When the noise of the sirens has dissipated, Tinik stops running and stands in the darkness. In the distance, she can see the lights of the advertisements from Krevax. Slumping into a ball, she cries in a slow wail. Far behind her, the burning truck was pulled to the ground.

No! I was so close to making it. How will I ever find you now? I will fix this.

Tinik wipes her face with her sleeve and takes a shaky breath. They may still offer me a spot, just for surviving the attack. Standing up, she resolutely begins walking towards the lights. I'm not dead yet. Just as she breaks out into a run, something crashes into her and pins her arms behind her back.

"What the fuck, get off me garbage fucker!" Tinik yells out. Twisting futilely, her head is pushed further into the dirt.

"Stop moving," the man says.

Tinik freezes. "What do you want?"

Cuffing her wrists, the stranger pulls her into a sitting position. "You're a red stripe!"

"Yeah, so shut up and listen. You're going to take me to your base and introduce me as one of the survivors."

"No way! I'll be killed if they ever find out you're a red stripe."

"Would you rather me kill you now?" he says, pressing his gun into Tinik's ribs.

She inhales sharply. "What are you going to do for me?" Maybe he can get me the file?

"This isn't a negotiation," he says, and grabbing her shirt collar, drags her to a standing position. "Let's go."

"Fine."

"What's the address?"

"It's in the Entertainment District," Tinik says.

"Are you going to show up with me in handcuffs?" They glare at each other.

"What's your name?"

"Tinik, what's yours, red stripe?"

"You can call me Khan."

"Are you going to uncuff me now, Khan?" she says, exaggerating the word Khan while rolling her eyes. He pulls out his gun and changes the dial.

POP

"Ahhh!" Tinik jumps. "What was that?"

"It's a tracker. I wouldn't mess with it either. It will blow up if you apply too much pressure." He takes off the handcuffs and shoves her a foot forward. "I'll find you in the Entertainment District."

"That's one way to start a partnership." She storms away, holding her right shoulder. Shit. I don't need this on top of everything else.

"See you soon, Tinik," the red stripe says.

With trembling fingers, she digs at the tracker, feeling it deep beneath her skin. I wonder if this thing will actually blow up if I try to remove it?

11 | BLOODY BODIES

PRATT

Pratt and Remi follow the group of red stripes winding through the Recycling District, Blackwell leading the way.

Watching the last row of advertisements disappear above them, an ad for the latest computer flashes in Pratt's eyes. *Enjoy Maximum Performance with Aurora. Embrace the Future of Gaming!*

Shaking his head, he attempts to erase the images of the various video games playing on a loop.

"Can you believe Blackwell got this tip anonymously?" Remi yells over the noise of the engines.

"I doubt it leads to anything," Pratt says, laughing.

Glancing back, he can see the advertisements of Krevax receding quickly behind them. Up ahead in the tunnel, the white headlights from the motorbikes bounce on the walls.

"Yeah," Remi says. "I hope he embarrasses himself."

"Have you ever been to the Dark Zone before?" Pratt asks.

The group slows as they move through a narrow part of the tunnel.

"Once or twice," Remi says.

Holes in the rusted walls of the old pipe reveal jagged rocks beyond the metal. A large cavern opens up ahead, enveloping them in an unnerving silence. He takes a deep breath, as the line of bike's speed up, following Blackwell's lead.

After continuing into the cavern for ten minutes, Blackwell puts his hand in the air, signalling everyone to slow down. Blackwell swipes his tracker and clicks on a green dot.

"This is the spot," Blackwell says. "Spread out."

The men turn off their engines and scatter into the dark, leaving behind only tracks in the dirt. Pratt looks for somewhere to hide his bike, eventually choosing a spot behind a large square-shaped boulder.

Walking a few feet forward, he sits in a cracked piece of sewer. He can't help but smile. It feels like a game, hiding in the Dark Zone. Looking up at the ceiling far above, he can see strange bits of metal jutting out of the rocks.

Was it all sewers and pipes for cities on the surface?

Picking up a handful of small rocks and metal debris, he lets it run through his fingers. It's all dust now.

Remi crouches beside him. "No Blackwell, at least."

"If he fucks up bad enough," Pratt says, grinning. "They could re-assign him."

"We may never work with him again," Remi says with a chuckle, and then they sit in silence, waiting.

The first hour passes quickly, then slowly into two, then strangely comfortably into three. Surprised by how relaxed he feels, Pratt doesn't desire vodka, for once.

Why did they have to make the entire ceiling in Krevax advertisements? Who wants to live like that?

He glances around at the quiet cavern. I think I would rather live here in the dark. I wonder if I could build a secret home out here? I could go in every day for work, have dinner with Serie, and then sneak out here to sleep. Enjoying the peacefulness, he draws circles in the dust with his finger. It's nice here.

"What do you think Blackwell's deal is?" Remi asks, breaking the silence.

"I don't know, he's a red stripe who lives in the Manufacturing District," Pratt says. "He's strange."

"Strange doesn't cover it," Remi says. "He's never mentioned a peon. Maybe he's a turncoat?"

"Maybe, but I don't think him not having a peon is proof," Pratt says, wiping the circles back into the dust. "I've heard Captain Lewis doesn't have a peon."

"What does he spend his money on then? Rent is cheap in the Manufacturing District."

"Doxies?"

"When do you think he will call it on this anonymous tip?" Remi asks, changing the subject.

Pratt looks up at the chute. "We'll probably be stuck here until tomorrow."

The sound of an engine echoes far above them and Pratt gives Remi a surprised look. The noise builds and then stops for a moment, then voices can be heard, but no one is visible yet. Metal clanks and then the tip of a large container can be seen lowering into the chute.

"On my signal," Blackwell's voice says through their trackers.

"Shit," Pratt says under his breath. "I guess he was right."

"This could be fun." Remi stands, ready to grab his bike.

Pratt nods, pushing himself up. In the distance, he can hear engines moving closer, until tiny figures zoom out of the darkness.

"They look like younkins?" Pratt says.

"Could be," Remi says. "Zorax doesn't care." The first bikes flood in the space below the chute.

"Now!" Blackwell shouts.

Running to grab his bike, Pratt climbs on, and revs the engine, rushing forward. Up ahead he can see Remi turn on his siren, so Pratt turns on his siren too. Bullets whiz through the surrounding air, making him duck in fear.

Pulling out his gun, he shoots toward the chute, hoping to stop the barrage of bullets. His wheel hits a large rock, and he is sent flying, rolling violently over the rocky surface, scraping his face. The shock of the fall courses adrenalin through his body.

Scrambling to his feet, he runs back to his bike. He feels his arms and legs for any damage. His face is bloody, but the wounds are shallow. I'm okay.

Picking up his bike, he looks back towards the scene. An explosion above causes him to drop the handlebars, and he leans forward to grab them again. Climbing on, he feels unsteady as he pushes on the gas with his gun raised.

The sound of screaming makes him shudder, and he lifts his foot from the gas, slowing. The terrifying scene in front of him unfolds like a dream. Screams of pain from the flames in the chute above, mix with the cries of terrified younkins below. Lowering his gun shakily, his head spins and he stumbles to the ground.

Up ahead, he can see Remi laughing joyfully as he smashes the jaw of a young Zorax recruit with a baton. The feeling of retching climbs up his neck, but he swallows it back as he holsters his gun.

"Pratt!" Remi shouts, his face speckled with blood. "Get up here. They need help with these chains."

Running forward, he grabs a chain connected to the truck above. The group of men pull until the truck tumbles through the chute and lands on the ground in front of them. Mercifully, the death screams from the crew are all silent now. Sweat and blood drips down Pratt's red face, his expression pained.

"Look at this heap of junk," Remi says. Nodding in response, Pratt forces a smile. "What's the matter with him?"

"Over here!" One of the lower-ranking red stripes calls, his voice steady.

They run half-way over, Pratt trailing, when Remi stops beside an injured younkin crawling on the road. Pratt jogs the last dozen steps and grabs a chain off the container, closing his eyes in fear. Behind him, Remi calmly stands over the crying younkin and shoots him multiple times. Pratt flinches with each bullet.

A moment later, Remi runs up beside him, grinning, and grabs another chain. Breathing in the vile air, as the smoke from the truck burns his lungs and eyes, he stares at the rubble.

Inside, he can see the crew still becoming ash in the burning wreck. The dead younkins bodies splayed on the ground flash in his vision, as he grabs box after box of nostaliem, loading them on the red stripe trucks.

Around him, the other red stripes ignore the bodies as their bloody footprints cake on the ground. Watching the bright red pooling into sludge around his own feet, he again fights the feeling of being sick.

"What have I done?" he says, whispering to himself.

After the nostaliem boxes have been loaded, the lower-ranking red stripes grab body bags, remove the trackers from the arms of the dead, and pile up the bodies in the truck.

A soot covered man runs over. "Do you want us to call in fire support?"

"No need. Those flames are already almost out," Remi says.

"Should we wait and clear the debris?"

Remi shakes his head, smiling. "Leave it for the Zorax gang."

The truck of bodies leads the way, as the red stripes grab their bikes and head back into the city. Pratt and Remi move to follow the noisy procession.

"Where the fuck is Blackwell?" Remi asks, stopping.

"Is that his bike?" Pratt sees Blackwell's silver bike abandoned behind them.

"What?" Remi walks over to the bike. "It is." He taps on his wrist. "Call Blackwell."

"Connecting."

"Blackwell, here." His voice huffs out through hard breath.

"We're standing beside your bike," Remi says. "Where are you?"

"I'm on my way." The call clicks off.

Remi shakes his head. "He's on his way?"

"He really needed a caffeine hit?" Pratt says, uncomfortably, shrugging his shoulders. "I'll wait. Find out what happened."

"Sure," Remi says, and turns, biking away without a look back.

Exhaling, Pratt sits on the ground and listens as the noise of the engines subside. I need a drink. The bloody bodies are imprinted in his mind in a terrifying collage. He can still hear the screaming in his head and instinctively grabs his neck.

What kind of pain would make you scream like that? No. Don't think about it.

Blackwell runs up a rock wall beside him, panting.

"Where have you been?" Pratt asks. Blackwell puts his hands on his knees, lowering his head while he catches his breath.

"I saw a man in one of the Zorax red masks," Blackwell says. "I thought I could catch him."

"On foot?"

"He was also on foot, but he had his bike at the edge of the city."

"Okay," Pratt says. "Let's go."

Blackwell nods and heaves his bike up with one muscled arm. Lumbering forward, Pratt grabs his bike, laboriously pulling it upright. They make their way back to the Enforcement District together until Pratt pulls off the road to stop at *Coffee! Coffee! Coffee!*

Walking straight into the bathroom, he grabs the last vodka bottle from behind the sanitizer dispenser. Gulping the bottle down, he stands looking at his flushed face in the mirror. Staring back is his sorrowful reflection, covered in deep scratches and congealed blood.

Gently prodding one of the wider scratches with a finger caked in red dirt, he sighs, feeling more exhausted than he had ever felt before. I didn't kill those younkins. I wouldn't kill younkins. Remi's laugh plays maniacally in his head.

12 | COCKTAIL PARTY
VIOLET

Tiptoeing over to the cupboard, Violet nervously puts away a stack of folded towels, sorting them by colour.

Closing the first door, she opens the next one, which contains a small pile of her belongings: a dog-eared copy of the *Book of Infinitum*, a palm-sized fake aloe vera plant, a white plastic hairbrush, two hair ribbons; one white, and one pink, both unused, and a brightly coloured poster. Touching each item gingerly, she takes out the poster and sits cross-legged on the couch.

In the poster, the Tzar of Krevax is standing in front of a beautiful willow tree, behind that a white-panelled house with a wooden door set against a clear blue sky.

A speech bubble above him states, "Win the Lottery, and you could have all this!"

Violet touches the willow tree in the image, imagining what a leaf might actually feel like. When I win the lottery, I'll also have a yard with an actual tree. An image of Remi's face flashes in her mind, making her flinch.

What if it takes too long to save for a ticket? Activating

her tracker, she clicks on her profile and reads '89 credits' in bright red.

Picking up the poster, she scans through the small print, tracing her finger along each line of text. Her eyes settle on '490 credits,' the colossal sum makes her throat feel tight. With my current income it would take me… Covering her masked face with her hands, she lets out a cry. Eleven years! I won't make it that long.

Tears pour down her cheeks and she crunches the poster to her chest. No, wait. She places the plastic poster back on the cushion and pushes out the wrinkles. I get ten percent of anything I purchase with his credits.

Maybe I can convince him to get a new screen, or buy a gaming system? Then I would have more credits in my account.

Swiping through the rows of icons on her tracker, she clicks on a Green Arrow, which opens to the list of all the advertisements in Krevax. Slowly scrolling through, she stops on an ad for a new motorcycle. That could be good. Saving it with a click of a heart, she continues searching.

After an hour of scrolling, she has saved the motorcycle, as well as an updated wall screen, gaming computer, gaming subscription, cocktail cart, luxury paste collection, and a weight set. If he purchases these, I will have just enough for one lottery ticket. I must convince him.

She makes her way to the bedroom and slides open the closet door. Alcohol could help convince him. Looking through the bottles of flavoured vodka in the closet, she formulated a plan.

I still need another bottle of blueberry vodka. Maybe something fruity?

She leaves the apartment and walks through the street, heading back to the shops. Up ahead, she can see a group of peons from her building walking towards her.

"That's her," one of them whispers as they pass. Facing forward, she pretends not to hear them, but her body still stiffens at their words.

"Poor thing," the tall one says. "Sally, do you think your owner would do something?" Please stop talking.

"No, he doesn't think it's any of his business." Quickening her pace until she can no longer hear them, she doesn't dare look back.

Her stomach aches at the thought of them knowing her shameful secret. Stifling a sob, she holds her arms tighter around her waist. It doesn't matter. Once I'm in the Orbs, I'll start a new life.

She turns into the alley of shops and beelines toward the liquor store. A bell chimes as she opens the door, making her jump. Moving purposefully through the aisles, she picks up the bottle of blueberry-flavoured vodka.

Placing the bottle on the counter, she stands silently in front of the attendant. Without looking up from a video on his tracker, he scans the vodka and then Violet's wrist. The sensor turns green, and she walks out into the street, making the bell chime again.

A block down, upbeat music blares from two speakers on the roof of *Pop-n-Yum's*, a juice and candy stand. She opens the door, slides in and grabs a bottle of cranberry soda, a tube of lemonade, and a package of strawberry marshmallows. I know he likes sweets.

"Looks like you're having a party?" the older man says, his teeth stained yellow with smoke.

"Something like that," Violet says, holding out her wrist.

Scanning it, he nods silently, watching her take the items and put them in a plastic bag. She can still feel his eyes on her as she pushes open the door and disappears into the crowd. Heading back down the street, she stops in front of her usual vending machine and scans her tracker. *"Violet, peon, 17, credits available - 89."*

Sighing, she selects two French Fry pastes and a gel hydration tube, watching as they drop into the drawer below. After picking them up, she looks around to make sure no one is watching and then slides in between the machine and the wall.

Sitting with her elbows on her knees, she opens one of the French Fry pastes. The drain flashes in her mind and she grabs her face, squishing her mask against her jaw as her mouth fills with puke. Forcing herself to swallow the mouthful of vomit, she stares at the scratches on the concrete wall to distract herself from the taste.

It will be over soon. In a few days, I will have enough money for a lottery ticket. Until then, I just have to prove I am strong enough to deserve to go. She forces herself to take a small bite of paste and winces as it still tastes like vomit.

Looking up, she watches as a man walks up to the vending machine and scans his tracker. He glances at her, and then twitches, his face morphing from relaxed to annoyed. Shit.

"What are you doing there?" he asks.

"Having a snack."

"Strange place to have a snack."

"I suppose," she says. Leave me alone.

"Why don't you come out here?" Violet wants to say no, but she doesn't feel she can. Standing, she slides back out to the street, with her groceries in two bags on one arm.

The man stares at her for a moment and then says, "no need to hide."

Balling her hands into fists, she nods, feeling confused. With a last look of approval, he strolls away. In a couple angry bites, she finishes the French Fry paste, and then marches back to the apartment. In the elevator's mirror, her tiny frame's brushed hair, clean uniform and well-secured mask seem to say nothing is wrong.

Lifting the edge of her mask up, she reveals her lips and nose. Inhaling sharply, she lets the plastic snap back into place. The features seem strange. She doesn't recognize them. The elevator opens, she walks through the hallway and steps cautiously back into the apartment. The real me is already in the Orbs. This is just a dream.

She puts the alcohol and candy in Remi's closet and then grabs a rag and the bottle of glass cleaner. I'm probably running through a forest of trees right now.

Standing at the window, she sprays the glass and wipes it with the rag, her mind elsewhere. My real body is waiting for me. I just have to buy a lottery ticket. After he's had a couple drinks, I'll mention the new wall screen, see how he reacts to that.

The panic rises in her chest at the thought of what could happen. It will be fine. He can't hurt you. You're not even here. Hours pass, but the hallway is still quiet. The real you is in the Orbs. She pinches her arm, hoping not to feel it. It's still not me.

In the hallway, footsteps walk from the elevator and stop outside the door. Violet holds her breath as the doorknob twists and it clicks open. Spraying the cleaner pointlessly on the glass, she wipes it away as Remi walks in.

"Take off my shoes," he says, pointing at his feet as he sits in the plastic chair.

Violet rushes over, but takes a frightened step back from the sight of him. He doesn't notice, as he's looking through the tubes of paste. There is dried blood splattered all over his muddy uniform and face. Feeling a fist tighten around her heart, she kneels in front of him, her hands shaking. It's not me.

Grabbing his dirty left boot, she unties it with weak

hands. Your body is already in the Orbs. Breathing in the smell of rust and dirt, she watches as red-soaked mud cakes off and onto her knees. Nothing here matters.

"I had a great day," Remi says, a smile in his voice. Without looking up, she grabs his right foot and begins taking off the boot.

Violet can't feel her tongue.

"That's nice," she mumbles, as she unties the laces.

After taking off his socks, she rubs his feet, her ears pulsing with the sound of blood rushing in her head. Touching his skin makes her feel nauseous, but she ignores it. It isn't your body. He picks up a tube of hamburger paste and eats it in one bite.

"I feel like celebrating!" He claps his bloody hands together.

Violet tenses. This is it. Unveil it as something you have for a celebration. It's something you're doing for him.

"I've been saving something special for a celebration!" she says, holding her breath.

"Really," Remi says, his curiosity peaked.

Standing haphazardly, she puts the socks and boots in the closet, and runs towards the bedroom.

"One minute, sir." Grabbing a plastic cup, she fills it with equal parts blueberry vodka, cranberry soda, and lemonade.

Ripping open the bag of strawberry candy, she tears a marshmallow nearly in half, and sticks it to the edge of the cup. Walking with rapid steps back to Remi, she places it in front of him.

"It's a berrylicious cocktail."

"Okay," Remi says with a nod, clearly impressed. He takes a sip. "Good."

"Good!" she says, and smiles, holding back tears from the relief.

"In the name of celebration, maybe you deserve a gift?"

Clicking on her scanner, she opens up the image of the wall screen and flicks it over to his tracker.

"I saw this today and thought of you." Please. Please buy it.

Remi shakes his head. "Watch yourself, my last peon got greedy too."

"No," Violet says, trembling with fear. "I just thought you might like it."

"Hmm," Remi says, swirling the cocktail in the cup. "Hold out your wrist."

Extending her arm, the memory of him running his fingers from her wrist to her elbow, describing the cut open doxy, floods into her mind. Closing her eyes to cope with the terror, she feels him click on her tracker.

"Eighty-nine credits. Hey, that's not bad." He pats her wrist twice, and she drops her arm, the skin still burning from his unwanted touch.

"Thank you," she says.

He smiles. "You're the first peon to do something nice for me. I might keep you around for a while yet."

Violet smiles back and says, "thank you, sir."

She feels exhausted. A while yet, a while yet, echoes in her head. Could that add up to eleven years? The shower alarm rings for the peons, startling her out of her spiral of despair. She looks up at him with wide eyes, pleading to go.

"Go." He waves and then watches her undress and wrap herself in a towel.

Will he be waiting? It doesn't matter. It isn't me.

13 | CHLORINE

CARR

CARR STARES AS HIS WIFE PLACES STEAK, CORN AND POTATOES on two dinner plates, his normally warm brown complexion, sallow from stress.

Thin red lines, like spider's web, have expanded in the whites of his eyes, which he struggles to keep open. With a concerned look, Wife Carr sits down and hands him a serving of food.

"Oh my, dear," she says, smiling with pearly white teeth. "You look exhausted."

"I'm sorry my love," he says, as he takes a bite of the meat, revealing his metal-pointed teeth. "Work has been distracting."

I shouldn't have given Charlie that assignment, he might get killed. No, he needs this task. It's the best way to get him here. Also, if I can find that lab, I can shut this whole thing down before anyone else gets involved.

"What's distracting you?" she asks, gently placing her porcelain-toned hand on his arm.

"Only a minor incident with the beasts."

Pushing her doll-like face against his shoulder, she whispers, "I'm sorry you're feeling stressed."

"My sweets." He holds her for a minute. "It will pass. Let's eat our food before it gets cold."

She slices the meat with a silver fork and knife. The phone rings and Carr swiftly stands up to grab it.

"Hello."

"The numbers are getting worse," Bouchard says. *"We've hit the threshold."*

"Right, I'll head in." Carr hangs up the phone.

"You're going in?"

"Not for too long," Carr says, standing over the table as he takes another couple of quick bites. "I should leave now."

"You didn't eat your vegetables," she says. "And the sun is nearly down."

Making a fake pouty face, Carr chuckles. "I'll eat them tomorrow, I promise."

With a peck, he kisses his wife on the lips and then walks out of the room. She runs after him and wraps her soft arms around his waist.

"I wish you didn't have to work so much."

"My dear," he says, turning to hug her. "As the General of the Livestock Association, it's my job to investigate every incident. I have to keep our men safe and our food supply strong."

"I know," she says. "Be safe."

Leaning down, he kisses her on the forehead. "I'm always safe."

With an easy motion, he picks her up and carries her through the kitchen to the yard, dropping her on the grass.

"Hey!" she says, laughing.

"Pick some blueberries," he says. "I'll be back for dessert."

She stands up. "You better."

Opening the gate to the front street, he glances back with a smile and then climbs into the waiting limo.

"Where to, General Carr?" the driver asks, his slightly pointed metal teeth glimmering in the rear-view mirror.

"Headquarters."

They pull away from the two-level, white-panelled house with a wooden door and billowing willow tree. Pristine tree-lined streets stream by, their leaves wide and green, or needles pointy. Up ahead the city breaks through the rows of matching suburbia.

Behind the highrises, three man-made mountains stand with snow-capped peaks. Leaning his head against the window, he closes his eyes and slips into a nightmare. Charlie's face flashes aggressively in his mind, then morphs into his own.

Suddenly, he's watching himself sleep in Charlie's small apartment. Feeling trapped, Carr tries to get up, to run, but he can't move despite all his efforts.

"Sir?" the driver says, as he shakes Carr's shoulders.

He glances up at his driver's concerned expression. "I must have fallen asleep."

Wiping away beads of sweat from his forehead, he climbs out of the limo and walks into the 50-storey Government building.

Pressing the button for the elevator, he taps his foot impatiently, climbs in and then watches the numbers move up to the 49th floor. The door opens and a team of muttering men, with varying levels of pointed teeth, surround him in the hallway.

"General Carr, thank you for coming in," Bouchard says, stepping forward, his wrinkled taupe skin and grey hair showcasing his advancing age, as well as his outdated perspectives.

"Nostaliem is a graver threat to our food supply than we

once thought." The group walks down a long hallway, Bouchard and Carr leading the way.

They enter a semicircular conference room at the end with black walls and a large screen. The men sit in leather seats around the screen. Bouchard stands at the front and uses a small remote to click on an image showing a graph with a steep rising orange line.

"Today we had a record number of suicides," Bouchard says, pointing up at the screen. "These new numbers show a disturbing trend."

A few of the men nod at this statement.

"I see," Carr says, shifting uncomfortably in his seat. "I'm looking at the same numbers, and I don't know if we should be concerned yet."

Bouchard bristles.

"Let's outline the worst-case scenario," he says, clicking the button, which switches the image to a new graph, one with a red line. "If the trend continues there's potential for us to face protein shortages."

"I don't agree," Carr says. "The trend is unlikely to continue. We're already implementing a three-pronged response: media, enforcement, and imitation products…"

"Let me break down the numbers for you," Bouchard says, interrupting as he clicks the remote.

The image switches to a faceless human body with lines sectioning it into pieces. "One animal creates 150 portions." He clicks the button again.

"We currently process a little over 3,000 beasts a day, or 1.2 million per year." Clicking to the next slide, the image shows the icon of a sad face.

"Suicide in Krevax is typically 1,072 per 100k, with the majority still going for processing." Bouchard clicks to the next slide.

"Now we're seeing a jump of 2,000 per 100k, and barely

any are going for processing. With a population of 120 million, that puts the previous total death rate at 1.07 percent of the population."

"I get it," Carr says, interrupting.

"No, you don't," Bouchard snaps back.

"Our current death rate is up to 3,000 per 100k, or 3.0 percent of the population annually, so the population is already below replacement level."

"We'll increase the quota for offspring," Carr says, standing dismissively.

"Travis," Bouchard says, shaking his head.

"This drug, nostaliem, it's only been available for a few weeks." He bares his pointy teeth. "This is just the beginning."

"What are you proposing we do?"

"We need to protect the system above anything else," Bouchard says, cryptically.

"Yes, but what does that look like?"

"A cull."

"A cull?" Carr says, frowning deeply.

"Yes," Bouchard says. "Before the infection spreads."

"How would that even work?" Fiddling with the hangnail on his thumb, he shifts his weight between his feet.

"We lock down all the districts and then flood Entertainment, Manufacturing, and Recycling with chlorine gas."

"That's how you want to stabilize the system?" Carr shuffles back a step. "It's an extreme overreaction to these numbers." Charlie lives in the Manufacturing District. I have to stop this.

"I'm not reacting to the current numbers, I'm trying to prevent the worst-case scenario," Bouchard says, leaning forward.

"We know gang activity is concentrated in those three

districts. It would stop the spread of nostaliem, and after the cull we would increase the birth rate to rebuild."

"No," Carr says, balling his fists. "You would kill all 20 million doxies. That alone would destabilize the system."

"The male animals killed in the three districts would mostly offset the gender imbalance. Instead of 54 percent male, we would have something like 58 percent male," Bouchard says, puffing out his chest. "The doxies can be replaced."

"I don't agree. It's too soon to take this kind of drastic step."

"You would rather stay the course, watch the suicides increase, and the system collapse?"

"Your way is just as likely to result in a collapse."

"My way is controlled," Bouchard half-shouts. "There would be no collapse."

"I can't agree to this," Carr says and takes a step towards the exit.

"I'll give you until the end of the week, but if the trend continues…" Bouchard takes a step towards Carr. "I'm taking this up with President Lehan."

"I'll set up a stronger propaganda campaign," Carr says. "We'll see where the numbers are in a few days."

Leaving the conference room, he walks numbly down the hall to his office. Shit. They're going after the gangs and I just hired Charlie to infiltrate one.

Sitting down at his desk, he wakes up the computer screen and types in a password. Charlie's face pops up with a play button over his left eye. Promptly clicking play, Carr feels his heart jump in his chest.

"I have infiltrated the ranks of Zorax. Once I become a member of the gang, I will send another progress report." The image clicks off and the screen goes black.

Reversing the footage, he pauses on a frame where his

eyes look directly at the screen. Moving closer to the image, he leans forward until he can see his reflection lined up with the eyes.

Where are you?

Clicking on his watch, he types in a passcode and taps on a tracker. Still at Gromwell Station. Good.

Watching Charlie's heartbeat for a moment makes him feel calmer, then he slides the tab away, sighing.

How am I going to stop this cull?

14 | ESCAPE PLAN

TINIK

IN EVERY SQUARE INCH OF SPACE, AN ELECTRIC MIX OF highlighter and neon rainbow made the Entertainment District dance and buzz.

Tinik scans the landscape of screens, holograms, and bright business signs, walking steadily through the packed street. A jumble of yelling, laughing, shouting, vomiting, music, and singing, clash with the noise of highway traffic.

Glancing down, she is immediately distracted by the screen below her, an ad for strawberry vodka yelling as she steps on it. Up ahead, the lockbox facility is squished between *Bright Angels*, a heaven-themed brothel, and *Birdie's Bonanza*, a mini-golf bar.

A doxy in a white halo and silver feathered wing costume attempts to wave her over as she walks by.

Opening the door to *Securawiz*, she walks into a narrow room and lines up behind a row of men. Pulling at her shirt sleeve impatiently, she counts the people in line: 12. She mindlessly scratches at the tracker in her shoulder. Popping her head out, she stares as one spot clears and the line moves forward slightly. Fuck.

How much time do I have before he shows up?

Up ahead, a heavy set man starts arguing with one of the attendants.

"Well, where is it then?" he shouts.

"I don't know. All I know is that it isn't in our system." The line moves forward a couple more people and Tinik grumbles audibly.

"You don't know!" the man shouts, stomping his foot.

"This is where it says to go on my tracker. I need that package. I need it, now!" He smashes his fist against the counter.

"Where is it?" With a judgmental side eye, Tinik shakes her head at the unfolding scene.

They say we're too emotional?

Finally, the man ahead of her is called to the counter. Now at the front of the line, she pretends not to see the man throwing a fit.

"Next," an attendant calls out. Walking up, she continues ignoring the tantrum next to her and hands the attendant a small key.

"A key?" he says, surprised. "Don't see too many of these nowadays."

With an excited grin, he turns it over a few times, scrutinizing it.

"You can never be too careful," Tinik says.

The attendant nods and disappears behind a door with the key in hand. What will I do if the box is empty? Don't think about it. It will be fine.

The attendant returns with an envelope and places it on the counter with the key. Exhaling slowly, she reaches out to take it, praying to the universe.

"It's two credits."

Discreetly unzipping a pouch hidden under her shirt, she takes out two plastic credits and hands them to him.

"Plastic too, hey," the attendant says with a laugh, putting down the sensor.

"You are careful, I haven't seen these in a while." Smiling, she picks up the letter and the key and walks past the man who is still yelling at the tired-looking attendant.

Outside, she stands below the neon blue sign for *Bright Angels*, hiding in its shadow. Lifting up a fake gold chain from around her neck, she puts the key back on and conceals it under her shirt. Gripping tightly, she holds the letter a moment before opening it. Saint Mary, if you exist, please make this good news. Holding her breath, she kisses the envelope and then rips it open, reading the note.

You know where to go. Have your passcode ready.

"Okay, let's do this!" she says under her breath.

Good luck finding me now, Khan. She runs up the street to a row of parked motorbikes. Across the street, doxies from Foxe Brothel blow her kisses and shout innuendoes. Fuck this place. Crouching down beside the last bike in the row, she watches the street for a minute.

A group of upper district drunk men wander aimlessly through, their fancy clothes wrinkled, coiffed hair messy with grease, bottles of booze hanging from their manicured fingertips. Debauchery was the ultimate escape from the mundanity of order and security for the upper class.

An intoxicated man in overalls plods by, holding a row of fried cockroaches on a stick. Tinik stares at them enviously, until the crunchy morsels disappear into the crowd.

Unzipping the small bag again, she pulls out a device that plays radio frequencies and examines the bike: it's a Pizyit. Holding the power button on the device, she toggles down the brand names of motorbikes and clicks on Pizyit. A list of models open and she plays the first sound. The bike is still off.

Stopping for a second, she looks around nervously but no one seems to notice. She plays the second sound. This time the bike powers up and she jumps on and bolts from the scene. Easy. You gotta love the Entertainment District.

On the highway, she speedily moves through the districts, weaving aggressively past the traffic. Glancing over her shoulder, she keeps expecting to see Khan following. I'm still alone. I'll be out of Krevax soon enough.

Expanding up ahead are the mirrored towers and blue advertisements of the Government District. Must be nice at the top.

I wonder if it's true they can see the surface in the penthouses? Nah, sounds like cockroach shit.

Slowing to a stop before entering the district, she gets off the bike and abandons it by the side of the highway. I don't need anyone looking for this bike and finding me.

She crosses over into the Government District on foot, still mindlessly scratching her shoulder, leaving her fingernails covered in dry blood. The air here was purified many times over, so it had no life left and was scentless.

A manufactured breeze moves through the district, making fake fabric leaves shimmer gently on the glass trees. Soft chirping sounds play over park speakers, although birds had not existed in ages. Tinik freezes. A guard standing at the entrance of one of the towers is watching her.

"What brings you to the Government District?" he asks, flashing his gun.

"Business," Tinik says, smiling.

He continues to stare her down, but doesn't move from his post. With a nod, she begins walking at a steady pace, her shoulders raised in fear. The eyes of the guard press into her back for a full minute before he decides she is not a threat and looks away.

Once out of sightline from the hired gun, she puts up her hood and walks swiftly into an alley. *Fucking racist. He would rather see me in copper chains. Categorized goods to be purchased present no threat, but the unlabelled, the unchained, well apparently were terrifying.*

Criss-crossing through empty alleyways, she avoids the busy roads where possible. Deeper in the district, the fake green-glass trees stand ostentatiously along every sidewalk. A peon with a gold-laced mask watches her cross one final busy road. Tinik ignores her, keeping her eyes set on the next alley.

Do you seriously think you're better than me? Idiot. No one is better than anyone. Maybe you'll figure that out when your owner gets bored and drops you off at the recycling facility in a year.

She glances up at the Salt Spike restaurant, behind where she will meet up with the connection from Zorax. *I made it!* Looking around the street, she breathes a sigh of relief, as the red stripe was nowhere to be seen.

She walks into the alley and stops behind the restaurant, peering through an ajar door. Inside pale men are yelling orders down the line in the busy kitchen. Tinik sighs. *Even the workers can't have dark complexions in the Government District, the wealthy are afraid to be polluted by the touch of a potential recycler.*

Moving further down the alley until she can no longer hear the cooks shouting, she sits with her legs out in front of her, stretching. *I wonder where they'll send me? I know the next step is collecting nostaliem. I hope it's somewhere in space.*

Looking up at the ceiling of ads, she tries to imagine stars instead. *How far below the ground can Krevax actually be?*

Have you considered offspring? An ad says to her.

Sliding her feet in closer, she rests her elbows on her

knees. I wish I knew your name. Closing her eyes, she brings back the memory of her baby's face, her bow-shaped lips, round eyes, and dark curly hair, her perfect tiny fingers holding tight. It's been so long.

What are you like now? Do you like to throw rocks? Or play pretend?

Tinik imagines her daughter running in the alley, flapping her arms, pretending to fly. She takes a deep breath, stopping herself from crying.

Or would you still need to hold my hand for balance? What's your favourite toy? It's all slipping away so fast. I thought I would have you back by now. How much longer will this take? What was your first word? Do you like to dance? Are you scared at night without me?

She buries her face in her arms, heartbroken about not knowing these answers. If you're anything like me, you probably have big moods. She laughs at this thought and then goes quiet. I wish I could have named you.

No, there was no way I could have, not like that. Not with us both starving, hidden in the sewers. I needed to know you were safe, then I would have named you. You were never safe, though. I'll have you back before the sorting. One day you won't even remember a time I wasn't with you. One day I'll tell you the story of how I tried to escape with you, how I was forced to leave you back in the Generation District because I couldn't keep you alive. How I spent every minute working to get back to you. One day, I'll tell you everything.

Holding her palms to her eyes to stop the tears, her heart fills with the pain of the lost time. No. Focus. I will find you and I will name you. Right now, though, I need to wait. First I need a shipment of nostaliem, then I'll become a full member of Zorax and I'll have enough money to find you and buy you.

Everyone knows a rich enough man can buy any female.

I'm going to be that rich man. A cook opens the alley door and pulls out a cigarette from his stained apron. Gazing down at the ground, Tinik hides her face behind the green hood. The cook walks over and kicks the edge of one of her shoes.

"You know you're in the Government District, right?"

Tinik looks up at him. "I know."

"Well, you won't want to loiter around here too long. Guards patrol every alley."

"Thanks for the heads up," she says. "I'm meeting someone."

"I don't give a fuck," he says. "Just thought you should know."

Standing, she stares at the cigarette in his hand.

"Do you have one to spare?" The cook pulls out another cigarette from his apron and lights it, handing it over to her.

Nodding a thanks, she takes a slow drag and watches as the cook turns back towards the open doorway. At the entrance to the kitchen, he takes one last puff and flicks the butt onto the ground. Sitting back down, she smokes the entire cigarette, unsuccessfully suppressing her hunger.

Where is this guy?

Rolling the cold butt between her pointer finger and thumb, she stares up at the advertisements. *Try the improved Very Berry Blueberry Blast! Extra sweet with a zing of sour!* The thought of food makes her head spin and her stomach growl loudly. I don't even like blueberry flavour.

Throwing the butt onto the ground, she shakes her head at herself. At least I lost my period. The smell of fried oil coming from the restaurant makes her mouth salivate. Won't this guy hurry! I need to get out of here.

Closing her eyes, she tries to block out the lights pulsing above.

What if no one shows up?

A motorcycle turns into the alley at the end of the next block. Tinik stares, trying to make out the features of the figure moving closer.

15 | ALARM

BLACKWELL

Walking past the elevators at Gromwell, Blackwell makes his way through the first floor, towards a bathroom he knows is typically empty. He keeps to the walls, hoping to avoid unwanted attention. Through the clear plastic ceiling, he spots a group of red stripes being briefed by Captain Lewis.

Staring at the holographic map for a moment, he sees a highlighted route that Zorax previously used to move nostaliem from Power to Entertainment. *I wonder if the lab is hidden in a facility somewhere in the Power District?*

He steps past the display case of black kevlar armour and pushes open the nearly hidden door just beyond it.

Inside the bathroom is quiet and he leans over, confirming the three stalls are empty. He locks the door and pulls a first aid kit off the wall. *This lab might be easy to find. Who knows, maybe I'll make it to the Orbs?*

Grabbing a small pair of scissors from the kit, he activates the dispenser on the wall and rubs sanitizer on his hands, wrists, and the blades. He opens the scissors and touches one edge to his arm. *This is happening. I'm cutting out my* tracker. Pushing the blade against his wrist, he pauses, taking a deep breath before breaking the skin. The blade is dull and he has to press harder than expected.

Holding his breath, he wills himself to keep going as he stares at the expanding cut. Blood drips down his hand and onto the floor. His arm shakes from the shooting pain. He can feel the blade scraping against the metal.

What if I just kept cutting?

No, a man's death should be from another's bullet, knife, or fist, not alone in a bathroom with a first aid kit. I know my death is waiting for me.

Exhaling a flustered breath out, he digs his fingernails into the sliced skin. He lets out a stifled cry as he rips out the tracker. Holding it to his stomach, he takes a second. He sprays the skin glue under his arm and slams the tracker on the glue. He closes his eyes. Breathing shallowly. Waiting for the possible alarm.

Don't go off. Don't go off. He opens his eyes. The room is still silent. He sprays the glue on his cut and holds the sides together for a full minute. The cut stays closed as he lets go of the pinch.

He wipes the blood away and places the first aid kit back on the wall. Now, I need something a gang member would wear? An idea hits him and he grins.

Leaning down, he grabs the garbage bag he had just filled with blood-soaked wipes and dumps them in the empty bin. Rolling the plastic bag into a ball, he stuffs it into the pouch on his utility belt.

He heads to an open elevator and pushes the button for the sixth floor. The doors open on the second floor and Captain Lewis walks in. Blackwell immediately moves his hands behind his body, hiding his removed tracker.

"Hello, sir," he says, with forced cheeriness.

"I've been looking for you," Lewis says. "Excellent job, yesterday."

"Thank you, sir." Blackwell picks at the glue on his wrist, willing the elevator to go faster.

"That's the largest seizure of nostaliem we've had. I'd say you're in line for a promotion." The doors open to the top floor.

"Thank you, sir." Go away.

"I see you're busy." Captain Lewis nods. "Come to my office when you have a moment. We'll discuss the details then."

"I will, sir," Blackwell says, as they leave the elevator and head in opposite directions.

He walks to the specialized equipment room, grinding his teeth the whole way. Now, I get offered a promotion. For a moment he feels bitter, but then cheers himself up with a new thought. I'll die a hero.

The vice detective who was so dedicated he infiltrated Zorax and discovered their secret lab hidden in a nuclear power plant. Everyone will know my name. He walks up to the secretary sitting behind the desk at the entrance of the poorly-lit equipment room.

"I hear you took an entire shipment of nostaliem from Zorax," he says, admiringly.

"Thank you," Blackwell says, as he leans forward impatiently.

"How did you know where they would be?"

"I'm afraid that's confidential."

"Of course, I'm sorry," he says, his neck going slightly red. "What do you need?"

"A tracker bullet remover."

"Sure." The man slides through the shelves. "We've got it."

He walks back and hands Blackwell the palm-sized device and then grabs a corresponding form.

"Sign here." Blackwell pulls out the camera pen from his pant's pocket and signs his initials, leaving it behind on the desk. *Fuck the Tzar. I'll never see him again anyway.*

The elevator comes to a stop and he walks out into rows of white plastic desks. Men congratulate him as he moves through the maze, making pride fill his chest.

Do I really want to leave? The weight of the tracker glued under his armpit pulls his focus. *I could probably put it back in my wrist? No. I can't stay here. What am I thinking? I hate this place. None of them will care tomorrow. I'm nothing to anyone, just a waste of space.*

He enters the evidence room and walks up to a wall screen. Leaning over, he awkwardly scans his tracker and types in the code 126300-BX.

Behind the wall, he can hear the machine sliding through the items. A drawer below the screen pops open and Blackwell picks up the white suit and green sequined top. *Thank you Kaliann.* Balling up the clothes, he puts them in the trash bag.

I wonder if this is how you felt when you ran?

He exhales slowly, his head floating with excited energy. Lifting his shirt, he raises his arm and navigates to *active tracking*. A bright orange dot blinks on a large schematic map of Krevax.

What? Why the fuck is he in the Government District? Suddenly feeling nervous he rushes out of the station.

At the exit he runs into Remi, who is blocking half the doorway.

"Taking out the garbage?"

"Just some junk I need to sort through."

"I hear the captain's happy," Remi snarls, staring up at him with furrowed eyebrows. "Have you spoken with him?"

"He mentioned it was the largest drug seizure on record."

"Did he say anything else?"

"No," he says, smiling forcefully at Remi, as he side-steps past him.

He'll be glad I'm gone. Jogging to his bike, he climbs on and heads away from the precinct. Remi and Pratt might even publicly get the credit for the bust. Maybe then, they'll like me, he grins angrily at the idea of people only liking him once he's disappeared.

Flooring the gas pedal, he moves dangerously fast up the highway. No, not even then. They hate me, always have, always will. Weaving through traffic, he watches the busy streets stream by, his heartbeat quick, fuelled by exhilarated anger.

Who cares if nobody likes me? I hate myself more than anyone. It's okay, I'll be dead soon. A full smile cracks onto his face.

I need to be quick. If that dealer gets away, my death might too. The thought makes him agitated and his smile disappears. Stopping outside a Natatorium, he parks his bike and rushes into the building.

Standing in front of a row of lockers, he quickly undresses and stuffs his uniform into a random cubby. He puts on the white suit and examines himself in the mirror. The green sequins flash tiny images of his disgusted face back to him. Running back past the pool, he ignores a strange look from a Shaxocs Caller and heads into the parking lot.

He lifts the green sequined shirt and taps his tracker to start the engine. The orange dot is still floating in an alleyway, close to the middle of the Government District. At least he hasn't moved. What could he be doing there?

He zooms out of the parking lot and onto the highway, speeding erratically through the rest of the districts. The air feels light in his lungs as he crosses into the Government District. Above him the mostly blue advertisements almost feel like a sky. I wonder if the chemicals cause my nightmares in the Manufacturing District?

Everyone there always looks exhausted. His reflection dances alongside him in the mirrored highrises as he races towards the alley. It doesn't matter now. He reaches the alleyway and slows down to scan the path ahead, spotting the younkin.

"You said the Entertainment District."

"Well, now they want to meet here."

"What?" Blackwell says. "Zorax is meeting you here? Now?"

"Anytime now," Tinik says indifferently, "could be one minute, could be two hours."

"Shit!" Blackwell grabs his arm. "Get on!"

"Why?"

"I still have my tracker. I need to get rid of it." No gang member is foolish enough to kill a red stripe.

"You're gonna get me killed." Tinik glares up at him, still refusing to stand.

"What about the tracker in your shoulder? You were just going to show up with that?"

"It wouldn't have mattered," Tinik whispers.

"Yes, it would have mattered; I can trace you anywhere with a signal," Blackwell says, pulling him up to his feet.

"What, were you going to leave Krevax?" Ignoring him, Tinik finally climbs onto the bike behind him and they ride down the rest of the alleyway.

"Where are we going? We might miss the connection!"

"Just give me a minute." Continuing down three more alleys, he finally stops the bike and they jump off.

"Turn around," Blackwell demands.

Tinik stands with his shoulder facing him. Powering on the tracker bullet remover, he pulls the younkin's shirt collar down and pushes the device onto the wound. The device makes a loud humming sound and the magnet pulls the bullet loose. Tinik lets out a yowl of pain and stares back at him angrily.

"Done." Blackwell grabs his arm. "Let's go." They turn into the street on foot, abandoning the bike in the alley.

"Where?"

"Somewhere busy." Blackwell leads them to a crowded road. "When I drop the tracker, continue walking. Don't run. Do you understand?"

"What do you mean, drop?" Tinik asks. Blackwell holds out his bandaged wrist. "Green."

The adrenaline pumping through him makes ripping the tracker off of his skin painless and after a couple more steps into the crowd, he drops it on the ground. The alarm blares out, making people all around turn to stare at the source of noise. Despite his heart pounding in his chest, he keeps walking at a steady pace so as not to look suspicious.

"It's a tracker!" someone in the crowd yells out and everyone scatters, not wanting to be arrested.

They turn the corner into another empty alley. Behind them, a Watchtower spotlight points at the tracker in the now empty street. Sirens audible in the distance close in quickly, blaring louder with each passing second.

"Shit." Blackwell stands at the edge, peering around the corner.

"Do you think they'll shut down the entire district for a missing red stripe?" Tinik asks.

"If it was any other district, but in the Government District," he says, shaking his head, "there will be resistance."

"Let's go!" Tinik runs down the alleyway ahead of him.

16 | BREATHING EXERCISES
PRATT

A notification beeps on Pratt's wrist, alerting him to a tracker removal. Pressing on it to turn off the alarm, he does a double take. Is that Blackwell?

An image of Blackwell floats on the screen. What happened to him? He runs to the elevator, pushing the call button repeatedly. Remi jogs up behind him and grabs his shoulders. The sight of him grinning like a younkin makes him feel immediately uneasy.

"Did you see?" he says. "It's Blackwell."

"Yeah, it's crazy," Pratt says.

"I bet Zorax removes all his teeth and fingernails before putting a bullet in the back of his head," Remi says, laughing as they climb into the elevator.

His excitement at Blackwell's violent death makes it hard to breathe. To hide his horror, he focuses on his work, clicking on a map to see the tracker's location. An orange dot blinks in the Government District. As the elevator opens on the main floor, their trackers ring and they both answer the call.

"*Remi, Pratt, did you see the notification?*" Lewis asks, his voice higher than usual.

"Yes," Pratt says, as he jogs beside his deranged partner through the lobby.

"We're headed there now," Remi says.

"*I'm sending in red stripes to search the district. This could be some kind of revenge from Zorax. Keep me posted on what you find.*"

"Will do." The calls click off.

"If they can take a detective from the Government District..." Pratt's voice trails off.

"I'm glad it was Blackwell!" Remi cackles, throwing open the station doors.

"I'm sick of him acting like he's better than the rest of us." Pratt nods, despite feeling confused by this statement.

He's a bit strange, yes, but I never found him to be pretentious. Remi leads the way around the circle of elevators, a mirthful energy to each step, as though on a treasure hunt. Watching with disgust, Pratt walks a foot behind him, not wanting to be a part of his sadistic game.

Thinking back on his many interactions with Blackwell, he comes to a new realization. I think he was sad most of the time. As he climbs onto his bike, he stares at Remi across the parking lot, disturbed that he ever considered him a friend. He swipes his tracker to turn on the engine and kicks forward.

I'm sorry Blackwell, I never did give you a chance. On the road, Pratt watches Remi up ahead, keeping his distance. They join a crowd of red stripes as they cross into the Government District.

"Detectives coming through!" Remi shouts, as they pull up to the spot where the tracker is lying. Tapping his tracker to turn off the alarm, Pratt clumsily gets off his bike to examine the scene.

"There's no blood," he says, feeling disturbed.

This is a message. Someone wants the red stripes to know what they've done. His head begins to ache and the thought of a drink crosses his mind. After looking around the pavement and seeing no other evidence, he grabs a pair of blue plastic gloves from his belt and puts them on.

"No blood?" Remi stares at the pristine crime scene and then chortles. "He's long dead then."

"I'll look up the location data," Pratt says, trying to ignore him, but his mind flashes images of Blackwell's tortured body lying dead at the bottom of a sewer, rotting into nothingness. I wish it wasn't true, but he's right, Blackwell is gone.

"Hey!" Remi calls out to the crowd of red stripes. "Shut down the district. We have a missing detective to find."

"No!" A man in an expensive green silk suit runs up. "You can't shut down the Government District."

"Who are you?" Remi asks, pointing a finger in the man's face.

"I work for Carlos Romell. You might know him as the mayor," the man says, jutting his chin forward.

"This is the Government District. You can't shut everything down and start interrogating politicians."

"Let me make a call," Remi says, swiping his wrist. *"Captain Lewis."* The screen goes from white to yellow and then back to white.

Remi exhales, his nostrils flaring, and then looks up at Pratt. "What does the location data say?"

"The stop before was at a Natatorium," Pratt says. "Could be where they removed his tracker, it would be an easy clean up there." Their trackers ring and they answer.

Captain Lewis yells through the microphone, *"They'll only let us shut down one block at a time!"*

"One block at a time," Remi says. "Are they serious?"

Pratt nervously takes a step backwards and grabs an evidence bag from his belt.

"What's happening there?" Lewis asks.

"There's no blood and no body," Remi says, "just a tracker, likely bleached of any evidence."

"I looked through the location data," Pratt says as he puts the labelled tracker in a pouch latched to his belt. "He last stopped at a Natatorium."

"Okay, Pratt, go search the Natatorium," Lewis says. *"Remi, get the red stripes to shut down one block at a time."* Turning on his heel, Pratt runs back to his bike.

"Yes, sir," Remi says.

Driving out of the Government District, he feels thankful to leave his deranged partner behind. Outside the Natatorium he parks his bike at the edge of the lot and watches as men walk out of the building, a peaceful expression on most of their faces. Everything seems calm, at least from here.

A Shaxocs Caller saunters along the edge of the pool, his emerald robes trailing on the tile behind him. Heading up the steps, past a large statue of an angel, Pratt enters the serene turquoise room, his eyes darting as he looks for signs of a struggle. The Natatorium is nearly empty, except for a few naked men praying in the water and two Shaxocs Callers. He walks up to the green-robed religious man at the side of the pool, his neck dripping in gold jewellery.

"Detective Pratt, do you have a moment?"

"Detective?" The caller stares dreamily out at the water.

"What brings you here?" Tapping on his wrist, Pratt expands an image of Blackwell's face.

"Have you seen this man?"

"Caller Lemieux had an interesting encounter this morning," he says without looking at the image, "perhaps it was him."

"May I speak with him?"

The caller looks slowly up at the tower above the body of water.

"He is leading a prayer," he says, and then strolls to the other side of the pool.

Shifting his weight from one foot to the other, Pratt breathes in the chlorine as he waits for service to end. Despite his anxieties, the sound of the water falling from the fountains clears his thoughts. Caller Lemieux yells out a low roar and the men in the pool submerge their bodies until the roar stops.

"Pa-uh, pa-uh, pa-uh," Lemieux calls out rhythmically.

The men praying copy the call, breathing out puffs of air in quick succession. Another roar and they slip under the water to hold their breath again. Watching their blissfulness, he becomes aware of a feeling of sadness tightening his chest. Almost makes me wish I believed. The breathing exercises end and Lemiuex speaks the *Message of Infinitum*:

"Let the breath leave your body to strengthen your soul. In this life, you feed the womb of Mary with your exhale, in the next, reborn with an inhale of the past. In this, in your last, in the next, flow up, through the body of Mary." The men slowly leave the pool, dripping water as they make their way back to the change rooms.

Keeping his gaze down to avoid the naked bodies, Pratt walks up to a small staircase leading to the tower above.

"Caller Lemieux, my name is Detective Pratt. Do you have a moment?"

"Yes, come up, boy," Lemieux says. Stumbling up the steps, he finds himself in a cramped office filled with books, mostly cased in green plastic, but some bound in the skin of doxies. I'm too sober for this.

Tapping on his tracker, he holds his wrist forward. "Have you seen this man?"

Lemieux looks at the image. "It was strange, he arrived dressed in uniform, did not pray, and then left in a suit, leaving his red stripes behind." The caller points at Blackwell's red stripe uniform, slumped in a pile at the corner of the wall of books.

"Was there anyone with him?"

"He was alone," the caller says, "and he seemed to be in a hurry."

"Did you speak with him?"

"No."

"Thank you." Picking up the uniform, he makes his way back down the steps.

What's going on? This doesn't seem like a violent kidnapping at all. Is Blackwell part of the Zorax gang? Maybe there was a bigger shipment than the one we busted?

He opens up the location data and chooses an address in the Manufacturing District. I bet that's his apartment. Examining the uniform, he notices specks of blood on one wrist. This is weird. He must have removed the tracker himself.

Walking back through the parking lot, he gets to his bike and shoves the uniform in the storage box. Driving steadily down the highway, his thoughts are on Blackwell, as he leaves the glass pyramids behind.

He makes his way through the middle districts into the warehouses, factories and truck stops of Manufacturing, a place he rarely found himself in. Stopping outside of a junky apartment, he parks his bike and shuffles through the garbage towards the entrance.

Of all places, why live here?

He looks through the list of renters and finds Blackwell's apartment, '1605'. Pulling out Blackwell's tracker from his utility belt, he taps it on the sensor. The door swings open and he makes his way to the elevator, where an out-of-order sign sits over rusty metal doors. Damn.

Opening the door to the stairway, he begins walking up to the 16th floor, as sharp pains of withdrawal shoot behind his eyes. On the stairs between the 11th and 12th floor, he plops down. *This better be worth it. I really need a drink.*

After catching his breath, he stands again, making his way up the final four floors. He hobbles over to 1605 and uses Blackwell's tracker to unlock the door. Inside is a nearly empty apartment with bare walls and a single mattress. Pratt slides open the small closet door, but nothing there is suspicious.

Could he have a secret apartment somewhere else?

Walking over to the bed, he rips the blanket off the mattress. Nothing. He flips the mattress onto its side, causing a bag of hair to fall to the ground. Picking it up, he rips open the bag and touches the red curls.

What? Why does he have a bag of hair? Grabbing a pen from his belt, he labels the bag:

Case #174020-HX; **Item**: Hair; **Date**: 13, 04, 181 A.W.; **Test**: DNA.

After searching the space one more time, he leaves the apartment and walks sluggishly back down the 16 floors. He adds the bag of hair to the storage box on his bike and swipes his wrist to start the engine. *Something strange is going on here.*

Was Blackwell a spy for Zorax?

Pushing on the gas, he pulls back onto the highway, the thoughts of Blackwell ebbing as vodka demands his focus.

17 | VERDICT

TINIK

Sirens blare from every direction, trapping them in the alley.

"Look what you did," Tinik says scathingly, pressing her body against the wall as she tries to be invisible.

"Would you rather I show up with a red stripe's tracker?" Khan says, snarling.

"What about your tracker?" He reaches to grab her wrist, but she pulls it out of his grasp, taking a step away.

"Don't worry about my tracker, no one from Zorax is going to show anyway."

"You don't know that," Khan says. "The district isn't shut down."

A bike pulls up from around the corner and stops a foot from them. The driver drops it, runs forward and shoves a knife against Khan's neck. Here's your chance. Get rid of him! Say he's a red stripe.

"Who the fuck is this?" He looks at Tinik for an answer. No. He could get her file. You need him.

"He's with me!" Tinik shouts.

"Why would you bring him?" He continues pressing the blade against Khan's throat.

"Khan has been selling nostaliem with me," Tinik says, somewhat convincingly. Shit. That's not allowed. What am I doing?

"You're not supposed to recruit sellers."

"It wasn't like that. I've known Khan for a long time." Tinik takes a step closer to the man. "I was just helping him make some extra credits and with the latest crew shot down…"

"This feels shady, boy. I don't have time for this." He drops the knife from Khan's throat and steps back, picking up his bike to leave. No! Don't leave.

"He cut out his tracker today," Tinik spits out, "so he could join Zorax."

The man pauses. "Did you actually cut out your tracker?" Khan holds up his arm and raises the sleeve on the white suit.

"You're a fool then," the man says, but stops walking mid-stride.

"I have nothing left to lose," Khan says.

"Go to Sweet Pink Brothel in the Entertainment District." The man climbs onto his bike.

"A decision will be made there." Disappearing down the alley, he leaves them in a puff of exhaust.

"You owe me," Tinik says. The advertisements above them turn white and sirens surround the block.

"Run!" Khan yells.

"Where?" Tinik pushes herself back into the alley wall, trying to hide from the spotlight.

Dashing across the alley, Khan pulls a grate off of the ground and jumps into a dark hole. Tinik jumps into the hole blindly behind him, landing in sludge. He grabs the sewer lid and they watch the bikes pull into view just as the lid clicks back into place.

"I guess we're even now," Khan says, gloating.

Tinik purses her lips. Fucking red stripe. Chuckling at her expression, he crouches down in the sewer and shuffles deeper into the tunnel. Moving through the muck silently behind him, she breathes calmer as the noise of the sirens melt away. After an hour of a crouched walk, they stop under another alley grate.

"It seems quiet," Tinik says.

Pushing the grate up, Khan briefly looks around and then climbs to the surface. Pulling herself up behind him, the brightness of the advertisements blinds her for a moment.

"We didn't even get out of the Government District."

"It's fine. They've moved on," Khan says. "Do you have enough credits to get us to the Entertainment District?"

"Sure," she says, and starts walking.

"Why don't you call the taxi?" Khan asks. "You know I don't have a tracker."

"I like to keep my business out of the data streams." Tinik continues walking. "There'll be taxis on one of the main roads." Mind your business red stripe.

"Fine." Khan follows her.

Up ahead there are taxis waiting outside a street of busy restaurants and Tinik walks up to the first one, smiling at the driver.

"Where to?"

"Sweet Pink Brothel," she says, and he nods.

Climbing on the bike, she squishes forward, so Khan has room behind her, and after a minute of awkward balancing, the bike takes off.

"What district are you from?" Khan asks.

Tinik turns back to look at him, glaring. "Why do you care?"

"I don't."

"Good," she says, turning forward again. Nosy cockroach.

Having not slept in days, Tinik finds it hard not to close her eyes and stares with blurry vision, as the upper districts streak by in a haze of colour. The bike finally stops in the Entertainment District and she climbs off after Khan.

"It's three and a half credits."

"Green." Turning away from the driver, she pulls out her credits from the hidden bag and hands the driver the amount owed. Poop. Only half a credit left. Broke again. The driver leaves with an annoyed expression on his dust covered face.

"Did you just pay with physical credits?" Khan asks, shaking his head.

"So?" They walk to the entrance of the Sweet Pink Brothel and a doxy with bubblegum pink hair greets them, grinning forcefully.

"How can I help you?" she says in a singsong voice.

"Just a drink," Khan says.

She leads them through rows of hot pink couches where men are drinking pink vodka and smoking pink cigars. Strawberry-flavoured smoke permeates the air in the bar, leaving a sweet chemical taste on their tongues. They sit next to each other on a pink couch, where a mural of a unicorn with large breasts takes up most of the space on the wall beside them.

"I think someone will come get us," Tinik says. A doxy struts over, her blue and white whippy ribbons bouncing with each step.

"What can I get you guys?"

"Still deciding," Tinik says, an apology in her eyes.

"You two, follow me." A sparsely-haired man discreetly directs them behind a set of black curtains.

Tinik and Khan follow, conspicuously looking around at the other patrons. Once through the curtains, the man presses on a purple rock, which drops open, revealing a handle. He pushes a key into the handle and opens it a crack into a dark stairwell.

"They're expecting you." They climb into the stairwell and he shuts the door behind them.

Tinik feels the space ahead, trying to find her way down the pitch black stairs. This is worse than the sewer. Khan stumbles down into her shoulders, almost making her lose balance.

"Sorry," he says.

Another door slides open, revealing a large, dimly lit red velvet room. Inside, there are four men in matching red masks on the lower part of their faces, standing stoically with guns. At the end of the room, two men sit at a large rectangular table, one of them is the man from the alley, and the other is wearing an expensive silver suit with a neon green triangle pattern, his gold watch ostentatiously placed above the fabric of his jacket sleeve's arm.

"Come in," the man with the gold watch commands. Walking ahead of Khan, Tinik looks around the gaudy room, her eyes still adjusting to the light.

"Tinik," she says, holding out her hand to shake. Laughing in response, he shakes her hand, his grin genuine.

"How old are you, Tinik?"

"Fourteen." Actually, 23, but you don't need to know that. Fourteen is believable for a boy.

"And you?"

"Twenty-seven, sir," Khan says.

"Hold out your tracker arms." Nervously holding up her wrist, she removes a black band, revealing an old scar.

"This scar is old," he says. "Why did you cut out your tracker?"

"I was set to be placed in the Purification District at 15," Tinik says. "I'd rather be doing this."

"Why Zorax?"

"I want to be rich."

"I like your spirit," he says, laughing. "What about you?" He looks at Khan.

"I hate my life," Khan says, staring with dead eyes.

"I see..." He looks at Tinik. "You're vouching for this man?"

"Yes, completely, he's not himself." She adds in a whisper, "he fell in love with a peon." Hah, like a red stripe could ever fall in love.

"Oh!" he says. "A peon?" Khan stares at Tinik with an annoyed expression.

"Females, they can't be trusted," the boss says, smiling again, "they only have credits in their eyes." He slowly looks them over.

"I think you both could be useful to me. I need to replace the nostaliem that was seized. There's a crew waiting for two final members. Are you prepared to go to the surface?"

"Of course," Tinik says. "Do we leave now?" How long will this take?

She plasters a fake smile on her face to hide her worry. I don't want to miss out on any more time with my daughter. What's the surface like, anyways? Could I die up there? Shit. There's no backing out now. If I don't do this, I'll never get her back.

"Yes, right now." He motions to a mirror at the back of the room, seemingly talking to someone behind the glass.

"Wait," Khan interrupts, "the surface?"

"Nostaliem is a substance found in the sands of an evaporated body of water. We mine it," he says, with eyes twinkling. "If you return a shipment, you'll be a part of Zorax."

"How long does the trip take?" Tinik half shouts, trying to sound excited.

"Eager, I see," he says. "It could take a week if the storms are severe. You should know, though, it's a war up there, we're not the only gang selling nostaliem in Krevax."

A round-faced man in Manufacturer's overalls walks into the room.

"Escort these two to the drop off point," the boss says.

The man nods and signals for Tinik and Khan to follow him. Tinik exhales slowly. *It's only a week, it will be fine.* Walking at a fast pace, he leads them through an underground garage filled with rows of fancy-looking motorbikes.

"Once you arrive, the crew will take off immediately," he says, as he climbs onto a rusty bike at the end of the last row.

"The crew leader will assign roles for you." Biting her lip nervously, she climbs on the seat behind him and Khan climbs on behind her.

The bike hums, spiralling down through the lower districts, all the way past the garbage heaps of the Recycling District. At the end of the advertisements, they drive through a tunnel and into the Dark Zone.

"Woop!" Tinik lets out a shout. *I did it. I'm one step closer to my baby girl. In a week I'll be a part of Zorax and soon after I'll be rich enough to buy her from anyone.*

Glancing back at Khan, she sees him staring emotionlessly out at the rocks. *Maybe the red stripe will still help me get her file, seeing how I got him into the gang? It's the least he could do to repay me.*

What if Zorax finds out he's a red stripe? Will I be blamed? He's not a problem yet.

Turning forward, she stares out at the vast cave ahead of her. Despite the red stripe and her worries, she can't help but smile. After what felt like at least an hour, the driver's tracker beeps and he stops, motioning at them to get off the bike.

"I can't take you any further, but up a few paces you'll find a hole in the sewer," he says, pointing ahead.

"Climb down and follow the arrows."

With a dip of his head, he does a quick half circle on his bike and revs forward. Darkness collapses in on them as the light from the bike bobs away.

18 | COUNTDOWN
VIOLET

VIOLET STARES OUT AT THE HALLWAY, TAKING A SMALL BREATH. Tiptoeing towards the bathrooms, she pulls the first stall open and then stops. Standing rigidly, she stares across at all four stalls, each door flashing a terrible memory. The horror of each one fills her with shame, making the pit in her stomach tighten.

Taking a step backwards, she goes into the stairwell and climbs two flights of stairs to the floor above. She exhales a breath she hadn't realized she was holding and opens a stall. Shutting the door behind her, she locks it and sits down.

Everything's okay, I'm sure there will be blood. She removes the clear plastic cup from her body and stares at it. Why is there still no blood? You know what this means. She quietly cries into her elbow, not wanting to be heard. No, it has to be something else. Still holding the cup, her hands tremble and she holds them close to her chest. If it's true… then a violent end is inevitable. Don't think about that.

Tapping her tracker, she navigates to a blue dot and clicks it. A calendar opens and she swipes down, scrolling past weeks prior.

Wait? Did I skip the last one too? I will starve myself until I bleed. What if I don't bleed? Then it will show itself, even if I refuse to say its name.

"Help me," she says to no one. "Please, somebody help."

Gripping her hair, she pulls it down in front of her eyes. "Why?"

After a couple of slow breaths to calm herself, she places a hand on her belly. It doesn't feel any different. I need to know for sure. Clicking on her tracker, she navigates to the tab store and chooses a pink button for generators. A new screen opens, full of sleep tools, breastfeeding guides, and diaper trackers, she scrolls past these to an image of a pink balloon and taps on it.

The pregnancy tracking app opens and she reads through the information. Detects pregnancy in as little as three days after the first day of your missed period. *Purchase for only 64 credits* flashes in soft pink wispy typeface. Sixty-four credits!

She shakes her head feeling hopeless and then resolutely touches the wallet icon to buy it. White plastic credits stream down the tracker's screen, until only 27 remain. The pregnancy tracker unlocks and downloads into her files. She scrolls down to the *Am I Pregnant* button and clicks it.

"Calculating," a cheery-baby voice says. After a torturous minute, the screen changes from white to bright pink. *"Congratulations! You are seven weeks pregnant."* No.

"No!" Throwing the empty cup at the door, she watches it bounce off the wall and onto the ground.

Standing shakily, she sanitizes her hands and turns towards the door. Seven weeks. The door opens to the empty hallway and her body floats through the hall where it pushes the button to call the elevator. Inside, a pitiful figure in a white mask stares at her in the mirror. Pathetic. It's not you. She's pathetic.

On the ground floor she calmly walks out to the street,

knowing exactly what she will do next. It's unspeakable, but as clear as the advertisements above her. Everyone knows what happens to a pregnant peon. She giggles to herself erratically.

Everyone knows that they die, whether from attempting to rip out the flesh themselves, or they end up killed when the truth is discovered. With eyes glazed over, her body presses forward through the busy road. Either way, they die; a nuisance to be cleaned from the street. No one cares about a dead peon. They're all garbage. I'm garbage.

Around her, motorcycles honk, bodies shuffle by indifferently, the advertisements buzz loudly and Violet's body walks on. Dead, dead, dead. Stopping in front of the Lottery Supplier, she puts her wrist up on the counter. In the Orbs, I won't be a peon.

Laughing deliriously, her voice says, "one ticket, please."

"It's 490 credits," the attendant says as he presses the scanner and 490 credits come out of Remi's wallet. He holds out a shiny blue piece of plastic with a long string of golden numbers across it.

"Good luck," he says.

Taking the ticket, she walks to her usual spot and slides between the vending machine and the wall. Slumping into a seated position, she stares at the ticket in her clammy hands. Studying the fluffy white clouds in the bright blue sky, she traces the edges with her eyes. My actual body is waiting for me. A feeling of peace comes over her and she inhales calmly. I'm finally going to the Orbs. I've proven myself and I am good enough.

She anxiously reads through the contest details on the back of the ticket. 'Find our draw countdown on the Lucky Lottery tab.' Clicking on her tracker, she navigates to the Lucky Lottery tab and it opens to a clock counting down. The next draw is in 24 hours. With slight desperation in her eyes, she smiles with a wide uncanny looking grin. Only 24 hours.

A terrifying thought presses down on her and she falls against the vending machine, her smile disappearing. That's still one more night I have to survive at the apartment.

Will Remi know I spent his money? What if he already knows?

A cold sweat breaks out on her chest and she stands in a panic, but dizziness overcomes her and she collapses back to the ground. He doesn't know. He's never mentioned anything money related before. He won't figure it out in the next 24 hours. Determined, she stands again and slides back out to the street, focusing on moving one step at a time. I'll be fine.

Back at the building, she takes the elevator up and walks briskly to the apartment, hiding the lottery ticket in her personal cupboard. Lying down on the couch, exhaustion forces her eyes closed and she slips into a deep sleep. The door clicks open, making her twitch awake and she bolts up right. Does he know?

"Get over here," Remi says. "Take off my boots."

Feeling relieved at his words, she runs over and leans down in front of him. Removing his boots and socks, she stands and places the boots in the closet and the socks in the empty laundry bucket before quickly returning. She picks up a foot and rubs his heel methodically. With her head spinning, she watches his eyes dart around the clean room. Everything is in place.

He seems agitated?

Remi mumbles to himself distractedly and picks up a tube of corn and beef flavoured paste, tearing it open. The smell makes her feel nauseous and she takes a slow breath, as she switches to his other foot.

"Why would he go to the Natatorium? Was he repenting

for a crime?" He continues mumbling to himself. She finishes rubbing his feet and stands in front of him.

"Would you like a drink, sir?"

He sighs. "Yeah, make it a double."

Nodding, she heads to the bedroom and pours him a mix of blueberry and pineapple vodka. *What if he gets a notification about the credits after I've fallen asleep?*

An image of him stabbing her awake flashes in her mind. Staring at the glass in her hand, she steps slowly back towards the table. *What if I broke it? Could I slit his throat?*

Sighing heavily, she hands him the glass as he stares past her with zoned out eyes. *He's too strong. I could never slit his throat.* Without looking at the glass, he takes a gulp. *Maybe while he sleeps… I could never kill someone.*

Taking a couple steps back from him, she stands against the wall, silently. He makes his way over to the couch and the screen lights up his face as he jumps through the channels. The sound of gloves hitting flesh blasts from the speakers and into Violet's head.

Watching him stare at the screen for a minute she imagines what he would look like dead. *I could give him sleeping pills?*

Sitting down at the table, she waits for her alarm by scrolling through sleeping aids. *Maybe a strong enough dose would keep him asleep until I was gone.* Grabbing a tube of strawberry paste from the vase, she opens it and takes a small bite. It doesn't make her feel sick and she mindlessly eats it. *I hate this place. I'm always waiting. Waiting for him to hurt me. Waiting for him to sleep. Waiting for him to arrive. Waiting to shower. Waiting for blood.*

She looks down at her stomach and then up at the clock above the doorway. *Only 20 hours left. I'm so tired of waiting.*

19 | FAMILY LETTERS

CARR

SITTING AT HIS DESK, CARR LOOKS PAST THE NEW PROPAGANDA posters for Krevax. His head is buzzing with thoughts of rescue and he can't focus. Clicking on his watch, he stares at the spot where Charlie's heartbeat used to transmit. I knew he might cut out his tracker, but now with Bouchard wanting to take out the gang strongholds...

Sighing heavily, he rubs his temples with his fingertips. I should have called him off when I had the chance. I didn't think it would end up being this dangerous. Why hasn't he sent any progress reports? I need to find him before it's too late. Picking up his desk phone's receiver, he dials the numbers 1-0-0-1.

Ring.

Ring.

"Captain Lewis here."

"Captain Lewis, it's the Tzar."

"Tzar! Of course, how can I help you?"

"You have a detective, Charlie Blackwell, I believe, who went missing recently?"

"Yes, Blackwell, he may have been kidnapped by the Zorax

gang, we're still investigating. He recently brought in a large seizure of nostaliem."

"I see. I would like his safe return to be a priority. We don't want the gangs to think they can take one of our detectives off the street. We need to show the people that we hold the control in Krevax."

"Absolutely. His two partners are already looking for him."

"Also, gather any information you can find about Blackwell. The city needs a hero to focus on. We should prepare a campaign."

"Yes, sir, I will let you know what I find out."

"Thank you," Carr says and hangs up the phone, refocusing on the advertisements.

This time, he actually looks at them. The first one is black with red flames stating, *FEAR THE WOMB OF MARY! Damnation waits for those who commit suicide! Damnation waits for those who use Nostaliem.* The poster recedes to the background of his mind and he sighs. What if they don't find him?

Attempting to distract himself from worry, he forces himself to review the next advertisement. In it a green-robed man points his finger forward at the viewer and whispers, *Fear of the LORD is the beginning of wisdom. Knowledge of the HOLY ONE is understanding. The HOLY ONE says no to Nostaliem! The HOLY ONE says no to suicide! MARY will curse those who use nostaliem.* Well, it doesn't get heavier handed than that.

Picking up the third poster, he drops it on the top of the stack. This one contains a bright blue sky with white fluffy clouds and cheerfully says, *Obey the HOLY ONE and choose recycling: Only sinners take Nostaliem! Heaven waits for the worthy.*

Pushing the advertisements to the far side of the desk, he leans back in his chair. If the numbers slow down, hopefully

Bouchard decides against this cull. I need more time to find Charlie. Reaching forward, he picks up the phone again and dials the numbers 0-5.

Ring.

"Hello."

"Bouchard, it's Carr. I've amped up the religious propaganda. I'm going to have the new advertisements take up 15 percent of the ad space city-wide."

"Good, I'll be watching the numbers." The call clicks off before he can reply. He slams the receiver down, his jaw clenched.

Bouchard is counting down the clock, even if the numbers improve—involving President Lehan is inevitable. Anger overwhelms him and he hits his fist against the desk. I need to calm down. I need to think. I've got to get Charlie to the Orbs. Looking up to make sure his door is locked, he stands, turns and stares at a painting of the three Orbs.

In the image the tropical orb sits in the middle, with the desert orb on one side, and the boreal orb on the other, all floating within the Earth's atmosphere, just above the dust. Removing the painting, he reveals a hidden safe, unlocks it and takes out a sealed folder. He unloosens the string tab and pulls out two disks.

After placing the first disk on the circular data reader, a video file pops up on the computer screen. Opening it, a passcode screen expands and he types in a 7-digit code and presses play.

His mother sits in a polka-dot dress, her long curly red hair and deep brown skin contrasted against the teal couch.

"Travis, I love you so much," she says, as a smiling child runs towards her and climbs into her lap.

"I love you, mama!"

Kissing his cheek, she then looks into the camera.

"I will always love you, my baby bear." The dark-haired boy giggles and disappears off camera.

She steps forward and the screen goes black. Grabbing the disk from the reader, he returns it to the folder, and then places the next disk on the device. The video file jumps onto the screen and he clicks on it, typing in the passcode and pressing play.

"I know you're smart enough to become the man I would have raised," his mother says, tears running down her prominent cheekbones.

"I would take you with me if it were possible, but it's too dangerous. One day, you'll understand why I had to leave." The video clicks off.

Carr closes his eyes. I don't understand, mother. If you really loved me, why would you leave?

After returning the second disk to the folder, he pulls out two letters and a time-stained photograph. The photo is of his mother holding a newborn baby, behind her a cave wall. In the picture she is smiling, admiring her newborn son. His chubby cheeks are lighter than that of Charlotte's rich skin tone, but the perfect match for Carr's. He places the photo back in the folder and opens the first letter.

Dear James,

I love you. I don't want to leave you. I am so sorry for hurting you and our son.

Every part of me wants to stay with you and Travis, but still I can't. I could not live with myself. There was so much I should have told you when we met. You looked at me and saw something I so desperately wanted to be, so I pretended it was true.

I wish I could have lied to myself, to convince myself of your truth. But I know what is real, and what is right. Now you need to see it too. I am pregnant with your second son and he will be born in Krevax. I will place him in the program you have created.

With your position in the agency, you can help dismantle this very program, and save him. You know the life you are leaving him with if you don't.

It is my dying wish that you act to save both our sons.

All my love,

Charlotte.

How could she be so selfish? Tossing the letter on the desk, like an apple with a worm in it, Carr composes himself and then opens the last letter.

To my son,

I am writing this letter on the eve of your wedding day. I know you have expressed some concern about not being able to give your wife a nickname.

I first want to let you know I am thrilled with your choice for a wife. She is lovely and will serve you well. Second, I hope to convince you that a nickname for your wife would be a mistake. I understand the desire to name your wife, as I am sure you want her to be an equal. But I implore you to remember she is not. She is much too emotional a creature to be your partner. That does not mean that you don't love her, just that your love is there to shield her, not to confide in.

I know you were devastated when your mother left and blamed me for what happened. I hope in this letter you will finally understand why. I was naïve when I chose Charlotte. I believed she would come to understand our way of life, but she was steadfast in her weak beliefs. Her betrayal of our family was her choice alone.

I wish I had found your brother, but she hid him well. Females are too emotional for facts. They cannot be trusted to choose logic. The Orbs are the last vestiges of our humanity, and no cost is too high to protect them. That is why a new law was implemented. One you are quite familiar with at this point.

The Law of Aegis which states that no female shall be named or learned. Females henceforth were taught their place is to care for men and children. This is for their own protection. I know now more than ever that I made the right decision.

I hope you will come to see that as well.

Your loving Father.

With a sad exhale, Carr puts the two letters back into the folder and returns it to the safe. Don't worry, Father, I finally found him.

"I promise I'll save him for you," he whispers to himself.

Turning off the light to his office, he walks into the dark hallway and makes his way to the elevator. Where are you now, brother? He walks steadily outside to the waiting limo.

"Where to, sir?" the driver asks as Carr climbs in.

"Home," he says.

The limo pulls out of the parking lot and onto the city street. Closing his eyes, he sees Charlie's face burned in his retinas, the brother he had spent years searching for.

His own flesh and blood trapped in the walls of Krevax. He stares out the window, trying to distract himself from his fears.

20 | SWIM LESSON
BLACKWELL

As Blackwell's eyes adjust to the darkness, he examines the barren cave. This is the perfect place to die. With a disturbed smile, he takes a step forward, ignoring the uneven terrain. Out here I don't even need to worry about my body ending up in a folder on some red stripe's desk.

"Have you heard of people going below Krevax?" Tinik asks, stepping cautiously forward in the darkness beside him, and then adds, "I've heard rumours but I didn't think they were true."

"I've never heard of it," Blackwell says, grinning. "We might get lost out here forever."

"I don't think so. Nostaliem is coming from somewhere," Tinik says, moving gingerly over the uneven surface.

"Besides, what else are we gonna do? I'm not going back to Krevax just to starve there." As Tinik trips, he automatically reaches out his hand, catching him.

"Sorry!" Tinik says.

"It's okay." Blackwell helps him stand upright, smiling at the unexpected moment.

Maybe I am good for something after all! I can help

thieves survive the Dark Lands. Despite his sarcastic thoughts, a tiny positive feeling floats in his head. As they continue walking together in the dark, he feels calmer than he could ever remember feeling before.

"It's strange not being watched, don't you think?"

Tinik looks up, reflexively searching for the Watchtower.

"I like it." He opens his arms wide. "Feels free! I'm not sure when we'll eat next though."

"I don't think we'll find any food out here." I would have preferred a bullet, but I guess I'm not good enough to be shot. You have to be someone to be shot, a real man, someone like Remi. I'm a fucking nobody. I deserve to starve.

Tinik smiles wryly in response.

"Who says there's no food?" He pinches Blackwell's arm.

Blackwell laughs. "No way you could beat me in combat."

"You don't know." Tinik kicks high into the air. "I could be an expert in the physical arts." Blackwell chuckles. He's funny.

"Do you see that?" Tinik says, pointing at a dim blue light in the distance.

Blackwell squints his eyes. "I think so."

Tinik breaks out into a run and he rushes after him. Up ahead a couple more steps, blue light is pulsing from a hole. As they get directly over the opening, they see cobalt flashing over the walls of a cave below.

"I think it's alive." Tinik leans down and brushes the surface with his fingertips. "It's soft!"

"A plant outside of the Farming District?" Blackwell whispers as he touches the feathery texture. I guess we couldn't kill everything.

"Beautiful," Tinik says, "like an ocean."

"Or maybe the sky." Blackwell smiles imagining a blue sky.

They climb down into the rocky structure towards a large tunnel that descends 10 feet into the earth.

Smelling the fresh scent of the fungus, he grins. "What if the surface is like this?" I hope I die soon, but it would be nice to see the surface first.

"Full of blue fungus?" Tinik asks, as he hops down the small stone steps.

"No," he says. "Alive!" They crouch down so their heads won't hit the stone ceiling and continue moving forward.

"That would make me mad, knowing we were trapped in Krevax and the whole time we could have been on the surface." After another few feet they can stand up straight again.

"True," Blackwell says. "Still, I hope there's something alive up there." Maybe it will be toxic. I wouldn't mind being an adventurer who succumbs to an alien environment.

As they reach the lowest point of the cave, blue fungus is glowing on every surface.

"I wonder if this is edible?" Tinik picks a small piece of fungus off the wall and bites it.

"Does it taste bitter?" Blackwell asks, staring at him.

"Tastes yummy," he says and then picks another chunk.

Disappointed, Blackwell looks away, only to be awestruck by the sight further into the cave where rocky walls open up to a vast subterrane of glowing blue fungus. Tinik yells excitedly into the cave.

"Hello!" he calls out, throwing his arms into the air. A moment later an echo returns and he looks over at Blackwell expectantly.

"Hello!" Blackwell yells. Another echo follows and then Tinik yells again, making them both break out into laughter.

Blackwell feels happy for a moment, but then looks down, feeling hollow. Staring at the ground, something bright red catches his eye.

"Look, an arrow, painted onto the rock there."

"This is going to be dangerous," Tinik states matter-of-factly and takes a small step forward.

Blackwell takes a step beside him. "Good, I like danger." They head further into the cave system stepping quickly over jagged rocks. Fungus dances on the walls ahead, lighting their way.

"Is that water?!" Tinik shouts.

A large pool of clear water expands out in front of them. Skipping forward to the edge, he leans down and picks up a handful and drinks.

"It tastes clean."

"You're drinking that?"

"I'm thirsty."

Crouching, Blackwell also drinks a handful of water. It tastes fresher than any hydration gel tube and he drinks another few handfuls.

"Look," he says, pointing down, "the arrows are in the water."

"Oh, they are," Tinik says in surprise. "Do you see a way around?" Standing on his tiptoes, he attempts to find a path carved into the rocks.

"I don't think so," Blackwell says, jumping into the pool.

Treading in icy water, his lips turn instantly grey. For a moment he hopes to sink, but he's too strong a swimmer. If I took a gulp of water, it could work, but if I got out, then it would be a slow death. Maybe I'll still get a bullet. I have to try.

"You getting in?"

Rubbing his arms nervously, Tinik mumbles, "I can't swim."

"You can't swim?" Blackwell stares up at him, stunned. "Didn't you learn in the Natatorium?" Tinik jumps into the water and immediately sinks, gulping in panic. Diving underneath him, Blackwell grabs onto his shirt collar and brings his head above the water.

"Thank you," Tinik sputters, grabbing onto Blackwell's arm.

"Do you know how to float?" Tinik shakes his head no.

"Lean back and don't move," Blackwell says, helping guide him into a floating position.

"I won't let go." Resting Tinik's head on his own chest, he holds him under his armpits and kicks out into the water. After a couple minutes of swimming, he can finally make out the edge on the other side.

"I'm c-cold," Tinik stutters.

"Not much further," he says, kicking harder.

Tinik's teeth chatter in his ears. When he reaches the rocky ledge, he pushes the younkin forward.

"Climb up," he says.

Tinik attempts to lift himself up, but his arms are too cold. Blackwell quickly climbs out beside him and then leans over and helps hoist him out of the water.

After they are both on solid ground, Blackwell immediately takes off the wet suit and starts squishing the water out. With his boxers back on, he looks over at Tinik, who's attempting to take off his pants, but his hands are shaking too badly. Blackwell helps him remove his pants and squeeze the water out, then he leans over to remove Tinik's shirt.

"Khan, wait," he says.

"We need to warm you up." Pulling off the shirt, he twists it and looks back at Tinik, whose chest is wrapped in black fabric.

Blackwell stares at him, slowly comprehending what he is seeing. He's not a boy? Leaning down, he wraps his arms around Tinik's small shivering frame. She's a female?

"Just say it," she whispers, "we both know you know."

"You're female," Blackwell says, staring at her small hands.

She's a female, and she thinks just as clearly as me. Just like Kaliann. They sit there silently until Tinik finally stops shivering. Standing, she turns away from him and begins removing the wrap. Politely looking away, he waits for her to twist out of the water and re-wrap herself. After getting dressed she turns back to look at him.

"What are you going to do?"

Blackwell turns to face her.

"What do you want me to do?" he asks, eyebrows furrowed in surprise.

"Nothing, I just want to be Tinik."

"Okay."

"Good." She steps forward towards the next arrow. "Let's go then."

Hastily, he puts the rest of his clothes on and follows her away from the water.

"What were you?"

"What do you mean?" she asks.

"Were you a generator, or a doxy…"

"It doesn't matter, Khan," she says, cutting him off, "peon, doxy, generator, in the end they're all the same— slaves."

"I'm sorry, I shouldn't have asked," Blackwell says, his cheeks flushing.

How could I have ever believed females were a subspecies? It doesn't even make sense.

"It's okay," Tinik says. "I know that's all they teach you about us."

"My name, it's not Khan."

"I know," Tinik says. The path narrows and Blackwell pushes himself through a small crevice, his shoulders getting stuck for a moment.

"It's Charlie Blackwell." He grabs his chest, focusing on

his breath, and squeezes through. "But everyone calls me Blackwell."

"Blackwell," she says, "I like it," walking through the crevice with ease.

"Are you actually fourteen?"

"Nah, I'm twenty-three," Tinik says with a laugh.

A booming thunders out. They freeze, confused, and then see the source of the noise above. An avalanche of rocks tumbling towards them.

"Run!" Tinik screams.

Blackwell grabs her shoulders and pulls her under a lip of the wall, protecting them from the boulders. Why did I do that? Getting crushed by rocks could have been a perfect death. It's okay. I don't need to be brave. I just need to put myself in a situation where death is inevitable and I'm already doing that. So I escaped this time, next time I won't. Motionless, they wait for the dust to settle around them. Who knows, maybe I'll still die in this cave, there's time.

"Can you move?" Blackwell asks, coughing as he slides back through the crevice and up to the entrance.

"Yes, but I don't think we can get through this way now," Tinik says, pushing her arm into the boulder.

"We won't be able to move those," Blackwell says. "We can find a different way."

Tinik growls, "we should've run for it."

"We weren't going to outrun a rockslide!" This is what I get for saving her? It doesn't matter what I do. I'm never good enough. I hate myself and I hate this place. I'm tired. I'm tired of everything.

"And you think this is better?" Tinik stares at him, her fists balled. "We've lost the arrows."

Blackwell stares back at her with his lips drawn in tightly.

Suddenly, he was whipped onto the cave floor, his flailing body dragging backwards into the dark. Screaming out in shock, his voice echoes back at him, bouncing off the cave walls. He tries to escape, but something has his leg in a vice-like grip. He turns to look.

A terrifying eight-legged creature is holding him with one of its two razor-sharp claws. In that second, he knows he is about to die, and suddenly, he wants to live. A switch is pulled, and the light in the room of his once dark mind is made clear and bright.

Please, I don't want to die! I want to live, to really live. Another scream calls out from his chest as he continues to be dragged behind the scurrying legs.

For a moment, his body bumps along the rocky floor like a rag doll, but then a small voice inside him shouts *fight*! He reaches out on the fast moving ground and grabs onto a rock. Hitting forward, he smashes the pincer. The creature screams and throws him against a wall.

His chest tightens as the wind is knocked out of him. The creature runs towards him. With a sharp inhale, he jumps up and runs into the dark. The creature snaps its claws just behind him. He rolls into a narrow trench and drops into a hole.

Above him, he can hear claws digging. There's no way out. He pushes his body against the rocks, staying just out of reach of the pincers. With every scratch, it pushes closer.

Eyes wide with terror, he picks up a handful of gravel, but it melts away uselessly. Turning, he tries to dig out of the trench. Panic overtakes him. He scratches at the rocks, hyperventilating. He covers his ears and shuts his eyes. The pincer catches the edge of his pants. He pulls his leg away. There's no more space to manoeuvre.

He freezes in terror. No one cares about me. I'm all alone. I'm going to die all alone.

21 | CLIMBERS

TINIK

"Blackwell!" Tinik crouches down as she watches his body ripped away.

What the fuck was that? Hearing him scream out a second time, her chest breaks out in a cold sweat as this one is much further away.

For just a second she thinks of leaving the red stripe behind, but his terrified screams keep playing in her head. Get up. If you wait, you won't be able to find him. With a breath, she leaps up and runs towards the scream. The echo takes her to a wide tunnel that spirals into a fast descent. Thin jagged rocks sit precariously above her, threatening death with every foot.

Stepping quickly, she moves lower into the earth, sticking to the edges. Her daughter's face flashes in her mind and she slows to a crawl and stops, cowering against the cave wall.

What if I get myself killed over a red stripe?

Closing her eyes for a second she thinks on the consequences of this decision. I would want someone to save my daughter. He's someone's son. He could have let me drown, but he didn't, even though I know his secret.

Resolute, she steps quietly forward, and as the decline becomes more gradual quickens her pace.

"Blackwell?" she whispers.

There's no reply, and fear is taking over, but she keeps moving. In the distance she hears a scraping sound and stops to listen. For a moment terror pushes her to run back up the tunnel, but the idea of leaving Blackwell alone to violently die feels too painful. With fists tight, she runs forward, pursuing the sound. The scratching is louder now. She slows and tiptoes around the next bend, freezing when she sees the creature digging just beyond reach.

Moving a step closer, she takes in its eight-legs, razor-sharp claws, curved tail, and stinger, its white shell exterior shimmering in the dim light. She picks up a sharp rock and takes another tentative step forward. The creature stops digging and turns towards her with two beady black eyes.

Tinik lets out a high-pitched scream and falls backwards onto the ground. The creature scurries forward, its stinger jutting violently.

Rolling back, she jumps to a stand, holding her position. Too late to run now. Adrenalin pumps through her body, making time flash in slow fragments.

The stinger propels towards her and she springs up, swinging the rock forward. The rock smashes the last segment of its tail. The creature lets out a hissing whine and lunges with a pincer. Jerking backwards, she just escapes its grasp. She wraps her fingers around another rock, leaving a knifelike corner exposed.

With her heart pounding in her ears, she charges and leaps off one of the extended pincers towards the creature's face. The rock plunges into one of its beady eyes as it swings madly around, trying to escape her grasp. She flies through the air, colliding with the cave wall. Collapsing onto the rocky ground, she pulls her legs into a ball as her vision of the cave fades out.

"Tinik! Wake up!" Blackwell shouts, holding her shoulders. "Can you hear me?"

She opens her eyes, disoriented, and says, "Green."

"Let's go!" Blackwell helps her stand, but she immediately falls back to the ground.

In the distance she can see the monster's body curled into a contracted ball, with its legs in the air.

"It's dead?"

"We need to get out of here. Now!" He picks her up, swings her frame over his shoulders and carries her through the crevice. She can hear his footsteps echoing. A scurrying sound comes from the dark.

"They're coming!" Tinik cries.

The noise grows louder, gaining quickly on their position. Blackwell pushes Tinik up to a ledge where the rocks open to a chamber of green-blue fungus.

"Can you climb?"

"Yes," Tinik says, although she's not sure she can.

Her head is spinning with pain as she does everything to focus on getting up the rocks. In the chamber below, Blackwell holds a stick-shaped rock like a baseball bat, bracing for a fight. Tinik watches the creature launch itself towards him. This one is smaller than the last, but its stinger is still razor sharp.

"Go for the eyes!" she yells.

Blackwell kicks gravel at the creature and swings with the rock, crushing its stinger. It retreats into the darkness with a terrifying screech. Tinik stares at the crevice at the top of the chamber, willing herself to keep moving. Blackwell scrambles up the rock wall, passing her quickly. Scurrying echoes throughout the chamber. Tinik climbs a few feet, but her pounding head keeps her slow. The sound of the scurrying increases to a roar.

"Hurry, Tinik!" Blackwell outstretches his hand.

Their screams catch in their throats in terror, as the creature slams its body around the corner and starts climbing the rock wall towards them. This one is at least twice as big as the first. Pulling her up by an elbow, Blackwell holds under her arms.

A pincer grabs onto her dangling foot. She shrieks as searing hot pain spreads up her leg. Blackwell kicks just below the creature's pincer and it hisses and recoils.

Tinik scrambles the last foot to the surface and collapses. Blackwell heaves up a boulder. The stinger swings up through the crevice. He comes down with the rock, hitting the segment behind the stinger. The white armour cracks, emitting a yellow sludge.

Launching forward, the creature lunges erratically with a pincer. Blackwell grabs onto the middle segment of the arm and kicks down with all his weight. His foot hits the creature's mandibles and they both tumble to the fungus-covered floor of the chamber below.

"Blackwell!" Tinik screams.

Crawling over to the edge of the hole, she watches him clamour back up the wall. Grabbing his hand, she pulls as he jumps up through the crevice. He tumbles a few feet away onto the rocky surface and lands face down. Picking up a large rock behind her, she stands and limps forward.

A pincer snaps through the opening and she smashes it as hard as she can. The creature spits a low whining sound. The rock shakes for a few seconds and then it frees its squashed appendage. Tinik and Blackwell stare at the spot in anticipation, breathing heavily as the silence continues.

"I think it's gone," he whispers after a full minute.

"I hope so," Tinik says, and taking a breath she finally

stops staring. Looking up she sees an ancient system of pipes shimmering on the expansive cave ceiling. Stumbling back, she falls, surprised by its eerie beauty.

Blackwell rushes to her. "Are you okay?"

"I think so." The wonderment she feels distracts her from her spinning headache and throbbing foot. Tinik points up. "Look."

Blackwell follows her gaze and inhales sharply. Goosebumps stand on her arms.

"It's so beautiful," she says, as her eyes linger over the crystal-covered pipes, "and strangely terrifying." She looks over at Blackwell.

"It's hard to imagine the people who made that."

He looks back at her, smiling. "You're crazy, you know that? You risked your life."

"I couldn't let that creature eat my only meal," Tinik says, laughing.

His smile disappears. "Why did you come back for me?" he asks, his voice cracking.

Tinik meets his eyes, surprised by his vulnerability.

"It was the only choice," she says.

Blackwell nods slowly and then stares at her as though to press further, but doesn't. Seeing him this way, Tinik feels thankful she decided to save him. There's more to him than just a red stripe. Sighing deeply, he gives a small smile and looks back up at the crystal sewers. She limps a few steps away, wanting to give him a moment to himself.

Surveying this new underground world from the top of the rocks makes her feel like something small, and yet vital. Here she was, underneath an unknown city, an ancestor of people now dust. In time these crystallized sewers would also become dust. She looks at her hands and imagines the bones hidden beneath her skin. Then she sees something unexpected through the holes between her fingers, small red arrows far in the distance.

"Holy Mary!" Tink shouts. "Arrows."

She points towards the line of arrows exiting the cave system below them.

"That's lucky," Blackwell says, grinning as he walks towards her.

Tinik takes a tentative step down the steep slope, but the pain from her foot still causes her to lose balance.

"Are you okay?"

"It's my foot," she says, sitting down.

Blackwell gently removes her shoe and sock and examines the dark purple bruise. Wincing at the sight of it, Tinik looks up, trying to lose herself in the crystals.

"It doesn't mean it's broken." Blackwell feels her foot and bends it into a walking position. "It doesn't look too bad…"

Laughing, she looks back down at her foot.

"No bones sticking out of my skin at least."

"Come on, I can carry you," he says, smiling.

Nodding, she wraps her arms around his shoulders.

"Let's get out of here!" Blackwell stands up slowly, holding tight to Tinik's legs and jogs down the hill. Stopping at the first arrow, they stare at the entrance to the cave system, thankful there's no movement.

"I think it's safe to say we destroyed Zorax's only route out of Krevax," Tinik says.

"I'm sure they'll just carve out a fresh path."

"Your boss would be happy, red stripe," she says, laughing.

"That's true." They follow the arrows for what feels like an hour underneath the crystal pipes.

At first Tinik is too exhausted to think, but slowly her head stops pounding and she can't help but picture her daughter.

"Blackwell." I'm sure he will give me her file now.

"Yeah?"

"Do red stripes have access to birth records?"

"The detectives do."

"So you do?" She holds her breath, wanting to believe her daughter is in reach.

"I did, not anymore, though."

"Right," Tinik whispers to herself.

It's okay, I'll find her. There will be another way. A blue glimmer of light catches her eyes.

"There's something up there," she says. Something is glinting in the distance, but not from the crystal ceiling.

"I see it," Blackwell says, "it might be them."

As they get closer, the mass of metal is less like a truck and more like a clump of garbage welded together, waiting for its chance to collapse in on the passengers and kill them. Tinik stares at it feeling slightly sick. Just because the outside looks like trash, doesn't mean it isn't sturdy. I have to believe this is going to work. She takes a breath to steady herself. This is going to work.

"I recognize those," Blackwell says.

"What?"

"The rockets on the sides, they're from cargo ships that took materials to the Orbs."

"They look old," Tinik says, barely containing her nerves.

"Old is right, they decommissioned them when I was a younkin. I used to play on them in the Manufacturing District."

"Good to know we're expendable," Tinik says.

Looking up, she sees a pitch-black hole in the crystals coming into view. Despite the obvious danger and her fears of being killed, the idea of the surface was thrilling. As excitement builds in her chest, she commits herself to faith. This is going to work. Once they get within a few feet of the heap of metal, the massive size of the truck becomes clear: it's two storeys tall and ten feet wide.

A large window bubbles out at the front, with a gun station on one side, and blue light pulsing from strips in the ceiling. A loud buzzer blares above them, signalling their arrival. Letting go of Blackwell's shoulders, Tinik stands and limps a few steps beside him, watching as a large ramp unfolds out from the side of the truck.

"Lookie here!" An intimidating muscular man steps forward onto the ramp, his expression a mix of annoyance and contempt.

Staring up at him, Tinik's fragile excitement dissipates, replaced again with the gnawing feeling of worry.

22 | GERTIE

ROCKET

ROCKET WALKS UP BEHIND GUNNER AND POPS HIS HEAD OUT of the metal doorway, a smile dimpling his warm sepia-toned cheeks.

Another younkin? He nods kindly at the two recruits, but privately feels concerned.

I know the crackdowns have been bad, but they shouldn't be sending younkins to collect nostaliem, especially not two on one mission. Looking over at Gunner, he watches him glare at the boy, his buggy eyes narrowing with increasing anger. Great, he was already in a rage over the first one.

What will he do now? Tightening his fists, Rocket prepares himself for an outburst, but after a full minute of awkward silence he realizes Gunner is holding back. Interesting, he must be sizing up that one.

He looks at the lean-muscled man staring up at them, and feeling pressure to fill the silence, braces himself. In his mind he sounds out the words he wants to say, removing any sign of his recycler's accent. Because of the difficulty of hiding his background, he tries to speak as little as possible, but, reigning in Gunner's anger was quickly becoming his number one priority. He had already spoken more in the last few days than he would in a typical week.

"Took you long enough," Rocket says with difficulty, breaking the tension.

He holds his breath, waiting for a reaction. This is going to be the longest week of my life.

"I'm Tinik!" the little one says, yipping in a high-pitched voice that suggested he was still far from puberty.

Stepping forward, excitedly, his short black stubbled hair framed a younkin-like face in the ramp's spotlight. I wonder if he's from the Recycling District? Looks malnourished and his skin is a fair bit darker than mine, maybe he's also hiding an accent. No one wants to be the lowest caste.

"Are you limping?" Gunner asks, stomping a few feet down the ramp towards Tinik.

With each step, the ramp shakes and his blocky head bounces uncomfortably on his oversized muscular neck. Watching keenly, Rocket tries to make eye contact with the two recruits, silently trying to warn them. Here we go, he already pinned Pickles against a wall, what will he do to this one?

"I had a run in with a giant bug, back in that cave system," Tinik says. "It pinched my foot, it's okay, though."

"How old are you?" Gunner asks, pointing at Tinik, his finger and thumb a few inches from his face.

"Fourteen."

"This is fucking bullshit," Gunner shouts, marching back up the ramp.

With a quick step out of the way, Rocket watches him lean down to avoid hitting his head on the doorway and disappear into the truck. I hate that he's double my height. In a fight, I'd have no chance. Exhaling slowly, Rocket thinks through the next few words and takes another step down the ramp to greet the recruits.

"Is everything okay?" the man asks, moving protectively beside the younkin.

This one's a Manufacturer. I'd bet all my credits, he looks to be middle caste and I can hear his elongated vowels.

"It's not his fault," Rocket says, referring to Tinik. He takes a breath, thinking through his words.

"These missions are dangerous and younkins…" He trails off.

"Right," Tinik says. "How many younkins are on this crew?"

Rocket holds up two fingers.

"How old's the other one?" Tinik asks.

"Nine," Rocket says.

"Do they usually have younkins?" the man asks. Rocket shrugs his shoulders.

"We're just a bunch of young punks, hey!" Tinik says, jokingly. The man chuckles in response.

"I'm Rocket," he says, stepping forward to shake hands. His muscled stature is only slightly taller than Tinik's.

"Khan, nice to meet you." With a slight smile, Khan turns and helps the limping younkin up the ramp.

Rocket pushes the button to close the ramp behind them. Zipper strides through the kitchen towards them, his long, straight black hair flowing with each step. Leaning against the metal wall, Rocket watches from the side, relieved to be done speaking.

"I thought I heard voices," the boss says, smiling. "I'm Zipper, the crew leader." He holds out his copper-brown hand to shake. "Welcome aboard!"

"Khan," the recruit says, as he shakes his hand.

"And you, younkin?"

"Tinik," he says, cheerfully.

"I know she doesn't look like much," he says as he pats the wall of the truck, "but Dirty Gertie here has strong bones."

Hiding a smirk with his hand, Rocket examines the new recruits' faces, reading their reactions to Zipper.

"Dirty Gertie?" Tinik says with an expression of genuine enjoyment.

"Well," Zipper says with a smile, "her parts have been scavenged from every part of Krevax, so you know, she's been around." Tinik nods.

"Come in!" Zipper beckons them forward.

Walking slowly, Rocket follows the group at a distance, examining Khan's face of queasy fear.

"That staircase in the back there, it goes to the sleeping quarters on the second floor," Zipper says, pointing.

"This here is the kitchen, our bathroom is through those doors, and there's a medical kit in there in case anyone gets injured."

Tinik stares at the wall of cupboards in the kitchen. Rocket recognizes the desperation in his eyes. He has the look of someone who's been hungry for a long time.

"Quickly now," Zipper says, getting Tinik's attention, "these pipes filter the air on the surface for us," he points up at the air vent system in the ceiling.

"And through here." He pushes a button, opening a sliding door, and says, "The driving pit."

Staring with a sour expression, Khan prods at one of the rusty metal walls. Each wall was uniquely dissimilar, bolted together with random bits and bobs.

"Okay, let's get everyone buckled in," Zipper says, leading them back to the kitchen.

"This is the best we can do, I'm afraid," he whispers, referring to the four seats around the kitchen table.

Each seat had a different fabric—one bright orange and the others in various shades of grey. They had all been stolen from offices in the upper districts, of course. Each seat had a hand-sewn seatbelt with the workmanship of someone who seemed to protest with every loop of the thread. The belt was neither secure nor in the proper location.

"We're going to the surface in these?" Khan asks. Rocket laughs.

"It's fine," Gunner says, walking up behind them, "if you're not a bitch." Sitting down in the largest chair, he closes a rusty metal buckle around his waist.

"How many of these trips have you gone on?" Khan stares at him.

"Three," Gunner says, "and I'm still here, but with two younkins, this might be my last." He looks over at Tinik, sneering.

"Don't worry about me," Tinik says, fearlessly, "I know how to pull my weight."

He sits down beside him in the orange chair and buckles himself in. Suppressing a laugh, Rocket stares at Tinik, as he sits down across from Gunner. He might hold his own after all, definitely a nerumoo.

Glancing up, he sees Khan, still standing in place, his expression one of intense contemplation. I bet he's wondering if he would have a better chance going back through those caves. Finally, Khan sits down in the last chair, exhaling.

"Great," Zipper says, a sliver of annoyance in his voice.

Turning from the group, he presses the button to close the sliding door between them and the driving pit.

"The good seats are up there," Gunner says with a growl, hitting the table. "I should be in one."

"Why aren't you?" Tinik asks, with a voice that expresses equal measures of kindness and concern. Wow, this one really is fearless.

"Because of that other fucking younkin," he says, staring at the metal door as though boring an invisible hole with his eyes.

"How did you guys end up here?" Rocket directs his question to Khan and Tinik, trying to distract Gunner from his rage.

"Assigned to the Purification District," Tinik says, shaking his head. "No way I was going to do that, so I cut my tracker out and started selling Glass and Rochaodil about a year and a half ago."

"You cut out your tracker?" Gunner asks, clearly impressed.

"Yeah." Tinik holds out his wrist, showing an old scar.

"Better than Pickles," Rocket says to Gunner, forcing a smile. "Has some scrap."

"And you, Khan?" Gunner looks over at him.

"I had nothing to lose," Khan says, although the nervousness in his voice seems to convey he thinks he has something to lose.

"Nothing to lose?" Gunner says, an edge returning to his voice. "Zorax is going to shit. We'll take anyone now. You used to need a calling to be a member, but now they'll take you, as long as you're still breathing."

"I just mean, I want something more than Krevax," Khan says and then shows them his recently cut wrist.

"Whoa," Rocket says.

"Seems desperate." Gunner shakes his head. "At least this younkin chose gang life."

"What about you?" Tinik looks at Rocket. The truck engine rumbles on, making their seats shake.

"I enjoy taking things apart," Rocket says, thankful the loud engine is muffling his voice.

"That's how I got noticed. A Rochaodil cook, Smalley, wanted me to repair a heater. After that, I was always doing odd jobs for him. When I started using it got messy for a minute." Taking a breath, he considers dropping in a fake reference to the Manufacturing District, but then decides it isn't worth the risk, and continues without.

"Smalley helped me get clean. Said I was wasting my potential. He was the one who convinced me to join as a mechanic." Rocket shrugs his shoulders.

Tinik and Khan nod in unison. Tapping his foot nervously against a bolted table leg, he obsesses over the words he just spoke, searching for any accent slips.

"And you, Gunner?" Tinik asks.

"I can introduce myself, younkin," Gunner says.

"Fair enough," Tinik says, unfazed by his anger.

With a long exhale, Gunner, now disarmed, shakes his head. "I grew up in Zorax. My entire block was gang members, so when I turned 13, they asked me to sell drugs." Seething, Rocket grins aggressively at him through clenched teeth. What lies! No way any of that's true, with that honeyed accent and his light skin.

Closing his eyes a moment, he inhales slowly, calming himself. Screw it, let him have it. I'm trying to hide that I'm a recycler. Who am I to judge?

"What about Zipper?" Khan asks. "Do you know his story?"

"Sounds like him and Gunner had a similar start," Rocket says, barely containing his sarcasm, but letting his accent slip through.

Despite his decision to accept Gunner's lie, anger got the better of him. He chews on the inside of his cheeks, hoping no one noticed.

"Could Pickles be from Zipper's block?" Tinik glances over at the driving pit door.

"No way!" Gunner says. "That tiny pale younkin is blonde and blue-eyed, he looks like he's straight out of the Government District."

You mean like you, your fucking poverty costume? I bet

I'd be as tall as you if I'd been given proper meals my whole life too. Gripping the table, Rocket takes another calming breath. It doesn't matter.

"Really?" Khan says.

"Yeah," Rocket says, trying to keep the conversation light, despite his fury, "I don't know why he's here." Good, that sounded perfect.

"Strange," Khan says.

"Hope you're all buckled in," Zipper's voice comes over the intercom, "I'm starting the countdown!"

An automated voice counts from 10. Looking at the faces sitting around the table, Rocket feels queasy with nerves. Beside him, Khan's face looks peaky too, as he stares intensely at the table. At least I'm not the only one who's nervous. Grinning widely, Tinik yells an excited "whoop" when the number gets down to three.

Still boring holes into the driving pit door, Gunner's anger seems unimpeded by the countdown. As the numbers get to one, Rocket slams shut his eyes.

The rockets ignite with a loud roar and the truck blasts upward through the air. With his jaw clenched, he feels the force of the acceleration pin him in his seat. Gertie shakes violently, causing his head to be thrown aggressively backwards and forwards, as though in the jaws of a monster. The pressure builds, and his chest compresses, threatening to collapse his lungs.

Time feels torturously slow, but it's only seconds until the truck pops out of the cave and light floods through the windows. One last burst of flames steadies the beast and Rocket looks out the window at the curious orange haze. The noise lessens as the landing protocol is engaged and the truck touches down, shakes, and settles its weight on the surface.

"That was awesome," Tinik says, punching a fist up.

"I feel sick," Khan says, placing his forehead on the table.

Laughing, Gunner unbuckles and stands, staring at Tinik approvingly. After a minute, Zipper walks into the kitchen, a small blonde younkin at his heels.

"Welcome to the surface," he says. "You know," he adds in a thoughtful tone, "from up here, Gertie even lets you talk to the moon."

Rolling his eyes, Gunner immediately looks ready to throw a punch again.

"So you're making that younkin lookout now?" he barks.

"This trip is going to be different," Zipper says, his eyes darting around the room, "we're all going to share roles because we all matter equally to this mission."

"What about the ranking system?" Rocket asks, aware of an intense growing feeling of panic.

Why are you doing this? Can't you see what a psychopath Gunner is. He bites the insides of his cheeks to keep from yelling at Zipper.

"Not this time," Zipper says. "Tinik, you and Gunner will take the first shift as driver and lookout. Khan and Rocket, you will start with the first break, and Pickles and I will be cleaner and cook. I'll let you know when we switch."

"You're just going to switch us arbitrarily?" Gunner shouts, standing threateningly over the small circle.

"No, I'm going to switch at specific landmarks," Zipper says, with a fake cheeriness. "I am very familiar with this trek, so everyone will be treated fairly."

"Right," Gunner says, as he stares at Pickles with a look of uncontained hatred.

The younkin looks down, his small shoulders hunched in fear.

23 | ORANGE HAZE

TINIK

Watching the younkin bounce from foot to foot at the driving pit door, Tinik feels an urge to hug him.

Why would anyone bring this little one here? The face of her baby daughter pops into her head. I have to help protect Pickles. Somewhere I know there's a mother who's worrying about him.

A knot tightens in her stomach upon a terrible realization. There was nothing to hold on to when the others were ripped away. Her tongue feels dry in her mouth as the guilt she feels spreads. I didn't get to see them. I was lucky to even know they were boys. The only peace I felt was knowing that. It was impossible to think about them, knowing so little.

Now though, seeing Pickles she knew that her peace of mind had been a fantasy, her sons had never been safe in Krevax. This younkin is just as vulnerable as my daughter, and my sons are just as vulnerable too. She chokes back the emotion in her throat. If I can find my daughter, I can find my sons. I'll get them all back.

"Do you need something, Pickles?" she asks, smiling from her seat at the lookout post.

"Zipper says I'm supposed to grab garbage," he mumbles.

"Speak up, boy!" Gunner yells.

"Garbage," Pickles says with a yip.

"Hurry then." Gunner grabs a handful of garbage from behind the wheel and throws it back. Tinik stares at him angrily.

"What!" he says.

Rushing forward, Pickles picks up the trash and then steps towards the lookout seat. She collects a handful of plastic paste tubes from the compartment in the door and gives them to Pickles. He runs back out to the kitchen with the garbage wrapped to his shirt.

"You know it's not his fault he's here," Tinik says.

"I know," he says, without looking over at her, "it's Zipper's." She picks up the binoculars and stares out at the endless orange haze.

This is going to be hard. I just have to survive. As long as I get back to Krevax, everything will be okay. What am I even looking for? Zipper isn't one to provide instructions. I'll just look for trucks from rival gangs. What else could be up here? I hope we don't run into any.

At first she feels nervous, but as the shift continues the boredom creeps in. Blinking her eyes slowly, trying to stay awake, she glances down at the black screen between her and Gunner. There's no scale?

Staring at the blinking orange dot, white arrow and the word *Gertie*, it looks like they're floating in one spot. She looks up through the binoculars, it's still just a bunch of rocks and the haze. The smell was also irritating to her, it wasn't the usual chemicals of Krevax, but something like sickeningly sweet paste with a hint of sewage.

Smacking her dry tongue to the roof of her mouth, she

inadvertently tastes the air, which is sour. To get rid of the strange taste, Tinik opens a chocolate caffeine boost and drinks it.

"The surface sucks," she says, through a sip of watery chocolate.

Gunner looks over at her laughing. "Yeah, it's terrible, and you haven't even seen the worst of it."

"What's the worst of it?"

"The surface men, they attack with blades, steal all the food, and usually pick off some of the crew to enslave."

"Sure," Tinik says, chuckling. Still believing fairy tales I see, this younkin is no threat.

"No, seriously." Gunner stares at her. "I've been lucky so far, haven't had a run in, but the men at the mine, they have some stories."

"You're saying there's people who live on the surface?" Tinik says, rolling her eyes. "I think some men at the mine were having a laugh."

"You'll see, when we get to the mine," Gunner says, smiling. "You really don't act like a younkin, do you?"

"You know what they say." Tinik grins. "There are no younkins in the lower districts." She stares dramatically.

"That's fair," he says with a nod. "Well, I'm glad you're not like Pickles. I don't think I could deal with that."

"I get it," Tinik says. That younkin shouldn't be here. It's not safe for him, or for anyone.

I'll do what I can for him, but it's not going to be easy if we get attacked. She holds her breath at that thought. Don't think that. Everything's going to be fine.

"You know, you might be right about there not being men on the surface."

"You think so?" Tinik laughs.

"Trust me, the men telling those stories, they believe it, but some of them helped build the mine, so they've been up here for months now," Gunner says, glancing over at her, "even a week in this shit makes me feel loopy."

"It's like we're floating in a large tank of orange water."

"That's exactly it. You just lose all sense of time or place," Gunner says.

"I've heard of some crews having to lock a member in the sleeping quarters because they go mad."

"I could see it," Tinik says. After only a week? Silliness. I'll just placate him, no reason to make an enemy, besides he's not that bad, once you get to know him.

Gunner grins. "Nothing scares you, huh?"

"Nope." She looks back through the binoculars, pretending to be invulnerable. Everything scares me. Not getting back to Krevax. Not finding my younkins. Not making this plan work.

A memory of her first labour plays in her head. That's also scary as fuck. At least, I won't have to do that again. She cringes, thinking back to the pain and the constant screaming in the Generation District. I'm lucky I only had three. The feeling of sadness mixed with guilt hits her again. How old would they be now? Seven and four.

Her chest aches at the thought of her younkins alone in Krevax. I'm gonna need to be really rich to buy all my younkins. Staring out at the unchanging scene, she sits silent in her thoughts as time continues to be frozen. After an hour, or maybe four, she can't tell, she drinks another caffeine boost and a hydration tube.

"I need to pee." She stands, holding the binoculars out. "Is there some kind of protocol?"

"Be quick," Gunner says. Nodding, she drops the binoculars in her seat and pushes the button for the sliding door. Limping through the kitchen, she presses the button to the toilets and turns to lock the door. No lock. Lice on ticks.

Turning in a half-circle, she examines the room. Two

urinals, one toilet, and three showers all out in the open. Lice on ticks on fleas. Sitting on the toilet, she quickly pees, staring at the door nervously the entire time.

She pulls up her pants and holds the handle on the toilet to let the pee out on the ground. She stares at her reflection in the small square mirror and pumps a splash of sanitizer into her hands. *I hope this goes by quickly. What if they want me to work in the mine next? I don't want to be away from my younkins for that long.*

She looks at her dust covered face and smiles at herself. *I'm so glad I look like a boy.* Walking the few steps back to the door, she taps the button and limps back through the empty kitchen. She hears something, standing still, she realizes it's crying. Leaning down, she sees Pickles sitting under the stairs, his face buried in his knees.

Tinik walks over. "What's wrong?"

Shaking his head, he doesn't look up. "I'm scared."

"It will be okay," she says, touching his shoulder. "Zipper is watching over you, and I'm around too if you need help."

Lifting his head slightly, he meets her gaze and nods.

"I have to go back to the driving pit now," she says. "You should try to get some sleep."

Standing shakily, he walks up the first few steps on the stairs. With a final glance back, Tinik pushes the button to the driving pit. Gunner steers the truck with half-closed eyes. *I hope he doesn't fall asleep.* She picks up the binoculars and stares out at the orange haze. What feels like only a moment later, Rocket and Blackwell walk through the door.

"You guys are off shift now." Rocket waves them out of the driving pit. Behind him, Blackwell waits at the entrance with an awkward smile.

"That did not feel like twelve hours," Tinik mumbles, feeling exhausted.

"That's the surface, man, every hour feels like a second,"

Gunner says, as he climbs out of his seat, "but every week feels like a year."

"I'll take those," Rocket says, reaching for the binoculars. Feeling relieved, Tinik happily hands them over.

"Is everything okay?" Blackwell mouths silently, facing Tinik.

"Yes, you?" she asks silently back.

He nods and sits down in the driver's seat. Tinik follows Gunner out to the kitchen and the driving pit door slides closed. The gas revs and the truck pulls forward, almost making her lose balance. She plops down in the orange chair and leans with her elbows on the table.

"What do you think about that Khan guy?" Gunner asks, sitting down beside her.

"He's actually alright," Tinik says, looking up at him, "we had a bit of a situation with the giant bug that messed up my foot and he came through."

"Something about him seems off to me," Gunner whispers, a suspicious expression on his face, "like he's an undercover red stripe or something."

"Really?" Tinik says, with a muted reaction. How does he know that? He's a good read. Going forward, I must be more careful around him.

"I know Zorax is desperate for men, but he didn't mention selling drugs, or working as a mule, or anything gang-related," Gunner says. "I think it's strange."

"Hmm," Tinik nods. "I hadn't thought about it. I can't imagine Pickles selling drugs though."

"True." Gunner yawns, leaning his head in one hand and closes his eyes.

Zipper walks down the staircase and joins them in the kitchen.

"Can I grab you guys anything?"

"A hydration tube and a cornbread paste for me," Tinik says. Zipper nods and then looks over at Gunner, waiting.

"I'll have a hydration tube and a french fry paste," Gunner says.

Turning towards the wall of cupboards, he opens one and swipes through the tubes, grabbing their requests. Like the rest of Gertie, none of the cupboards match, but at least magnetic latches keep them closed. With a tired smile, he puts the tubes of paste on the table and then marks off the numbers on a chart hanging from the upper cupboards.

"You should try to get some sleep," Zipper says to both of them.

"I've never had much luck," Gunner mumbles. Nodding without reaction, Zipper turns and walks into the driving pit.

"He's probably right," Tinik says as she finishes eating the tube of cornbread paste. "The sleeping quarters are up those stairs?"

"Yeah," Gunner says.

Standing, she limps towards the stairs and slowly trudges up the steps, her pinched foot throbbing. Inside the room of anchored sleeping bags she can see one in the middle, still wrapped in plastic. The dark room smells like old armpit, sweat and stinky feet, but that doesn't dampen her excitement for sleep. In the corner near the front of the truck, Pickles is already snoring. Removing the plastic off of the last unclaimed sleeping bag, she climbs in and zips the scratchy fabric up and over her head.

The smell of strong chemicals is surprisingly comforting because it reminds her of Krevax. Pulling off her shoes and socks, she examines her purple foot and is relieved it doesn't look worse.

Without another thought, she closes her eyes, and immediately falls deeply asleep.

24 | DINNER PARTY

GARCIA

Alvaro Garcia picks up a bag of flour and drops it in the cart. A gangly man with grey-streaked black hair, he had spent most of his life sitting at a computer, but that wasn't what worried him. Pulling out a piece of paper from his pocket, he adjusts the spectacles on his slightly crooked nose, and reviews his wife's drawings.

Walking to the fruit and vegetable section, he grabs corn, peppers, peas, tomatoes, potatoes, onions, and a bunch of bananas. Oldest walks up, her wavy black hair covering most of her face, and drops a stack of magazines in the cart; the kind for teen girls with no text and glossy pictures on every page.

"Isn't it amazing we have blueberries now!" Garcia says enthusiastically, waving his warm beige-toned hands.

Rolling her eyes, she turns away from her father and heads towards another aisle.

"You were just a toddler when the Agricultural Division re-introduced them." Garcia calls after her, feeling frustrated.

"The grapefruit research is coming along," he says,

mumbling to himself, and then awkwardly makes eye contact with another shopper who is avidly listening.

After giving a curt nod, he turns the cart, his cheeks flushed red. *I look like a fool. I hope they didn't notice my metal-less teeth.*

"Papa!" His younger daughter runs up holding a box of Fruitylicious Kernels, her pigtails swinging.

"Can I have these?" She stares up at him with pleading eyes.

"You can," he says, "but you can only choose one treat, so if you decide on the cereal, that's it."

She stares at the brightly coloured box in her hands, clearly weighing the pros and cons of sugary cereal, and then tentatively places it in. Garcia grabs steaks and ground meat, and continues to the deli, picking smoked luncheon meat and pâté from an impressive display. After, he turns into the cheese aisle, Oldest walks up again, this time holding a container of ice cream.

"I thought the magazines were your treat?" Garcia asks.

"No," she says, glaring at him. "You buy your stock market reports. I follow the trends, too."

"Okay," he says, watching her place the ice cream in the cart, sighing as she walks away again.

I hope she's out of this stage, before the youngest one starts her teen years. Watching Youngest skip down the aisle ahead of him, he smiles at the memories of his own childhood, when he would run down store aisles with his mother. He grabs cheddar cheese, yogurt, sour cream and milk.

In the next aisle, he chooses between spaghetti and lasagna noodles, and settles on lasagna. A few aisles further, he finds himself in front of an enormous selection of flavoured jerky, staring at the different options.

One sticks out to him, a new brand of jerky he had never

seen before. Picking up the bag, he examines the image of a regal-looking Wildebeest standing in an extensive field of green grass. The bright lights far above it shine down on its mane, its talons glinting.

This must be what Krevax actually looks like! I mean, obviously the Wildebeest is a fantastical image, but the humanoid species down there must roam large fields of grass, just like this one. He smiles at the thought. *Chef's Cut - Sweet Smoked Jerky*. That sounds yummy. He drops the jerky into the cart and continues pushing it.

Youngest runs up with an excited grin, a gap in her upper teeth. "Papa, can I ride in the cart?"

"Of course," he says, holding out his hand to hoist her up. Running fast, he pretends to crash into the aisle walls.

"Ahh!" his daughter screams and then breaks out into laughter.

Turning the cart into the alcohol aisle, he picks up a bottle of vodka and a bottle of wine. This should be enough for the dinner party. I'm glad I still have a level-six friend. I just hope I get an advancement soon, if I'm still stuck with un-filed teeth at retirement... He shakes his head, not wanting to ponder the thought any further.

Oldest runs up behind him and grabs his shoulder. "Could I try some wine tonight?"

"No, dear, you're still too young."

"But I'm fifteen!" she whines.

"I'll talk to your mother about it, if she agrees, you can try a small sip," Garcia says, smiling.

"What about me?" Youngest asks.

"You're not even thirteen!" Oldest snaps back.

"Not yet, my little one," Garcia says, patting her on the head.

Looking away grumpily, she folds her arms around her waist. With a sigh, he ignores the reaction and heads to the bakery. I'm sure by the time I'm forty-five I'll be a level-seven, who knows I might actually make it to level-eight, there's still time. He picks up a bag of lemon rolls and a box of sesame buns and they make their way to the checkout.

After bagging the items, Garcia places them back in the cart around his daughter, who is now happily singing about wedding dresses.

"That will be $72.55," the attendant says, his un-filed teeth exposed with each word.

Nodding, to hide his own natural teeth, he pulls out his wallet from his back pocket and taps the card on the sensor. Why do attendants and government workers have the same clearance level? It's ridiculous.

Feeling aggravated, he quickly pushes the cart out to his car. The oldest slides into the front passenger seat and shuts the door.

"Okay, sweets!" he says. "It's time to get out of the cart."

Reaching in, he offers his daughter one of his skinny arms, which she holds onto as she climbs out. They put the bags into the trunk together and Garcia puts the cart away. He sits down in the driver's seat, buckles himself in, and starts the engine.

"Everyone buckled?"

"Yeah!" Youngest cheers, smiling at him in the mirror.

Looking over at his other daughter, he sees the seatbelt buckled around her waist as she continues to ignore him. He pulls out of the parking lot and onto a suburban road. Reaching over to the dials, Oldest turns on the radio, making orchestral music softly play, which she swiftly switches to pop.

"This is 101.7," the host says in an over-the-top bubbly voice, "the hottest pop music in the Boreal Orb!"

The volume increases to a roar, making Garcia grind his teeth, as they continue down the road for nearly four annoying pop songs. Half-way down a picturesque block sits their small yellow house. He turns off the engine, stopping the pop music once and for all.

As he climbs out, Youngest runs ahead of him, opens the trunk and grabs a bag of groceries. He follows her with the last of the bags, heading up the path to their front door. At the entrance he attempts to lock the car doors, but Oldest is still inside, staring at her reflection in the visor mirror.

"I need to lock the doors," Garcia shouts. Sneering at him, she closes the visor and climbs out of the seat, slamming the door behind her. Garcia holds his breath. It's only a stage, she won't be like this forever.

"Thank you for shopping," his wife says, calling from the kitchen and runs over to grab the bags.

"No worries, dear," Garcia says as he takes off his shoes. "How's the baking coming?"

"I'm nearly done." She smiles, leaning back through the doorway, as she puts the perishables into the fridge, "I just need to ice the cake."

Walking over, he kisses her, then leans in to examine the dessert.

"Looks delicious," he says.

"Thanks, honey," she says, her eyes bright. "Would you mind getting the burgers going? I want to finish my hair and makeup before they arrive."

"I'm on it," Garcia says, grabbing the container of ground meat and placing it on the counter.

He washes his hands and dries them on an ironed, bleached-white towel. Opening the lid to the meat, he grabs a chunk and rolls it into a ball. Behind him, his wife quickly finishes layering and icing the cake and then runs out of the kitchen. He continues rolling the balls until he has eleven patties. Taylor does like his burgers, but that should be enough.

After soaping and rinsing his hands, he closes the container of ground meat and puts it in the fridge. The doorbell rings.

"Can you get it?" his wife asks from the bathroom, "I'm almost done curling my hair."

"No problem," Garcia says, as he strides over and opens the door, excited to see his friend.

"Garcia!" Taylor, a stout man with a small potbelly, grabs his arm. "It's so good to see you." Wife Taylor smiles in agreement.

"Taylor, Wife Taylor, it's been too long. Come in." They walk into the hallway and take off their shoes. After a minute, Garcia's wife joins them in the hallway, her perfect brunette curls bouncing.

"Taylor! Wife Taylor, I'm so glad you're here!" his wife says, greeting them enthusiastically.

"Wife Garcia," Wife Taylor says, stepping forward, "can I help you with anything?" She holds up a bottle of red. "We brought wine."

"Thank you!" Wife Garcia says. "That's so appreciated. Come, come to the backyard, we've set the table out there." She waves her forward with a fair hand.

"How are things?" Taylor asks.

"Good," Garcia says. "The kids are happy, the wife is happy, things at the lab have been going well. How about you?"

"Also good," Taylor says and then smiles, bearing his freshly metal-capped teeth.

"Your teeth!" Garcia shouts, his eyes wide. He feels an intense pang of jealousy, but hides it with a smile. "When did this happen?"

"Last week," Taylor says. "I signed a contract to take the lead position on the commissioning of a lake."

Walking into the kitchen together, Garcia uses all his effort to keep smiling.

"Well, congrats friend, anything you can tell me?" he asks, laughing awkwardly.

Taylor shakes his head slowly. Garcia waves a hand in the air, as though throwing the last question away.

"I was hoping Freddie would be here today?" He picks up the plate of meat and leads Taylor out to the sunny backyard.

"I know." Taylor shakes his head. "It's hard to get him away from a screen these days."

"No worries," Garcia says, smiling too widely as he lights the BBQ, "teenagers."

Taylor nods sympathetically, which Garcia feels is more about the metal teeth than the teenagers. Placing the patties on the grill, he takes a slow breath of air in, feeling embarrassed. Taylor has sharpened teeth now. Taylor! What do I have to do to get to level-seven? I'm way smarter than him...

"Taylor, would you like white wine, red wine, or vodka with a flavoured syrup?" Garcia's wife asks.

"What kinds of syrup do you have?"

"Orange, cherry, and vanilla."

"Orange for me, thanks," Taylor says.

Wife Garcia nods and then walks away.

"Did you see the baseball game last night? I couldn't believe the pitcher."

"I know." Garcia nods. "They should trade Brock." He smiles again, feeling uncomfortable.

"Who would you want to see in his place?"

"I've always liked Sanchez, but that new pitcher this year, on The Capitalists, Larson, he could be good."

"Larson! Yes, I'm impressed by him too," Taylor says. Garcia's wife hands them each a glass and Taylor takes a sip.

"Thank you, Wife Garcia." She smiles and then sits down at the table across from Wife Taylor.

Garcia drains his drink, burying his feelings, and flips the patties.

"I'm hungry," Youngest says, running up.

"Dinner's almost ready," Garcia says, "why don't you tell your sister to come to the table?" She nods and skips into the house.

"She's getting so tall. Looks just like you, that one," Taylor says. "Really, they both do."

"I know," Garcia says with a laugh, "my wife is always complaining that she made two clones of me."

"Freddie looks a lot like his mother. Maybe that's the secret," Taylor says. Garcia nods.

First, he gets a son, and now he also gets filed teeth. Garcia looks down at the burgers, feeling bad for himself. Why haven't I gotten to level-seven?

"Everyone, grab a plate," Garcia calls out.

Walking away burger-less, Taylor sits down at the table and waits for his wife to make him a plate. Youngest runs up with a bun on a plate, jumping from foot to foot impatiently. Forking a patty, he drops it on the bun and she grins. Wife Taylor walks over with two plates, one with a single bun, and one with two.

Distractedly, he places three patties on the buns, and she nods a thank you and walks away. Oldest holds out her plate, which has no bun on it and stands in front of him with an expression of annoyance.

"Aren't you missing something?" he asks.

"No," she snaps in a bitter tone.

With eyebrows raised, he slides a burger onto the empty plate. Garcia's wife holds out two plates, again one with two buns, and the other with only one.

"You okay," she whispers, as Garcia puts the burgers on them.

"Yes," he says, convincingly, "everything's perfect."

Wife Garcia kisses him on the cheek and waits for him to turn off the BBQ. They walk back through the grass to the table together and sit down with everyone. Grabbing a spoonful of pea salad, he puts it beside his burger and then squeezes sweet and sour sauce on the bun, throwing on two cheddar slices on top for good measure.

"You know, our lab is working on recreating the grapefruit," Garcia says.

"We know," Oldest says.

"Are you?" Wife Taylor asks. "That is really something."

"Yes, it's complicated work, but we're nearly there," Garcia says. "I love the science of it all."

"Now," Taylor says, laughing, "that we know."

"Okay, okay." Garcia grins. "I know I can be a bit science-focused."

"A bit!" Taylor roars goofily. "I remember when I met you back in school. You always had your head buried in some kind of chemistry textbook."

"It's true," he says, "but you were the same with your landscape studies."

"Yes, but everyone loves a good landscape."

"He's right," Wife Garcia says, "which reminds me." She stands and bolts into the house, returning a moment later with the bag of jerky Garcia had bought earlier. "Look at this!"

"Neat." Wife Taylor nods. "Is that actually what Krevax looks like?"

"It must be," Wife Garcia says.

"They should offer trips there," Wife Taylor says. "I would love to see the Wildebeests roaming in those fields." Garcia and Taylor laugh.

"What?" Garcia's wife asks. "I agree with Wife Taylor."

"I'm sure that it would be considered a risk to the food supply," Garcia says, reaching for his wife's hand. Sometimes I forget she's just a level-five, at least I'm not a level-five. I'll be a level-seven soon. I know it.

"The Wildebeests must be protected," Taylor says, also smiling at his wife.

The men give each other a knowing look. Garcia feels another pang of jealousy shoot through his stomach. His children would never get to level-six, because they were both girls, but Taylor's son Freddie would. I wish I'd had a son I could talk truthfully with. My daughters can never truly know me or what I really do at work.

Picking up his burger, he takes a bite, making the juices run down his chin. He sighs, feeling momentarily comforted by the taste.

25 | THE PRESIDENT

CARR

In his white-walled office, Carr sits, staring at Charlie's face on the computer screen. Pressing play, he listens to the report for what feels like the 20th time.

"I have infiltrated the ranks of Zorax. Once I become a member of the gang, I will send another progress report." The image clicks off.

Carr leans his head against the computer screen. Charlie, where are you? How hard is it to send another report?

Closing the image, he opens a live footage stream of Krevax and toggles through various security camera angles. He stops at one that looks directly into Charlie's apartment. Does the bed look unmade? Could be hiding out there?

Bouchard walks into his office and Carr automatically closes the tab showing his brother's apartment.

"The religious advertisements are not having an effect," Bouchard says, dropping a stack of charts on Carr's desk. "The suicide rate is increasing beyond even what I predicted. We can't wait until the end of the week to report this. We need to talk to President Lehan now."

"You're right," Carr says. "We need to report this before it looks like we were hiding information." Picking up the phone, he dialled the President.

"Thank you," Bouchard says. Carr puts the call on speakerphone.

"You've reached the Office of the President."

"This is General Carr and General Bouchard. We have a time-sensitive report for the President."

"I'll patch you through." The call is silent for a minute.

"Generals, What do you have to report?" a deep-voiced man asks.

"We have a contaminate in Krevax that's leading to a rising suicide rate," Carr says.

"What kind of contaminate?"

"They call it nostaliem," Bouchard says, referring to the novel drug. "It is described as living in a dream, but the result is a stark increase in suicides."

"The suicides are increasing, but we are addressing it," Carr retorts.

"When did the suicides climb?" Lehan asks. Bouchard slowly paces around the room, waiting for Carr to respond.

"It's only been a few weeks, the situation has been evolving quickly,"

"We need to cut out the source of the drugs," Bouchard says, "the gangs in Krevax."

"No," Carr interjects, shaking his head. "We need time to investigate this substance."

"There's no time!" Bouchard shouts.

"How much stock would we lose if we went after the gangs?" Lehan asks.

"Three districts' worth, including all the doxies." Carr holds his breath.

"Okay, we should only use that tactic as a last resort," Lehan says. *"Find out how the drug works first, maybe we can make an antidote?"*

"I'll get a sample as soon as possible," Carr says. Good, I can use this trip to search Charlie's apartment. If he's hiding out there, I can get him back to the Orbs before he's at any risk.

"I'll get the propaganda team together," Lehan states. *"We'll call it a disease outbreak, in case we have to slow down our protein supply. Ensure you provide progress reports."* The call clicks off and Bouchard and Carr stare at each other, both men with furrowed eyebrows.

"We need a scientist to test the sample," Bouchard says, breaking the silence, "someone who can create an antidote."

"Fine," Carr says.

"I'll find the right man." Bouchard turns and disappears through the doorway.

The reports are still scattered on his desk, but Carr doesn't pick them up, he knows what's written in them. Instead, he clicks on his watch and scrolls to a tab with the image of a tracker, dialling in a 10-digit code.

Ring. The call connects.

"Is now a good time?" Carr asks.

"Green," a man says in a half-whisper.

"Thank you for the information on the nostaliem drop off, everything went as planned. Did you see the credits I transferred?"

"Yes, I saw them," he says.

"There's another 5,000 in it for you, if you can track down a man who removed his tracker."

"Do you want me to kill him?"

"No, I want to speak with him. No harm will come to him."

"Okay, what can you send me?"

"Not much. His name is Charlie Blackwell. He's 27, and he just joined Zorax. I'll transmit a photo now," Carr says, and clicks on an old photo of Blackwell, obliviously looking into a vending machine.

"I'll get my men to listen in on Zorax's communications. If he's alive, we'll track him down."

"Thank you," Carr says, biting a hangnail on his thumb. The call clicks off.

I hope he can track him down before the trip tomorrow. He pushes the stack of charts into a desk drawer and leaves. Clicking the button for the elevator, he stares down the hallway at Bouchard's office. I really hate him, he's too extreme. The elevator doors open and he climbs in.

Sighing heavily, he closes his eyes as he moves down the building. The doors slide open and he walks through the lobby and out into the parking lot. His limo driver spots him and jumps up, opening the back door for him.

"Headed home, sir?" he asks. Carr nods curtly and climbs in, resting his head against the window. What if Charlie is already dead, and all this has been for nothing?

At home, he finds his wife lying in the backyard, staring up at the pink-streaked sky. Carr lies down in the grass beside her and wraps his arms around her. Smiling, she curls in towards him, her head lying on his chest. Scrunching his eyes from the sunlight, he then closes them feeling the warmth on his skin. Where are you, brother? I've had your heartbeat beating along mine since I found you.

Carr instinctively touches his watch, even though the connection had been lost. Now you're gone.

"My love, are you okay? You're breathing so fast?" his wife asks as she sits up to look at his face.

"Everything's fine, my sweets, just work."

"What's wrong at work?"

"Some kind of disease is spreading in Krevax. I'm worried we won't be able to get it under control."

"I'm sure it will get better, but even if the worst were to

happen, some animals will survive and they will produce more resilient young in the future. Isn't that how survival of the fittest works?"

"You're right!" Carr says in genuine surprise, resting his hand on his wife's leg.

"I know things." She grins, batting her eyelashes. "Here, have a blueberry, they always make me feel better because they're so sweet."

Reaching up, she picks a small round berry off of the bush and places it on his tongue, giggling.

"Delicious," he says, biting into the berry with an exaggerated chomp. She eats her own handful of blueberries and cuddles back into his side. Behind them in the living room, a green light pops on the screen.

"The news is out," he says, helping his wife stand.

They make their way inside, where she sits on the couch in front of the screen and he stands behind her. A man with heavy orange-tinted foundation grins maniacally from behind a desk.

"I'm Stanley Hughes and you're watching *Orb News*. President Lehan released a statement about a potential protein shortage," he says as he points to a terrifying image of the animal in question; a blood-splattered hairy-brown cow, with the face of a lion and enlarged black eagle talons for feet.

The screen's image switches to President Lehan, a well-fed man with broad shoulders and a pale face, standing at the podium.

"Currently, there is a disease spreading through the Wildebeest population in Krevax. I have been in contact with the Generals of the Livestock Association, and they have assured me that the situation is under control. There is a possibility of protein rations in the future, but the animal population is not facing an extinction level event, and is resilient enough to be regrown to regulation standards."

The clip ends and returns to the image of Stanley.

"In other news, the Miss Mother Pageant will begin this Saturday and we have exclusive interviews with the top three candidates." The camera pans over to reveal three attractive girls sitting across from Stanley.

"So tell me, what are you most excited about?" In response to the question, the girls look at each other and giggle. Carr turns off the propaganda and looks over at his wife.

"Have you ever had a secret name?" Carr asks.

"My name is Wife Carr," she says in surprise, a look of fear in her eyes.

"I know, but I mean a name just for you?"

"In school I was called Sixteen."

"Sixteen… that's not very personal. What about a nickname?"

"Sure," she says lightly, but not without hesitation, "when I was younger, we all had little nicknames for each other, but I outgrew that."

"What were you called when you were a little girl?"

"Well, my mother would sometimes call me 'Listen,' but that's only because I was always misbehaving and there were three other girls in the house," she says, laughing a bit too loudly, clearly uncomfortable.

"Do you ever feel upset about not having your own name?"

"No, I've never had one," she says, looking taken aback. "I understand my role isn't to take the lead, it's supporting my husband. You, my love, you're my life. At least for now, I'm sure one day soon we will have children to look after too."

"And you're okay with that?"

"What do you mean?" she says, staring up at him. "Do you think less of me for not having my own name?"

"No, that's not it at all, love," he says and leans over to pull her into his arms, "it's just, I'm afraid you're unhappy."

"I could never be unhappy with you," she says, her head on his shoulder.

"I'm sorry if I upset you, my love." He kisses her on the forehead. "I need to tell you, early tomorrow I have to go to Krevax."

"For how long?"

"Not long at all. I'll be back late tomorrow."

"Do you want me to wrap up a meal for you, for when you get home?"

"That would be wonderful, my dear. Speaking of food, is dinner ready? I'll be getting up at 4:30. I can't stay up late."

"Of course," she says and disappears into the kitchen. Moments later, she returns with a plate full of meatloaf. Inside the meatloaf were chunks of carrots and peas.

"It's great!" Carr says, through his first bite. "Do we have any milk?"

"Yes!" she says, rushing back into the kitchen to grab a carton of milk.

On the side of the carton was an image of another lion-faced Wildebeest, only this one looked demure compared to the image on Orb News. She pours a glass of milk for each of them and sits down beside Carr.

"This disease the animals have..." She stares at her glass. "Do you think we could get it?"

Carr pauses from eating his meatloaf. "No, it would be very unlikely for the disease to jump species like that. Not something you should worry about, my love."

"Okay," she says, and takes a sip of milk. After they finish dinner, she washes the dishes and when the kitchen is clean, they head upstairs and brush their teeth.

"Carr…" she says, as she puts on a silky pink nightgown.

"Yes?"

"I'm ovulating tomorrow."

"Okay, I'll be late, but we can still make time."

"Good." She climbs under the blankets.

Rolling onto his side, Carr pointlessly closes his eyes, knowing he won't sleep. After a minute, he can hear his wife lightly snoring beside him. With his mind racing, sleep feels impossible, he twists and turns as his body vibrates with an unpleasant energy.

After a few hours, he gives up and shuffles out of the room to do push-ups downstairs; he keeps going until he can feel his arms shake with exhaustion. Lying down on the carpet for a moment, he breathes slowly and then stands to sneak back into the bedroom.

Under the covers, he focuses on his breathing, but images of his brother keep popping into his head. Sleep slowly pulls him into the nightmares he'd recently found himself living in. His mother stares out from Charlie's eyes, her grin growing wider and wider until it takes up her entire face; her white teeth turn yellow, and then from yellow to blood red.

One by one they fall out of her mouth, revealing bloody gums and a swollen tongue. The tongue continues to swell until it's so big it looks as though it might burst.

Waking with a start, Carr's body is soaked in a cold sweat.

26 | RED HAIR

PRATT

Sitting at his desk, Pratt watches the footage from the Natatorium. What were you up to? He zooms in on Blackwell exiting the pool in a white suit. Why does that ridiculous suit look familiar?

A notification beeps on Pratt's tracker and he clicks on it: 'DNA Analysis Complete'. Let's find out whose hair you had. He opens the report and reads through the details: 'Match - Designation: Doxy, Number: D-432-99-77A, Name: Kaliann.' He stops reading. Holy Mary! The dead doxy. Why did he take her hair? When did he take her hair?

Scrolling further down the report, he finds two current DNA connections: 'Designation: Doxy, Number: G-806-09-12K, Name: Scarlett; Designation: Male, Name: Charlie Blackwell.' Charlie Blackwell?

"No way," he says to himself, his mouth gaped open.

He clicks on the name and Blackwell's face pops up. Is he related to the doxy? Inhaling sharply, he's hit by a realization. That's where I saw that white suit, it was in the motel! He closes the footage and navigates to a symbol of the Watchtower, clicking on it.

Scrolling through the districts, he pauses at the Technology District and enters the date 12, 31, 181 A.W. The screen fills with small video feed squares, and above them, he types in the address of the Sweet Dreams Motel.

Four video streams remain and he expands the first image and toggles through the timeline, stopping on a frame with the white suit. That's definitely the same gaudy suit. What? Blackwell took clothes from an active crime scene?

He watches the footage of the man in the white suit walking up to the motel, but can only see an angle that shows his back. Minimizing the video, he clicks on the next screen, expanding it. This one shows the same footage, but at a viewpoint slightly further away. The last two videos are just as useless, as no face is revealed in either of them.

Closing the screen, he opens the database for active cases and types in the number #162300-BX, he scrolls through the report and clicks on a link showing related footage. Three videos open.

The first shows the man in the white suit, the one he had just watched. The second captures Kaliann outside the Red Foxe Brothel, her decorative metal gleaming in the light an hour before she disappeared. In the last video, a peon pushes a large crate filled with folded towels.

What? When did Kaliann go into the motel? Shaking his head, he clicks on the report's corresponding notes.

"A man in a white suit enters the motel and soon after, a peon arrives with the laundry cart that the doxy was hiding in." That's the working theory? Really. Holding his head in his hands, he exhales huffily.

When did Blackwell take her hair? What if it was shaved at the brothel?

Clicking on the Watchtower again, he types in 'Red Foxe Brothel' and slides through the timeline. There he is! The man in the white suit. How did they miss this?

Watchtower red stripes, they're all useless idiots. Scrolling through the footage he stops at a point where the man in the white suit has fallen back onto the ground, a red stripe staring down at him.

Wait, is that Blackwell? Why is he with the man in the white suit outside Foxe? Pratt zooms in on the man's face, it's a perfect image of him looking up at Blackwell with an expression of terror.

Something is strangely familiar about the features, and he clicks back to an image of Kaliann earlier that day, standing outside the brothel. Zooming in, there's no mistaking it, it's the same face, only without the red curls.

Holy Mary! The man in the white suit is Kaliann. No one is going to believe this. She shaved her own head, that's how Blackwell got her hair, it was at the brothel. Was he involved in her escape? He must have known they were related.

Getting up from his desk, he quickly turns towards the elevator. I need to tell the captain about this. Dashing through the rows of desks, he jumps into an elevator, drumming his hands on his legs, as he waits for the doors to open on the sixth floor.

If Blackwell helped the doxy escape, where did he take her and why? Could she have reached out to him for help? Where could you hide a doxy in Krevax, anyway?

With the Watchtower there's no place a red stripe couldn't see, except maybe in the Recycling District, but that would be no place for a doxy. The doors open on the fourth floor and Remi walks in. Holding his breath from fear, he stops drumming and locks eyes, immediately aware of the tension between them.

"I haven't seen you in a minute," Remi says.

"I've been busy." Pratt forces a chuckle. "Did I tell you about the bag of red hair I found at Blackwell's apartment?"

Remi laughs. "I knew he was a loser, but... yikes. I don't

want to know what he did with that." He switches to a whisper and adds, "Maybe he wore it." The elevator doors open.

"I don't think so." Pratt exits the elevator. "I got it DNA tested, and…"

"What?" Remi chases after him. "That's stupid. Why would you DNA test some female's hair? Just throw it out."

"I have the results and…"

"He was a turncoat with a hair fetish," Remi growls, his eyes narrowing.

"We're his partners, no one can know about this." He follows him through the hallway, his face twisting with anger. "They might think we're turncoats with him."

"I'll make sure that it's only my name on the file," Pratt says. "The hair, it was Kaliann's, they were related."

"Who the fuck is Kaliann?" Remi shoves Pratt's shoulder into the wall.

"The doxy," Pratt says, his hands instantly clammy from fear, "the dead doxy in the Sweet Dreams Motel."

Remi taps his foot. "What does it matter?"

"It might matter." Pratt clicks on his tracker and scrolls through the report again. "They were half-siblings and…"

"It doesn't matter," Remi says. "You're wasting everyone's time. For all you know, we're half-siblings. Being related to someone means nothing in Krevax."

"I'm still going to report it to the captain."

"Why?" Remi's eyes widened. "Why would you do that?"

"Because Blackwell knew," Pratt says and slides away, rounding the corner to the captain's office, Remi at his heels.

Walking into the large office, Pratt immediately begins shouting, "Captain Lewis, I've discovered something about Blackwell."

"No, he hasn't," Remi says, just behind him.

The captain looks at each of them, but settles on Pratt. "What is it?"

"Blackwell and the recently deceased doxy, they were half-siblings," Pratt says.

Remi crosses his arms. Pratt holds his breath waiting for the captain to reply.

"That's something the Tzar would want to know," Lewis says as he picks up a physical phone on his desk. "I want you both on this call."

Ring.

"Hello."

"Tzar, it's Captain Lewis." He pushes the speaker button. "Detective Pratt has new information." He nods at Pratt to continue.

"Blackwell and a missing doxy we are investigating, they were half-siblings."

"Half-siblings?" The Tzar says intensely.

"Yes, and she died taking nostaliem," Remi interrupts. Pratt flashes him a look of annoyance, but Remi's violent glare back makes him feel queasy. The call is silent for a minute, except for the sound of the Tzar breathing.

"Were there other DNA connections?"

"Yes," Pratt says, clicking open the report, "one other half-sibling. A doxy, named Scarlett."

"What about the generator who birthed them?"

"Nothing on that," Pratt says.

"Send me the report and find the generator."

"Yes, sir!" Pratt says.

"Good job, men," the Tzar says, and the call clicks off.

"Why does the Tzar care about a bunch of females related to Blackwell?" Remi barks.

"He wants Blackwell to be a heroic figure to show the people that the red stripes still control Krevax," Lewis says, puffing out his chest.

"Some bloodlines are better than others. He wants to confirm Blackwell comes from a higher caste."

"I see," Remi says, and then stomps out of the office.

Pratt stands there, silent for a moment, thinking. If the Tzar wants Blackwell to be some kind of hero, maybe it's better I don't tell Lewis about him taking Kaliann's hair, or possibly helping her escape, or knowing that they were related?

I don't know if Blackwell is the hero the Tzar wants to believe. There's still a chance he's working for Zorax. I'll keep this to myself for now, until I can gather enough evidence, then I'll present it. I don't want the captain to think I'm a fool.

The best thing I can do is track down Blackwell, then he will have to answer for all of this himself. I don't believe he was kidnapped, I think he's hiding, or maybe even planning something bigger. All I know for sure is that Blackwell is more than just a red stripe.

"Good work today," Lewis says, smiling up at Pratt.

"Thank you, sir." Pratt's face fills with pride and he turns to leave the office.

He thinks I'm doing good work. Serie will be so proud of me! Smiling, he walks through the hallway in a daze. Remi grabs his neck, pulling him into the elevator and slamming his head against the wall. The shock of it takes his breath away as his head pounds from the impact.

"You embarrassed me," Remi shouts into Pratt's face, spraying spit.

"I'm sorry," Pratt cries out. "Come on Luis, we're friends! It wasn't intentional."

"Fine," Remi says, letting him go. He presses the button for the first floor. "Don't let it happen again."

"Of course not," Pratt says, fear coursing through him.

"Let's find this damn generator." Remi grimaces.

27 | SKY BLUE

VIOLET

Clutching the sky blue lottery ticket, Violet traces over the raised numbers with her fingers, despite having memorized the sequence hours prior.

Imagining herself walking through a forest of trees, she can almost feel the sun dancing on her skin, the ocean breeze blowing through her hair. *Once I'm in the Orbs, I'll feel the bark of a tree, touch strands of grass in a meadow, run with bare feet through the sand, swim in the waves of the ocean…* She looks up, through the advertisements, out at an imagined paradise, her eyes glazed over with delusion.

Clicking on her tracker, she nervously opens the tab for the draw, which shows two minutes left. Taking a shallow breath, she closes her eyes and keeps her mind blank, barely breathing.

After nearly two minutes she opens her eyes and watches the last seventeen seconds countdown, pacing in front of the apartment window.

The screen flashes white and then opens to fireworks surrounding an announcement: *'Congratulations 209-627-456-234-9762-92!! You're a winner!'* She stares at the numbers, but they're not right. Continuing to stare, she is at first unable to comprehend the meaning of it, but then her cruel reality comes into focus. Around her, the room feels off balance as she leaned her head against the glass to stay upright.

"I didn't win," she whispers, collapsing.

I'm not good enough. She cowers into a ball, her forehead touching the ground. I was never good enough. I'm garbage. Sobbing, she rips off the mask and throws it across the room. Turning towards the window, she stares at her transparent reflection in the glass, watching tears slip down her cheeks. Nothing matters anymore.

Remi will find out and he will kill me. Standing angrily, she feels a new unexpected sense of peace at this thought of inevitable demise. My death can be my decision. I won't give him the satisfaction of killing me.

Storming out of the apartment, she walks purposefully to the elevator, with the intense energy of someone going into battle; war drums beating in her head. I know what I'm going to do. Smiling at herself in the mirrored elevator, she takes in her angry reflection and feels powerful.

The doors open on the ground floor and she exhales, feeling relieved that nothing matters anymore. It's over. It's finally over. Clicking on her wrist, she navigates to a tab with an image of a lime green motorcycle and taps on the button for a ride; the icon flashes green and she looks up at the advertisements, waiting.

Try Shello gel nails! Doesn't chip, even after a full week of scrubbing, washing, and working with household cleaners. Choose a brand you can depend on, choose Shello! Violet looks down at her plain, slightly cracked nails and laughs. Why not? Cancelling the ride, she runs back into the building and then takes the stairs two at a time to the second floor. Striding over to the apartment door, she quickly opens it, grabs a towel, and a clean grey dress, and rushes back to the elevator.

Pushing the button for the basement, she revels in the moment of freedom. Only the wealthiest shower when they want, but today I'm going to be wealthy. Giggling as she enters the empty shower stalls, she undresses, and then holds her tracker to the scanner.

"Welcome," the automated feminine voice says. "Please choose an option."

The screen below the shower head shows three choices. Violet clicks on the most expensive, 150 credits for a 15-minute hot shower. The sensor beeps and 150 credits come out of Remi's wallet.

The water turns on and she stands underneath it, letting it fall down her bare face. The warmth comfort's her and she finds herself unexpectedly crying. I should have done this every night. I deserve to feel warm, don't I?

She sighs. I'll make up for it. On this one day, I'll do everything I've always wanted to. The water turns off, but instead of getting out, she pays another 150 credits from Remi's wallet. Fuck you, Remi! I'm going to spend as much of your money as I can.

Beaming, she imagines his reaction at discovering she is gone. If I spend enough, he won't be able to afford another peon, at least for a while. The water is still running, but now she has a plan, so she dries off, dresses in the fresh uniform, and abandons her towel and dirty clothes. Outside, she calls for another ride, bouncing on her heels as she looks down the road for her ride.

"Where to?" The man stares at her, clearly confused by a maskless peon.

"Government District," Violet says. I'm going to see every district before I die.

"Green," he says and hands her a helmet.

She awkwardly lifts her leg over the seat behind the driver and grabs onto the bar in between them, barely centering herself before the bike lurches forward. The excitement of the moment overcomes her and she giggles uncontrollably. The driver focuses on the road, ignoring her illegal outburst of emotion.

As she watches the familiar black glass of the Enforcement District turn into the pyramids of the Devotion District, her laughter stops, and she stares in awe. *I wish females were allowed in the Natatoriums.* Closing her eyes, she imagines what it would be like to swim in one of the pools. When she opens them, the statue of a pregnant generator catches her eyes and she looks down at her belly, feeling uncomfortable. *It still looks the same,* but a wave of nausea hits her.

They pass through the marble towers of the University District. *I wonder what the men study? What would I have studied?* She shakes her head at herself. *It doesn't matter.* A strange smell makes her wrinkle her nose, but then it's gone.

Up ahead, the screens on the spiralling towers of the News District flash the same image–a blonde reporter speaking aggressively.

"The threat to the public is high. If you see anyone selling nostaliem, report it immediately, you might save a life." *Selling nostaliem?*

The reporter talks about an award of 2,000 credits if a tip results in an arrest of an active gang member. Violet looks away, trying to avoid his intense stare. *What's nostaliem?*

The News District turns into the Technology District and she gawks up at the thin metal towers. *The upper districts have so much height!* Leaning back, she almost falls off the bike trying to see the top.

Whoa! The driver stops as soon as they cross into the Government District and she stumbles off the bike. She hands the helmet over to the driver without meeting his eyes, as she can't stop staring at the massive mirrored towers.

"Why are the advertisements all blue here?"

"That's two credits," the driver says, ignoring her question.

Reaching for her wrist, he scans the tracker and drives away without another glance. Walking excitedly, she heads further into the Government District, glaring back at the men in business suits who stare at her bare face. I'm dead anyway. What does it matter?

Feeling powerful for the first time in her life, she walks confidently up to the entrance of a particularly fancy-looking tower.

"Can I go to the top floor?" she asks.

"On what business?" the gun-toting guard asks.

Violet stares at him, unsure of what to say, but then she smiles.

"I'm getting my nails done." The guard steps aside and she jumps forward, pressing the button for the elevator.

Once inside she scans the gold buttons in admiration and presses the number 401, the top floor. As the elevator ascends, the back wall opens to a glass chute, where she stares out in awe at the mirrored district expanding below.

Up here, everything is bright blue and shiny, like a fancy perfume bottle. Behind her, the doors open into a vast white hall filled with expensive shops. Turning, she walks out of the elevator and into the luxury mall. After a minute of gawking at all the store fronts, she spots a nail salon.

An attendant greets her, "Oh my!" he says in a syrupy voice. "What happened to your mask, dear?"

"Someone stole it," she says.

"How terrible. Was it expensive?"

"Yes, it had copper lace on it."

"I'm so sorry to hear that," he says and grabs her arm, guiding her to a seat in the back of the salon.

"What colour would you like for your nails today?"

"Sky blue." She grins.

"Of course!" He leaves and a peon in a crystal adorned mask walks over with light blue polish, her eyes smile in greeting behind her mask.

Sitting down, she places Violet's hands in a warm bowl of water and then pats dry each hand, before methodically applying polish to the first nail. At the front of the shop, Violet watches a group of peons chatting as they get their nails done.

Seeing them looking so happy, she can't help but feel envious. I wish I could have ended up in the Government District, maybe I would have come to this shop every week.

"Here," the attendant says, walking up with a case of masks. "We have copper-laced if you'd like."

"How much for the diamond encrusted one?" Violet asks. If I have to wear one, it might as well be the most expensive.

"1,200 credits," he says, his face twisting into a greedy smirk.

"I'll take it," she says, "And do you have eyelash extensions?" Maybe I'll be able to spend Remi's entire savings?

"We do!" He gently places the mask over her face.

Exhaling sharply, a twinge of discomfort hits her, as the mask obscures her face from the world; as though she's gone from person, back to object, in an instant. Something about wearing it makes fear creep back into her. Everyone knows objects are to be used. A moment later, he returns with the eyelash extensions.

"Maliy will apply them for you once your nails are done."

"Thank you," Violet whispers, as the peon places a completed hand under a dryer.

Moving the mask to line up better with her eyes, she watches Maliy paint her other hand.

"Would you like an eyeshadow?" she asks, as she places the hand under the dryer.

"Yes," Violet says. "Whatever you think would look nice." I hope it's expensive.

She smiles, "with your skin tone, I would say something orange or gold."

Standing, she grabs a peach and gold-flecked coloured eyeshadow from the wall and then returns and sits in front of Violet. Leaning forward, she opens the case and brushes on the eyeshadow. Violet holds back her welling emotions, she couldn't remember the last time anyone touched her kindly.

"I'm going to add a little dark gold eyeliner, yes?"

"Sure," she says, her voice shaking. Breathing slowly to prevent tears, she keeps her eyes closed as the peon applies the eyeliner and then gently presses on the fake eyelashes.

"Perfect!" she says.

Violet opens her eyes to see Maliy holding a mirror for her to look at the work. "It looks so pretty on you."

"Thank you," Violet whispers, surprised by her reflection; pretty tear-drop shaped eyes, adorned in gold, peach and diamonds.

Moving the dryers, Maliy checks the nails are dry.

"All done, let me walk you out." She leads her to the exit, where the attendant is waiting.

"That will be 1,325 credits," he says, scanning her wrist. She holds her breath waiting for it to be approved. After a second of terror, the light on the scanner flashes green. "Have a great day, dear."

Walking back to the elevator, she catches another glimpse of herself. The reflection is a peon of an extremely wealthy man. Remi wouldn't even recognize me! Good. She stares at the unfamiliar figure in the mirror and laughs.

People look at her as they pass, nevertheless, she can't

stop laughing at the absurdity of the moment. The elevator doors open and she presses the button for ground level, laughing uncontrollably as the doors close. Above her, the advertisements are dimming.

Taking a slow breath, she stops her laughter. He'll be off work soon. This is it. She taps her tracker to connect to a ride and walks out into the glass-tree filled street, where the motorcycle is waiting.

"Where to?"

"The Recycling District."

The man stares at her for a moment and then asks, "Are you getting recycled?"

"Yes."

"Could I have your mask?" He rocks on his heels. "I mean, once we get there... it's just I could sell it, if you aren't going to use it anymore."

"You can have it," she says. "Actually you can have my credits too, if you want?" Good! Take Remi's money.

"Really!"

"Sure, I don't know how much is in the wallet though."

"Could I try scanning for 1,000?"

"Let's try," Violet says, holding up her wrist. She watches as the scanner turns green.

"Let's do another!" She inhales excitedly. The driver's eyes widen and he types in another 1,000 credits, scanning her wrist with an excited yip. Again, it turns green.

"Again?" he asks.

"Yes." Fuck you, Remi! This time he scans it and it turns red. "Try 500 credits," she suggests.

"Okay," he says and scans away 500 credits.

"Let's see if there's 250!" She grins. He types in 250 and scans her wrist. This one turns red.

"Try 100." He nods and scans for 100 credits. It turns green.

"Try 75." After another moment he scans away 75 credits, his smile is so wide now, Violet can see his molars.

"Thank you!" he cheers, punching his hand in the air. "You've just changed my life!"

"No problem," she says, grabbing the helmet.

Climbing onto the back of the bike, she holds on tightly to the handlebars as the engine revs. They ride down the highway, spiralling through the districts.

Holding her breath as they pass through the Enforcement District, she stares at all the faces in the street, hoping not to see Remi's among them. It's okay. You're invisible. He can't hurt you anymore.

Once they enter the Education District, she breathes a sigh of relief. Parts of it look familiar enough, but all of her memories were made in the basements of the district. One enormous building in the distance catches her attention, something about the shape of it sticks out to her. I wonder if that's where I was trained?

Fidgeting with the plastic on the handlebars, she looks away. It doesn't matter. Nothing matters anymore. Seeing her bright blue nails makes her smile and for a moment her indifference was spiked with joy. I'm glad I did that. She giggles. I actually spent all his money!

As they move into the Generation District, Violet watches the pregnant bellies move in the glass bridges above, each one chasing her like a starving animal she can't escape. I won't be pregnant anymore. I won't be anything.

Closing her eyes, she doesn't want to see any more round bellies, but they're still there in her mind's eye. The noise of the Entertainment District startles her, and she watches the men crowd around the brothels, stumbling through the streets buzzed from booze.

The fumes of the Manufacturing District made her nausea worse, and she presses her masked face against her elbow. Here the men walk through the streets like zombies, their dust-encrusted uniforms erasing any sense of individuality among the horde.

The smell is much worse as they move into the Purification District and she closes her eyes to stop them from stinging. In the Power District, the noise, heat, flashing sparks, and smell is all too much, so she doesn't bother looking around. Everything in the lower districts seemed terrible to her, and for just a moment she felt thankful she'd been brought into the Enforcement District.

In the Farming District, she finally opens her eyes again and rebalances herself on the bike, taking a slow breath. Almost there. Looking up, she sees the bright lights feeding the plants above her. I wonder who I'll come back as? I hope I get to be someone in the Government District. No, I hope I get to be someone in the Orbs.

They leave the Farming District and the motorcycle stops in front of a towering white stone building; completely windowless and with the hum of a factory. Standing stoically, Violet hands the driver her diamond mask.

He looks at her in surprise. "You're so young."

"That's true," she says. "But I feel old."

He nods in understanding. "Thank you for this."

Smiling, she walks up the steps to the expansive entrance way, queues, and then watches him drive away. The line moves fast and her heart is beating hard in her chest. I can't go back. There's nothing but violence there. I will finally have peace.

"Next," a recycler calls her up.

"Scan here," he says. With tight fists, she lets him scan her wrist.

"Peon, age seventeen, is that correct?"

"Yes."

"Remove your clothes," the man instructs.

Tears stream down her cheeks as the finality of her choice hits her. *I have no other option.* Removing her grey dress and underwear, she ignores the other naked people around her, instead watching the recycler as he takes her items and drops them into a chute behind the desk.

"Follow me." He leads her to another room with five doors, each with a label: *Man, Generator, Doxy, Peon, Younkin.*

Opening the door labelled *Peon*, he waves her in, his expression indifferent. Violet walks through the doorway into a long white hallway and watches the man shut the door behind her.

Turning back, she grabs the doorknob and twists it, but it's locked. Inside it's eerily silent compared to the constant noise of Krevax. She slides down the wall onto the floor, her breath quick. *You have to do this.*

"Walk to the end of the hallway," a voice rings out over the intercom.

Standing, she walks towards the end of the hall, where it opens into a small blue room with a metal table. Beside her, a white circular pill and a gel hydration tube sit on a ledge in the entranceway.

"Take the pill and lie down on the table," the voice commands.

Swallowing the pill with a gulp of water, she then lies down on the cold metal. Wiping the tear streaks from her face, she wraps her arms around her small naked frame, but the cold only sinks deeper.

After a minute her fear disappears and she finds she feels sleepy. Hazily, she looks up, staring one last time at the blue ceiling with blurred vision. *I'm glad the room is blue.* Her eyes close.

28 | LEVEL-EIGHT

GARCIA

Perched on his chair, Garcia scrolls through the list of Government-controlled artificial flavours. He taps on a file labelled *butter* and prints the instructions for the chemical compound used to mimic the flavour. The printer beside his desk drones to life.

"I was thinking, for the tweaked cheesecake pudding recipe, we should start with a butter base," Garcia says, holding the printed recipe in his hand.

A square-faced man in a matching lab coat turns to look over at him.

"Starting with the easiest recipe this week," Willis says, exposing his white teeth.

"You know me," Garcia says, gliding through the lab equipment, machines whirring around him. "I like to knock out a few simple recipes before I hurt myself trying to get cinnamon again."

Willis sighs. "Aye, cinnamon, it's our dragon."

After sticky tacking the recipe to the whiteboard, Garcia reads through the week's list of requested recipes. Willis joins him at the whiteboard, a steaming cup of coffee in his hands.

"I can't believe they want another Blueberry Blast flavour," Willis says, his forehead creased with irritation.

"It seems silly, but I like the idea of the humanoids enjoying the flavours we make in their feedstock."

"That's true," Willis says. "But I can't see why they would need a third version of Blueberry Blast." Willis takes a sip of his coffee. "What do I know though?" He chuckles. "I'm only level-six."

Garcia nods, feeling slightly stung and turns back towards his desk. An email alert pops up on his computer screen. Settling down into his seat, he scans through the message. It's a level-six memo describing a sudden increase in the death rate of Krevaxers.

"A substance of unknown origins, officials have labelled *nostaliem*, has poisoned large portions of the Krevaxer stock..." he whispers to himself.

"A search for an antidote has begun, as well as an investigation into the source of the contaminant."

"Are you reading this?" Willis says, glancing over from his desk.

"Yes." Garcia looks over at him. "Seems like we'll be taking a break from synthesizing artificial flavours."

"I don't know, this is high-level stuff," Willis says. "We're only a level-six lab."

"That's true, but we're the chemical experts, and this is the Orbinian Institute of Food in the Agricultural Division," Garcia says. "Who else could they ask?"

"I've always said that scientists should have the highest clearance," Willis says. "Not these military men with their flashy metal teeth."

Forcing a laugh, Garcia automatically runs his tongue along his natural teeth.

"What can you do?" Garcia says. "I would love to know

who was poisoning Krevax."

"It sounds like it could be political," Willis replies. "President Lehan isn't exactly popular right now."

"True, but attacking everyone's food security seems extreme."

"The Geites attacked the outer shell of the Tropical Orb back in the 80s."

"Yeah," Garcia says with a shrug. "But they were cult nuts who believed they could only ascend to heaven if humans lived on Earth." He scratches his black beard. "And that attack was poorly executed, whereas this poisoning seems organized."

"Hmm." Willis vocalizes, nodding. "An orchestrated attack? Do you think level-five's got the same memo as us?"

"I don't know." Garcia shakes his head.

"I'm going to look it up." Willis turns back to his computer. After a minute of clicking, he looks over at Garcia. "Looks like they're calling it a disease outbreak."

The door to the lab swings open and a grey-haired general steps in, a severe expression on his face. Inhaling a quick breath, Garcia stares up at him, hiding his excitement. An actual Orbinian General is in the lab! Beside him, Willis takes a step closer, an intrigued twinkle in his eyes.

"Doctor Garcia," the man says, beckoning him forward. "I'm General Bouchard. I would like a word with you in private."

"Of course, General Bouchard," Garcia says. Hopping out of his chair, he follows the general through the hallway to a black elevator at the end of the hall

"Let's talk in my office." Bouchard presses the call button and the doors open.

Standing rigidly beside the General, Garcia hides his excitement by focusing on his breath. I can't believe I'm going to a level-ten floor right now! At the forty-ninth floor, the elevator stops and they head out into a long hallway.

The general leads Garcia half-way down to a leather-filled, smoke-stained office. The general shuts the door behind them and directs Garcia to sit. He watches the general sit across from him, his eyes bright with anticipation. This is it. I'm finally going to be a level-seven.

"Did you see the memo on nostaliem?"

"Yes," Garcia says. "I read it." Staring at Bouchard's sharply-pointed teeth, he angles his head down to hide his own normal teeth.

"I need a material scientist to identify the components of this drug and create an antidote. Are you up for it?"

"Of course," Garcia says, and then smiles with his lips closed.

"Let's look at your clearance." Bouchard types on his keyboard. "You're only a level-six?"

"Yes," Garcia says, feeling nervous.

"Hmm." Bouchard stares at the screen, clearly making a decision. "Level-six, remind me, what does a level-six know? I haven't been one in years."

"I think the easiest way to break down what I know is to share what a level-five believes. Level-five thinks Krevax is a large farm filled with Wildebeests. An animal created by the propaganda arm of the Government to protect the vulnerable from the truth." Garcia pauses for effect. "I know that is a lie."

"Can you tell me about Krevax?"

"Krevax is full of Krevaxers, a lower humanoid species," Garcia says confidently. No woman wants to eat something that looks like her child, even if it's no smarter than a 20th century pig, they're too sensitive.

"Animals," Bouchard corrects. "Would you be up for going

to Krevax? I need a scientist on the ground for this operation."

"Yes, I would be comfortable going to Krevax," Garcia says with a nod, trying to contain his glee. I'm actually going to see a Krevaxer in the flesh!

"Right, but let's be clear," Bouchard says. "You understand anything you see in Krevax must be kept secret."

"Of course."

"This would mean you would need to be a level-eight."

"Sounds good," Garcia says. A level-eight! I wonder how pointed my teeth will be? Taylor will be so jealous!

"Are you sure you want to be a level-eight?" Bouchard stares at him sympathetically.

"Yes," Garcia says. "I want to serve the Orbs at the highest level." Why wouldn't I want to be a level-eight? What a ridiculous question to ask someone.

"Right." Bouchard taps a few more keys. "It's done, you have officially been granted level-eight access."

"When are we going to Krevax?"

"Early tomorrow morning you and General Carr will go to collect a sample of nostaliem, and a subject to test it on. I want to see the drug's exact effect on its brain."

"How should I choose the subject?" Garcia asks. Would a male be best to ensure potency, or perhaps a female, to highlight potential side effects?

"They're all obsessed with seeing the sun, just take one out of the processing plant and mention the lottery." Bouchard leans forward. "Do you have any more questions?"

"No," Garcia says, standing. "Thank you."

What lottery? He continues to stand in place. And what does he mean by they're 'obsessed with the sun'? Who? Just ask. Quick, do it before it's too late.

Bouchard opens the door for Garcia and ushers him out with a final demand.

"Make sure the subject is small. Having one of them up here is dangerous enough."

The door shuts as Garcia stupidly nods. It's too late. Walking back through the hallway, he almost has enough confidence to turn around, but instead pushes the button for the elevator. Fiddlesticks, I should have asked. No… maybe it's for the best I didn't. I don't want him to think I'm a fool and put me back to level-six.

The doors slide open and he clicks on the number three. I can figure this out before tomorrow. Looking up, he watches the numbers countdown as the elevator descends. I suppose Krevaxers could have some simple understanding of our language? Neanderthals made stone tools in the past. I'm sure they would do the same if we hadn't domesticated them.

"What happened?" Willis asks, as Garcia enters the lab.

"I'm going to Krevax." Garcia laughs.

"No way," Willis says, shaking his hand. "I envy you."

"I know. I can't believe it."

"Well, you'll have to tell me what it's like. I've always wanted to see how they run that operation."

"I'll tell you… if I'm allowed," Garcia says, tilting his head playfully.

"They put you up to a level-seven?"

"Level-eight," Garcia says, grinning.

Willis pats him on the back. "You lucky bastard! This is what I get for starting three months after you."

"I'm sure they'll give you access soon," Garcia says. "I'll probably need help managing the subject."

"They're bringing a Krevaxer into the Orbs!" Willis punches up into the air. "Awesome."

"Oh man, I probably shouldn't have told you that."

"I won't mention it." Smiling, Willis turns back to his desk.

Garcia sits down at his computer and attempts to gain

access to the level-eight catalogue, but web administration had yet to grant access. Level-six bureaucrats. Fudgsicles! Just approve the request already.

Closing his eyes, he exhales nervously and picks up a pen from his desk, chewing it. What if I don't have access to the catalogue before my trip tomorrow? I should have asked about the lottery. The back of his neck breaks out in a cold sweat. I'm a fool.

29 | COMPASS

BLACKWELL

BLACKWELL STARES OUT AT THE HAZE, GRIPPING TO GERTIE'S peeling plastic steering wheel. Everything really is dead on the surface. A feeling of sadness expands in his chest, but then dissipates. It doesn't matter. All that matters now is that I get to the Orbs.

Twisting the truck through a particularly thick section of boulders, he glances down at the black screen to realign the arrow with the blinking dot. The map, which is disorientating, doesn't show the four cardinal directions, North, East, South, and West. I wonder if I can make a compass? I'm pretty sure I made one as a younkin.

Glancing at the still-healing cut on his wrist, he feels frustrated by his inability to search for information. How am I going to report this location to the Tzar if I can't even figure out what direction I'm going? I should have brought that damn pen, then I could have documented the route with video.

Sighing, he glimpses over at Rocket looking through the binoculars. I know north has the strongest magnetic pull, so if I can figure that out, I can solve this problem. Where can I find a magnet though?

Leaning forward, he stares out at the rocky wasteland that stretches in every direction. No way humans survived on the surface. I wonder how Tinik is doing? I hope no one else finds out she's female.

Looking down at his wrist again, he wishes for a moment that he could find out Tinik's past identity. He shakes his head at that thought. Even if I had my tracker, it would be wrong to search for that answer. She'll tell me if she wants to.

Why did she ask about the birth records? Was she a generator? I shouldn't think about this. If I can't get the Tzar his answer, maybe I'll join Zorax for real, then I could stay with Tinik... Krevax might not be so bad with a friend?

"Did Zipper mention what to look for?" Rocket asks, breaking the silence.

"He hasn't really given any instructions," Blackwell says.

Removing the binoculars from his face, Rocket glances over at him. "I'm looking for anything that moves, but I haven't seen anything yet."

"Probably not much out there, but sounds reasonable enough," Blackwell says. "What are you going to do if something does move?"

"Shoot it," Rocket says.

Blackwell nods slowly. That could go poorly. Someone might shoot back. Shouldn't joining a gang include some kind of training? I hate that I want to live now. It's stressful trying not to be shot.

"Makes sense, if it's an obvious threat," Blackwell says.

After side-eyeing him, Rocket looks back through the binoculars. I guess they don't really care if we die, there are always more men. With his eyes glazed over, an image of the kitchen cupboards jumps into his mind. Those might use magnets? What else do I need to make a compass?

An image of a bowl of water and a floating needle on a plastic cap leaps into his head. Right! That's how you make it. Hopefully, those cupboards use magnets. Then it's just a needle, and I bet I can find one in the bathroom medical supplies.

"I need a bathroom break," Blackwell says, slowing down the truck. "Should you take over driving?"

"No," Rocket says. "It would be best if I waited for you."

"Sure." Turning off the engine, he stands, stretches and walks out of the driving pit.

At the edge of the doorway, he glances back at Rocket, who is still staring out at the haze. Walking quietly into the kitchen, he nervously looks at the wall of cupboards. Slowly opening one, to avoid making noise, he can feel the pull of a magnet on the latch. He pries off the chunk of magnet and examines it. I need to be fast. I don't want to explain this to anyone.

Grabbing three gel hydration tubes from the cupboard, he tiptoes to the bathroom and pushes the button to shut the door behind him. Leaning underneath the sink, he pulls out the first aid kit and unzips it, finding the needles in a small plastic case.

He walks over to the empty toilet bowl and twists open the three caps from the gel hydration tubes, pouring the water in. Outside the bathroom, he hears a weird clanking sound coming from the kitchen.

"Rocket, is that you?" he calls out, but no one answers.

Someone else must be up. I need to get out of here! He runs the magnet along the needle a few times and then pushes it onto the plastic cap and places it on the water. It slowly turns and then stops at what must be north.

Orienting himself to face north, he puts his arms up to

get a sense of the direction they're moving in. So that means we're going north-west. Grabbing the needle out of the toilet, he flushes the water, caps, and tubes down onto the ground. With a squish of sanitizer he cleans the needle and his hands, and returns it to the kit back under the sink.

He conceals the magnet in his hand and presses the button to open the door. Plastering on a fake grin, he prepares to covertly side-step to the cupboards and put the magnet back in place.

As the door slides open, he freezes. Instead of one of the crew, he sees three figures in ornately carved white shell masks and woven blue fungus robes. Their long hair, which is sandy blonde, raven black, and jet black respectively, are braided with intricate spiralled circles of blue and orange beads.

Still unaware of his presence, they are frantically grabbing tubes of paste out of the open cupboards and stuffing them into blue pouches. Blackwell drops the magnet in shock, startling the small group of thieves.

They stare at him, all frozen for a moment, their bright orange painted skin showing through the eyeholes of their masks. Staring back at them in shock, Blackwell can't help but notice one is clearly female. She grabs an obsidian blade from her back and points it in his direction.

"Abrax, Dahhaak, sgiobalta yatrak wăng wài zŏu o keia!" she yells.

Falling back terrified, he can't make himself move. She takes a tentative step backwards, towards the ramp. After another step, the two men follow her lead, their side pouches bursting with plastic tubes.

Rocket opens the driving pit door and looks around the corner.

"Heloise! Kipanniq me," a man shouts, and they turn and

run down the ramp. Blackwell picks up the magnet, hiding it in his hand and jumps to his feet.

"What's going on?" Rocket sprints to the ramp exit, staring out at the group running into the dust.

Behind him, Blackwell steps to the open cupboard, secretly pushing the magnet back into place.

"Shit!" Rocket yells, as he pushes the button repeatedly to close the ramp that won't budge.

Blackwell looks out at the orange haze trying to spot the three figures, but their dark blue clothes have become shadows in the dust.

"Help me close this!" Rocket shouts.

Grabbing the far chain connected to the ceiling, Blackwell pulls the ramp half-way up, just as Zipper barrels into the kitchen.

"Why are we stopped?"

"Khan had to pee," Rocket says, throwing his hands in the air.

"No!" Zipper yells, directing his anger towards Blackwell.

"You never stop out here." He stares with an enraged look, and grabs the chain on the other side of the ramp, dragging it the rest of the way closed.

"Quick, go start the engine," Zipper says, as he slides the lock on the ramp door.

Rocket rushes into the driving pit, starts the engine, and slams his foot on the gas, jolting them forward. Blackwell and Zipper fall backwards to the ground from the movement.

Feeling terrible about what just transpired, Blackwell stands again and stares guiltily at Zipper. "I can take over the lookout position."

"Did you actually see any of them?" Zipper asks, fear in his voice.

"Yeah, three actually," Blackwell says. "They stole some paste."

"What!" Zipper grabs the cupboard doors and starts looking through them.

"What is with the racket?" Gunner shouts, stomping down the stairs.

"Khan stopped the truck and surface men took at least half of the paste," Zipper says, slamming a cupboard door.

"What!" Gunner growls. "What do you mean surface men took our paste?"

"I didn't know I shouldn't have stopped the truck," Blackwell says, defensively.

Gunner runs over and shoves him into the rusty wall. Blackwell stumbles back, momentarily disoriented, and then rebalances, ready for another attack.

"Gunner!" Zipper says. "That's not helping." Gunner steps back, seeing Blackwell hold his ground.

"How much paste is left?" Gunner asks, his voice vibrating in anger.

"I'm counting," Zipper says.

Blackwell walks back into the driving pit and sits down in the lookout seat, putting the binoculars to his eyes. I can't believe this is happening. Pressing a fist to his chest, he can feel his heart pounding from the stress. What will Tinik think?

Behind him, Gunner lumbers hostilely into the driving pit. "Zipper locked all the cupboards!"

"I'm sorry," Blackwell says, calmly looking up at him.

"He's sorry!" Turning on his heel, Gunner stomps away, leaving Rocket and Blackwell alone.

Blackwell looks over at Rocket, but he doesn't look back. He won't say anything? Dammit, now everyone will hate me here, too. Looking back through the binoculars, he chokes down his feelings. Tinik would have hated me eventually. A moment later, Zipper walks into the driving pit, a ball of nervous energy.

"The surface men got a good chunk of our food, but they left all the hydration tubes."

"That's a relief." Blackwell looks over at him, but Zipper ignores him and continues to speak in Rocket's direction.

"The food supplies are quite limited. Rations will be required, so I will stay on as cook for the rest of the trip, to prevent any misplaced tubes. Only one tube of paste a day going forward." Rocket nods.

Zipper turns to leave, but then glances back.

"Oh, and Pickles will stay as cleaner, but I expect everyone to pitch in." The door closes and Blackwell stares through the binoculars, thinking about what just happened. Only one tube of paste a day.

Everyone is going to hate me, even the younkin Pickles.

30 | MATCHMAKER
TWENTY-TWO

Sitting at a wooden desk, Twenty-two gazes up at the rafter ceiling as she waits for her only friend to arrive. Sunbeams shine through the classroom window, making her black wavy hair sparkle like some kind of picture book princess.

The other girls whisper to each other from their seats, intermittently flashing back cruel glances. Slouching forward, she tries to hide her body. I wish I was invisible. Twelve finally walks in and sits down beside her, impervious to teenage judgement.

"Did you see Chao yesterday?" Twelve asks.

"Yes," Twenty-two whispers, leaning closer. "He bought me an ice cream!"

"That is so sweet!" Twelve squeals. "I wish a boy liked me."

"I'm sure there are lots of boys who like you," Twenty-two says.

"Not enough to buy me an ice cream. Are you seeing him again after class?" The door slams closed and Mr. Raymond walks to the chalkboard, cutting their conversation short.

"Everyone, up front, in a line," he says, flashing a

threatening, un-filed grin. The girls stand and get in order of their numbers: One through Thirty-Two.

"Twenty-two, put your shoulders back, stand up straight," Mr. Raymond says, as he whacks her wrist with a metal ruler, leaving a red mark on her skin.

"Sorry, sir," she says, and hides her red wrist behind her back, straightening her shoulders.

The row of young women stand in a perfect line, waiting for further instruction. Glancing over at her friend, Twenty-two rolls her eyes, and Twelve discreetly smiles back.

Rushing over, Mr. Raymond grabs her neck with a pale hand. "Twenty-two, you're not paying attention."

Standing limply, she helplessly waits to be released, but he doesn't let go. Her breath quickens with adrenalin as thoughts stream through her head. Please let go! Why are you doing this to me? Stop. Still holding the base of her neck, he leans in.

"I should give you a beating," he whispers into her ear.

It takes all of her mental energy to stop herself from crying. Closing her eyes, she tries to imagine the sun streaking pink and orange across the sky, but she can't.

Instead, she can feel his breath on her face as he presses against her, running his hand down her neck, between her breasts to her waist.

"You're lucky, you're so pretty," he says, as he finally lets go of her and steps back.

With her face burning, she stands straight and stares forward, wishing no one could see her. Everyone is silent. Almost forgetting to breathe, she repeats the moment over in her head. Did that really just happen?

Mr. Raymond pulls out a stack of charts. "Today we have a special guest and we all need to be on our best behaviour."

"Yes, sir," the girls say in unison. Twenty-two scratches her nails into her thighs, just above her dress line. Across the room, there's a knock at the door and Mr. Raymond walks over.

"Welcome!" He ushers an old woman in.

"Girls, this is Wife Shwall, she has been given the special task of finding a husband match for each of you." Excited giggles fill the room as the moment before is forgotten by almost everyone.

Twelve catches the eyes of Twenty-two. "You okay?" she asks, silently.

"Fuck this place." Twenty-two whispers, smiling, despite her intense distress.

Why did he do that? What if it happens again? I want to leave.

She stares at the old woman, trying not to see Mr. Raymond, but his dirty blonde hair keeps bobbing in and out of her circle of vision.

"Silence!" Mr. Raymond yells. "Please, Wife Shwall, begin." The older woman steps forward with all the energy of an anxious baby deer.

"Hello girls," she says in a high-pitched voice. "You are all beginning the journey of blossoming into future wives. In this sensitive time you must learn to showcase your looks, find the best husband match, and maintain your purity; all while you train to please your future husband. Whores will not be tolerated. If you can't control your body, or present yourself in a way that avoids inappropriate attention, you will be punished."

"Yes, and I will see to that punishment," Mr. Raymond says, interrupting, and then looking directly at Twenty-two.

What is he staring at me for? I'm not doing anything?

Staring down at the ground, she feels sick. I would never be like one of those girls.

"I see some of you are already done blooming," Wife

Shwall says, and walks over to Twenty-two, cupping her breasts with her hands. "What bra size are you?"

"I'm a 32 D," Twenty-two whispers, her cheeks are so red now, she can feel the blood tingling her skin.

"I see," she says, stepping back. "That should be in your chart." She walks over to Mr. Raymond.

"Do you have this girl's chart?" Nodding, he grabs a file out of the stack of folders on his desk.

"That's Twenty-two," he says, handing Wife Shwall the file, which she immediately opens and begins reading.

"Fifteen, I see," she says with a glance over at Twenty-two. "With a body like that, we could have you married off this week."

Looking back down at the notes, she continues reading.

"But I see your parents have denied approval for early marriage. A pity, pretty girls rot quickly."

Closing the file, she walks over to One and examines her body.

"You're too skinny, my dear. No curves at all." Twenty-two looks down at her hands, trying to shut out the classroom.

Why is it always my stupid body?

Taking a slow breath, she tries not to cry. After a minute to calm herself, she looks up at Wife Shwall, watching her fill out the notes for another of the girls. Twelve looks in her direction, fear in her eyes. The old woman slowly makes her way down the line until she stops at Twelve.

"A bit thin, dear," she says, feeling Twelve's waist. Twelve nods apologetically.

"Quite a pretty face though, besides the dark tone." Turning back to the desk, the old woman writes in Twelve's file.

Twenty-two lets out a breath she'd been holding. At least

she said something nice about Twelve. Next, the horrible woman walks over to Thirteen.

"Oh no, dear," she says, shaking Thirteen's arms. "You've been eating too many sweets."

Covering her face with her hands, Thirteen bursts into tears.

"Restrict, restrict, restrict, with a face like that, you need a perfect body." Wife Shwall walks back to her notes, indifferent to the slashing she'd just done.

She then continues down the line, ignoring the sobs filling the room. Twenty-two looks away from the line of girls. Please skip me. She already asked me about my bra size. I'm sure she won't examine me again. Skip me. The woman steps in front of Twenty-one.

"Now dear, you are acceptable, not too curvy, not too pretty. You will not stray from your husband." Twenty-one stares at the old woman, her eyes wide, unsure of how to react. Wife Shwall walks over to the file.

"Oh good! I see your parents have approved you for early marriage, with a round face like that, an older man would love to have a baby with you." Twenty-one's face pales.

The woman drops her pen and stands back in front of Twenty-two. You already did me. Go away.

"Look at this figure!" The woman presses Twenty-two's dress into her waist.

"Hand me the measuring tape, Mr. Raymond." Twenty-two holds her breath, rigid with fear.

Why? They didn't measure anyone else! The teacher walks over with the measuring tape, staring at Twenty-two.

Wife Shwall takes the tape and puts it around Twenty-two's bust line.

"Write this down for me," she says.

Although she's trying not to look over at the line of girls, she can feel them watching her. Walking back to the desk, Mr. Raymond picks up the pen and nods that he's ready.

"Bust 38." She lowers the tape down to Twenty-two's waist.

"Waist 25." Again she lowers the tape.

"Hips 40." Stepping back to the notes, she takes the pen from Mr. Raymond.

"With those measurements, full lips, and big eyes, this one is going to make some man very happy."

"Or maybe one special teacher," Mr. Raymond says.

Twenty-two winces at his words and grinds her teeth to keep from yelling. *I would never marry you, you monster.*

"Yes, perhaps," Wife Shwall says humorlessly.

Doing her best to shut out the room, she waits for the old woman to finish examining her classmates.

"Thirty-two, last, but certainly not least." Glancing over at Thirty-two's fearful face, she continues grinding her teeth.

"Blonde hair and blue eyes, that will give you an edge," Wife Shwall says, then walks back down the line, filling out her own page of notes.

After a minute of reviewing, she steps forward with a small stack of folders in her hands.

"Okay girls, I need those approved for early marriage to come with me. That's Three, Eight, Nine, Fourteen, Twenty-One and Thirty." The girls step forward and follow Wife Shwall out of the room.

After they've exited, Mr. Raymond steps forward, a pleased grin on his short face.

"I suppose the rest of you can leave early," he says. "As a special treat from me."

Twenty-two runs to Twelve and grabs her arm, pulling her into the hallway.

"That was horrible!" Twelve says.

All she can do is nod in reply, because her stomach is still twisting. They head out the front doors of the school together.

"Hey," Chao calls, from the bottom of the stairs.

When she sees him, her anguish disappears, replaced by excited butterflies. She beams down at him. With this greeting, Chao begins walking up to her.

"Go," Twelve says, smiling. "I'll see you tomorrow." With one last glance at the pair, she turns, leaving Twenty-two with Chao on the concrete steps.

"Hey," she says back.

"Can I walk you home?" he asks.

"Okay." Reaching out he takes her hand, his fingers interlaced with hers, making her head dizzy.

"Anything exciting today?" he asks.

"No, boring stuff, like the difference between laundry detergent and dish soap." Twenty-two says, laughing. "What about you?"

"We learned about rockets today."

"Wow!" Twenty-two exclaims. "My classes aren't that interesting."

"Yeah, it was awesome. We actually got to build one and everything."

"I wish I could do that," Twenty-two says.

"Nah, what you're learning is important, too. I know you'll make an amazing wife someday," he says, smiling. Twenty-two blushes. "You look so pretty in the sunlight."

"Thank you," Twenty-two whispers. She leans in close to him, and for a second, she thinks they might actually kiss.

"What are you doing?!" her mother shouts, stopping the car beside them.

"Mother?" Twenty-two says, jumping in surprise. Looking over, she sees her mother and little sister through the car windows.

"Get in the car, now," her mother says, her expression twisted with rage.

She climbs into the back seat of the car and stares back at Chao, watching him disappear behind a row of trees.

"Who is that boy?"

"He lives in the neighbourhood," Twenty-two says, defensively. "He's nice."

"I can promise you he's not nice," her mother says. "Boys are dangerous."

"Yeah!" Her little sister looks at her from the front seat, giggling.

"When did you bleed last?" her mother asks.

"I think it was a couple we...weeks ago," Twenty-two stammers, feeling embarrassed.

"We will look at your chart when we get home. I don't want to see you with that boy again," she says, staring at her in the rearview mirror. Twenty-two looks away from her gaze, not wanting to agree.

"Oldest, do you hear me?"

"Yes!" Twenty-two shouts, rolling her eyes at her mother.

Her mother sighs in annoyance, leaving them both feeling exasperated.

31 | GROMWELL STATION
CARR

Carr runs up the ramp of the OD12 Passenger Drone and sits down in a leather seat. Impatiently fidgeting with a crack on his fingernail, he stares through the window, looking for the scientist.

A limo pulls onto the tarmac and a gangly man climbs out. That must be him. Pulling two straps over his shoulders, Carr buckles himself in. I only have so much time to make this happen; I need to grab the nostaliem, look for Blackwell, and get Scarlett, all without raising suspicion.

Tapping his foot on the blue diamond-patterned carpet, he anxiously watches the scientist walk towards the ramp. At least Bouchard isn't here, he wouldn't have let me out of his sight. A plan had been percolating in his mind since he found out about his half-sisters.

He touches the small vial of ketamine in his jacket pocket, thinking through the steps he needs to take, and then closes the zipper. Clicking on his watch, he slides the screen to a map of the Entertainment District and zooms in on the *Dark Lotus*. I can't leave her in Krevax with those animals, she doesn't belong down there, even if she is a half-breed.

Watching the orange dot blink inside the walls of the brothel makes him feel calmer. I wonder if they found my mother? A feeling of hope at this thought flickers in his chest, but then goes cold. Don't hope, you know she's not alive, she'd be too old. Slumping slightly in the seat, he feels consumed by the thoughts of his family history.

Did my father know they made her a generator? He said she was killed in the tunnels. Or did he have his own children in Krevax? No, I don't believe that, Krevaxers disgusted him.

"General Carr, I'm Doctor Garcia," the scientist says, smiling with natural teeth. "It's nice to meet you."

"Garcia, of course, glad you could join me," Carr says.

Why doesn't he have his teeth filed? I've never heard of a higher-level choosing to forgo the procedure? Curious, perhaps he doesn't care if others know he's important or not. Surprised to find himself feeling impressed by the scientist, Carr wants to speak with him further.

"Ten, nine, eight…" The automatic voice counts down in a comforting tone.

"This is my first trip outside of the Orbs," Garcia whispers nervously, as he buckles himself in. The feeling of admiration immediately dissipates. Who is this man? Is he even a level-seven?

"Bouchard mentioned you will collect the subject for the study?" Carr asks.

"Yes, it would be unethical to test the antidote on an Orbinian." A low hum revs and the craft lifts vertically, seemingly with little effort.

"Of course," Carr says, feeling annoyed by the strangely patronizing words. "As you're the scientist, you go to the processing plant and pick the best subject for our work. I'll collect the nostaliem."

"I can do that," Garcia says, and then adds in another whisper. "Who do you think is behind nostaliem?"

Carr stares at him for a confused moment. "The gangs, of course."

The scientist's eyes widen, but he doesn't say anything. This is who Bouchard chooses? This man knows nothing. Shaking his head to himself, he looks away from Garcia and leans back in his seat. For the best, this rube won't threaten my plan.

The drone moves into a clear chute, as walls of plastic open to let them pass out into the atmosphere. Beside him, Garcia's excitement is palpable as he looks through the bubble window. Carr can't help but stare at his reaction. Once they have cleared the Orb barrier, the drone starts its steep descent into the haze.

After watching Garcia for a minute, he closes his eyes, ignoring him. With the scientist distracting Bouchard and Lehan, the cull might be weeks away. The drone shakes, making the seats vibrate, as it's hit by a powerful gust of wind. He looks out at the stormy haze, holding tightly onto the handles as he waits for the turbulence to pass.

As the craft stabilizes, he clicks on his watch, and stares at the unchanged orange dot. I need to be quick, even with this scientist out of my way, something could still go wrong.

At the bottom edge of the windows, blue light appears, highlighting the way into Krevax. The drone drops into the chute, leaving behind the orange haze, and casting them into the dark. Lights flash from the chute walls on their faces as they descend.

After less than a minute the drone lands with a gentle wave and Carr unbuckles. At the front of the passenger bubble, the metal doors automatically open and the ramp unfolds. He walks quickly down the ramp, Garcia trailing at his heels.

At the edge of the tarmac, the limo driver—one of a handful of Orbininan's who works in Krevax, opens the door for them. Inside, a wide-faced guard with a gun strapped to his chest, greets them with a friendly wave.

"It will be interesting to see a Krevaxer in the wild," Garcia says cheerfully, climbing into the limo.

Exhaling a breath, Carr nods, refraining from responding to this ridiculous statement. What does he think he's about to see? A goddamn savannah? What was Bouchard thinking? He should have retired years ago.

"We're going to Gromwell Station," Carr says to the driver. "Then you can take Doctor Garcia to the processing plant."

The driver nods and starts the engine, pulling away from the tarmac. They enter a dark tunnel, which winds lower into the earth.

"Gromwell Station?" Garcia asks.

"Every station will probably have nostaliem in evidence, but I have a relationship with Captain Lewis."

"Is Captain Lewis an Orbinian?"

"No," Carr says, indifferent to Garcia's naivety. The tunnel opens and they enter at the West wall of the Government District.

Gasping at the towering, mirrored buildings and bright blue advertisements, Garcia stammers. "I... thought it would be more natural looking."

"There is nothing natural about Krevax. The Orbs are where we have preserved nature." Outside the limo, men move through the street in wedge heels and brightly coloured suits, their eyes covered by screened glasses, animating every frame of their lives.

"I see that now," Garcia says, and then leans closer to Carr. "Who built the towers?"

"Krevaxers built the entire city, we just excavated the structure," Carr says. "Doctor Garcia, what's your clearance?"

"Eight," Garcia says. "I'm sorry, I had a different expectation."

"Oh, come now, don't tell me you fell for the propaganda." Carr chuckles cruelly.

"I know they're humanoid," Garcia says. "But I didn't expect them to build all this."

Looking back out the window, Garcia gazes up at the ceiling of advertisements with a perplexed expression.

"They're animals," Carr says. "Disgusting vermin we need to keep caged."

Garcia looks back at Carr. "Why is there no grass or trees?"

"They believe there are only a few surviving species of seeds left. Part of a fear tactic." Everyone knows if the animals grew their own food, then we wouldn't be able to control them.

"I see." Fidgeting with his watch, Garcia looks away.

Carr closes his eyes. Imbecile. The limo stops outside Gromwell Station. Pulling open a small drawer from the wall, he grabs a set of dentures wrapped in plastic, rips them open and pops them over his pointed-metal teeth.

"Pick me up here when you have your subject," Carr says, and then shuts the door.

Tapping his watch on the sensor, he steps into the entranceway of the Watchtower and walks around the circle of elevators. At the tiger-carved door, he taps his watch again and walks into the station.

A secretary at the front desk of the cube greets him. "Tzar!"

"Is Captain Lewis in?"

"Yes," he says, in an excited yip.

"Let him know I am on my way up." He steps into an elevator and pushes the button for the sixth floor.

Standing outside the doors is Captain Lewis. "How can I help you, Tzar?"

"I need a large sample of nostaliem," Carr says, continuing to walk towards the captain's office. "And I need to talk to your detectives on the Blackwell case."

"Of course." Lewis runs ahead of him, holds open the office door, and then sits down at his desk.

"I'll call them now," he says, clicking on his tracker. Carr sits down on the other side and stares.

"Pratt, Remi, I need a moment with you in my office," Lewis says and then clicks the call off. "How large of a sample of nostaliem?"

"Large."

He taps on his wrist. "Morrey, it's Lewis. I have a task for you."

"*Yes, sir,*" Morrey's voice says through the tracker.

"The Tzar is here for a sample of nostaliem. Prepare a large crate, one that's 24 by 36, and make sure it has wheels."

"*Green.*"

"We'll be down there soon to collect it," Lewis says and then clicks his tracker off.

"I have a private matter to attend to in one of the lower districts," Carr states. "I need transport for the afternoon."

"You can take one of our motorbikes."

"I need something bigger," Carr says.

"Of course." Lewis nods apprehensively. "How about an armoured truck?"

"Thank you."

After a minute, Remi enters the office, his uniform and hair dishevelled. "You wanted a moment." Lewis beckons him in with a wave.

"Tzar!" Remi says in fake admiration.

A second later, Pratt walks in behind Remi. "Holy Mary!"

"Pratt, please!" Lewis shouts. "The Tzar has some questions for you both."

"Yes, Tzar," Pratt says, smiling. "Of course."

"Have you found anything on the generator?" Carr asks.

"Yes, actually," Pratt says. "She has no data before the year 157. It's like she came out of nowhere?"

"Where is she now?" You shouldn't have asked. You know.

"Died during labour, back in 160," Pratt states emotionlessly.

Taking a sharp inhale, Carr clenches his fists as anguish floods his chest. Maybe it isn't her. My father could have had a child in Krevax?

"Can I see the file?" Carr asks.

Opening the file on his tracker, Pratt holds out his wrist and Carr stares at the small image of his mother. It is undoubtedly her, but her cheeks are hollow, and her eyes empty. Nothing like the woman he remembered. What did these rabid dogs do to her?

"What was her caste?" Lewis asks. Carr looks away from the image and presses his palm over his mouth. In 160, you were only nine. You could never have saved her.

"Power District," Remi shouts impatiently.

"I see," Carr says, composing himself. I can still save Charlie and Scarlett from this place.

"That's a shame." Lewis shakes his head. "What about Blackwell's paternal side? His skin was not that dark?"

"We haven't looked into that," Pratt says. "But we will find out."

"Is there any information on Blackwell's current whereabouts?" Carr asks, interrupting them.

"No, none," Remi says. "He's completely disappeared." Clicking on his wrist, Remi scrolls distractedly.

"Okay, thank you for your work." Carr stands and exits the office. "I have some other matters to attend to."

"I'll walk you out!" Captain Lewis runs after him, leaving the two detectives behind.

"I'm sure Blackwell's father was at least a Manufacturer, he didn't have the look of the lower caste and his accent was only slightly noticeable," Lewis says, jogging beside him.

"Sure, he spoke with elongated vowels, but his language pattern was that of the upper districts, no recycler slang ever slipped through."

"I see," Carr says indifferently, as he pushes the button for the elevator. The metal doors slide open and they step inside.

"You should have heard Remi's accent when he first started," Lewis says with a laugh, and then seeing Carr's face pivots back to the matter at hand.

"As for finding Blackwell, I've got men in the Watchtower pulling all the footage we have of him over the last two weeks." He pushes the button for the second floor and the doors close.

"Excellent, send me what you have."

"Of course." Lewis nods. "Even if he's dead, though, we could still rectify the situation. Everyone loves a fallen hero."

"Something to consider," Carr says, as he walks out of the elevator.

His stomach churns at the thought of Charlie as a 'fallen hero.' Lewis follows him silently, a foot behind, and then runs forward to open the evidence room door. Inside, Morrey is waiting with the large plastic crate of nostaliem.

"Is this good?" Lewis asks.

"Yes, thank you," Carr says. Morrey nods and exits the room.

"I've got it from here." Carr looks over at Lewis, waiting for him to leave.

"No problem," Lewis says, stepping out of the evidence room. "I'll have a truck waiting for you in the parking lot."

"Thank you, Captain Lewis," Carr says, waiting for the door to shut.

Opening the crate, Carr examines the plastic bags of nostaliem. Good, I can easily make space. Tilting the crate up, he wheels it back through the hallway and into an open elevator and pushes the button for the ground floor.

32 | PROCESSING PLANT

GARCIA

WITH AGONY SPINNING IN HIS GUTS, GARCIA WATCHES THE general enter Gromwell Station. The limo moves steadily out of the parking lot as though the world wasn't destroyed. Casting a terrified glance out the window, he sees the innocent people walking through the streets, their faces flashing in his mind. They're not Neanderthals at all? They're us.

Dropping his head in his hands, hyperventilating, he wonders how this happened. Rubbing his sweaty palms on his knees he looks back out, staring at a group of boys. He can hear them yelling cheerfully as they throw a ball into the air.

Muffling a sob with his hand, he closes his eyes, not wanting to see anymore. The thought of the meatloaf his wife made for dinner fills him with nausea. Why is this happening?

With clenched fists, he takes long slow breaths to steady himself. Glancing up at the guard, he is confused to see the man looking calmly out the window. Seeing his apathy,

Garcia is filled with a new rage. It's men like you who let this happen! With your cold indifference.

How can I go back to the Orbs and pretend that this is okay? None of this is okay.

With his beliefs crushed by this new clarity, he feels off balance, like a tree in a storm fighting forces beyond its control.

"You're an Orbinian, how are you okay with this?" Garcia half-shouts.

The guard looks at him sympathetically and then back out the window. Thinking of his conversation with General Bouchard, he remembers how he'd asked him if he was sure he wanted to become a level-eight. I was not prepared for this, I should have stayed at level-six.

Flinching as a motorcycle loudly passes them on the highway, he grips the seat with his fingers. If only Willis had started the job at the lab before me... The terrible scene outside the limo flashes erratically, as his heart thuds in his chest.

If Willis was here instead of me... I would be in the lab right now, blissfully unaware of this nightmare. Between the guilt and the revulsion, he can't seem to sit still, and his noisy fidgeting catches the attention of the guard again.

"It will get easier," he says.

"Will it?"

"Yes." The guard leans forward. "I know it's disturbing, but the system began out of necessity, and now it's just part of a greater good."

"Part of a greater good," Garcia whispers to himself.

The guard leans back, unfazed, and stares out the window again. Despite the advice, Garcia can't get the image of the Krevaxer children playing out of his head. Have I ever eaten a child? The thought brings another wave of nausea and horror.

"Wait!" Garcia shouts. "How do we have milk?"

The guard glances at him, a streak of annoyance in his eyes. "You should try not to think about it." Garcia can feel it, the contents of his stomach moving up into his throat.

"I'm going to puke," he says.

"Pull over," the guard calls up to the driver. The limo stops abruptly and he jumps out, falling onto the pavement, puking. The guard slides out of the limo and stands beside him.

"You okay?"

Wiping his mouth with the sleeve of his sweater, he whispers, "I don't know." He stares up at a large glass bridge where he can see a line of pregnant women being led by a man holding onto a copper chain.

The women are all wearing the same floor-length white dresses, chains connecting their wrists and bellies. "Why are those pregnant women in chains?"

"Don't you know how the system in Krevax works?"

"I just became a level-eight," Garcia says, looking at the guard sorrowfully. The guard guides him back into the limo and sits down beside him. The limo moves forward again.

"Let me explain," he says. "In Krevax, men are taught that women are a subhuman species, basically they're used by men and to incubate offspring, but nothing more." Wrapping his arms around his thin body, a cold empty feeling pierces Garcia's chest.

"So, the women, they're treated like animals here then?"

"Probably," the guard says. "But their sacrifice keeps the entire system stable. Without the work of these women, the men would not submit." Garcia closes his eyes.

What kind of greater good is worth all this? Hours of anguish follow as no answer he can think of justifies the system in Krevax. The limo finally stops outside a large white marble building and he climbs out, shakily. Wiping sweat off his forehead with the back of his arm, he looks back at the driver with a desperate stare.

"Where are we?"

"This is the processing plant."

"I see," Garcia says, looking up at the people standing in line.

No. No, this isn't right. This can't be true. Why would they agree to this? Walking up the stairs with his stick legs, he queues at the back of the line, his mind lost in chaotic thoughts. Behind him, the limo driver rushes forward and grabs his arm, leading him back down the stairs.

"Our entrance is there," he says, pointing to a camouflaged door hidden behind the stairs.

"Thank you," Garcia says.

Turning, he walks towards the door and attempts to open it, but it's locked. Knocking softly, he hopes no one will answer. I want to go home. The door opens with a creak and a heavy-set, grey-haired man waves him in.

"You must be the doctor," the metal-toothed Orbinian says. "I've been waiting for you."

"Yes," he says. "I'm Doctor Garcia." The man guides him through a long hallway that smells of bleach, to a room full of metal doors.

"It's through here," he says, and pulling out a key opens a door in the middle.

Garcia closes his eyes. I don't want to see this. Then he opens his eyes and follows the Orbinian through the doorway. Inside is a room full of naked people lying unconscious in clear plastic boxes, stacked on top of each other like items in a fridge. Garcia gasps. This can't be real. Then beyond the stacks, he sees something worse.

The noise, immediately identifiable as saws, is terrifying. Red pools on the floor as the bodies move through high-speed blades; cut into perfect portions he recognizes from any grocery store.

The vision before him disturbs him so completely, he almost falls over, his head floating as the smell of blood overcomes him. Trying not to wretch, he follows the Orbinian further into the room. We're eating the flesh of humans. He covers his mouth. I've eaten people.

The man leads him through the maze to a control panel at the end and uses the key to activate the device. I'm a cannibal. Closing his eyes, he can't help but picture his daughters' faces. My daughters are cannibals.

"General Bouchard mentioned you needed someone small," the man says.

"We received these last night and they've already undergone disease testing. Let's start with the youngest on the line and see if they work." Garcia nods.

The man presses a few buttons and a machine moves one of the plastic containers out of a stack and pushes it into a dark tube, where it disappears.

"Follow me," he says. Garcia shuffles behind him, counting slowly in his head to distract himself. Just get through it. You're almost done. They leave the factory floor, walk down a hallway, and enter a small room. Taking a shallow breath, he is relieved the smell of blood is gone. The man shuts the door behind them, muting the noise of saws butchering the meat.

"It's just being washed," the man says.

The body of a teenage girl slowly enters the room through a connecting tube, lying naked and wet on a metal table. Garcia shakes his head. She looks the same age as my eldest.

They wait as the tube fills with blowing air, drying her small frame. The metal table slides out of the tunnel and stops in the centre of the room. The man opens a drawer, removes a bottle of liquid, and after soaking a cotton ball, rubs it under her nose.

She immediately sits up and starts sobbing. "What's happening?" she asks between breaths, curling her body into a ball.

"There's no need to cry. You won the lottery!"

Pausing, she looks at the man, confused. "No, I didn't?" She glances at Garcia, clearly terrified.

"It's true, you won a place in the Orbs," the man says with a warmth that seemed utterly impossible.

"How?" She giggles. "I thought I was being recycled?"

"Once you have started the recycling process, there is a final draw for one lucky name of the day, and today it's you!"

"I get to live?" Confusion contorts her smile and she sobs violently into her hands.

"Yes, but it's a long process, so I hope you are ready for that. What's your name?"

"Violet," she whispers. "My name is Violet." Her name is Violet? They name the females in Krevax?

"Excellent, that is step one," he says. Opening another drawer, he pulls out a plastic-wrapped outfit. "Put this on."

Violet takes the grey sweatsuit, but she is too distraught to unwrap it. The man grabs it back and unwraps it for her and then attempts to pull her leg out to put on the underwear. Falling over onto the table, she crunches into a tighter ball. The man sighs, exasperated.

"There's no rush," Garcia says, walking over to the girl. "My name is Doctor Garcia. I'm here to help."

"Don't touch me," she says with a yelp.

"I won't," he says kindly. "Take your time."

Sitting up slowly, still crying, she reaches for the underwear and puts them on. After a minute, she composes herself and puts on the rest of the clothes, and then standing, wipes the tears away from her puffy cheeks.

"Follow me," the man says, leading them to the exit.

Watching her get into the limo, he feels the anguish hit him again. I didn't know it would be like this. He glances at the guard, as the man gives him another sympathetic look. Garcia watches Violet pinch her arm.

33 | DARK LOTUS

CARR

ON THE HEAVILY USED ROADS OF THE MANUFACTURING District, the armoured truck shakes from the potholes. Carr's nose wrinkles in disgust from the smell of chemicals. Past dust-caked warehouses and a plastics factory, he can see Charlie's apartment building.

A feeling of hate burns through him, imagining his brother trapped in this prison. Krevaxers, rats, all of them. My poor mother and sister, dying in this wretched place.

Pressing on the brake, he turns into the garbage-spewed lot and parks outside the decrepit doors. He gets out and takes an unfiltered breath of the air, which stings his throat. I hate this place.

Opening the back of the truck, he lifts the lid off the crate and pulls out a bag of nostaliem, holding it a moment. After deciding it feels close to 25 pounds, he drops it on the ground. His eyes dart around the empty parking lot and up to the connecting street before returning to his task, confident no one has noticed him.

After dropping four more bags of nostaliem onto the

concrete, he turns and examines the space in the crate. That will be enough, the doxies are always underfed.

Putting a bag of black powder under each arm, he leans down and picks up the other three, gripping them in his fingers. He makes his way to the entrance of the apartment building and uses his watch to open the door.

An out-of-order sign hangs over the rusty elevator. Shit. Turning towards the stairs, he walks up all 16 floors at an angry pace and kicks open the door to the hallway, huffing. God dammit, Charlie. He taps his watch to the apartment sensor, pushes the handle open with an elbow and slides in.

The door shuts behind him and he drops the nostaliem on the ground. His hands hurt from the heavy bags and he stretches his fingers. Searching the small apartment for any signs of his brother, he is immediately disappointed. Why did he live like this? It's nearly empty.

"Charlie," he calls out, despite knowing it's pointless.

After no one replies he opens the entrance way closet and kicks the bags of nostaliem in. He shakes his head at himself and shuts the closet door. I'm sure he's okay, he must be with Zorax.

Clicking on his watch he scrolls through the tabs searching for any messages, there are none. He taps on a tracker icon and types in the contact code for his informant.

Ring.

"*Hello,*" the man says.

"Is now a good time to talk?"

"*It is, but I haven't found the man you're after.*"

"Have you learned anything about his whereabouts?"

"*He could be collecting nostaliem? If he was selling black powder, I would have found him by now.*" Good, he's alive. Carr exhales a small breath. Just far away.

"How long does that take?"

"*Could be a week, depends when he left.*" Carr taps his foot against the wall. A week. President Lehan could intervene with the gangs at any time, maybe I can find him before he returns to Krevax?

"And you still don't know the location of the lab?"

"No, I've asked around. Crew members don't even know. Most tell me they followed an arrow that points towards a blinking dot on a black screen, and with all the dust on the surface, it's anyone's guess." The informant pauses. *"I never said it was a lab, though."*

"You didn't? I thought you had," Carr says in surprise. "What is it?"

"A mine." The gangs are digging this stuff up?

"Let me know if you hear anything else," Carr says.

"Green." The call clicks off and he leaves the apartment, walking down the hallway in a haze of thoughts.

What is nostaliem, if it isn't being made in a lab? Moving slowly down the 16 floors, he feels confused and intrigued by this information. They say it lets you live in a dream. He's still lost in thought as he opens the armoured truck door. What kind of dream?

Climbing into the seat, he starts the engine and moves the gear into drive. Maybe the doctor can explain this. Driving back up through the districts, he barely notices anything around him, as he's absorbed by the mystery of black powder.

Once at the edge of the Entertainment District, he refocuses and checks the map on his watch. She's still there, at the brothel.

"Dark Lotus," he whispers to himself as he parks the truck.

Walking through the busy street towards the brightly lit purple building, he can see doxies dancing, each one adorned with a tattoo of a lotus on their stomach.

Clicking on his watch, he sees the orange dot blink back. A few feet away he spots dark curly red hair in the row of doxies. With a nervous breath he moves a step closer and watches as a stranger with his mother's features looks out at the street of men.

Stepping in front of her, his heart pounds in his chest as he asks, "Scarlett?"

"Yes." She stops dancing. "How can I help you, sir?"

Carr stares at her face, taking in all the ways she differs from their mother; her eyes aren't round like hers, they have a parallelogram shape, and her skin is lighter.

"I have something I need to discuss with your director." Nodding politely, she leads him to the brothel entrance.

A man in a bubblegum pink suit, standing behind the desk, looks up at them. "How can I..." he stops mid-sentence. "Do I know you?"

"I'm the Tzar of Krevax."

"Tzar!" the man says in recognition. "How can I help you?"

"I would like to purchase this doxy," Carr states.

"For how long?"

"Not for an amount of time, but outright. How much did you pay for her?" Scarlett looks up at Carr, concern creeping into her smile.

"I see," he says as his eyes widen.

"Let me look up the numbers." He taps on his wrist. "We paid just over 550 for her, but the price for a new doxy would be closer to 675, now."

"How does 1,000 credits sound?"

"That sounds perfect!" The man picks up the scanner expectantly, and then looks befuddled when Carr holds out his watch.

After a moment of hesitation, he scans the watch, grinning when the screen turns green. Grabbing her hand, Carr leads Scarlett back to the truck, as she shoots him nervous glances.

"Can I get my ribbons?" she asks.

"You won't need them." Carr opens the door to the back of the truck and waves her forward. Staring with intense fear, she reluctantly climbs into the truck. He closes the door behind them and pulls out the vial of ketamine from his pocket.

"Drink this," he says, opening the stopper.

"Okay." Her voice trembles.

"Don't worry," Carr says, smiling kindly. "I promise you'll be alright."

Taking the vial, she drinks it in one gulp and stares at him for another intense moment, before slumping over, unconscious. He picks her up and carefully positions her body in the crate of nostaliem.

Once inside she looks so small, like a child. Was my mother this small? He closes the lid, sighing slowly, relieved to have his sister. Looking up, he imagines his mother's energy floating in a bright blue sky.

"I hope you know I saved her," he says, as he shakes his hands out nervously.

She's not safe yet. I still need to make it back to the Orbs.

Climbing over the seats, he positions himself behind the wheel and starts up the engine, determined to get his sister home.

34 | CLASSIFIED

GRINNING, PRATT WATCHES CAPTAIN LEWIS RUN AFTER THE Tzar. I can't believe the Tzar of Krevax thinks I'm a good detective! Serie will be so jealous that I met him.

He looks up at Remi expecting to see him smiling, instead his face is contorted with anger as he clicks furiously on his tracker. Taking a step away, he creeps a foot into the hallway, hoping to evade his partner's attention.

"Fuck!" Remi shouts, glancing up.

"The Tzar seems pleased with our work," Pratt mumbles, trying to appease him.

"I don't understand why he's so interested in Blackwell?" Remi stomps into the hallway ahead of him.

"Why not make one of us the hero for the campaign?" Pratt walks quickly beside him, keeping up with his agitated pace. With a seething expression, Remi punches the button for the elevator.

"Now we're supposed to track down his paternal side, too. What a complete waste of time."

"I can go to the Government District, follow up on my own," Pratt says. "If you prefer." The doors slide open, but his stare is locked with Remi as his partner flashes him an enraged look, and then climbs into the elevator. Without a word, he steps in beside him, holding his breath.

"You're not cutting me out," Remi says threateningly.

"Of course not!" Pratt says. "I didn't intend to cut you out." Shit.

Silence fills the space between them with tension. The elevator doors open on the ground floor and they walk through the lobby and out to the circle of elevators in the Watchtower. Without another word, Remi exits into the parking lot and heads towards his bike.

Fidgeting with his sleeve, Pratt climbs onto his bike and starts the engine. Does he know I'm afraid of him? Dammit.

I should have asked him why he was upset. I need to convince him I still see him as a friend. Even if he's a monster, I still have to work with him.

Taking a breath, he kicks forward and heads up towards the ramp. Maybe I can fix this?

Remi's motorcycle pulls up behind him, but not close enough for them to talk. Glancing back, the hairs on his neck prickle, as Remi's eyes bore into him. Tapping on the gas pedal, he tries to create some distance, but with each change, Remi swerves close behind. Is he trying to intimidate me?

As they enter the Devotion District, the streets widen and Pratt presses on his brake, positioning himself beside Remi. I don't want him to be a threat.

"What's got you worked up back at the station?" Pratt shouts over the noise of traffic. Remi looks at him for a moment, deciding on a response.

"It's my damn peon," Remi says. "She spent my savings."

"No way!" Pratt shakes his head dramatically. "I can't believe a peon would do that?" Good, he's confiding in me.

"I know," Remi says, baring his teeth. "I just got the notifications this morning."

"I'm sorry. Have you confronted her?"

"No, she's in the recycling facility."

"She recycled herself?" Pratt asks. Poor thing, she must be terrified of him to do that.

"Possibly," Remi says. "Her stats show she's alive. I think she must have hidden in there, but when she leaves, I'll be waiting."

"Can you get your money back?" Pratt asks.

I hope she recycled herself, it would be a better death than anything Remi would have in mind. He stares ahead at the road, hoping to hide any sliver of his true feelings. I don't want to think about what he would do if he caught her.

"I don't know." Remi sighs deeply. "I've made a few calls, but no one has told me either way."

"That's terrible," Pratt says, glancing over at him with a forced look of concern. "I'm sorry, man."

Remi nods slowly. "Thanks."

Pulling ahead, he is relieved the conversation is over. Letting his mind go blank, he feels the sensation of wind on his hands and face. The upper districts go by in a blur and he parks his bike. He waits for Remi at the edge of the archival building.

Nausea creeps into his head and he looks down at his shaking hands. I forgot to grab a bottle of vodka.

Searching the unfamiliar mirrored towers and clean streets of the Government District with his eyes, he feels at a loss. Where do I find vodka here?

All you had to do was stop for coffee, and you couldn't manage that one thing. Grinding his teeth to lessen the judgmental voice in his head, a slow panic builds in his chest. When did it get this bad?

Scanning the road, he realizes he still can't see Remi. I wasn't going that fast? Clicking on his tracker, he presses on a photo of his partner's unsmiling face.

Ring.

Ring.

"She left the recycling facility!" Remi's voice rages through the tracker.

"Okay, no worries," Pratt says, his shoulders hunching up in fear.

"Fucking bitch!" The call clicks off.

Wiping sweat off his upper lip, he replays the memory of Remi smashing the younkin's jaw in his mind. You can't do anything for her… Trying to forget the peon, he turns and walks up the grand stairs. Outside the doors an armed guard waves him forward, his oversized muscles pushing grotesquely through his uniform.

"Your tracker," he demands, holding out a sensor.

As his wrist is tapped, Pratt's withdrawal symptoms melt away for a moment, as he's so distracted by the young man's chemically enhanced physique. Is this what rich Krevaxer's are doing now?

The sensor screen turns green and Pratt walks through the door. Just inside a second guard is waiting, this one with normal proportions.

"Stand in the scanner," he commands.

Pratt walks into the body scanner, sucking in his gut as the machine circles around him.

"Your gun will have to stay."

"Sure," he says, unclipping the gun from his belt and placing it in the drawer.

The guard pushes the drawer into an open gap in the wall, locks it and walks back with the key. Pratt takes the key and walks into the foyer, where a secretary in a white and black mask greets him.

"How can I help you today, sir?"

"I'm looking for paternal genetic records," Pratt says, his head pulsing in pain from the lack of vodka.

"Do you have a name?"

"Charlie Blackwell." The secretary clicks on the screen for a few seconds.

"We have quite a few men by that name," he says, looking back up at Pratt. "What is his personal number?"

"Let me look." Pratt clicks on his tracker, his head throbbing now. "It's 578-589-2L."

"Got it." The secretary clicks a button and a plastic card punches out of the machine. "This is the location of the records." He hands it over.

"Thank you." Turning towards the elevators, he walks slowly, feeling dizzy.

After pushing the button for the elevator, he examines the card: Floor: 203; Block: Seven; Row: Three; Label: Paternal Line Younkins B-Year 157.

The doors open and he taps on the button for 203. The shiny towers outside the ascending elevator leave no impact on his spinning head, as he is solely focused on controlling the nausea twisting his stomach. He stumbles out into a marble hall with rows of files stacked impressively high. A secretary watches as he hunches over for a moment.

"Are you okay, sir?"

"I need vodka," Pratt whispers.

The secretary stares at him a moment and then disappears. Great. It's okay, no one will believe the word of a secretary over a vice detective.

He shuffles towards Block Seven, sweat soaking through his shirt. Leaning on the metal shelves in Block Five, he closes his eyes to shut out the fluorescents for a moment.

"Here," the secretary says, holding out a mug of coffee. Pratt accepts it, feeling confused, and then tastes the cherry vodka.

"Thank you," he says.

The secretary nods and walks away. He drinks the entire

cup in one gulp and takes a few slow breaths. After a minute, his head stops throbbing, leaving behind only a dull ache, and he takes a steady step forward. *I can do this. I can't stop all at once, but I can deal with this. I'll start with a little less alcohol every day.*

Walking into Block Seven, he scans the third row and leans down, grabbing a small stack of files labelled, "Paternal Line Younkins B-Year 157."

He brings the files to a desk at the end of the row and sits down. Opening the first book, he scans through the names *Babbage* to *Becks* and then closes it.

Looking quickly through the next few, he finally finds the name *Blackwell* and matches one to the personal number. He reads through the line of text, stopping at "Paternal Line: Unknown." *Unknown? How?*

Looking through the lists of the other paternal lines on the page, he sees each one was assigned a name. He closes the book and rereads the title: *Paternal Line Younkins B-Year 157.* *Year 157? Wasn't that the year the Generator showed up?* Clicking on his tracker, he opens the file for her. *It is. Both year 157. I wonder?* He clicks on Blackwell's red stripe file. *What year were you assigned to the Enforcement District?*

Scrolling half-way down the page, he finds the year 168. *That would make him only eleven, not fifteen? Unless he wasn't born in 157? When and where was Blackwell born?*

Taking a photo with his tracker, he saves a copy of the page in his files, and then walks back to the elevator. *Who is Charlie Blackwell's father?* He taps on the *Red Stripe Database* and types in "births outside Krevax."

The screen turns white and a notification pops up— Access denied–classified topic. *What?* The elevator doors open and he presses the button for the ground floor. *Access denied? What could be classified from a red stripe?* He presses on Captain Lewis's picture.

Ring.

"Captain Lewis, here."

"Hi captain, it's Pratt. I'm trying to find information on Blackwell's paternal side, but I am getting an access denied message."

"Oh, that's interesting," Lewis says. *"Don't worry about it then. Just focus your efforts on finding Blackwell."*

"You don't think there's a way for me to get access to these files?"

"No," Lewis says with a laugh. *"I don't even have access to those kinds of files. We'll fabricate an upper district paternal line for him. It's fine."*

"Right, no problem," Pratt says and clicks off the call.

If a captain doesn't have access, then who does? He turns and watches the Government District expand beneath him.

35 | LOTTERY WINNER
VIOLET

Sitting in the back of the limo, Violet watches the streets blur by, lost in a stream of thoughts. She pinches the skin on the inside of her arm. *This is real. I'm going to the Orbs. This is actually happening. I'm not dead and I will not die today, or tomorrow, or the next day.* She almost laughs from the intense feelings flowing through her. *I knew it! I am good enough.*

Exhaling, she taps on her wrist, wanting to know how long she was in the recycling facility. It's been nearly 18 hours without a single memory. The cold metal table flashes in her mind, causing terror for a second.

With a slow inhale, she dissolves the image into specks, obliterating it. *Nothing in Krevax matters anymore.* Swiping away from the clock, she scrolls through at least a dozen threatening messages and then peeks nervously out the window. Relieved to not see Remi among the motorcycles, she sits back against the seat. *I'm safe here.* Across from her the doctor is staring.

"How long until we get to the Orbs?" she asks.

"We have to drive up to the Government District, and

then, from there, it's about an hour to the Orbs," he says, smiling. "How old are you, Violet?"

"Seventeen," she says, anxiously picking at her fingers.

"Why were you at the processing plant?" he asks with a concerned expression. "You're so young?"

"Processing plant?" She shakes her head. "Do you mean the recycling facility?"

"Yes, of course, my mistake." He laughs uncomfortably. "The recycling facility."

"My owner was going to kill me," Violet says bluntly.

"Oh!" The doctor sits up in his seat. "Couldn't you get help?"

She shrugs her shoulders. "Who would help a peon?"

"There are no laws to protect the workers?"

"Do you mean the men?" She tilts her head.

"You called yourself a peon, yes?" the doctor asks, scratching his head. The man with the gun gives him an intense look, which confuses her.

"Yes, I was designated a peon when I turned nine." She looks down at her hands, staring at the fingernail marks in her skin. "Because I wasn't pretty enough to be a doxy or a generator."

"I see," he says. "I'm sorry for the questions. The Orbs are a little different."

"What are the Orbs like?" Violet grins, looking up at him.

"They're nice," he says, clearly relieved to be changing the subject.

"Lots of trees, blue sky and sunlight." Tapping her feet on the ground in excitement, she almost forgets about Remi.

Her tracker rings and looking down, she sees it's a call from him. I shouldn't answer it. Staring at it wide-eyed, she can't seem to stop herself and clicks on the phone icon.

Remi's voice blares into the limo.

"I'll fucking kill you, you little thief! I see you right now in the Farming District. I'm going to smash your face into the ground until all your teeth break…" Violet clicks the call off and stares at the doctor, who is staring back at her.

Her mouth feels dry. "Is there a hydration tube?" she asks.

The guard pulls out a plastic water bottle and hands it over to her.

"Thank you," Violet whispers, taking a sip.

Despite her best effort, she coughs it back up. Dizziness overtakes her and she leans into the limo wall, feeling as though she can't get enough air. The doctor sits beside her and holds her steady.

"That man on the call, he can't get to us, can he?" he asks the guard.

"No," the guard says in a relaxed tone. "The limo is bulletproof." Violet sobs. He can't get me. I'm okay.

"I'm sorry," she says, crying.

"No, don't apologize." He pats her arm.

"You have every reason to feel upset. That's not a nice man." She giggles. Not a nice man? He's a monster.

"Thank you," she says. "I feel better now."

Sitting up straighter, she takes another sip of water and this time she swallows it. After another slow breath to steady herself, the dizziness fades. I'll be in the Orbs soon.

Leaning against the window, she closes her eyes, exhausted by the intense emotions. Too overwhelmed to think, she let herself slip into the blackness of sleep. The limo brakes hard, making all three of the passengers fall forward.

"Sorry about that!" The driver lowers the partition.

At the front of the vehicle, Remi is swerving on his motorcycle, his red stripe uniform flashing in the car's headlights. Violet stares at him through the black glass. His eyes are raging.

"Don't worry, he can't see you," the armed guard says, patting her on the knee.

Remi brakes and slides left, positioning himself beside the window. He smashes his fist into the glass repeatedly. Cowering in fear, Violet slams her eyes closed.

"Stop!" he yells, his voice muffled. "I command you to stop!" The limo keeps going. Outside, Remi pulls out his gun and points it at the driver.

"Pull over now." The limo slows down and Violet feels her stomach move into her throat. Oh, no! They're stopping. They didn't know he was a red stripe. She pukes onto the ground, coating her bare feet.

"I'll deal with this," the guard says, as the vehicle comes to a stop. The doctor takes off his jacket and wipes the puke off Violet's feet. Tears stream down her cheeks as she faces her imminent murder. This is it. He's going to beat me to death like he always said.

The guard, who is a full foot taller than Remi, and a good chunk wider, handles him with little effort, easily grabbing his neck and holding his gun arm in the air. Violet holds her breath in fear as she watches Remi attempt to fight back. The guard rips the gun from Remi's hand and shoves him to the ground.

For a moment, she can't comprehend what she's seeing. The idea that someone could be more powerful than Remi had never occurred to her before. As he lies there, the guard turns and walks towards the limo, a look of calm on his face.

Remi stands and runs forward, but the guard has already climbed back into his seat. The limo lurches forward, leaving Remi standing there. I'm okay. Taking a small breath, she lets herself imagine the possibility of escape.

Outside the window she can see Remi get on his motorbike and start chasing after them. The guard holds down a button to open the window and points his gun towards Remi.

Bang!

The bike swerves and he rolls over the handlebars and onto the highway. With desperate relief, Violet watches his body slump to the ground, blood pooling around him.

Staring hard through the glass, she wants to know without any reservations that he is dead, but the limo keeps moving and soon he is only a shadow on the road. Breaking her gaze, she looks down, surprised to see the doctor at her feet.

"I'm sorry," she whispers, finally noticing the puke he is cleaning up.

"It's okay," he says. "You're not the only one who got sick today."

He winks. The guard opens another compartment in the limo and hands the doctor a plastic bag. Putting the puke-soaked jacket in the bag, he ties it in a knot and places it beside him. The guard hands Violet a piece of tissue paper, which she uses to wipe the tears from her cheeks and blow her nose.

"Do you think he's dead?" she asks.

"I'm sure he'll be fine," the doctor says.

She stares back out at the road. I hope he's dead. After driving through a couple more districts, the limo parks outside the Watchtower. Taking in the scene, she can see her apartment building in the distance.

"Where are we?"

"This is Gromwell Station," the doctor says. "We're picking up General Carr."

"Oh," Violet says. Gromwell Station.

This is where Remi works. Feeling weary, she closes her eyes for a moment. A knock on the window startles her and she looks up to see the man from the lottery posters standing in front of her, causing her to inhale sharply. I guess he would be here, wouldn't he? I won the lottery! A small smile creeps onto her face. I beat you, Remi. I won.

The guard steps out of the limo and walks over to an armoured truck. A wave of nausea hits her and she looks down at her belly. No. I can't have that monster's baby. Her muscles tense in fear as the reality of her situation becomes apparent. Should I tell them I'm pregnant?

In the parking lot the men pull a large case out of the back of the truck and wheel it over. I'll wait until we're in the Orbs. Curling her feet up under her to stay out of the way, she watches as the driver opens a second set of doors and they slide the crate in. The general climbs into a seat beside the doctor, the guard following in after him.

"What happened here?" the general asks, referring to the smell of vomit.

"I get motion sickness," the doctor says, holding up the plastic bag.

The general stares at him a moment and then nods a hello to Violet. She nods back. The limo pulls out of the parking lot and continues up to the Government District. Everyone is quiet.

As a tunnel opens up ahead of them, she finds herself feeling something wonderful, hope. Once they are through the doorway, her tracker flashes, as the advertisements lose connection.

The screen displays the message 'out of range,' and then goes black. The limo stops and she follows the general and the doctor out of the backseat.

"Congrats on winning the lottery," the guard says with a final nod.

"Thank you," Violet says, as the door shuts, leaving her alone on the tarmac with the two men.

Looking back at the tunnel, she says goodbye to Krevax. At first, she's hit by a rush of energy as she follows the doctor up the ramp, but overwhelmed by the intensity of the moment, she buckles herself in and immediately falls asleep.

It feels like only seconds later that the doctor is gently shaking her awake.

"I thought you would want to see this," he whispers.

Violet looks out at the vast orange haze and then stares up at a dark blue sky of tiny shining specks. The beauty of the sight feels overwhelming.

"What are those?" she asks.

"Those are stars," he says. "But I want to show you that."

He points at three large Orbs, as they come into view above them. Gasping at the bright blue and green orbs, she feels awestruck.

"Each one has a unique ecosystem," he says.

"That one closest to us, that's the Boreal Orb, that's where we're going today. It's colder than the other two. We even have two months of snow every year to mimic winter." He grins. "That's my favourite."

Leaning forward in her seat, she stares at the dark green orb, watching as more details come into focus. I can't believe this is going to be my new home! I'm so lucky. As they move closer, large bodies of blue water meet rocky coastlines, which grow into snow-capped mountains.

"I can't believe this is real," she says, crying tears of joy. The doctor smiles back.

36 | HOMESICK
ROCKET

ROCKET STARES OUT THE WINDOW AT THE ORANGE HAZE, steering Gertie. With nothing visually changing, it feels strangely still. Leaning over to examine the surface, he hopes to see something that will ground him, but it's just a blur. The driving pit door slides open and Gunner walks in, grumbling.

"I'm fucking hungry," he says, slamming his fist into the back of Khan's seat.

It had only been 24 hours since rations started, but everyone was feeling on edge. Rocket's stomach spins nervously, distracting him from his own hunger. I hope Khan doesn't tell him what I said about stopping the truck. He hasn't said anything yet. Khan looks back at Gunner. Rocket holds his breath.

"Shouldn't you be sleeping?" Khan asks.

"I can't sleep," Gunner says gruffly.

Khan picks up the binoculars, ignoring him. Feeling relieved, Rocket refocuses back on his driving and Gunner disappears into the kitchen.

"You could take some of the blame," Khan says, looking over at him. "Let them know we both stopped the truck."

"I don't know what you're talking about," Rocket says, avoiding eye contact. Shame fills his face, but he buries it.

Anything is better than Gunner turning on you. He's dangerous.

"Right," Khan says angrily.

Gunner walks back into the driving pit and leans against the wall behind Khan.

"Look at this fucking pussy. I can't believe this plucked pubic hair can call himself Zorax!" Tinik walks into the driving pit behind Gunner.

"I'd call you a pussy too, but you lack both the warmth and the depth," Tinik says and then bursts out laughing at his own joke. Rocket chuckles, trying to diffuse the tension.

"Stay out of this, Tinik!" Gunner shouts.

"Why don't you ask Zipper for your tube of paste for the day?" Khan says. Gunner glares at him.

"Come on man," Tinik says, reaching up and patting Gunner on the arm. "You can have my tube today, you're way bigger than me anyway. I'll be fine."

"I want his tube of paste, not yours," Gunner says.

"Well, I'm not as nice as Tinik." Gunner takes an aggressive step forward.

"There are consequences when you fuck up," he growls.

"Let's turn it into some kind of game," Rocket says with a half-shout, his accent breaking through.

He bristles at the long vowels, and "o" for "ay" sounds in 'to,' 'some,' and 'game,' which were unmistakably from the Recycling District. The truck shakes as he steers them through a steep section.

Zipper walks into the driving pit. "Everyone go buckle up, this area gets rough."

"Did you still want me to drive?"

"No," Zipper says. "I know how to handle Gertie best."

Rocket stops the truck and stands, letting Zipper quickly take over. He heads back to the kitchen to buckle in with everyone else, leaving Khan and Zipper alone in the driving pit. What if Khan tells Zipper what happened while they're alone? He closes his eyes. I hate this.

The truck bounces, throwing his head forwards. I can't wait to be back in Krevax. Even the Recycling District is better than this. When I get home, I'm going to the first kitkits I can find. I'm going to get super drunk and eat all the cupsawags and I'm never going to think about any of these people ever again.

"This is probably the best part about collecting nostaliem, most people in Krevax will never see what we're looking at right now," Zipper says, his voice shaking through the intercom with the movement of the truck.

Gunner rolls his eyes, gesturing to the endless orange haze. Rocket chuckles in response. I hope he likes me. He seems unstable. It would be best if he liked me.

"Hey, I didn't notice your accent before," Gunner says. "What district are you from?"

Shit. I wish he hadn't noticed.

"Recycling," Rocket says, as he holds his breath, waiting for the inevitable question.

"Really," Gunner looks at him in surprise. "Your skin is so middle caste, I thought for sure manufacturing?"

"I'm not sure why," Rocket mumbles defeatedly.

"It's interesting though," Gunner says. "Your paternal side must have liked them dark, dark like Tinik."

Tinik sneers at Gunner, a smile in his eyes. Gunner grins back. They seem to get along now?

"I'm not sure," Rocket says. "I thought that your paternal line decided your birth caste."

"That's right. So how did a recycler get access to an upper

caste generator?" He scratches his chin. "I bet there's an interesting story there. Maybe he was rich."

"Could be," Rocket says, feeling deeply uncomfortable.

"Really, I should have known. You've got scrap like me. Those upper district boys are all too comfortable. In the Devotion District you knew your place." He stops talking, aware that he let a secret slip.

He's from the holy district, no wonder he's so fucked up. For younkins, nothing good happens there. This is my chance to make him feel accepted.

"Yeah, that's true, but if I ever have to sleep in garbage again…" he says, smiling, letting his full accent come out. "I think I'll just have to kill someone."

"Exactly man!" Gunner says, laughing. "It's the same for me, but with cleaning. When I think back to scrubbing those pools…"

He shakes his head, his expression twisting darkly.

"I want to rip someone's face off." Rocket nods, his breath shallow. The murderous words he said as a joke sounded much truer coming from Gunner.

"Have you ever tried nostaliem?" Tinik asks, looking up from a clapping game with Pickles.

"Nah, I stay away from all drugs now," Rocket says, thankful for the change in subject. "How about you? Have you tried it?"

He breathes a small sigh of relief. For once he could speak without painfully thinking about every word he planned to say.

"No, honestly, the Government warnings got to me," Gunner says. "I don't want to." He pretends to cut his neck open with a blade. Rocket nods.

"Obviously, Pickles hasn't tried it, but what about you Tinik?" Rocket asks.

"Oh, I've tried it," Tinik says.

"Oh, come on!" Gunner says, grinning. "Don't lie."

"Fine, I haven't tried it," Tinik says and they all laugh. He seems to have a handle on Gunner. That's good.

"I've definitely been curious about it, though," he adds.

"Yeah, if the rumours are true, it could be amazing," Rocket says.

"What, that you get to swim in the ocean," Gunner says. "And run through green fields, and..." He moves his arms in the air. "Frolic in the sun." Tinik laughs.

"Exactly," Rocket says, beaming. The truck bounces high, throwing them all backwards.

"I don't believe it," Gunner says, after the truck returns to a steadier rumbling.

"We'll have to try it to find out," Tinik whispers, grinning.

"You first," Gunner says.

"I'm out." Rocket shakes his head.

Pickles looks up at them, smiling.

"I've tried it," he shouts, "and I've swum in an ocean before."

Gunner rolls his eyes and Rocket gives a sympathetic nod.

"Thumb war?" Tinik asks Pickles, holding out his hand.

"Can you believe the bastard up there lost our paste?" Gunner growls, referring to Khan.

"At least we have all the hydration tubes," Rocket says, feeling uncomfortable.

"This is my third mission and I've never seen a crew member turn off the engine and just leave the driving pit." Gunner shakes his head. "Khan shouldn't get any tubes of paste."

"It's not right," Rocket says, immediately feeling guilty. "But he's still got to eat." He shrugs his shoulders.

"It's not right," Gunner says, hitting the table. Rocket nods. He's being a little intense. We still have enough food to survive.

"We'll be back in Krevax soon enough," Rocket says.

"You think that, but this orange haze." He grabs his own head. "It plays with your mind. I'll tell you what, there's no fucking way I'm coming on one of these trips again."

"I hear you." Rocket nods.

"I'm tired." Gunner sighs and closes his eyes, resting his head in his arms.

Rocket watches Pickles and Tinik quietly thumb-wrestle. I hope he goes to sleep soon, then I won't have to talk to him until shift change. Pickles giggles when Tinik clearly lets him win. The truck slows down.

"Rocket, you can come drive again," Zipper says through the intercom. "Everyone else can unbuckle."

He stands and heads up to the driving pit. Zipper moves aside, and he quickly sits and puts the truck back into drive, pulling forward.

"I'll bring you two each a tube of paste," Zipper says. Khan nods.

I wonder if Khan said anything while they were up here alone? Rocket glances over at him, but he is staring through the binoculars. Zipper returns after a moment.

"The surface men were avoiding the plain ones." He hands them both a tube of plain paste and a gel hydration tube.

"Thank Mary for plain paste then," Rocket says.

Zipper nods and leaves. He swallows the paste in two bites, but his hunger is still ravenous.

37 | STORM CHASERS
TINIK

"I'M SORRY ABOUT THIS," ZIPPER SAYS, DROPPING THREE TUBES of paste on the table. Tinik picks up a strawberry paste. He's saying it like it's all Blackwell's fault, but he's the one who didn't give explicit instructions.

"Don't be," Tinik says. "Still more than I got back in Krevax. This might as well be the Government District—a tube of paste every day."

Zipper nods. What a cockroach, I guess as long as the heat isn't on him, he doesn't care. Gunner grabs a tube of hamburger paste, examines it, and then opens it in acceptance. How can I help Blackwell? I don't want him to get hurt, he's the only one I trust.

Pickles takes the tube of plain paste and opens it without complaint. I really do trust him, don't I. She feels surprised by the revelation. I never thought I would trust a man. Should I tell him about my younkins? I'll decide that later, what's most important is that we get back to Krevax together.

Zipper stands at the wall of cupboards, locking them and then walks back to the table.

"You two should get some sleep," he says, addressing Gunner and Tinik.

"Have you had a run in with the surface men before?" Tinik asks. That question should throw him for a loop.

Zipper stares at her for a moment, his large eyes looking sorrowful. "My second trip, before I was crew leader."

"Really," Gunner says, looking up from his empty paste. "Why didn't you tell us about that?"

Good, this is it, this is the moment Gunner forgets about Blackwell.

"It's rare to have a run in with them and I didn't want to scare anyone," Zipper says, glancing at Pickles.

"I think it would have been safest to have known the risks," Tinik says. Zipper stares at her for a moment and then turns and walks up the stairs without responding.

"You look like you're getting tired," Tinik says to Pickles.

"A little," Pickles whispers in a meek voice.

"You should go lie down," Tinik says, patting him on the shoulder.

Nodding, he takes his hydration tube and runs over to the stairs, quickly climbing them. She waits until he is out of earshot and then leans closer to Gunner.

"I think Zipper should have warned us, don't you?" Tinik whispers.

"Probably," Gunner says indifferently, "but I already knew they were out there."

"If he had, there's no way, Bla..." Shit! I almost said Blackwell. "Khan, would have stopped that truck."

"Maybe," Gunner says, his eyes glazed over. "Have you been able to sleep?"

I guess that's the end of the conversation. He's probably fine with Zipper, now that Pickles is the official cleaner.

"I've been able to sleep," Tinik says.

It's quieter than the Generator District and better than

sleeping on the streets in Krevax, but I've always been a deep sleeper. I wonder why he can't sleep? It's not that bad here. I hope when I get back my payday is enough to rent an apartment, then I'll have somewhere safe to bring my younkins.

"That's crazy," Gunner says, deep circles under his eyes.

Tinik stares at her half-full tube of strawberry paste. He's not used to being hungry, best to keep him happy. If he snaps... She exhales slowly. All that matters is getting back to Krevax. I'll be hungry for as long as it takes.

"You should have this. I'm like half your size," Tinik says, handing him the tube. Besides, if I eat too well, my period might return.

"Thanks." He takes the tube. "I still think Khan should have less than the rest of us."

"A little sugar will cheer you up," she says, nodding.

Well, tick-a-lice, there's nothing much else I can do to make him stop hating Blackwell. He squishes the strawberry goo up the tube and eats it in one bite. If he sleeps, he'll be less dangerous though.

"Have you ever tried the red stripe method for sleeping?" Tinik asks.

"No," Gunner says with a tired laugh. "Do I want to know how you know this?"

"You can learn a lot from the streets," Tinik states, grinning.

That first match for offspring, he never stopped talking. She cringes, thinking back to him.

"Basically, you focus on relaxing every part of your body, starting with your face and working your way down to your toes."

"I guess I'll try it," Gunner says.

"I'm sure it will help." Staring at Gunner's buggy eyes, she feels he's unravelling.

If he doesn't sleep, it might be him we have to lock in the sleeping quarters. Of course someone would actually lose their mind during the trip I'm on. I really hope he sleeps. No one would have a chance against him.

"Do you know what they do to younkins in the Devotion District," Gunner says, turning towards her, staring with an empty look.

Tinik shakes her head, holding her breath. "Anytime I think back to it…" he whispers and then takes a deep breath. "You know there're no peons there, and doxies are impure…" His voice trails off again and he looks down.

"I'm sorry," Tinik says, holding back tears.

I'm so sorry Gunner, you were little once too. I can't believe I let myself think my boys would be safe. They're not safe, no younkins are. Gunner stares at the table for a minute and then shuffles over to the stairs. He's not okay. Nothing about this is okay. I need to talk to Blackwell. Tinik stands and makes her way to the driving pit door.

"Khan, Zipper needs a moment with you," she says.

"Oh!" Blackwell stumbles up from his seat, rushing out into the kitchen. She closes the door to the driving pit, giving them privacy.

"Where's Zipper?"

"It's just me," Tinik whispers. "Are you okay?"

Blackwell nods, a small smile on his face.

"I've been trying to get a moment with you," she says. "Gunner hates you and I'm thinking he might actually become dangerous. He's unravelling."

"I know," Blackwell says. "I'm sorry about the paste."

"Don't be, it's not your fault." Tinik shakes her head. "Zipper should have told us about the surface men."

"I was worried you hated me."

"Of course not." She jabs him in the side with her elbow,

laughing. "We survived a giant bug attack, nothing can destroy that."

Blackwell grins. "Okay," he says and then looks around the empty kitchen. "The surface people I saw must live in those caves, they wore white masks made from the shells of the bugs we fought."

"That's so green! I'd lose that food all over again just to know that people are living outside Krevax," she cheers. "Maybe we could join them instead of going back?" After I get my younkins, of course.

"I don't know if they would take us," Blackwell whispers with a laugh. "There's something else, though. One of them was female."

"Really."

"Yeah, and she dressed like the men."

"Well, it's settled then," Tinik says. "We're definitely joining them, I already fit in." Blackwell looks down.

"What's wrong?"

"I can't believe I ever thought that females were a lower species."

"It's not your fault," Tinik says. "We've all been told lies in Krevax."

Blackwell nods. She looks away for a moment thinking of her younkins and then looks back up at him. They stand silently staring at each other.

"Well, that's all I wanted to say, so you should go work before Zipper kicks you off the truck," she says with a grin.

"Yeah, you're right," Blackwell says, also smiling, and then awkwardly turns and pushes the button for the driving pit, stumbling through the doorway.

He looks back at Tinik, his cheeks red, and closes the door. Why did he blush? Tinik's stomach spins as she heads up the stairs, her face getting warmer with each step. Best not to think about it. She goes quietly over to her sleeping bag and zips herself in. Across the room, she can hear Gunner groaning, still awake. Despite the noise, she closes her eyes and falls asleep immediately.

"Shift switch," Zipper says as he shakes her sleeping bag.

Yawning, she unzips herself and climbs out. Gunner is already standing there, looking dishevelled, and she follows him down the stairs. She moves quickly past the kitchen, trying to ignore her hunger. In the driving pit, she gives Blackwell a nod of hello, which makes his cheeks blush again. Also blushing, Tinik takes the binoculars from him and sits down.

"I'm hungry," Gunner shouts as he buckles himself into the driving seat. Tinik glances over at him nervously. I don't know if he should drive?

"I'll bring you a tube of paste when you're halfway through your shift," Zipper says, and then shuts the driving pit door, isolating them.

"What a fucking cockroach," Gunner says under his breath.

Tinik looks through the binoculars, pretending not to hear him. He's in an awful state, but I can't stop him from driving.

For a while she can hear voices from the kitchen, but then it's silent, except for the sound of the engine and the wind. She looks over at Gunner. His eyes are dazed with large bags hanging underneath and a vein pumping on his forehead. If he's already in this state now, what will it be like in a few days?

She stares out at the orange haze, feeling anxious. Glancing down at the map, she feels hopeful the truck has made some progress. Inhaling slowly, she stares back out through the binoculars, and then spotting something dark in the distance, leans forward. As they move closer the details of a black cloud of dust materializes on the horizon.

"There's something out there," Tinik says. This could be bad.

"What?" Gunner growls.

"It looks dark," she says, hoping for a reasonable response, but he only shrugs his shoulders. "It could be a storm, I can wake up Zipper."

"Don't!" Gunner shouts. "If Zipper sees it, he'll make us go around, we could be out here an extra week, and that's only if we don't hit another storm."

"Wouldn't that be safer, though?" Tinik asks.

"I thought you weren't afraid of anything." He glared at her.

"There's a difference between bravery and stupidity."

"Are you saying I'm stupid?" Gunner says with a terrifying stare.

"No, that's not what I said." She watches him fearfully.

"Good," he says, looking away.

The wall of dark dust spins ominously larger. Shit. Gunner presses harder on the gas pedal, steering erratically through the terrain, a deranged expression on his exhausted face. I can't stop him. Zipper can't stop him. No one can stop him. Please, if there's anyone up there, let me survive. This time when she looks up, she doesn't need the binoculars to see the wall of ominous clouds.

The wind is howling and she can see flashes of light and hear booming seconds after. She holds her breath as they drive into the storm. It's completely black, except for when a flash of light hits, which makes everything a bright grey. She holds her hands over her ears to dull the deafening noise.

Gunner laughs maniacally, pressing on the gas pedal even harder. The wind pushes the truck off course. He leans on the wheel to straighten Gertie out, as dust cakes on the windows. The air filtration system turns up to the highest setting, as dust seeps in through cracks in the walls. Zipper runs into the pit, bounces off the edge of the wall and grabs onto the back of Gunner's seat.

"What are you doing?" he shouts, his eyes wide with fear.

"My job," Gunner says. Staring through the binoculars, Tinik can see a slice of orange light in the distance.

"We're almost out!" she cries.

Zipper grabs the binoculars from her and stares out the window. A bolt strikes just in front of them, sending out a burst of bright orange flames, as the thundering shakes the windows. Gunner swerves around the black smoke. Pickles runs into the room, tears streaming down his cheeks and grabs Tinik's hand.

"We're almost through," she says. Blackwell and Rocket run into the room behind him.

"What's happening?" Rocket asks.

"Keep going!" Zipper yells.

Gunner twists the wheel to line up with the map. The wind is still howling, but the wipers are finally working as the wall of dark dust in front of them evaporates and they are reborn into light.

"Get out!" Zipper shouts at Gunner. He slows the truck but doesn't stop.

"If it wasn't for me, we would be on this trip for another week," Gunner says. Zipper throws the binoculars at Tinik, stomps into the kitchen and returns moments later.

"There," he says, tossing the tubes of paste, and then still shaking his head, walking out. Watching it all, Pickles, Rocket and Blackwell stand awkwardly between the two seats.

"Take Pickles," Tinik says to Blackwell.

Nodding, he grabs the younkin's other hand and leads him away; Rocket sleepily following behind them. Tinik looks back through the binoculars and sees its clear. She exhales slowly. I hope this shift is almost over.

38 | SUNSHINE
VIOLET

UNBUCKLING HER SEATBELT WITH SHAKY HANDS, VIOLET stands and follows the doctor down the ramp. A clear blue expands above in every direction as she moves out into the light. *I did it! It's real!* With her face angled up, the sun tingles her cheeks, and she embraces her tears of elation. *This is my real home.*

She takes a deep breath, and feeling the fresh air in her lungs, spreads her arms out like an eagle in flight. The sound of bubbling water flows in the distance as a breeze in the air makes her hair fly out behind her. The doctor beckons her forward, and she walks in a daze towards him.

"The limo is this way," he says hurriedly.

Staring out past the limo, she sees a line of trees in the distance and laughs to herself. *They're smaller than I imagined, but still lovely.* A driver opens the door for them and Violet climbs in, feeling sad to leave the open air. Looking out the window, she sees the general wheeling the large crate down the ramp.

"Where are we going?" she asks.

"To a safe-house," the doctor says. "We have to do some

final tests to ensure you are ready to live in the Orbs." Violet nods.

I wonder what tests? Hopefully, it won't take too much time, but if I can see the sky, I'll be happy. Looking up again at the blue, she notices her painted nails are almost an exact match.

Oh right! For one dazzling instant everything is picture-perfect, and she laughs giddily, but then a wave of nausea twists her stomach. I need to tell them. Sighing heavily, she closes her eyes. I hate that Remi still ruined this moment.

"Open the double set doors," the general commands.

The driver unlocks the second door and opens it, leaving a big enough space for the crate. Violet sits with her feet underneath her, to stay out of the way as they push in the heavy box. The general climbs in, wiping sweat off his brow and the three of them sit in silence. Maybe I should tell them I'm pregnant now?

The engine starts and they pull away from the tarmac, the general tapping his foot rapidly on the ground as he stares ahead at the road. I'll wait until I can talk to the doctor alone.

Violet looks out the window and watches the trees get closer, noticing the dark green needles shimmering in the sunlight as they pass them. They're so pretty! The sight is overwhelming as she closes her eyes to keep from crying. I could never have imagined it would be this beautiful. Everything here dances in the sun! A cityscape unfolds, busy tree-lined streets flashing past the window.

The limo turns off the road and descends into an underground parking lot. Violet feels sick staring up at the fluorescents. I hope I never have to see another advertisement ever again.

"This is our stop," the doctor says. She climbs out of the limo behind him and they watch the general pull on the large crate.

"You two go ahead," he says.

The doctor nods and bolts away, with Violet running behind him. They climb into an elevator and he pushes the button for the seventh floor. I should tell him now, before other people come around. She watches as he taps his fingertips together, his face pale. He seems nervous.

"Doctor," Violet says. He looks over at her. What if he makes me carry the pregnancy?

"You can call me Garcia."

"Garcia, I'm pregnant." Violet holds her breath.

"Oh!" Garcia says in shock.

"Can you help?" she asks, staring up at him. "I don't want to be."

"I'm sure that can be addressed," Garcia says with a small smile.

The elevator doors open and they walk into a white hallway. What does 'that can be addressed' mean? She exhales slowly. I just have to believe he will help me, he already helped me get to the Orbs. They walk to a grey door near the end, which he opens for her.

"Wait here," Garcia says. "I'll be back."

He shuts the door leaving Violet alone in a spotless studio apartment. Looking around she sees there are no windows. She sighs, disappointed, and then spotting another door, jogs over. Inside is a small windowless bathroom with a shower and sink. Stepping in, she turns on the sink spout, making a stream of water pour out. Water whenever I want!

Gasping, she holds her hand under the cold for a minute. Above the sink, she notices the mirror and stares at her face. Exhaling slowly, she really looks at herself for once, studying her teardrop-curved eyes, rounded nose and heart-shaped lips. She smiles as the features finally seem to fit.

"Violet," Garcia calls. Walking back into the room, she

sees the doctor standing with an older man. "This is General Bouchard."

"Hello." Violet nods politely.

"I hear you're pregnant," Bouchard says. "I have a pill for you."

"Thank you!" She rushed forward, taking the pill from his hand, her expression a mix of desperation and relief.

Doctor Garcia pulls a cup out of the cupboard, fills it with water and then holds it out for her. Grabbing it, she immediately swallows the pill.

"I'm not pregnant anymore?"

"It will take a few hours to work," Bouchard says. "But yes, you will no longer be pregnant,"

"Thank you so much!" she says, crying. Bouchard exits, leaving Garcia alone, staring at her with a strange expression.

"When can we leave the safe-house?" she asks. "I've always wanted to see the ocean!"

"Soon," Garcia says, cryptically. "Are you hungry?"

"Yes." With a slow step he goes to a metal door beside the cupboards. Opening it tentatively, he pulls out a rectangular box, unwraps it, and sticks it in a larger plastic box.

"What's that?" Violet asks.

"It's a TV dinner," Garcia says. "I'm heating it up for you."

With a click of a button, the box lights up, making a humming sound.

"That makes the food hot!" Violet exclaims.

"Yes. It's a microwave."

"Wow!" After a minute, the microwave beeps and Garcia pulls out the TV dinner and puts it on the table. Then he grabs a metal thing out of a drawer and puts it beside the food.

"Enjoy," Garcia says. Violet sits down and examines the food. It doesn't look like anything she's seen before.

"What is it?" she asks.

Garcia picks up the plastic he had ripped off and reads it out loud. "It's lasagna with garlic bread and blueberry crumble."

"Blueberry!" Violet shouts. Garcia nods.

"Yes, that one is the crumble," he says, pointing at a small brown square with a dark purple base and then turning away. "I have to go now."

"Oh! Okay." Picking up the metal thing, she examines it and then attempts to stab it into the blueberry crumble. "Will I see you tomorrow?"

"Yes," he says, halfway out the door. "Get some rest."

He shuts it without looking back. Violet puts a small bite of blueberry crumble into her mouth. It's the most delicious thing she's ever tasted, nothing like the paste in Krevax. Wow! The metal thing is too hard to use, so she drops it and picks up the rest of the square with her fingers, putting the whole thing in her mouth.

Chewing it slowly, she feels the satisfying texture and enjoys the sweet and sour flavour. With the blueberry crumble eaten, she picks up the piece of garlic bread and smells it. It has an unusual and pungent smell and she takes a bite expecting to dislike it, but it's also delicious.

She picks up the lasagna, but it's sloppy, and half falls back into the container. Leaning over, she shovels the food into her mouth. It doesn't taste like anything she's ever had before. I can't believe this is real! After finishing the TV Dinner, she undresses and climbs in the shower. Standing under the hot water, she giggles joyfully. There's no timer! I could stay here all night if I wanted. After soaping, she stands under the hot water until her fingertips are pruned. Sufficiently warmed, she wraps herself in a fluffy towel and walks back out to the room.

Beside the bed was a set of long-sleeved white pyjamas,

underwear and a sports bra. Squishing the last of the dripping water from her hair, she drapes the towel over the back of a chair and excitedly puts on the clothing. Unlike the plastic-based clothes in Krevax, the fabric feels soft on her skin. She lifts the collar to her nose and smells the clean, chemical-free scent. Examining herself in the mirror, she smiles and then spins in a circle, making herself dizzy.

Leaping excitedly towards the kitchen, she opens the door Garcia had grabbed the TV dinner from and looks through a stack of eight options: Wildebeest steak with potatoes and sugar pie, wonton soup with bubble tea, Wildebeest with all the fixings, pineapple pizza and chocolate chip cookies, nachos and flan, Wildebeest burritos with sweet potato and caramels, fried Wildebeest with coleslaw and pecan pie, and Wildebeest pot pie with vanilla pudding. *What is Wildebeest?* She closes the door to the cold box. *It must be something that can survive in the Orbs, but not in Krevax, like the trees.*

Walking across the room, she tries the handle, but it's locked. *I guess that makes sense...* She tries to reason with it being locked, but an anxious feeling grows in her. *Everything's okay. At least I'm not pregnant anymore.* Tiptoeing over to the bed, she climbs under the blanket and closes her eyes. *I have my own room! I never have to worry about being hurt again. So what, the door is locked?*

I'm in the Orbs! I'll be free soon enough.

She falls to sleep quickly, but her dreams are pierced by nightmares of a rat running on a wheel.

39 | MINT CONDITION

GARCIA

Knocking on General Bouchard's door, Garcia holds his breath, preparing for the conversation. The door swings open, and Bouchard waves him in as he goes to sit back down. Garcia stands awkwardly beside the desk, not wanting to sit in the leather chair. That was somebody's skin... The faces of the children running in the street flash in his mind and he closes his eyes a second to ward off the faintness.

"Do you have the subject?"

"Yes, but there may be a problem."

"What's that?"

"She's pregnant," Garcia says.

"That doesn't matter," Bouchard says dismissively. "Once we have our results, we'll dispose of her."

"I see," Garcia says, inhaling sharply. "She seems quite upset about being pregnant, though."

"Okay," Bouchard says in an annoyed tone, but then flashes a strange smile. "Well, I have a mint."

He opens a small metal container and pulls out a white circular mint.

"A mint?"

"We'll tell her it's a pill to end her pregnancy," Bouchard says, grinning. "It will be hilarious." Garcia nods, feeling sick.

"How long do you expect to keep her for the testing?"

"We should be done within three days," Bouchard says, standing, the mint in his hand.

He leads the way out of the office. Only three days and then they'll kill her? Garcia feels dizzy as the elevator moves down the floors.

Glancing intermittently at Bouchard's cruel smile, he is disgusted by the metal teeth pricking over his bottom lip. The doors slide open and they walk to the room.

"Violet," Garcia calls, watching her come into view. "This is General Bouchard."

"Hello," Violet says.

"I hear you're pregnant," Bouchard says, chuckling. "I have a pill for you."

"Thank you!" Violet runs forward and takes the mint out of Bouchard's hand.

Garcia hands her a glass of water and stares in horror as Bouchard watches her swallow the mint, an expression of delight on his horrid face.

"I'm not pregnant anymore?" Garcia looks away, feeling sorrowful, not wanting to hear the lies.

"Thank you so much!" she shouts.

He watches as Bouchard leaves the room and then stares back at Violet, overcome with guilt.

"When can we leave here?" she asks. "I've always wanted to see the ocean!"

"Soon," Garcia says, with a hollow voice, as images of the ocean splash in his mind.

She probably won't see anything outside this room again.

"Are you hungry?" He crawls over to the fridge, not wanting to face what's inside.

"Yes," Violet says, smiling.

Opening the fridge door, he pulls out a TV dinner at the top of a stack without looking. While unwrapping it, he keeps his eyes averted, determined to not to see what it contains. Don't think about it. She still needs to eat. Resolutely, he sticks the meal in the microwave.

"What's that?" she asks.

"It's a TV dinner." He clicks on the one-minute button. "I'm just heating it up for you."

"That makes the food hot!" Violet exclaims.

"Yes," Garcia says. "It's a microwave."

"Wow!" He pulls out the TV dinner and puts it on the table with a fork, still avoiding the contents.

"Enjoy," he says, holding his breath. Violet sits down.

"What is it?" Sighing defeatedly, Garcia picks up the plastic label.

"It's lasagna with garlic bread and blueberry crumble." The noise of the saws from the processing plant roar in his head, making him feel feverish.

"Blueberry!" Violet shouts excitedly.

"Yes, that one is the crumble." He points at the square and then turns away. "I have to go now." I can't watch her eat this.

"Oh! Okay. Will I see you tomorrow?"

"Yes," he says. "Get some rest."

Garcia shuts the door. Standing there waiting is Bouchard, fidgeting impatiently with an unlit cigar.

"General Carr submitted a sample of nostaliem for chemical analysis," Bouchard says. "Can you explain what it means?"

Nodding, he follows Bouchard back to his office and looks at the readings on the computer screen. One thing is crystal clear, no amount of testing would find a cure, as it would mean turning off the brain.

"It seems to be some kind of hallucinogen," Garcia says.

"Can you make an antidote, preventing it from taking

effect?" Bouchard asks, staring at him. No, but if I told you that, you'd probably kill Violet immediately.

"Possibly," Garcia says.

"Hmm." Bouchard sighs. "I'll follow up with you tomorrow."

Garcia's head spins with thoughts as he walks alone down the hallway. Maybe I can use this time to prove Violet is like us? How many people know the truth? It can't be many. If I write a scientific report explaining the case for reunification, I could save all Krevaxers.

He presses the button for the third floor and walks down to his old lab. Staring at Willis through the glass panel in the door, he watches him bumbling around the lab in his usual way. Garcia looks down, feeling sad for himself. I should have never left level-six. He turns back to the elevator and heads down to the parking lot.

What if no one cares Krevaxers are human?

Opening the door, he climbs in and leans his forehead against the steering wheel. Enough people will care, I just have to get it published. He turns on the engine and drives out into the late-afternoon sunshine.

Watching the people moving about, he drives in silence, stuck in his thoughts. You see an animal, but I see a child. Where you see a farm, I see a prison. Will the dead not call out their names and beg you to leave their bodies untouched?

Not the dead, they cannot stop you. Not the Krevaxers, dispossessed, who you confine in fluorescent walls, subjugated by your ideology. He takes a shallow breath. Orbinian ideology. What have we done?

It's the death of our own humanity. It can't be too late to make a change for all the children of Krevax. Should I tell my wife? No, not until everyone knows. It would put her in danger. Parking his car, he walks up to the front door where his youngest daughter is waiting.

"Papa!" she screams in excitement. Garcia picks her up and hugs her tightly.

"Hi, my dear!" he beams at her, as his wife walks to the doorway of the kitchen.

"I hope you're hungry," she says, smiling. "I made steak."

Garcia puts his daughter back on the ground. Steak. His sudden awareness of the smell of the meat cooking makes him feel queasy and he has to sit down to take off his shoes. I must publish this report before General Bouchard knows what I'm doing. Once it's out, we'll all be safe. He walks over to the dining room table and sits down, gripping his chair. Wife Garcia enters the room, holding a set of plates.

"You look pale?"

"I'm feeling a bit off," he says.

"Oh, no!" She walks over and puts her hand on his forehead. "No fever, at least. Do you think you could eat?"

"Maybe some vegetables?"

"Of course. I'll wrap you up a piece of steak for lunch tomorrow."

"Thank you, dear," he says and kisses her.

The thought of the meat being wrapped up for him makes him feel ashamed. He stands for a moment, feeling dizzy, and then walks into the bathroom, where he stares at himself in the mirror. How am I going to keep this a secret?

I wish I could cut this out of my mind. Washing his face in cold water, he walks back out to the living room and sits down again. His youngest daughter looks up excitedly as his wife walks in with the platter of steaks.

"Where's Oldest?" he asks.

"She has a bit of a stomach bug," his wife says, as she grabs a slice of steak and starts cutting it up.

Looking away, he picks up a piece of corn and eats it slowly. All around him he can hear his wife and daughter chewing bites of their medium-rare flesh. Trying to shut it out, he closes his eyes, but the sound of the grinding and the smacking, and the smell of it all, makes it too hard to swallow his corn. His wife taps his shoulder.

"Did you want to lie down? You don't look well," she says with concern.

"Yes," Garcia says. "Maybe I have the same stomach bug as Oldest."

Dropping the ear of corn on his plate, he stands and makes his way out of the room and up the stairs, where he lies down on the cold bed. Nothing is ever going to be okay again. I need to get Violet out. My report won't be published in the next three days.

He stands up and walks over to a set of drawers, opening the top one. Inside there is an old photo book amongst his wife's socks and underwear. Opening the first page to a picture of his wife's family, he touches the face of the youngest, a toddler in his wife's arms. She died of leukaemia when she was little. I could use her family details to hide Violet at a wife school. I could tell them her identification was destroyed in a fire that killed her parents. That could work.

He closes the book, shuts the drawer, and lies back down on the bed. If the right people read my report, it will change things, but first I need to make sure Violet is safe.

Staring up at the ceiling, he balls his hands into fists, his eyes wide with worry.

40 | BITTER PILL
TWENTY TWO

TWENTY-TWO RUNS HALFWAY DOWN THE STAIRS, LEAVING behind her friend.

"Where are you going?" Twelve asks, holding her paper-bag lunch in the air.

"I'm meeting Chao!" Twenty-two replies. "I'll be back for fourth period."

"What?" Twelve says, taking a step down. "Where?"

"At home," Twenty-two says and then runs down the rest of the way.

At the bottom, she glances back and sees her friend's worried expression. Everything's fine. We just want some time alone together. This is the only way I can see him, now that my mother knows about him. Twenty-two continues running down the tree-lined block. Up ahead, she can see Chao turn the corner and she slows to a walk, taking a deep breath to compose herself.

"Hey!" Chao says. "How long until you need to be back?"

"My next class is in 55 minutes," Twenty-two says, as they walk within a few paces of each other.

"Same." Chao grabs her hand. "Are you hungry?"

"Not really." Twenty-two smiles nervously. "You?"

"I ate."

"That's good."

"Where's your house?" Chao asks, as he looks up the street at the row of two-storey homes.

"Around the corner," she says, her eyes darting at the passing cars.

"Are you sure it's okay I'm coming over?"

"Definitely!" She nods. "No one will be there."

Twenty-two pulls Chao behind her. "It's the yellow one."

They run to the front entrance of the house and she confirms the doorknob is locked before pulling out her key. Grinning at Chao, she opens the door and they step inside.

"Hello!" she calls out, waiting, and when no one answers they run down the hallway together. Shutting her bedroom door behind them, she steps towards the bed and sits down.

"When do your parents get home?" Chao asks.

"I'm not sure, but we'll be back at school before that." She looks up at him.

Chao sits down beside her and grabs her hand again. Twenty-two smiles, feeling excited as she awkwardly stares, unsure of what to say. After a tense minute, Chao leans in and kisses her on the lips.

"I think you're perfect!" Chao exclaims.

"You do?" Twenty-two asks, laughing nervously.

"Will you wait until I can marry you?" Standing, her mouth gapes open in surprise and she bounces on her toes.

"You mean it?" she asks.

"Of course!" Chao says. "I would do anything to have you as my wife."

Giggling, she sits down beside him again, leaning in to kiss him. The door slams open and Twenty-two's mother stands angrily in the hallway, a bag of groceries hanging off one arm.

"Get out!" she screams and Chao leaps up and runs out of the room. The front door swings open and he runs down the steps.

"What are you doing in my room?!" Twenty-two yells.

"I told you to stay away from that boy!" her mother shouts, dropping the bag of groceries on the ground, enraged.

"He wants to marry me." Twenty-two stands to face her.

"Did you have sex with him?" Her mother bolts over and grabs her arm, examining her clothes.

"No! Of course not," Twenty-two says, stepping back in shock as her mother reaches down and feels her belly.

"Stay here," she orders.

Twenty-two leaps onto the bed and pushes her face into the blankets, crying. A moment later her mother returns.

"Drink this," she says, holding out a small cup with a shaking hand, her face flushed red in anger.

"What is it?"

"It will ensure you don't get pregnant."

"I didn't do anything," Twenty-two begs, looking up at her. "I swear!"

"Drink it!" her mother screams, pushing the glass to her lips.

It tastes disgustingly bitter and burns her throat, making her cough, but her mother keeps forcing more into her mouth. Finally, the cup is empty. Twenty-two stares up at her, feeling frightened, as tears well in her eyes. Without explanation, her mother walks away, only to return a moment later with an empty tub of ice cream.

"What do I need this for?" Twenty-two asks angrily, burying her fear.

"You'll be sick," her mother states emotionlessly as she stands at the door. "I'll let the school know you're unwell."

She shuts and locks the door, leaving Twenty-two crying, curled in a ball. Why does she hate me?

She sobs for the next hour and then falls asleep, waking to the sound of her father getting home.

"Papa!" her younger sister shouts.

"Hi, my dear!" he says.

"I hope you're hungry," her mother says cheerfully, "I made steak."

Twenty-two stands to leave the bedroom, but is overcome with nausea, and slumps to the ground. Grabbing the bucket, she holds her head over it, puking, just as the door opens and her little sister runs in. The smell of minty vomit hits her nose, making her nearly wretch again.

"What's wrong?" Youngest asks.

Their mother walks in behind her and taps her sister's shoulder.

"Go sit at the table, your sister has the flu." Youngest skips away, leaving Twenty-two alone with her. She steps closer and kneels beside her.

"It will pass by the morning." Twenty-two pukes into the bucket again, her thoughts full of anger for her mother.

Why didn't she believe me? I've done nothing wrong. I hate her!

Looking up, she sees the door is slightly ajar. Her mother walks in with a glass of water and helps her sit up. Twenty-two takes the cup and sips the water, watching her mother leave with the bucket of puke. Lying back down on the ground, her head still spinning, she can't stop the tears. After a couple minutes, her mother places the now empty bucket back beside her.

"I swear I did nothing!" Twenty-two says, staring up at her mother.

"No more talk of this. Garcia is home," she whispers. "I'm

sure he had a stressful day at the lab. He doesn't need to be exposed to any female talk."

Kissing Twenty-two's forehead, she stands and shuts the door. Holding onto the bucket as another wave of nausea builds, Twenty-two stares at the carpet trying to make the room stop spinning. Outside the room, she can hear her family having dinner, pretending she doesn't exist.

Closing her eyes, she hopes for sleep, but the nausea makes that escape impossible.

41 | FRIENDS

BLACKWELL

UNZIPPING SLOWLY, BLACKWELL GLANCED AROUND THE ROOM. The sleeping quarters are completely silent, except for light snoring. Pickles, Rocket and Zipper must be asleep by now. He climbs out and tiptoes over to Tinik's spot, smelling the fabric; it has a subtle sweetness, a soft fragrance that makes him want to be physically close to her.

What am I doing? He drops the material and climbs back into his sleeping bag, a pang of guilt shooting sparks in his cheeks.

"Do you love him?" Zipper asks from the dark. Jumping in surprise, Blackwell twists himself to face the other sleeping bag.

"I didn't know you were awake," he half-shouts, feeling embarrassed.

"Don't worry. I won't say anything," Zipper says.

Then he's silent for a moment, before adding in a whisper, "I loved someone once, but he died a long time ago."

"I'm sorry," Blackwell says.

This must be why he doesn't like the ranking system. The

only thing lower than a female in Krevax is a black stripe. I hate I bought into all of it. Zipper's right, the system's wrong.

"So, do you love Tinik?"

Blackwell thinks for a moment. "How do you know if you love someone?"

"You just do," he says. "You should tell him you love him. I never got the chance to."

At that admission he closes his sleeping bag. Shutting his eyes, he thinks about Zipper's advice. Do I love Tinik? His heart aches at the thought of the trip ending and never seeing her again.

Can anyone love in Krevax? Zipper did, even with the risk of arrest, he chose love.

After hours of racing thoughts, he falls into an uncomfortable sleep. A woman with dark curly red hair reaches towards him, her beautiful face contorted with fear as she screams out in terror. A loud bang reverberates through the truck, and the walls shake violently for a full minute, waking Blackwell with a start.

"We're under attack!" Tinik's voice rings out over the intercom.

Bolting out of his sleeping bag, Blackwell leaps down the stairs, Zipper and Rocket following quickly behind. They rush into the driving pit where everyone is puzzled by the unexpected scene. Gunner is shooting at a smaller truck just in view, as Tinik steers them backwards. He looks half-crazed as he holds down the trigger to the gun, releasing a stream of bullets. The other truck is moving closer, and fast, as Tinik struggles with being in reverse.

"Don't fire!" Zipper yells at Gunner. "You'll make it worse!"

Another blast hits the side of the truck, causing the walls to shake.

"Hit the gas!" Zipper barks at Tinik. "We can outrun them."

Tinik jams her foot on the gas and twists the wheel, putting the truck back in drive as she punches it forward. Blackwell holds a pipe in the wall to steady himself as the truck springs over the rocks. Crouching beside Tinik, Zipper guides her through the larger boulders, gripping onto the seat to stay upright. The other truck slowly recedes in the distance. Gunner grips the smoking gun as he stares out the window, his angry expression covered in a slick sweat.

"Where's Pickles?" Zipper asks.

"I'll find him." Blackwell heads into the kitchen where he sees bullet holes in Gertie's side. "Pickles!" Oh no.

The kitchen is empty, and he presses the door to open the bathroom. Inside, Pickles is cowering in the corner. Blackwell walks over to him and leans down.

"Are you hurt?" he asks.

Pickles shakes his head, no. Wiping the tears off the younkin's cheeks, Blackwell was hit by a wave of sympathy which surprised him, as he had always felt disgusted by emotions before. He's so little. Of course he cried. He tries to think back to a time he had cried as a younkin, and the nightmare flashes in his mind.

Could that be a memory?

He helps Pickles stand, feeling confused by the question spinning in his thoughts. He never considered his nightmares may have been real.

"It's safe now," Blackwell says, leading Pickles into the driving pit.

Upon seeing the younkin, Zipper breathes a sigh of relief. Blackwell gives him a small smile. He really does care, doesn't he. At the lookout station, Gunner has refocused his attention on the binoculars. Across from him Tinik is silently driving, a pained expression on her face. Rocket stands to the side, keeping out of the way.

"Tinik, realign to the map. I don't think we'll see that truck again," Zipper says. "Each gang has their own route." She turns the steering wheel, slowly this time.

"Do you think we'll run into another?" Tinik asks.

"Doubt it," Zipper says. "I'm surprised we ran into that one. They have their own mining location, too. Just bad luck." He glances over at the lookout seat. "Gunner, aren't you supposed to be driving?"

"Tinik didn't have the backbone to use the gun," Gunner growls. Tinik is silent.

"In the future, if you see a rival gang, always try to outrun them first. Violence is a last resort." Blackwell looks at Rocket, who averts his eyes.

"Green," Tinik says, even though her voice is tense.

"It's only an hour until the shift switch. Let's just call it now, Gunner, Tinik, go get some sleep." Zipper guides Pickles out of the driving pit, ignoring Gunner's anger.

Tinik slows down the truck, puts it in brake, and quickly slides from the seat. Rocket climbs in, puts the truck into drive, and immediately moves forward. Blackwell tries to get Tinik's attention, to check if she's okay, but she has already disappeared into the kitchen.

Defeated, he walks toward the lookout seat as Gunner stands and aggressively steps into him, hitting his chest with a shoulder. Ignoring the pain, he sits down and picks up the binoculars. His eyes look extra buggy today. I hope he's not angry with Tinik. He could hurt her. I wish I was stronger than him. Sighing, he looks through the binoculars and out at the endless haze. Let's just get this trip over with. He feels Rocket staring at him. What does he want?

"Thank you for not saying anything," Rocket whispers.

"You should have said something," Blackwell says, lowering the binoculars.

"I know." Rocket looks down.

"Why didn't you then?" Blackwell asks.

"You know I'm from the Recycling District, right?"

"Yes."

"I know what happens to the powerless in this world," Rocket says.

"You don't seem powerless to me?"

"Not anymore." Rocket glances up at him. "But I'll never risk being in that position again. You don't have to understand that."

"If we all fought Gunner, we would win," Blackwell says. Rocket laughs.

"We both know Zipper will not get involved, he's a pacifist." He shakes his head. "And you think Tinik and Pickles could help? Combined, they probably weigh less than one of his legs."

"So, you're scared of him, then?" Blackwell states matter-of-factly. He's probably right to be afraid of him.

"I'm not afraid, but I won't risk him coming after me, either." Shit. He's not wrong, he's just a prick. Blackwell sighs.

"So if it comes down to it, I'm on my own then."

"It won't get that far. We might even get to the mine this shift," Rocket says, smiling assuringly. "We'll all be back in Krevax soon enough."

"Right," Blackwell says.

No way to know if we're still going northwest, but better than nothing. I doubt the Tzar will consider the job a success, though. I'll probably have to go on another one of these trips. Maybe I can find something useful at the mine? Like an actual fucking map.

"What district are you from?" Rocket asks.

"Manufacturing."

"Mm, I used to steal a lot from that district, back when I was using rochaodil," Rocket says with a laugh. "They have some interesting stuff there."

"I suppose, but mostly it's just Lablinx junk." Blackwell shrugs his shoulders. "Weapons, medical gear, agricultural equipment, construction supplies, plastic and electronic gadgets, dollar store trash, clothes, soap, makeup, tubes of paste—it's all made by Lablinx Co."

"This was something else," Rocket says mysteriously. "I had this friend from the Manufacturing District who showed me this one building. It had high fences with barbed wire and no doors or windows."

"I know that building, it's a weapons warehouse."

"No, it isn't," Rocket whispers.

"How would you know?"

"Because I broke in," Rocket says, smiling knowingly.

"No, you didn't." Blackwell rolls his eyes. "You would be recycled for that."

"I didn't get caught."

"Fine." Blackwell grins. "What did you find?"

He looks back out at the orange haze, convinced Rocket is lying.

"I was a lot thinner back then. I broke a small grate and shimmied in through an air duct," Rocket says, as he taps on the brake to go around a boulder. "I thought I would find guns, or something like that, stuff I could sell, but it was all products I had never seen before."

"What do you mean?" Blackwell lowers the binoculars.

"I mean literal shelves of products that they don't sell anywhere in Krevax!"

"Come on," Blackwell says, looking through the binoculars again.

"I'm serious," Rocket says. "I think it was going to the Orbs."

"You're saying the Orbs have their own products?"

"Yes!" Rocket nods excitedly. "Mostly food, and none of it was in plastic tubes."

"What was it then?" Blackwell asks, intrigued.

"Boxes, shelves of all different boxes. I tried one called Dreamios. Inside were two rows of sugary circles with some kind of white sugary paste in the centre."

"Hmm." Blackwell tilts his head forward. "What else did you see?"

"I didn't get to look through everything, as I didn't want to get caught, but there was a shelf of 'Wildebeest Jerky' that I'll never forget."

"Wildebeest Jerky?"

"Yes, it had a picture of this strange creature on it, standing in a large, open green space with bright yellow lights shining down."

"That's weird," Blackwell says.

"I know." Rocket looks over at him. "After I saw that, well, I always just thought that creature must live somewhere on the surface, but this looks nothing like the image in the picture." He shakes his head. "I don't know. It's confusing." Blackwell feels uneasy. He appears to be telling the truth. It would be a very elaborate and pointless lie to tell.

"It seems like they have some kind of meat source, then?"

"Exactly, but what?" Rocket asks, shaking his head.

"Could be bugs," Blackwell says, his eyebrows raising for a moment and then scrunching down. "Why are you telling me this?"

"I don't know." Rocket shrugs his shoulders. "I never trusted anyone enough to tell them before. I don't want trouble."

"But you trust me?"

"Yes." Rocket nods. "You keep secrets. Besides, there's no one else to talk to on this trip."

Blackwell looks back at him feeling grateful. I guess not everyone hates me, in fact, maybe only Gunner hates me.

"Well, thanks for telling me," he says, smiling. "It's freaking me out, but I'm glad you shared."

"It is freaky, isn't it?" Rocket chuckles.

Still smiling, Blackwell looks back through the binoculars.

42 | RED SUN
ROCKET

Rocket stares out at the rapidly changing scenery. Where boulders had once been, strange bars of jagged black metal stick out of the ground, like bones from a ribcage. The orange dust, which has morphed into dark red sand, moves like waves with the gale. A high whining sound in the wind makes the hairs stand on the back of his neck. The eerie feeling grows with each second and he grips the steering wheel harder.

"Do you feel like we shouldn't be here?" Rocket asks nervously. Khan lowers the binoculars, giving him a serious look.

"There's something about this place." Khan shakes his head and stares back through the binoculars. "Hopefully, we'll get through it quickly."

Rocket looks down at the map. The tiny icon of the truck looks to be almost over the top of the blinking orange dot. Outside, the rows of growing jagged bars appear to be pulling them into an expansive spiral. How do I get out of here?

He can't help but hold his breath in fear as the bars get

bigger with each passing minute. The pit in his stomach grows heavier as he looks up at the towering structures.

What is this place? He closes his eyes a moment, taking a slow breath. We shouldn't be here. I know it. Without warning, the map emits a loud beep. Jumping in his seat, he looks down; the once blinking orange dot has turned green and has stopped flashing.

"The map," Rocket says, slowing down the truck, but not stopping.

"I don't understand, this is where the mine is?" Khan stands. "I'll get Zipper."

Rocket nods as fear tingles the back of his neck and shoots down his spine. Zipper walks into the driving pit, ahead of Khan, a relaxed smile on his face.

"Good job you two, this is it," he says. "You can stop now."

"What about surface men?"

"No need to worry, they seem to be afraid of this place," Zipper says.

Rocket feels the blood drain from his face. The surface men are afraid of this place.

What's here then? He stops the truck and turns off the engine, but doesn't move from his seat; ready to punch forward. Above, even the sun looks red, as though painted with blood.

"I'll go wake the others." Zipper leaves the driving pit.

Khan and Rocket stare out at the spiralling rows of metal bars, so thick now, even Gertie wouldn't fit through.

"I don't want to go out there," Rocket whispers, "do you?"

"No way," Khan says, "but we don't have a choice."

"Hurry, you two," Zipper calls from the kitchen.

Reluctantly leaving their seats, they find everyone standing in a semi-circle around a box of gas masks, one already on Tinik's face.

"Here," Zipper says, handing a mask each to Rocket and Khan, "we all need to wear one of these."

Once everyone is masked, Zipper presses the button to the ramp and an unexpected heat floods in. Holding out some kind of beeping device, he leads them outside and into an intense wind. A low whining sound rings out from the metal bars. Panic grows in Rocket's chest, but he ignores the urge to run back to the truck, continuing to trudge forward through the blowing sand.

The beeping device leads them to a man-made tunnel, nearly half an hour's walk from the truck. Once a few feet into the tunnel, a thick metal door shuts automatically and they find themselves thrust into darkness. Another door opens ahead of them and the room fills with an orange glow. A tall, muscular man with mousy brown hair comes bounding into the room.

"Pickles!?"

"Yes!" Pickles shouts, pulling off his mask as he runs towards the man's outstretched arms. Rocket takes an uncomfortable step back as they embrace in a hug. They know each other?

"I'm so glad you're finally here!" Beaming, the man turns towards Zipper and shakes his hand. "Thank you."

"Of course," Zipper says, smiling. "I'm glad I could help.

"Welcome everyone, I'm Ritter." He greets the group. "I'll show you to the loading dock where we'll grab the crates of nostaliem."

"How do you know each other?" Tinik asks, his voice muffled through the mask.

"Pickles is my son," Ritter says.

"What do you mean your son?"

"Have you ever tried nostaliem?"

"No." Tinik shakes his head.

"Well, change that," he says, "nostaliem knows the secrets of your blood."

Zipper nods knowingly beside him. No way I'm trying another drug. I don't care about finding long-lost relatives. What does it matter in Krevax who you're related to?

"For now, though, let's sort out these crates," Ritter says, as he leads the group into a room with windows overlooking the mine.

Below, floating orange orbs light up the vast heaps of black powder. Around the piles, dozens of men in metal bulldozers funnel the nostaliem into industrial-sized containers.

"Do all Zorax members have to work at the mine?" Rocket asks. I hope I can skip this part. It seems horrible.

"Anyone in Zorax who wants to become a crew leader has to do 12 months in drug production. I started out with rochaodil and they moved me here once nostaliem was discovered." Ritter opens the door to the mine. "You all should put your masks back on now."

Rocket hastily puts his mask on, but the strangely appealing smell of decay has already hit his nose. For a minute his head spins, but he doesn't lose sight of the mine. Ritter leads them down a winding stairwell as the buzz of the machines make his ears ring.

"Nostaliem is a cool substance," Ritter says, "but if you take too much, people seem to lose their minds."

They move through the hive of activity to another door which opens to a room filled with crates of nostaliem.

"Don't worry, you won't have to carry anything up those stairs." Ritter smiles as he shuts the door behind them. "We have a separate exit on the loading dock for that purpose." Leaning down, Khan examines the crates.

"I try to stay out of the mine." He laughs. "It's too bloody loud in there."

"How did Zorax find this place?" Khan asks, still kneeling.

"I actually don't know," Ritter says. "When I started, there were rumours that surface men traded the location of the mine for a crate of gold medallions, but that's ridiculous."

"Why do you want to know?" Gunner shouts threateningly, staring at Khan, his face hidden by the mask.

"It's interesting," Khan says and stands. Ritter presses a green button, and the elevator moves up, revealing the red sky above. After a slow incline, the elevator stops at the sand-covered surface.

"Let's go!" Ritter picks up one of the heavy plastic crates.

Pickles tries to pick up a crate, but he can't lift it. Gunner steps towards him and kicks him in the ribs. Ritter drops his crate leaps back towards Gunner and shoves him to the ground.

"Don't touch my son!" he yells, pressing a gun to Gunner's head, his voice muffled by his mask.

"I won't," Gunner says in shock, his hands in the air.

Standing slowly, Ritter continues to point the gun.

"Go, now," he says.

Rocket holds his breath, waiting for a reaction. Gunner stands, picks up a crate and walks toward the truck. Putting the gun down, Ritter guides Pickles to the elevator. Rocket picks up a crate and begins trudging through the sand, following Gunner and Zipper. They walk a full thirty minutes before they can see the outline of Gertie through the red sand, and then it's another painful fifteen minutes before they're finally standing outside the ramp. Rocket slumps down beside the crate, exhausted. Zipper waits for Khan and Tinik, and then, opening the ramp, they all stomp onto the truck with their crates.

Once inside, everyone falls to the ground as Zipper shuts the door. Taking off his mask, Rocket wipes away perspiration from his mouth and sits silently in a pool of his own sweat, breathing too heavily to talk.

"You never get used to that," Zipper finally whispers.

"Where's Pickles?" Tinik asks, still wearing his mask.

"Before I forget, we should grab the crates of paste," Zipper says, ignoring Tinik's question. He leans over and unlocks a secret compartment under the kitchen table.

"What!?" Gunner shouts. "You told me we didn't have any extra paste! I'm starving. I only got one tube of paste a day and this has been here the whole time!"

"One tube of paste is enough to get by on. Our first responsibility is to ensure there is a steady paste supply coming into the mine," Zipper says, glaring.

With a roaring scream, Gunner rips off his mask and throws it against the wall.

"I won't take those!"

"Fine, the rest of us will manage." Zipper hands a crate to Khan, who takes it and prepares to go back out.

Tinik takes a crate and stands behind Khan. Avoiding Gunner's stare, Rocket leans over and picks up a crate.

"Fuck this, I'm done," Gunner says, beads of sweat rolling down his face as he turns towards the stairs.

"Are you serious?" Zipper shouts irately through his mask. Ignoring him, Gunner runs up to the sleeping quarters.

"Ready?" Zipper asks the rest of the crew.

Everyone else stands in silence as he presses the button to lower the ramp. Red sand blows into the truck as they plod into the heat, each holding a crate of paste.

Once Rocket reaches the elevator, he drops the paste and picks up a crate of nostaliem, slowly turning back towards the truck. This time Ritter joins them, but Pickles is nowhere to be seen.

The hair on Rocket's arms stands each time he walks past

one of the whining metal rods. With fear building, he tries to focus on his breathing, but that is difficult with the gas mask. When he arrives back at the truck he waits for Zipper to open the ramp and once everyone is there they climb back inside.

Ripping off the mask, he sits quietly for a few forgiving minutes, until Zipper stands signalling the end of the break. He puts his mask on as the ramp opens back up to the heat. Picking up a crate of paste, he walks out into the terrifying landscape, keeping pace with Zipper and Khan. Far ahead already is Ritter. It's too bad Ritter isn't coming back to Krevax with us, he's as big as Gunner.

Rocket watches Ritter put down his crate and jog back towards the truck with a crate of nostaliem. Dropping his own crate of paste, he picks up a crate of nostaliem and turns slowly back towards the truck. On his way back, he passes the others and then sits on the red sand beside Ritter. Zipper opens the ramp when Tinik gets within a few feet of the truck. Shuffling up the ramp, he lies down beside the crates. With the mask off, Rocket takes a full breath of the filtered air.

"This is the last trip," Zipper says, as he puts his mask back on.

Feeling exhausted, he picks up the final crate of paste and struggles down the ramp, watching Ritter effortlessly move through the sand ahead of everyone.

Stopping for a moment to catch his breath, he feels sweat roll down his skin behind the mask. Ritter is so far ahead now, he can't even see him anymore. Glancing back, he sees Tinik has only made it a few feet from the truck. Fucking Gunner. He should be helping.

Pressing painfully forward, he continues trudging until he can finally see Ritter again, this time moving towards him with a crate of nostaliem. The wind grows stronger, pushing against his side, forcing him to lean into it to keep upright.

Is Tinik still standing? Looking back, he can see Tinik heading towards the truck with a crate of nostaliem. Ritter has taken his crate of paste and is marching back towards Rocket. Good thing Gunner isn't here to see that. The whining sound rings out louder. Rocket moves forward hoping Ritter won't pass him again. Finally at the elevator, he drops his crate of paste and picks up his last crate of nostaliem. Ritter passes him on the way back.

Zipper opens the ramp for the last time and they all crawl up it like slugs. Once the ramp is shut, they lie there, unable to move. Slowly standing, Zipper unlocks one of the cupboards and hands out hydration gels and strawberry cheesecake tubes.

"I've been saving these," he says, smiling.

Opening the hydration gel, Rocket drinks the entire tube in one swig. It's not enough to satiate him, but it makes the thirst bearable. The sweetness of the tube of strawberry cheesecake makes the pain in his muscles briefly melt away.

Ritter takes off his mask and drinks a hydration gel tube. "Are you going to get by without Pickles?" he asks.

"We'll be fine," Zipper says.

"Wait!" Tinik pulls off his mask, revealing a bruised eye. "Where's Pickles?"

"Pickles is staying with me," Ritter says. Tinik looks at Ritter with a strange expression Rocket can't decipher.

"Take good care of him," Tinik says. Ritter nods. Zipper puts on his mask to let Ritter leave.

"Thank you for bringing me my son," Ritter says. "Have a safe trek home."

The ramp opens and Ritter waves goodbye. Zipper pulls out the storage box and everyone throws their gas mask in.

Leaning down, he picks up Gunner's abandoned mask, placing it on the top of the heap.

43 | REUNITED

CARR

Sitting across from the hotel bed, Carr watches his sister sleep, mentally preparing himself for their talk. *Everything will be okay. It will be a shock, but I can introduce things slowly.* He nervously glances down at his watch without registering the time. *The most important thing is that she doesn't learn about the farm until I've had time to educate her.*

Looking down again he notices the number 1:02 P.M. in white text. *The effects should have worn off by now.* He double checks his dentures are secured before walking over and gently touching her shoulder.

"Scarlett," he whispers, making her stir slightly.

"Scarlett," he says again, this time louder. She opens her eyes and looks up at him.

"Where am I?" she asks, slowly sitting up, eyes darting around the cream-coloured room.

"I've brought you to the Orbs."

"The Orbs," she whispers, as she closes her eyes, cupping her face in her hands.

"I'm your brother," Carr says, sitting down on the bed beside her. "You were never supposed to be in Krevax."

"My brother?" she asks, looking up at him confused.

"Yes, our mother was trapped in Krevax as a generator." Standing, he turns and opens the curtains, revealing large pine trees outside the window.

"You see," he says, gesturing at the trees. "I rescued you. The Orbs are your rightful home." Still in her decorative metal, she stands and looks out the window.

"You need to change your clothes," he says, and then opening a drawer, picks up a folded yellow dress with white daisies.

Staring at it a moment, as though undecided, she tentatively removes her metal plates and then takes the dress. Holding it in front of her with a disturbed expression, she unzipped it and pulled it over her head.

"Here." Carr reaches forward. "I can zip it for you."

She angles her back towards him and he zips the dress up.

"You also need to take the ribbons out of your hair." Carr picks up a plastic comb from the bedside table and hands it to her.

Quickly removing the ribbons, she brushes her dark red hair until it looks long and frizzy.

"What do you think of Krevax?" he asks.

Scarlett turns to look at him, placing the comb on the bedside table. Carr inhales sharply. In the daisy dress and with her hair down, she looks just like their mother, albeit with slightly less coiffed curls.

"Krevax is a tough place," she says, without conveying any emotion.

"Yes," Carr says, "it's a terrible place." She doesn't respond, but watched him silently. "You will live here in the Orbs now."

"What will I do here?" she asks, her voice cracking.

"I will enrol you in school to become a wife," Carr says, smiling. "I've already reached out to the right people to get your papers in order."

"What's a wife?"

"You will marry a man here in the Orbs and take care of him."

"Like a peon?" she asks, her shoulders tensed.

"No." Carr shakes his head. "More like a peon, a doxy and a generator combined."

"I can't be a generator." She shakes her head. "Doxies are sterilized."

"Yes, that's true," Carr says, sitting back down on the bed, "but I may be able to reverse that."

"Reverse it?" she whispers to herself. Clicking on his watch, he scrolls down through his contact list and taps on the number for the doctor.

Ring.

"Doctor Privok, it's General Carr. I have something private to take care of."

"An abortion?" the doctor asks.

"No, not that, a sterilization reversal."

"I see," he says in a surprised squeal.

"Time is a matter," Carr states. "Would I be able to bring her in now?" The man inhales sharply.

"Yes, I will set up a team immediately."

"Thank you, doctor."

"Of course, general." Carr clicks off the call.

"Are you ready?" he asks, stepping towards the door.

"I don't know?" she says, shaking her head. "I've never considered being a generator. This is all…" She stares out the window at the trees, lost in thought.

"It's very important that your fertility is intact." Carr grabs her hand. "Otherwise the only option will be the cleaner track."

"Then I would be a peon?"

"Yes." He nods.

"I'll do the surgery," she whispers.

Good, first step done. This is going to be fine. Feeling relieved, he leads her out of the room to an elevator at the end of the hallway. Carr pushes the call button, his eyes locked on his sister. Her face is expressionless as she wraps her arms around her ribs. What is she thinking?

The doors open and they step into the elevator.

"There's something else," Carr says.

"What?" She looks up at him.

"Women here are not given a name, so no one should know you have one."

"I'm not Scarlett anymore?"

"Not anymore." Carr watches her expression, but her face is unrevealing, leaving him disappointed.

The doors slide open and they walk into a fancy foyer with a grand piano and gold chandelier. Televisions in each corner of the room play Orb News, as Carr leads the way to the front desk. An attendant nods in acknowledgment as they get to the counter.

"I need a cab," Carr says, and the attendant picks up the phone. A commercial for Chef's Cut–Sweet Smoked Jerky plays on all the screens.

"You shouldn't watch that," Carr says, grabbing Scarlett's hand. "There's still things I need to explain about the Orbs."

"What's Wildebeest jerky?" she asks. Carr takes a slow breath.

"I'll explain after the surgery."

"Sir," the attendant says, "your cab is waiting outside."

"Thank you." He leads Scarlett to the bright orange cab.

"Where to?" the driver asks.

"Rutherford Hospital," Carr says as he holds the door open for her to climb in.

She slides in and he sits down beside her, shutting the door. The cab takes off down the road and he watches his sister staring awestruck at the sky. Everything's going to be okay. He feels momentarily relieved and then nervously fiddles with his wedding band. I'm sure she'll come to understand our way of life. Once she's acclimatized, I'll introduce her to Wife Carr as a distant cousin.

He looks up at the fluffy clouds. It really is beautiful here. I should have brought Charlie here when I had the chance. I don't know what I was thinking with this undercover assignment. I'll find him soon. The cab stops in front of the hospital.

"It's twenty-four dollars," the cab driver says.

Carr holds out his watch to be scanned, and then having paid, opens the car door and climbs out.

"Dollars?" his sister asks, as she climbs out beside him. "Not credits."

"Money is different here." He leads her to the hospital entrance. "You don't need to worry though, I'll always be here to take care of you."

A circular room with a white front desk greets them. An attendant looks up as they get to the glass barrier.

"How can I help you, sir?"

"I have a patient for Doctor Privok," Carr says.

"Of course." The man nods. "Room seven, on the second floor."

Carr guides Scarlett to the ramp behind the lobby desk, which winds up to the second floor and opens to a long hallway.

"General Carr!" Doctor Privok greets them from behind a surgical mask. "It's good to see you again." The men shake hands like old friends.

"You as well," Carr says, smiling.

"You must be our patient," the doctor says, staring at Scarlett.

"Yes," she says and the doctor waves them forward, leading them to room seven.

"This is Lamb. He'll be your anaesthesiologist. Barker is our healer for the operation, and Adesina will assist me." She nods at the three men in white face masks and scrubs.

"Go behind that sheet and undress," Privok says, pointing to a blue curtain at the side of the room. "There's a hospital gown for you on the chair."

Exhaling slowly, Carr watches as she disappears behind the curtain. "You can wait downstairs, if you prefer?"

"In a minute," he says. The doctor nods in acceptance. Scarlett walks out from behind the curtain wearing the beige hospital gown.

"Excellent, lie down now, dear." She climbs onto the metal table and lies down.

"Count back from ten." The anaesthesiologist places a mask over her face.

Carr watches her eyes close, a stream of tears flowing down her cheeks. Why is she upset? Tomorrow will be better. It must be the shock from escaping Krevax.

"She's out," the anaesthesiologist says.

"Thank you, Lamb." Privok finishes scrubbing his hands and puts on gloves.

"Scalpel." Adesina hands him the blade.

Turning away, Carr opens the door, but then glances back as the doctor cuts into his sister's flesh. This better work. Taking out the dentures, he puts them in his pocket and walks down the hallway to a waiting room. A few other people are already there, praying for their loved ones. Sitting down in a blue fabric chair, he closes his eyes, just for a second.

Charlie's face stares at him, his forehead protruding

forward, expanding until the entire room is filled with skin. Carr runs down a long tunnel that doesn't lead anywhere. A gigantic hand moves towards him, stretching to grab him. He runs as fast as he can, but the hand is too quick. He gasps as he's locked in the grip of giant fingers and pulled from the tunnel.

The room is spinning and Charlie's maniacal laughter is strangely slow motion. The giant opens his mouth and crushes Carr's back with its teeth, ripping away a chunk of the skin. Carr's scream pierces through the laughter, and then the pain that just a moment ago felt unbearable, disappears.

Now Carr stares at himself screaming in the giant hand, his hand, and watches as his face flashes from protruding, to normal, to protruding. Suddenly, Charlie's eyes look out of his, and terrified, he recoils.

Carr jolts awake, soaked in sweat, and takes a deep breath. Damn nightmares. Looking around the waiting room, he's relieved it's empty, embarrassed by his exposure. He stands and walks into a small bathroom. Get it together. He rinses his face with cold water and steps back out.

"General Carr, she's up," the doctor walks over.

"How did it go?"

"Perfectly," he says. "I'd say she'd be ready to make a baby by the end of the week."

"Thank you," he says, following the doctor down the hallway to a small hospital room.

The doctor opens the door for him and leaves. His sister is watching the screen above the bed.

"How are you doing?" Carr asks.

"What do they mean when they say there's a disease spreading in Krevax?" Carr walks over and clicks the TV off.

"I'll explain everything soon." He holds her hand. "Right now you need time to recover."

"What would you like for your meal, dear?" A healer walks in pushing a cart with stacks of plastic-wrapped trays. "We have meatloaf or steak."

Clearly confused, she stares at the man and then whispers something to herself, but Carr can't make it out.

"She'll have the meatloaf, thank you," he says, taking a tray from the cart. The healer leaves, and he places the tray beside the bed. "Are you hungry?"

"They called Krevax a farm," she half-shouts, distress creeping into her face. Oh no. I can still fix this.

"Yes, well, that's where the fruits and vegetables are grown," Carr says.

"What is this?" With wide eyes, she stares at the meatloaf, recoiling from the tray.

"It's food," Carr says, crossing his fingers behind his back.

"Your teeth!" Gasping, she stares up at him. "Why are they sharp?"

Shit. He smacks his hand across his mouth. I forgot the dentures.

"It's a sign of status in the Orbs," Carr states, trying to stay calm.

Leaning forward examining the meatloaf, her face pales. "Are you eating Krevaxers?" Damn it all. There's no going back now.

"Hush, sweetheart." Carr sits down beside her, shaking his head. "Krevaxers aren't like us, they're animals."

"No, they're not!" she yells. "You're eating us!" She throws the tray and attempts to stand.

"Help!" Carr calls into the hallway as she struggles to her feet. Doctor Privok walks in.

"Is everything okay?" he asks with a startled voice.

"No!" she screams, backing into the wall.

"I think she's having some kind of breakdown," Carr says. "Do you have something to relax her?"

"Of course." The doctor quickly opens a drawer, takes out a needle and walks towards her, cornering her. "Don't worry, dear, this will help."

"I'm not having a breakdown!" she yells. "Krevax is full of people!"

The doctor laughs and stabs her with the needle, making her immediately fall back into the bed.

"It's always hard when a woman comes across level-six material," he says, smiling. "I'm sure once she understands they're more like pigs than us, she'll be okay." Carr nods. Fuck.

44 | THIEF

PRATT

THE SMELL OF ARTIFICIAL COFFEE WAFTS THROUGH THE crowded cafe as Pratt fidgets with a bottle of vodka in his pocket. Beside him a man impatiently taps on the counter. Sighing, he stares at the man, wanting the irritating noise to stop.

Ring.

Ring. He taps on his tracker, stepping closer to the wall to hear better.

"Pratt here."

"It's Lewis," the captain pauses, his voice strained. *"Remi was driven off the road."*

"Oh!" Pratt says, trying to convey concern. With his anger issues, he probably provoked it.

"I want you to go home and lie low. I believe Zorax is sending a message."

"Of course, sir." No way Zorax cares about Remi.

"If you have time, go visit your partner, he's in rough shape."

"Where?"

"Saintly Angelic Hospital, second floor, room 23."

"I will." Pratt clicks off the call.

"Not," he adds to himself. *I wonder if his peon got away? I hope she did.*

"Pratt." The attendant calls, placing a coffee on the counter.

He steps over and picks up the cup, smirking at the man still tapping his finger. Turning away from the waiting people, he cracks open the vodka and discreetly pours it in his coffee.

Here's to you, Remi! He lifts the cup in celebration and takes a sip. *May you rot in hell.* At the exit he dumps the empty bottle in the garbage and walks out into the Enforcement District. Clicking on his tracker, he taps on a picture of Serie.

Ring.

"Hello," Serie says.

"I've got the afternoon off!" he shouts exuberantly. "Can you hang out?"

"Sure!"

"See you soon," he says through a swig of coffee and climbs on his bike.

I can't believe it! Remi's gone and I get the rest of the day off. Gulping down his drink, he squishes the cup and tosses it in the bin. Driving through the black towers back to his apartment, he feels completely at peace.

"Afternoon, sir," the attendant says, as he opens the door.

Nodding cheerfully back, Pratt takes the elevator up to the third floor and walks to the door of his messy apartment.

"Video games?" Serie asks, grinning as she moves her grey-streaked dirty blonde hair behind her pink-tinged ears.

"Yep," Pratt says, taking off his shoes.

"I'm thinking, *Gold Thieves*, which is a train robbers game, or *Super Speed 12*, which is obviously going to be the greatest racing game of all time, because *Super Speed 11* was awesome." Serie steps forward excitedly, rocking on her heels. "Notice anything interesting about those choices?"

"Oh I know!" Pratt laughs. "You might be the only thief who brags to a red stripe about stealing though."

She does a goofy twirl and then sits down on the orange polka-dot couch.

"Well, they shouldn't make it so easy," she says, her upturned eyes dancing mischievously. "You should see what some of the other hackers brag about on the community board! There's one guy on there who claims he created counterfeit credits."

"I could use those," he says as he picks up a controller. "Gold Thieves?"

Nodding, she clicks on the game. The screen opens to a large golden field with a track running through it. A horn calls out, and an animated train chugs in the distance. They choose through a rag-tag team of characters and the game begins.

"How do you jump on the train?" Pratt asks, as his character, 'Cowboy Cooper,' runs towards the track.

"I think you hold 'a' to jump, and 'x' to roll." Holding down the buttons, Serie's character, 'Busty Betsy,' jumps into the air and rolls forward, her red cowboy boots emitting sparks as she lands.

"Oh, shit! It's the train. Go!" Her nose scrunches as she focuses on the game.

"Oh, no!" Pratt laughs as his character jumps in front of the train instead of onto it, his cowboy hat flying into the air.

"Hah!" Serie shouts, "I'm gonna steal all the gold."

"I'll steal it from you then." His character respawns, and he jumps on the caboose. "You know… I should actually do that."

"What?" Serie asks, as Busty Betsy fills a bag with gold.

"Steal."

"Steal what?" She glances over at him, confused.

"Blackwell's classified file," he says, staring at the screen, "maybe I could steal it."

"Why? He was probably just born in the Orbs?"

"I don't think it's classified because he's from the Orbs." Cowboy Cooper grabs a handful of gold. "I think it's something else."

"Well, I don't think you'll be able to steal it," Serie says, looking over at him, "even I don't know anyone who's hacked the red stripe system." Pratt puts down the remote.

"I think I might know someone." He clicks on his tracker.

"Pratt!" Serie pauses the game. "This sounds dangerous."

"It's fine," he says, smiling. "I've known this guy since we were younkins. I've gotten him out of a few tight spots over the years." The tracker rings. "He owes me."

"Hello?"

"Rowley! It's Trevor."

"No way! Trevor, how are you?"

"Green man! How are you?"

"Nothing to complain about."

"I've got a favour to ask. Are you still connected?"

"Does crime still pay?" Rowley chuckles. *"What's down?"*

"I need access to a restricted file on the red stripe database."

"Whoa! You're talking about a recycling-level crime there!"

"Can you help?" Pratt asks. Serie stares at him, shaking her head.

"I know someone who can handle that, but we're even after this."

"Of course!" Pratt says, laughing.

"He goes by Theus. I'll call him."

"Thanks Rowley, you're the best."

"No problem! If he can do it, is there a location that works? He doesn't like to choose the meeting spot."

"Uh…" Pratt thinks for a second and then grins. "Saintly Angelic Hospital, second floor, room 23."

"*I'll text you the time when I know.*" Pratt clicks off the call.

"Whose hospital room is that?" Serie asks.

"Remi's." He looks over intently, waiting for her reaction.

"No way!" She pinches his arm playfully. "I can't believe you didn't tell me that! What happened?"

"Well, I just found out," Pratt says. "He got run off the road."

"Will he live?"

"Probably, he's built like a barrel."

"Well, I'm glad you won't have to work with that psychopath for a while at least. I can't believe you're doing this, though!"

"I have to know the truth," he says, shaking his head, "it's driving me nuts."

"I bet its something completely innocuous."

"You wanna bet?"

"Sure, I'll bet you 100 credits," she says, grinning.

"You don't have any credits!" Pratt laughs. "Otherwise you wouldn't always be spending mine."

"You don't need credits when you know you're going to win!"

"Fine, 100 credits, but if I win, you have to clean there, and there," he says, pointing at messes in their apartment, "and there, and there." Serie rolls her eyes.

"I don't think you should do this," she says seriously. "It isn't worth it."

"It's going to be fine." He picks up the controller. "You're worrying for nothing."

"Pratt, even your buddy called it recycling-worthy."

"I know, but I'm a red stripe. Who would stop me?"

"I don't know." She stares at him. "How about another red stripe?"

"Nonsense," he says, smiling. "I'm a detective. I'll just say I was undercover."

"You have an answer for everything," she growls angrily.

"After this, I'll let it go, I promise."

"I hope that's true."

"Don't you think it's interesting?" Pratt stares intensely. "Someone born outside Krevax?"

"Yes, it's interesting, but not worth dying over."

"I agree, but I'm not planning on dying," he says, chuckling. "Besides, the meeting might not even happen."

"I hope it doesn't." Serie sighs. Pratt's tracker beeps and he reads the text. It's from Rowley, telling him to meet up with Theus tomorrow.

"It's him, isn't it?"

"Yeah." He smiles. "I promise I'll be careful."

"Okay," she says defeatedly. Pratt clicks play on the video game and the train horn calls out. I'm finally going to find out the truth.

45 | MULTI-VISION

TINIK

Pushing the button for the bathroom, Tinik nervously flashes a look back at Rocket and Zipper. They are focused on moving the crates of nostaliem into the compartment below the table. Gunner is still nowhere to be seen. Fuck it. I have to shower. I can't stand another moment being this disgusting.

Closing the door, she quickly rips off her clothes and stands under the shower, which sprays a disappointing mist. Wiping her dusty, sweat-caked face, she winces when going over her bruised eye. Glancing back at the door, she pumps liquid soap into her hand and scrubs her body. In the mist, the soap is slow to rinse away. The door to the bathroom slides open and she twists, hiding her body.

"Hurry! Rocket and Zipper are right behind me," Blackwell says, his voice facing away from her as he shuts the door.

"Thanks!" She runs towards her dirty clothes, shakes them and dresses, the fabric sticking uncomfortably to her wet skin.

"What happened to your eye?" Blackwell asks in a whisper.

"It doesn't matter." Tinik shakes her still dripping head as the door opens.

Rocket and Zipper walk in and start undressing and she slides by them out into the kitchen. Holy Mary! That was close. Standing at the edge of the table, she looks down into the open compartment with the nostaliem. This is my chance! I need to try it. If what Ritter says is true, I could find all my younkins. The bathroom door opens and Blackwell walks out, still dusty.

"Don't you need to shower?"

"I'll shower later." He walks towards her, looking morose. "Are you okay?"

Tinik takes a quick inhale. "I need to tell you something." He looks at her earnestly.

"I joined Zorax so I could get my baby back," she says.

"Your baby?"

"Yes." Tinik looks down. "I was a generator."

Blackwell nods slowly.

"Usually they don't let you see the baby," she whispers.

"They make you trade?" Blackwell asks in shock.

"Yes, that way the bond isn't as strong." She looks down at the ground. "My last baby, though, arrived five weeks early. They don't take premature babies away from the biological generator because the death rate is too high." She pushes on her eyelids before any tears can fall.

"What happened?"

"Before that moment, I'd never gotten to hold my baby before." She inhales sharply. "I tried to take her."

Blackwell stares at her, his eyes wide and then slowly nods.

"I couldn't find enough food to eat, so I put her back."

"I'm sorry," he says, gripping her shoulders.

"There's more." She looks up at him. "I have two older boys." She exhales slowly, shaking her head. "I need to find them."

"How can I help?" Blackwell asks.

"I want to try nostaliem." She stares intensely. "If Ritter can find his son using nostaliem, then I can find my younkins."

"Okay," Blackwell says. "When?" Tinik looks down at the open compartment where the crates are.

"Now," she says and leans down, slowly opening a crate to keep the noise low.

She grabs a handful of black powder and puts it in her pocket. Blackwell also grabs some and puts it in his pocket. After quietly closing the crate, she leads the way up to the sleeping quarters. Gunner is shifting in his sleeping bag, but thankfully he ignores them. Tinik climbs into the bag and zips herself in, and Blackwell does the same beside her.

She collects a pinch of the powder from her pocket and inhales it. The dark room dissolves away and her mind fractures, splitting into three clear images. In each one, a younkin appears.

In the first, a boy with black curly hair and a deep brown complexion pulls her forward. He kicks a ball behind a concrete building, laughing joyfully. Zooming into the image, and into his mind, Tinik loses the edges of herself, piece by piece.

Running after the ball again, I laugh as it zooms by me.

"Leo!" Zachary runs forward. "Pass it here."

Kicking the ball, I run towards him and watch as he kicks the ball back. It bounces through my legs. Chasing after it, a truck honks, startling me as I grab the ball from the road.

"Younkins!" Trainer Pam runs out from the school, her eyes glaring at us from behind her mask.

"Get back inside, now!" I run up behind Zachary, still kicking

the ball. She picks up the ball and grabs my ear. "What did I just say?"

"Sorry," I whimper and she lets go.

I run up beside Zachary, my face burning with anger as I press my painful ear against my head. Zachary looks down at the ground, avoiding the angry stare from Trainer Pam as she opens the door. We run to the far room at the end of the hall, avoiding her.

"This is the Education District," she calls out after us, "you're too old to be acting like this."

I giggle nervously and hide behind a large couch. The peon disappears into the room of vending machines and Zachary crawls out from behind a chair.

"Want to play 'the floor is lava'?" he asks.

I nod and jump onto the couch across from him. Murray, Trevor and Garret see us from the other room and bolt over. We all fight for space on the cushions.

"Ahh! The volcano erupted! Run!" I yell, laughing.

"That's enough." Mr Vahn ushers us into a small classroom where others are already sitting. I move behind a desk as he walks to the front and starts writing on the board.

"Today we'll be learning the Krevax Anthem." He writes out the words and I lie my head down on my hands, feeling bored.

"Leo, pay attention."

"Sorry, Mr. Vahn."

"Now, together everyone, recite the following." He taps each point on the board as he sings them out.

Oh, Mary Bless Krevax, the last humans of Earth

Oh, Mary bless our bold men, and tall cities,

Thank thee light of the Natatorium

Built out of rubble and fight

Our sturdy walls and watchful tower keep us safe

Our advertisements banish the evil night

Thank thee, the red stripes watch over

Not one moment missed towards our collective positivity
Our laws cheered by every voter
Land of the strong and moral
Always let the womb of Mary guide our way
For there is no need for quarrel
And when your body grows weak, do your duty
Recycle for the greater good
And we will sing praise, as the new collective we
Oh, how we love our land of the strong and moral
"Again," the teacher calls out.

I stop singing half-way through and look down at the carpet, running my foot along the bumpy texture.

"Leo!" the teacher walks over and smacks me on the top of my head. I choke back the tears, but one falls despite my effort. "Don't you cry, younkin. How old are you?"

"Seven," I stammer. Some of the other younkins in the room giggle.

"Seven, and you still cry? I expected better of you. Go, now, back to your dormitory. There will be no dinner tonight." I quickly stand and sprint out of the room, my face hot with embarrassment.

"Bye, crybaby!" Danny calls sneeringly behind me.

In the hallway, I can feel my neck pulsing and I grab my throat in panic as the icy feeling moves down into my chest.

The image zooms out and Tinik slowly becomes herself again until she can see all three images in equal-sized segments of her mind.

This time she moves into the middle image, where a boy with blonde curls and warm brown skin sits at a table playing with a strand of his springy hair. The image expands around her and she feels her own thoughts fade away.

My stomach growls from hunger. Trainer Tara reads through the letters of the alphabet. Outside the window, men are yelling.

"G is for generator." She points at the picture of a female with a round belly.

"Joey, are you paying attention?" I look back from the dust-covered men in overalls.

"Yes, Trainer Tara," I mumble, pulling on a curl of my hair.

"Stop playing with your hair or the Education District won't take you." She stares at me angrily behind her mask. "Don't you want your caste to move up?"

I drop the strand and she looks back at the book.

"H is for Hell." She points at a picture of a scary-looking cave filled with tortured faces and fire.

I want to look away, but I keep staring, too afraid to make her angry again. She turns the page, which shows a picture of a girl in a white dress.

"I is for inferior." A loud horn beeps outside the window and I look over, picking up another piece of hair and twisting it again.

This time I chew on the end with my teeth, lost in the noise outside. Trainer Tara turns the page.

"J is for jewellery. Joey! Pay attention." I let the hair bounce out of my teeth. "Do you want me to shave your head?"

"No?" Tears well up in my eyes. She glares at me as she turns the page.

"K is for Krevax." I stare at the image of the spiralling city, holding back my sobs.

The scene zooms out and Tinik finds herself again, but before she can think about what just happened, she's zooming into the last image. As she gets closer to the small toddler with black curls and deep obsidian skin, the sliver of awareness of her own mind disappears.

The person with the covered face stares down at me. I don't know what she wants. I see a tube and I reach for it. Smack! Her hand hits mine hard. It hurts. I cry.

"No!" she shouts. "I said smile."

I don't know what that means. I just want the tube. I keep crying and reach for it again. Smack! It hurts more this time. My hand pulls back. My face feels hot.

"Everly, smile!" she says, louder. "You need to smile if you want it."

I don't know how. I cry harder and she yells again.

"Stop crying!" But I can't stop. I want the tube. I don't know what she wants me to do. She turns away and talks to someone else. "These recyclers are always the slowest to learn."

Tinik opens her eyes, finding herself back in the sleeping bag. No. The image of her three younkins were burned into her and she cries angrily, feeling their pain. *I need to get back to Krevax. They can't wait, they need me! Everly.* They called her Everly.

She exhales slowly, letting her anger melt away. *Leo, Joey, Everly. I will find my younkins. I know Leo's in the Education District and Joey is in the Manufacturing District. Where is Everly, though?*

She must be somewhere in the Education District, but she's too little to know where, so her memories can't tell me. Reaching into her pocket, she collects the last of the nostaliem and inhales the powder, hoping to find out where Everly is.

The drug takes effect, making the dark room evaporate around her. At first she sees waves in an ocean moving with the tide and then her own awareness slips away.

Pushing my toes further into the sand, the sun dances on my skin and I breathe in the sea-soaked air. My son splashes in the water and I smile, feeling at peace with this life. I picture my grandmother's kind face, hoping she can see our happiness. I remember her stories and the violence she faced at the hands of the descendants who put our ancestors in chains. I will be free for all of them, but especially for her.

"Malik, don't go too far!" I see him dip his head below the waves. Running into the icy water, I swim out to him and dive under, grabbing his toes.

"Mom!" he says in surprise. I laugh and splash him with a handful of water, the taste of the salt on my lips.

"It's deep here," I say.

"I like the enormous waves!"

"I know, but it can be dangerous." My son looks out at the horizon, wanting to go further.

"Come on, let's go get ice cream."

"Ice cream!"

"Yep! I'll race you there." I pretend to dive forward and then watch him swim safely back to the shore.

I remember my grandmother again. There was no safe shoreline for her to swim to. I look up at the sky and thank her for building one for me.

Tinik opens her eyes, tears streaming down her cheeks. The moment felt so real. Who were they? Something about them was familiar.

Whoever they were, they've been dead a long time. They were free, but they had ancestors who weren't... my ancestors too. I know what I need to do. There's no safe shoreline in Krevax. It would be better if the entire city burned.

The only option is to escape and create something new. That's what her grandmother did. I'll get my younkins and go. Fuck it, we can live in the caves with the surface people.

Tinik unzips herself, resolute in her plan, and walks over to Blackwell who's still lost in the nostaliem.

46 | FAMILY TREE
BLACKWELL

Taking a small portion of black powder from his pocket, Blackwell nervously inhales it. The room spins and then disappears, replaced by a bright surgical theatre. For a moment, he feels as though he'll puke and then his perception vanishes.

The smell of bleach stings my nose. I watch the doctors shuffle around me. One man leans over and places a mask over my face.

"Count back from ten," he says.

What if they're lying to me? No, I can trust them, right? I feel the tears flow down my face. I'm too scared to stop them from falling. He didn't even ask me if I wanted to leave! Would have I stayed? I didn't get to say goodbye to her. Kali's smile flashes in my mind. What does it even mean to be a wife? What if I get pregnant? I don't think I even want that. I could be stuck with a monster. It's one thing to deal with a bad client, but that...

What if the surgery doesn't work and I can't get pregnant? I know nothing about this place. I just want to go home. Will I still get recycled when I'm 35? I stare up at the man in the mask, feeling confused. I'm so tired. I feel cold. Am I dying? Stop. Please stop. Everything goes black.

Blackwell comes to, feeling confused and frightened. Who was that? She was from Krevax. Why was she in the Orbs?

He takes another small pinch of black powder and inhales it, hoping it will provide an answer. A large room expands out in front of him, with doxies sitting in a row, and then, once again, his thoughts melt away.

Nothing but bodies, empty vessels for angry men, beautiful animals, soulless, mindless, weak, pathetic. That's what everyone says. Objects to be used. That's what they say. What's more important than beauty when you're an object? I pinch my skin. I'm human, aren't I?

I tie a small braid from the base of my neck to my hairline. I pull the loose ends forward until it looks like a lion's mane, grinning angrily. Now I see the object. I see the beautiful animal. Men. They're just as much animals as we are. Lying to themselves like younkins. Fine. I will be an animal then. A wild animal.

Blackwell opens his eyes. Kaliann? He stifles a breath, as the intense anger he felt as her is overwhelming. The painful memories of her life as a doxy make him feel sick. How did I not know she was like me?

He closes his eyes, trying to center himself back in his own body. I didn't help her. Shame fills him. I just shoved her to the ground and ran past her. Picking up another pinch of black powder, he inhales it, wanting to forget her.

The room fades out and the scene opens to a hospital room, where a woman with long curly red hair is screaming in pain. For a moment Blackwell wonders who it is, but then he's gone.

Gripping the hospital bed arm, the pain twists my stomach and shoots out in every direction. For a moment it feels as though I might die, but I can't stop.

"Just one more push," the midwife says. "You're doing so good, Charlotte."

The burning of the contraction builds again in my back, shooting sharp blades down my legs and up my arms. I close my eyes, pushing as hard as I can, screaming uncontrollably.

"It's a boy!" The midwife places the baby on my soft stomach as the contractions disappear. Love floods through me as I stare down at him, barely believing he's real.

"Time to cut the cord, Dad." I glance up at James with tears streaming down my face.

He has the biggest grin as he cuts the cord, his fair-toned hand steady. The midwife helps me hold my son to my breast. I nurse him for a minute and then he looks up at me, melting into my arms. The doctor comes over with a needle and stabs me in the thigh. I jump at the pain, but then look down at my son's perfect puffy face. He looks like a little old man with a bewildered expression. The doctor pushes on my belly as he pulls out the placenta. I grit my teeth to get through the pain.

"What should we call him?" I whisper, watching as his belly breathes in and out.

The love I feel for him overwhelms me and I can't help but cry. I touch his perfect curly black hair with the palm of my hand. A sharp pinch shoots up my body as the doctor stitches up the tear. I hold my breath, waiting for him to finish.

"I like Travis," James says, leaning over and kissing our son.

"Travis." I touch his tiny fingers. "Travis is good." I lean in and kiss him, he smells sweet, like honey and warm milk.

"Hello, Travis, I'm your mama," I say with a sob. James laughs, kissing me on the forehead.

"Charlotte, why are you crying?" he asks, shaking his head.

"I'm so happy," I whisper. "I can't believe we made him."

Blackwell opens his eyes feeling more confused than ever. What's happening?

He grabs his empty stomach, the pain from the contractions still sharp in his mind. Where's my baby? That's not my baby.

He shakes his head. Who's Charlotte? Her red hair sticks in his mind like a shadow just out of reach, as something unknown feels so familiar about it.

What does it mean? It's just like Kaliann's hair, like the woman's from the first vision... Scarlett.

Feeling sick to his stomach, but determined to find out, he grabs the last of the powder and inhales it. The sleeping quarters disappear and he finds himself in a large, brightly lit cave. He watches as a man with brown hair and light beige complexion runs towards him and then his awareness slips away.

"Charlotte!" Robin grabs my arms.

"What is it?" I take in his sorrowful expression. "They're here, aren't they?" I whisper.

"Yes." He holds out a pistol for me to take.

"No, if we fight back, it will end in violence." I take a step towards the door.

"There's no time," Robin says, still holding the pistol, "go get Charlie ready. I'll try to slow them down."

He runs back towards the tunnels. My breath is shallow as panic climbs up my throat and I am frozen for a second. Go! Now. I turn and run. I stop outside the door and slowly open it, not wanting to scare my son. Inside I can see him sleeping, perfectly, peacefully. I walk over and pick him up.

"Mama?" he whispers, still half asleep.

"Hello, my sweet boy," I say and kiss him on one chubby cheek.

"There are some people coming. They're going to take you to the new home." I choke back my tears. "Do you remember what I said about the new home?"

"No!" he shouts and then cries.

"Charlie," I wrap him tighter in my arms. "I need you to listen to what I am telling you."

"I don't want the new home!"

"When you get there, it's very important you tell the adults that you're James Carr's son. Can you say that name for me?"

"Ja-mes." He pauses, thinking through the words, and then says, "Carr."

"Your father will come for you," I whisper, mostly to myself.

Charlie holds onto my neck, his face buried in my curls. I hear a loud bang in the distance as men's voices grow closer. No. We're not ready. He's still so little. What if he can't remember me?

"Quick, baby, it's time to get dressed." I grab his jacket, socks and boots, and throw them over his pyjamas. A banging at the door makes me jump. "I love you so much, Charlie." I kiss his cheeks. Charlie cries harder. Men run into the room and pull him out of my arms. Please! No!

"Mama!" Charlie yells as he disappears into the tunnel.

"No!" I scream. "Please, don't take him!"

I rush to grab him, but the men push me to the ground and wrap a black bag over my head. They drag me through the tunnels, gripping tight to my arms. I can hear the engines of the military's armoured trucks at the entrance. A child cries in the distance, but it isn't my son. A car door opens and the men drop me onto a seat and shut the door. I rip the bag off my head.

"James!" I sob. "Did you see Charlie? Do you have him?"

"I saw him," James says with an unfamiliar coldness, his tall frame sitting aggressively over me.

"Will you take him to the Orbs?"

"No," James says, "you wanted him here, so he will stay here."

"No! Please James, I never wanted to have him here." I look up at him pleadingly. "I only wanted you to see the truth. I always knew you would come for him."

"You didn't keep your word," James says.

"What do you mean?"

"In your letter, you made it sound like you would kill yourself." He laughs. "But here you are."

"I couldn't leave him," I whisper.

"But you could leave Travis," he says, staring angrily, "and me?"

"I knew you were safe." I turn to look out the window. "Where's Charlie? He was so scared."

"It's been almost four years, and that's all you have to say." James hits the window pane beside me.

"Where's Charlie?" I plead again.

"Where's Charlie?" James says mockingly. "Do you know how many nights Travis asked for you?"

"I tell Charlie about you and Travis every night. He's excited to meet his father and his brother."

"I'm not his father," James spits. "He's nothing to me, and Travis will never know him."

"Please," I beg, "please." I reach out to hold his hand, but he pulls away.

"That boy will be placed in Krevax," James says coldly.

"No!" I shake my head. "I won't leave without him."

James stares at me, a terrifying look in his eyes. "Do you think I'm bringing you back to the Orbs?" I look at him, confused.

"You wanted to have a baby in Krevax," James says cruelly, "now you will have all your babies in Krevax."

"What do you mean?" I whisper, terrified.

"You're going to be a generator," James says. I shake my head in disbelief. No. He's just trying to scare me. James opens the door, and a man dressed in camouflage walks over.

"Can I help you, General Carr?"

"Yes, take her," he says. "I'm done here." The man grabs my waist and drags me backwards out of the car.

"James! No!" I scream. "Don't leave Charlie here!" The door shuts.

I try to escape the military man, but he punches my stomach and I fall over, landing hard on the rocky ground. Blood drips from a cut in my eyebrow as I sob into my arms. The man drags me up by my hair and pulls the black bag back over my head.

Blackwell jolts awake, sobbing uncontrollably. Mama!

The nightmare was real. This whole time it's been a memory. He feels overwhelmed by the feeling of love his mother had for him. The Tzar... Travis. He's my brother.

Blackwell's mouth gapes open and he presses his hand to it, continuing to sob. My mother was a generator. That means Kaliann was my sister. That's why I couldn't submit her hair as evidence. She had the same hair as our mother. Is Scarlett my sister too? She must be.

That's why Travis has her in the Orbs! Blackwell weeps, tears falling down his face. Tinik unzips the sleeping bag and stares at him, looking concerned.

"Are you okay?"

"No," he covers his face with his hands as he slowly regains composure. It feels so strange to cry and he lets out a heavy sigh, as a weight was lifted from his chest.

"My mother," Blackwell whispers, "she loved me."

"Of course she did," Tinik says, smiling kindly.

"The Tzar of Krevax is my brother," Blackwell states numbly.

That's why he offered me this job. He wants me in the Orbs with him. This was all a ploy to get me into the Orbs.

"What?" Tinik stares with wide eyes. "How?"

Blackwell feels the blood drain from his face, as a terrifying realization hits him. Charlotte left the Orbs because she wanted to stop cannibalism. Blackwell crawls out of the sleeping bag and falls onto the floor, hyperventilating.

"What's wrong?" Tinik asks.

"We're being eaten!" Blackwell says.

"What do you mean?"

"Orbinians! They're cannibals."

"No!" She shakes her head. "That can't be true."

"Tinik!" Blackwell grabs her arms. "It is! My mother left the orbs to fight against it. That's how I'm the Tzar's brother."

Her face goes pale and she continues to shake her head, not wanting to believe.

"Tinik, Gunner," Zipper calls from the bottom of the stairs, "it's time to go."

Gunner unzips himself and glares at Blackwell and Tinik as he walks past them.

"Do you think he heard what I said?" Blackwell asks.

"No." Tinik looks back at him. "He's too angry and tired to hear anything right now." She pulls herself away from Blackwell. "I need to go. Try to get some sleep." Blackwell nods.

"Will you be okay with Gunner?"

"I'll be fine," she says and turns to leave. The image of his mother screaming flashes in his mind. How could I sleep ever again?

47 | HOSPITAL

TWENTY-TWO

Opening the bathroom door, Twenty-two sees her mother standing in the hall, staring at her with a concerned expression.

"How are you feeling?" she asks.

"Fine!" Twenty-two says, as she pushes past her and slams the door to her bedroom.

Don't pretend to care now, when you're the one who made me drink that disgusting shit. She throws her towel on the ground and bangs open her closet door, grabbing her school uniform from a hanger. You don't care about me, and you don't believe anything I say either. After dressing angrily, she swings open the door and jumps, not expecting her mother to still be standing there.

"You're not going to school today."

"Why?" Twenty-two stares at her. "Are you going to lock me up?"

"No," her mother says, shaking her head, "there's something I want to show you."

"What?" she asks, her voice sharp with anger.

"After we drop off your sister." Her mother walks away.

Sighing defeatedly, Twenty-two follows her to the dining room.

"Where's Papa?" Youngest asks, through a mouthful of toast and bacon.

"He left early today," their mother answers. Twenty-two sits down at the table and picks up a piece of plain toast.

"I'm glad you're better." Her little sister grins, revealing her green braces. Twenty-two nods. I wish I had an older sister to help me. At least I'll be able to do that for her.

"Oldest is coming with us to drop you off at school today," their mother says.

"I still want the front seat!"

"Fine!" Twenty-two says, taking a small bite of her breakfast.

"Alright, finish up girls, it's time to go." Tentatively eating one last bite of toast, Twenty-two stands slowly, still feeling sick.

Her little sister takes the last piece of bacon and then runs to grab her backpack. As she treads to the front door, her mother smiles at her, looking for connection, but Twenty-two doesn't smile back. She better be taking me out to apologize. I was sick the whole night. I couldn't even sleep! As her angry thoughts build, she pulls the strings on her shoes, tying them too tight. If she doesn't apologize, I'll run away.

"Where's my poster?!" her little sister yells, running around the living room frantically.

"I have it," her mother says, holding up a large poster with a picture of her sister's dream kitchen.

Bolting forward, she grabs the poster and continues out to the car. Twenty-two slowly follows and climbs into the backseat, where she stares out the window. The elementary school is just around the corner, and after a few minutes driving, Youngest is climbing out of the car.

"Bye mom! Bye sister!" She runs towards the playground.

"Bye sweetheart!" her mother shouts, waving. "Have a good day." Leaning back in her seat, she stares at Twenty-two in the mirror.

"Why don't you come sit beside me?" Reluctantly, Twenty-two climbs out of the back and moves into the front seat beside her mother.

Holding back tears, she watches her little sister swinging on the monkey bars, remembering when she was younger, and her mom used to rub her back every night while she fell asleep. The car revs forward, weaving through the suburban streets, until they reach the highway. Twenty-two glances over at her mother. Why does she hate me?

"Where are we going?" she asks.

"Across town," her mother says cryptically.

Rolling her eyes, she stares back out the window, watching cars speed down the highway. I wish I had a car. I would leave and never come back here. After half-an-hour, they pull off the highway and park beside a hospital, sitting in silence.

"What are we here for?" Twenty-two complains.

"Just wait," her mother says.

A small car drives up a few spaces away and pulls into a spot labelled *Cleaner Eight*. After a minute, a woman with short blonde hair climbs out, a large bag of cleaning supplies hanging off of her shoulder. Completely fixated, her mother stares at the woman, with tears welling in her eyes.

"Who's that," Twenty-two asks, feeling confused.

"That's your aunt," her mother says, watching the woman disappear through the hospital doors.

"No, it isn't."

"Yes, it is," she says, and then turns to face Twenty-two. "She was my youngest sister."

"Why haven't I met her then?"

"Our family erased her for getting pregnant when she was thirteen."

"Erased?"

"Yes." She looks back out the window at the place her sister was standing only moments before. "My mother had to protect the reputation of her other daughters, so she had her sterilized and put on the cleaner track. When we went back to school the next year, we told everyone she died of leukemia."

"What happened to the baby?"

"They aborted," she says, looking back at Twenty-two. "She wasn't approved to have it." Grabbing her hands, she stares desperately at her daughter. "Do you understand why you can't see that boy again?"

"I didn't do anything though," Twenty-two says.

"Maybe not this time, but boys are dangerous, you can't risk it." Her mother wipes a tear from her face. "I can't lose you, too." Twenty-two stares at her feeling shocked and slightly guilty.

"You won't lose me," she whispers.

Her mother pulls her into a hug. "Promise me."

"I promise." *What do I do now? Chao wants to marry me. She'll understand once he's old enough to propose. Besides, I'm not going to have sex before marriage.* Her mother lets go of her, still staring intensely.

"You must stay far away from all boys."

"I will," Twenty-two says, lying.

"When I was your age. I made a mistake." Her mother looks away. "If I hadn't had a miscarriage, I would never have been able to marry your father."

"You had sex with a boy?" Twenty-two gasps. *That's why she treats me this way, because she was a whore!*

"I guess," her mother says, staring out the window

vacantly, "I didn't agree to it. It just happened." Twenty-two tightens her fists, feeling upset.

"Boys are dangerous." Her mother looks over at her and asks, "do you understand that?"

"Yes," she whispers, thinking of Mr. Raymond grabbing her neck.

"If something were to happen, promise me you'll come and tell me immediately." She grabs her hand.

"If it's early, the brew I make can fix it." Twenty-two nods. After a minute of silence, she lets go of her hand and turns the key to start the car.

"Did you tell your mother about what happened?" Twenty-two asks, making her mother laugh angrily in reaction as they pull out of the parking lot.

"No, my mother didn't believe my younger sister. She would never have believed me either." Twenty-two looks out at the highway feeling frustrated.

I told you the truth and you didn't believe me.

48 | CHEMICAL WARFARE
ROCKET

WAKING ABRUPTLY FROM THE SOUND OF SCREECHING BRAKES, Rocket's body swings forward in his sleeping bag. Yelling echoes up the stairs. Could it be more surface men? Unzipping himself, he listens, but then it's quiet.

"Something's wrong." He shoves Khan's sleeping bag.

"Why are we stopped?" Khan asks, as he unzips himself and jumps out.

"I don't know." The yelling starts again and Khan leaps down the stairs.

Rocket runs behind him and stops at the edge of the kitchen, watching as Zipper and Gunner face off.

"What the fuck are you trying to say?" Zipper shouts, his face red with anger. "If you're threatening me, you better just do it properly."

"Fine! I'm going to kill you, you fucking bitch," Gunner spits. "How's that?"

"You're going to kill me?" Zipper laughs. "You could never kill me."

Then he darts forward, his fists extended. Gunner grabs Zipper by his long hair and easily pulls his arm back.

"What's happening?" Khan hollers. Tinik runs forward and kicks Gunner in the shin.

"Let him go!"

"Get back!" Gunner screams as he pulls out a pocketknife. Everyone takes a step back, as Gunner holds the knife to Zipper's throat.

"Gunner," Zipper says seriously, "you don't want to do this."

Gunner laughs, his face distorted with rage. "Yeah, I do," he whispers and slits Zipper's throat in one fluid motion.

With the whites of his eyes round in shock, Zipper grabs his neck and stumbles forward, blood pouring out of his throat and splashing onto the ground.

"No!" Tinik screams, reaching forward to help Zipper, but the slash is too deep.

Rocket watches in shock as Zipper stares up at him, his body twitching and contorting in panic. Finally, with one final sputter, he grows still and slumps over.

"Upstairs!" Gunner yells, his eyes bulging. "Now!" Rocket shuffles back in terror. "Get out!" Gunner roars.

At that, Rocket turns and bolts up the stairs. Gunner chases after all three of them, his bloody knife thrusting forward. Khan slams the button just as Tinik leaps into the sleeping quarters. They stare in fear, listening to Gunner breathing behind the closed door. Rocket's heart pounds in his ears as he imagines what Gunner will do next. There's a strange clicking sound and then a bang.

"He's locking us in," Tinik whispers. "Jamming the door."

"What do we do?" Rocket asks. Tinik looks at Khan.

"We'll wait until the truck's moving," Khan whispers. Tinik nods.

After a minute, Gunner stomps back down the stairs. With a deep breath, Rocket sits on the ground, taking a second to calm down.

"Poor Zipper," Tinik cries, wiping away tears.

Rocket nods slowly, feeling numb. The last violent moments of Zipper's life replaying in his mind. He exhales slowly, feeling a mix of sorrow and relief. I'm glad it wasn't me.

"What happened?" Khan asks.

"Gunner was enraged when he found out Pickles was gone," Tinik says through a tearful breath, "and he wanted someone to be named cleaner. Zipper told him everyone was equal on the truck and that he needed to clean up after himself. After that..." Tinik shakes his head.

"He slammed on the brakes and followed Zipper into the kitchen to kill him."

"I'm sorry," Khan says, pulling Tinik into a hug.

The engine turns on and Gertie moves forward. Rocket feels sick thinking of Zipper's body rolling on the ground below them.

"Should we try to get out now?" Rocket pushes the button for the door, but as expected it doesn't open.

Feeling too distraught to think clearly, he moves aside. Khan pulls on the latch, but it still won't budge.

"What if we just knock it down?" Rocket asks.

"He'll hear us," Khan says.

Leaning down, Tinik stares at the bottom of the door. "Maybe we can lift it off the track it rolls on?" he says.

"Rocket, can you push at the top corner there?" Khan asks.

Nodding, Rocket pushes on the top edge of the door as Khan and Tinik pull the door up from the track at the base. It twists up and forward, sitting at an angle in the doorway.

"Good thinking, Tinik!" Khan says.

After Rocket and Khan lift the door out of the frame and quietly place it on the ground, all three of them tiptoe down the stairs. At the bottom they find a pool of blood in the kitchen. Zipper's body is gone, a trail of red up the wall where the ramp lowers.

"What now?" Rocket whispers, feeling sick.

"We should drug him," Tinik says.

"What?" Rocket blurts, as he gingerly follows Khan into the kitchen.

"Let's do it," Khan says and leans down under the table, attempting to open the compartment to the nostaliem.

"I don't know." Rocket shakes his head, feeling nervous.

"It's locked," he whispers. Tinik pulls out a small bag from under his shirt.

"I've got it," he says, unzipping the bag and grabbing two tiny picks.

He pushes one into the lock and twists it while he taps slowly with the other. The lock clicks and he opens the door and steps aside, so Khan can pull out a crate of nostaliem.

"We should throw an entire crate at his face!" Tinik whisper-shouts.

"What if he crashes the truck?" Rocket asks.

"Rocket's right," Khan says quietly, as he places the crate on the table. "We need him to stop the truck first."

"I'm more worried about him stabbing one of us than the truck crashing," Tinik says.

Rocket looks up. "We could drop it on him through the vent. That way he can't hurt us." He points up at the vents above them.

"That's a good idea," Khan says, "but we'll probably end up drugging ourselves too."

"The gas masks!" Tinik jumps up anxiously.

"Right." Khan nods. "Do you know where they are?" Tinik and Rocket both shake their heads no.

"I hope they're not in the driving pit," Tinik whispers. Rocket nods and starts searching the cupboards, stepping carefully over the splashes of blood.

After looking through the last empty cupboard, he whispers to himself, 'Gunner took everything.' I'm sure he'd be happy if we all starved. He could tell any lie he wanted. He would be a hero for surviving and returning with the nostaliem on his own.

Khan searches at the other end of the truck, near the stairs. Tinik presses the button to slide open the bathroom door and tiptoes in. Staring at the empty kitchen, Rocket feels unsure of how to proceed. Khan waves at both of them, holding up the box of masks.

"They were under the stairs," he whispers, as Rocket and Tinik rush forward.

"Good job," Tinik says, smiling. Khan grins back. Grabbing the box, Rocket opens it and shakily grabs a mask.

"I'll set up the box of nostaliem in that vent," Tinik says, pointing to the spot just above the driving pit entranceway.

"We should tie him up," Khan says.

Nodding at this suggestion, Rocket tiptoes towards the stairs. "I'll grab the ropes that hold the sleeping bags."

After a few minutes of untying knots, he has the ropes from two bags and brings them down. Outside the driving pit entranceway, Khan is helping Tinik climb into the vent. Feeling nervous, Rocket wearily laces the rope through the arm of a chair. I hope this works.

Khan pushes a crate of nostaliem into the vent behind Tinik and creeps over to Rocket, tying the second rope to the other arm of the chair.

"We'll lure Gunner out of the driving pit, then Tinik will dump the powder," Khan says.

"How are we going to get him to come out?"

"Let's throw the broken door down the stairs. That will get his attention." After the knots were secured on the chair, they move quietly back up the steps, and Rocket walks over to the far side of the door and picks it up. Khan picks up the other side and they lift it over their heads, getting the weight balanced.

"On three?" Rocket asks.

"Yeah," Khan says.

"One, two, three," they say in unison and throw the door down the stairway.

It makes a series of loud banging sounds as it bounces to the floor below. Gertie screeches to a stop. Putting on the gas mask, he stares through the scratched plastic, feeling unnerved by his impeded sight. The door to the driving pit opens and he can hear Gunner run into the kitchen and then stomp quickly up the stairs. No! He's coming.

Rocket rips off his mask, not wanting to fight with his vision impaired. A cloud of black powder fills the room. He falls backwards onto the ground, reaching for the mask in panic. The air tastes strongly of a mix of dirt and metal in his mouth, but there's a strange sweetness to it as well. He can't see anything and it feels as though he's floating in a body of water.

Looking down at my round belly, I gently feel the taut skin. A small foot kicks the palm of my hand, making me laugh.

"Oh, hi there, baby," I say. "I hope you can hear me."

Only one month left until you're due. I hold my breath in fear, dreading the moment they take my baby away.

"I wish I could keep you," I whisper.

Why is this always so hard? I know this is what I'm supposed to do, but it feels wrong. Everything feels wrong. I hug my belly, trying to imagine what it would be like to hold them.

Black clouds expand out, erasing the scene. For a split-second Rocket remembers where he is and fearfully feels the ground for the mask, but then his thoughts fade out and a new scene emerges.

Fiddling with the settings of the composting machine, I sigh in frustration. If I can just get this right, I'll be able to grow corn in the soil. I pick up a handful of the compost and smell it. It's not right. It's just not right. I grumble, picking out a small piece of blue plastic. There's got to be a way to make this process work.

The scene fades away and Rocket finds himself again, still helplessly searching for the mask. This time his fear was tinged with unexpected emotions. Those were my parents. I know it. The room is still thick with black powder and after another breath in, the sleeping quarters fade out.

The warmth of fire licks at my legs as I watch it dancing in the dark.

"You know, this is probably the last time it will be just the two of us," Sasha whispers. I look over at her smiling as she places my hand on her belly.

"We still have five months to go!" I say with a laugh.

"Yes, but when will we be alone in the woods like this again?" She looks up at the dark, star-filled sky.

"That's true." I lean close and kiss her.

"Do you like the name Samuel for a boy?" she asks.

"I like Samuel. What about if it's a girl?"

"Alicia?"

"No, my old boss was Alicia." I shake my head. "Camila?"

"Camila! Really?" She laughs. "No, I don't think so. What about Naomi?"

"Hmm, I don't love it." I pull her into my arms, staring up at the stars.

"Keisha?"

"I dated a girl named Keisha."

"Well, fine, I guess we're having a boy," Sasha says, shaking her head.

Black clouds expand around the sleeping quarters as Rocket opens his eyes. With a panicked breath, he spots the gas mask and lunges forward, but then his awareness disappears.

Sasha and our son play in the waves as I run through the sand towards them. The cold water spreads goosebumps over my skin and I dive into the water. I grab Sasha's foot and she screams out in surprise, bursting into laughter when I bubble to the surface.

"Jordan! I thought you were a sea creature!"

"I'm a shark!" I say, grinning, reaching for my son.

"Daddy!" he yells excitedly. I pick him up and throw him into the air, listening to him giggle.

The picture goes black, but Rocket can still hear the child giggling. Forgetting the mask, Rocket reaches towards the sound in confusion, hoping to hold his son one last time. A large wave crashes over him, making salt sting his eyes and he closes them. Silence immediately follows.

Samuel sleeps beside me.

"He's getting so big," Sasha whispers, brushing his hair behind his ear.

"I know," I whisper back. "I can't believe it. Soon he'll be moving out." I say sarcastically.

"Don't say that!" Sasha pokes me in the arm, trying not to laugh.

"He's only eight," I whisper, smiling back.

49 | SPEARMINT

VIOLET

LOOKING AROUND THE WINDOWLESS ROOM, VIOLET FEELS stress blur the edges of her vision. When can I leave this place?

It's been three days and all I've seen of the Orbs is this stupid room. Moving from sitting on the bed to a chair at the small table, she traces the lines in the wood grain. I hope my blood returns soon. I thought I would bleed after taking that pill? Garcia opens the door to her room.

"How are you doing this morning?" he asks.

"I'm okay," she says. "Will I get to join the Orbs today?"

"Soon," he says, as he unwraps something covered in foil and pops it into his mouth.

What does soon mean? Tomorrow, next week, a month? Garcia extends his hand, holding another piece of foil out.

"Would you like a piece of gum?" Violet takes it, and unwraps the gum, revealing a lime green colour. She chews it twice, but then spits the gum out into her hand. Eww.

"You don't like it?" he says, laughing, as he sits down across from her.

"It tastes like dental gum in Krevax. Is it supposed to be good?"

"It's spearmint!" He hands her a tissue for the discarded goody. Violet smiles a nod of thanks.

"So, what should we start with today?" he asks.

"We can start with questions, if you want," Violet replies politely, but there's a nervousness in her voice. Is he stalling? Maybe they don't think I'm good enough to join the Orbs?

"Questions it is! Number one, can you tell me if 12 people shook hands with each other before and after a meeting? How many total handshakes occurred?"

Violet thinks for a second and then says, "132."

"Correct!" he says, grinning. "Very good."

"Garcia," Violet begins tentatively, interrupting his note taking.

He glances up at her, "mm-hmm," and then continues writing.

"How is it going in here?" General Bouchard opens the lab door.

"Great!" Garcia stands to greet the general.

"Can I speak with you for a moment?" Bouchard motions with his hand to the hallway.

"Yes," Garcia says, leaving quickly.

General Bouchard shuts the door behind them. Fiddling nervously with a loose thread on her pyjamas, she tries to hear, but can't make out the words, and after a full minute, the door opens again.

"Let's move forward to the next step," Bouchard says in a commanding tone.

"Violet, please follow me," Garcia calls to her, a new seriousness to his voice.

She follows them through the hallway to a room with a gigantic machine. Garcia explains the machine measures brain waves, and she jumps up on the table.

"Will it hurt?"

"No, you won't feel any discomfort at all," Garcia says. "Here." He holds up a device with a pump on it.

"You just breathe in through your nose." Breathing in slowly, she feels a spritz of something hit her nostrils, and then relaxes onto the table, feeling dizzy.

"I'm Lucas," a stranger says with a smile. "So, what's your name?"

"Toni," I say as I watch the bus pull away.

"Do you want a piece of gum?" He extends his arm towards me.

"Thanks," I say automatically. It would be rude to say no.

I reach out and take the foil-wrapped candy. He walks beside me as I unwrap the gum. It's green. I put it into my mouth. Spearmint! I hate spearmint. I smile a nod of thanks.

"So, where are you headed?"

"Home," I say, sneaking a glance at him. It would be best if I didn't talk to him.

"On a Friday night? Is there a party there?" he asks jokingly.

"I'm just leaving work."

"You should have fun on the weekend," he says. I look down, feeling embarrassed.

"Someone as pretty as you, that is." I continue walking, unsure of how to respond. "So, Toni, do you like wine?"

"I guess..." No, I hate wine. It's for old, rich people.

"You know, you should come hang out. It's only 7:00 after all! Who goes home on a Friday night at 7:00?!"

"I don't think I should," I mumble.

"Oh come on now! Don't say no," he says, grinning. "Come with me. It will be fun!"

"Okay," I whisper. Why did I agree? I really should go home.

"Yes?"

No! Say no. I look up at him trying to muster the courage to say 'no', but then I say, "Okay."

Why can't I say no? Why did I agree? Maybe I can still run off... He grabs my arm and leads me away from my route home. After a few minutes he stops, still holding onto my elbow.

"This is it." We walk up to a one-story house with white panelling and he opens the front door.

Inside the entrance is a messy shoe rack and I pull off my heels and let my bare toes relax into the linoleum. He walks away, turning on the lights as he goes. I glance back nervously at the door. It's still unlocked.

"Here!" He hands me a glass. "Cheers!" We clink glasses.

I take a sip, swallowing the spearmint gum, unsure of how to throw it away. The wine is bitter, but I continue to drink it.

"It's a Cabernet-Sauvignon. What do you think?"

"It's delicious. Thank you!" I take another drink, hiding a grimace.

"Let's go downstairs," he says, and I follow obediently.

At the bottom of the steps, he opens a door to a dishevelled bedroom. I stand at the entranceway, unsure of what to do, as he switches on a lamp.

"Sit," he says.

The only place to sit is the bed. I don't want to sit on the bed, I want to go home. I don't know how to leave. I sit on the bed and take another drink of the wine.

Turning on a small television set at the end of the bed, he clicks the dial until he gets to a pop music channel. He sits down beside me while placing his wine on the bedside table and leans in and kisses me. He smells like tea tree oil. I don't move, even though I don't want to be kissed. He grabs the wine from my hand and places it beside the other glass. He kisses me again and takes off his shirt.

Please stop! Why don't I say anything? Why can't I say anything? He kisses me a third time. I still can't move. I want to run away, but I feel trapped. He lifts my dress over my head, revealing my bra and underwear. Why can't I say anything?

Terrified, Violet curls into a ball, hyperventilating.

"What did you see?" Bouchard asks.

After a minute, she sits up screaming. "What was that? What did you give me?" Bouchard steps forward, staring at her.

"Tell me what you saw."

She laughs hysterically. "You're not going to let me live in the Orbs are you?" she shouts through her tears. "What is this place?"

Bouchard places his hands on each side of her head.

"What did you see?" he yells.

She smashes her head against his forehead and he falls back, stunned. Then she smashes her own head against the metal table as hard as she can.

Garcia grabs Violet's thrashing body and drags her back to the lab.

"Calm down!" He lets her fall onto the ground. "What happened?"

"What happened?" Violet says, sobbing.

I can't say no. I'm not allowed to say no. I am nothing but an object. It doesn't matter where, in Krevax, in the Orbs. I am nothing.

"I'm sorry this is happening to you," Garcia says, reaching for her hand. Violet stares up at him, confused.

"Why are you sorry when you're the one doing it?" He pulls his hand away, still looking at her.

"I'm sorry!" Violet cries.

I'm an object to them. I'm an object to everyone. Garcia places his hand on her forehead for a moment.

"No need," he whispers.

Lifting a blanket up from the bed, he wraps it around her shoulders and then brushes the hair away from her puffy, tear-streaked face.

After a minute of standing over her, he turns and disappears into the hallway.

"Why am I here?" she whispers to herself. What do they want?

50 | A HISTORY OF VIOLENCE AND DOMINANCE

CARR

CARR WATCHED HIS SISTER AS SHE STARED AT THE WHITE WALL, her arms wrapped in a straight-jacket.

"How has she been?" he asks the healer at the entranceway.

"She's still suffering from severe delusion," he says.

"Her eyes seem glazed?"

"Yes, well, she was a danger to herself, so we gave her some drugs to calm her down."

"Can she still understand me?"

"Of course," the healer says, waving him forward. "You have until 2:00."

Carr sits down on a stool beside the bed, and the healer exits the room. Pulling out a large, leather-wrapped book, his hands tremble as he opens to an earmarked page. I need this to work.

"I want you to have a good life here, but you can't do that until you accept our beliefs. I've brought a book to read, it's called *'Orbinian Superiority: A History of Violence and Dominance.'* It will help you understand. If you can adjust to our way of life, you can leave the sanatorium and enrol in a school." His sister continues to look at the wall, her expression unchanged.

With a slow breath, Carr braces himself and reads out loud: "Two million years ago, our ancestors started hunting and gathering, and as our intelligence increased, our brains outgrew the hips of our mothers. We had to be born into this world small and helpless, like animals." He looks over at his sister.

What if she doesn't understand me? Maybe it was a mistake to bring her to the Orbs? She is half Krevaxer. Charlie will understand.

He continues to read, "sometime between 200,000 and one million years ago men began sharing their food over hot fires. We danced, chanted, and felt the power of our bodies flowing with the cruel and kind seasons of the sun. Feast and starvation. Solstice and equinox. We told stories in the pause of darkness. Positioning ourselves in this world as ephemeral, we embraced the beauty and harshness of our breath. We lived in tribes and raised our children communally until money demanded our servitude." Scarlett's eyes stare wide from the effects of the drugs.

"Under capitalism, we broke further down into family units so that we could not be a threat. We lived in homes with white picket fences and empty values." Carr pauses, staring at his sister a moment.

This is the only option. I can't let her run through the streets again, screaming about Krevax being full of people. If she gets caught, they will kill her.

He continues reading. "When the state faded away and both men and wives needed to work to support a home, this confused the role of females in society. Exhausted, the females no longer made food for their children, instead they bought fast-food burgers and TV dinners packed frozen."

Carr pauses, hoping to see any kind of reaction from his sister, but there is none and he turns the page.

"The magic of fire building, hunting, and star gazing faded in our collective memories. Now even the art of cooking is gone. Microwaving was the only way. As we consumed more and more. Clothing, electronics, jewellery, furniture, cars, junk, trinkets, garbage, every item we bought, removed us further from meaning; from the true flow of our bodies and our breath. Isolated from the support of a community, the family unit grew weaker, burdened, and finally broke." Carr inhales slowly, staring at her, as a queasy feeling grows in his stomach. She can't hear a word of this. I'm a fool to read to her.

He continues. "And so, the family met their demise, and in the new world, everyone stood alone. Perfectly packaged meals for one at every corner of every street. Silent and isolated, depression and insanity seeped into every mind." Carr closes his eyes for a moment.

There's a chance she can hear me. Somewhere underneath the haze of drugs, she can hear me. I'll come back in a few days, hopefully she'll remember my words.

"When they weren't working, they were buying, looking for meaning in material goods. The consumption piled up in landfills outside the city, but then these overflowed and garbage heaps obstructed the view of the land. The year is unknown, but a switch took place and within days, the trees crumbled, the oceans evaporated, and the sky turned red. Terrified, lonely, insane people ran into the roads in search of food, but the vending machines were all empty. Cannibalism became rampant and violence unavoidable. Soon, even the air choked them. The sky danced with red lights every night, and then the sun faded into an orange haze, as dust enveloped the surface." Carr leans over and touches his sister's hand. She doesn't move.

"I hope you hear what I'm saying. Cannibalism was the only way any of us survived the famine." He looks back at the page. "Orbinians rose from the ashes. Men of every colour and creed stood victorious to begin a new era in the Orbs." Carr closes the book.

"Scarlett, you were always meant to be an Orbinian." He leans down and kisses her on the cheek. "I'll be here when you're ready."

Standing, he waves to the healer, summoning him over. With a nod, he unlocks the door, allowing him to leave. Outside the sanatorium, his limo is waiting. *I'll get through to her… eventually.*

"Home," he demands.

"Yes, sir," the limo driver says, as he opens the door for him. As Carr climbs in, the phone on the wall of the limo rings.

"Carr speaking."

"General Carr, this is President Lehan. I've just read Doctor Garcia's report on nostaliem. I am concerned about our ability to create an antidote."

"Yes sir, of course. You have every right to be. We're still testing the subject. I'm confident we will have a breakthrough soon. Doctor Garcia will send you another detailed report on our progress."

"I'm giving you until tomorrow night," Lehan says, *"and if you have nothing new to report, I'm implementing the cull."*

"I see."

"We'll talk tomorrow."

"Yes," Carr says.

The phone clicks off and he drops his head onto his knees, hyperventilating. *I can't let that happen. Charlie could be anywhere.* He waits a moment until he's calm and then presses the button to open the partition between him and the limo driver.

"Change of plans. Take me to the office." Carr closes the partition and dials the number to reach his wife.

"Work is going to keep me at the office late tonight." He pauses, listening to his wife's understanding response. "No, I won't be home for dinner. I love you too."

Once in the building, he takes the elevator up to the 40th floor, where he opens a storage room and grabs a small cup of the nostaliem. After, he heads up to the 49th floor. I need to find out what this does. It's the only way I can stop the cull.

Inside his office, he locks the door and closes the curtains that view the hallway. Sitting frozen, he stares at the lines of black powder he has formed on his desk. If I try it just once, I'm sure I'll be fine. Then I'll have an answer for Bouchard and Lehan. Carr takes a deep breath and snorts the first line of nostaliem.

The room around him peels away like old wallpaper, revealing a new office underneath, one with a velvet couch and a fireplace burning in the corner. Carr stares at the scene, feeling dizzy, and then his thoughts vanish.

"Have you prepared her room?" the stern-looking man asks, a stethoscope hanging from his neck.

"Yes, sir, all accommodations were accounted for."

"You may leave us."

"Of course, sir," she promptly leaves the room.

"Charlotte, do you know why you're here?"

"No." I turn away, embarrassed by my tears.

"How old are you?"

"Seven."

"What can you tell me about the famine?" He stares through a glass window, out at people rocking in their seats, their arms tied with white fabric.

"My mama said the famine started when she was young. That everyone was starving, and they had to do terrible things to

survive. It's better now though, and we'll get to live in the Orbs soon."

"Yes, that's true, but not everyone is good enough to go to the Orbs. There's still a limited food supply. Do you think you're good enough?"

I stay silent, unsure of how to respond.

"You must hear them every hour, like the rest of us," he says, turning towards me, "the laws blaring over the announcement system."

He then recites: "Those deemed unfit for parenthood must be sterilized. If you have conceived without approval, ensure you seek abortion. If they deem you fit, you can apply for approved conception. Report unfit individuals and secret pregnancies to ensure application approval. Do your part to create a stronger society." He looks down at me. "Do you know if you are strong or weak?"

I shake my head, confused.

"Charlotte, your mother was mentally ill. She was exterminated." I sink onto the floor.

"No...no! Mama!" I shriek.

The man in the lab coat moves towards his desk and opens a drawer. Inside, he picks up a needle and fills the syringe with a clear liquid from a small bottle. The sobbing has alerted the nurse, who is now at the entranceway.

"Hold her down," he says.

The nurse grabs my wrists, revealing bloodied fingernails from where I was digging into my back. The man kneels beside me and inserts the needle into my arm as I sob.

"Take her to the operating room."

"Yes, sir." The nurse picks up my small immobile frame and places me on a cold table.

She pushes me through a hallway and into a large open room. I try to call out, but I can't move. The lights are too bright, but I can't look away. The man stands over me and removes my clothes until I am lying naked on the table.

"Please clean the area, and hang the sheet," he moves away and the sound of a faucet turns on.

I try to sit up, to run away, but I can't move. I scream at the top of my lungs, but no sound emits. I thrash and kick my legs, but my body remains motionless. I feel the nurse spray my stomach with a cold liquid and then wipe it away with a cloth. I try to look, but all I can see are the top edges of a white sheet, placed just below my neck. The man steps forward, a mask now over his mouth.

"Charlotte, you are being sterilized. Our world does not need mental illness. If you prove yourself to me, I might permit you to live in the Orbs. If you disobey me, I will bring you back to this room and cut you open again, only this time I'll take something more important." He moves behind the sheet.

My body vibrates with fear. A sharp blade cuts just below my belly button. I scream again, but still only silence. The cutting keeps coming deeper and deeper into my flesh. Then a hot, burning sensation rips into me. I want to push away. I want to fight back, but I am trapped. I sob uncontrollably in my mind. The pain becomes too much to bear and the room goes black.

I wake up on a mattress, gasping in fear. The pain in my abdomen throbs. I walk forward slowly and reach out, searching for a doorknob, but there is none. I'm locked inside. I slam my arms into my chest in terror. I lie back down on the mattress, as a heavy, cold feeling fills my chest. No one in the world loves me. I am completely alone.

"Goodbye, Mama." I sob quietly.

Carr wakes up on the floor, drenched in sweat and yells, "Mom!"

After a minute of sobbing, he frantically leaves his office. It's nearly 3:00 in the morning and everything is sleep-silent, except for the sounds of clocks ticking, ticking, ticking.

Running erratically into the street, he screams at the top of his lungs.

"Sir?" his driver asks in a surprised squeal.

"Take me home," Carr says, as he walks towards the limo, averting his eyes.

51 | SALON GOSSIP
SERIE

"YOU SAY THAT LIKE YOU'RE OLDER THAN ME OR SOMETHING," Serie says, laughing as she opens a gel hydration tube. Pratt grins back at her as he grabs his shoes from the front entrance closet.

"May I remind you I am two years older than you?" He sits down at the table beside her, tying his laces.

"Don't get cocky, it's 18 months, and we both know I'm the mature one." Serie rolls her eyes, while looking through the tubes of paste for something sweet.

"When I got here, you didn't even own a hairbrush!" she says, selecting a vanilla pudding paste.

"Okay, so you were right about the hairbrush, but I'm right about this." Pratt shakes his head, still smiling as he stretches out his arm to put on the red stripe jacket.

"You want to risk being recycled?" Serie says, dropping the tube of paste and standing, her smile now gone. "For what? So you might find out who Blackwell's father was."

"Don't worry." Pratt reaches out and touches her wrist. "I'm a red stripe. Remember, I'll be fine." Serie looks away, sighing heavily.

"Besides, with no one to recycle you," Pratt says, grinning, "you could live until 100!"

"Like you would ever recycle me." Serie steps closer and hip checks him as he opens the apartment door.

"Of course not." Pratt smiles warmly. "Alright then, I need to check in at work. Did you…"

"I'll restock the vodka."

"And you know…"

"About the new spot in the hospital, yes," Serie interrupts, staring at him seriously. "This meeting. When is it?"

"Later today."

"Okay," Serie says, her heart racing in her chest.

"Don't worry about me." Pratt steps into the hallway. "I'll see you tonight."

"See you," Serie whispers as the door shuts.

Standing frozen for a minute, she wants to run after him, but instead stares at the closed door, feeling frustrated. He's going to get himself killed. Sitting down at the table again, she picks up the vanilla pudding paste and takes a bite. There's nothing I can do to stop him. At least he's been happier lately. I wish he wouldn't pretend his death wouldn't matter, though. It'll be okay. He'll probably get an answer today and there won't be anything else to take risks for.

Serie stands, leaving the empty plastic tube on the table and reaches into the closet, pulling out the white mask. I hate this thing. At least I don't have to wear it at home. She puts it over her face, snaps the strings underneath her hair, and grabs a large bag from the closet. Swinging open the door, she strides to the staircase and races down three flights to the apartment building's foyer.

"Hey Serie!" Shannon, another peon, calls from the open elevator. "Will you be at the nail salon later?"

She follows Serie out of the apartment building and into a street of the Enforcement District.

"Yep, these," Serie holds up her hands, "need a new colour."

"I like the pink on you," Shannon says. "What colour are you thinking?"

"Lime green," she says, grinning. "Anyway, I'll see you later. I've got some things to take care of." Serie runs towards a waiting motorbike.

"Hey, are you picking people up?"

"Where are you going?" the driver asks.

"Saintly Angelic Hospital."

"Sure," he says, handing Serie a cracked helmet.

Taking it, she laughs silently to herself. This is safe? At least I'm going to a hospital. Staring at it a moment, she inspects it for lice, and then puts it on, tightening the frayed straps around her chin. The seat on the back of the bike feels shaky when she climbs on, and as expected, the driver punches the gas.

Serie holds on tight to the handlebars, her eyes darting between the road and the steering wheel as she watches him swerve through the traffic. I guess I should have been more worried about my life today. The glass bridges of the Generation District expand in the distance.

Outside the hospital, the driver slams on the brake, sending her swinging forward, almost falling off the seat. She jumps off the bike, relieved to be on solid ground again.

"It's two credits." Nodding, she pays him from Pratt's wallet.

The driver turns on his heel and punches the gas, leaving a cloud of exhaust. I don't think he cares much about being alive. She watches him disappear down the road, speeding dangerously, then climbs a set of stairs entering the hospital. Inside, a map shows the different wings of the building.

After a quick glance, she heads down a hallway, climbs a second set of stairs, and enters the first room on the left.

Inside the small white room, Remi lies unconscious in the hospital bed. Ignoring him, Serie walks to a vase of fake flowers, opens her bag and pulls out a handful of miniature vodka bottles.

Lifting the roses, she drops the bottles into the vase, and then rearranges them until all the spaces are even between the petals. With a quick tap on her tracker, she sends Pratt an image of the flowers, and then leaves. Okay, one down, five to go.

She heads back to the staircase and races to the hallway below, promptly exiting the hospital. From the top of the exterior stairs, she can see there are no motorcycle drivers in the parking lot. Glancing at her wrist, she thinks of calling one, but then spotting a coffee station in the distance, decides to walk. After a quick trip, she pulls open the door and stands at the back of the line. As the customers move forward, Serie reads through the menu options.

"What would you like?"

"I'll have the mint hot chocolate latte," Serie says.

"Name?"

"Serie."

"That will be three credits." Serie taps on her personal wallet and holds out her wrist. The screen turns green, and she stepped to the side.

A man waiting for his coffee stares at her and then angrily asks, "How old are you?"

"How old are you?" Serie asks back as she tucks a grey streak of hair behind her ear. The man glares at her.

"Luke," a worker calls, as he places a coffee cup on the counter.

The man picks up his coffee and leaves. She lets out a held breath of air. Best if no one knows how old I am. She looks down at her hands, examining them. Maybe they are showing my age. Should I wear a hat and gloves? An older peon was quite unusual outside the lower districts.

"Sara-lee." Grabbing her coffee, she quickly leaves and heads towards the highway.

Men who can't even handle seeing an older peon—they're terrifying. I'm only 38 dammit! Still shaking her head, she looks up at the generators walking in the glass bridge, copper chains connecting their wrists and bellies. If I'd been a generator, I would have been recycled three years ago. Hell, even if I'd been a doxy, I would've been recycled three years ago.

She takes a sip of her latte, trying to let the upsetting thought go. I'm lucky I ended up with Pratt.

A row of motorcycle drivers is waiting up ahead near the entrance of the highway. She finishes her drink and drops the empty cup in a garbage can before jogging over. A group of red stripes across from the taxis are watching the road with vacant expressions.

"Can you take me to Gromwell Station?"

"Get on," the driver says, as he hands her a helmet.

This one isn't cracked, and she puts it on without inspecting for lice. The engine starts and they slowly pull onto the ramp to access the highway. Serie breathes a sigh of relief. At least this driver is sane. The motorcycle stops outside of Gromwell Station and she pays two credits and then strolls to *Coffee! Coffee! Coffee!* hoping to run into Pratt. She opens the door and side steps down the line, walking to the bathroom instead.

Locking the door behind her, she takes out a small tool from her side bag and unscrews the sanitizer dispenser. She puts a couple of handfuls of vodka into the hole, and then pulls the dispenser back into place, and twists the screws back in. With her task completed, she exits the bathroom and quickly leaves the cafe.

From there she heads to a small french fry restaurant, where Pratt sometimes grabs lunch. Once again, she sneaks into the bathroom and hides a handful of vodka bottles, this time in a hole behind the mirror. Serie walks a few blocks down to a taco shop, where a man at the entrance, wearing a large taco costume, yells,

"Are you taco-ing to me?" Serie can't help but laugh as she steps into the restaurant.

Sliding behind a large fake plastic palm tree in the corner, she hides vodka bottles under a cracked tile that the plant obscures. Then she heads back towards the entrance and sits down at a small pink table, looking through the menu. The 'Spicy Taco,' made with fried bean and chilli paste, topped with cream cheese paste, looks the best to her.

"What can I get you?" the server asks.

"I'll have the Spicy Taco," Serie says.

"Would you like anything to drink with that?"

"Uh." She looks back down at the menu. "Grapefruit soda."

The server nods and takes the menu. Serie clicks on her tracker. It's 11:50 AM. I wonder if Pratt is meeting with the tech peddler now?

Looking up, she hopes the taco mascot will distract her from her worry, but he's disappeared. Instead, she clicks on a game of virtual golf and holds down the icon of a club to make it swing at the ball.

The server places a basket with the spicy taco and a tube of grapefruit soda in front of her. Opening the cap from the tube, she takes a sip of the zingy fizz and then a bite of the taco. Yum.

A three-piece mariachi band ambles through the restaurant, serenading customers. She smiles to herself, humming along with the lyrics of *Krevaxer Dream*.

After listening to the music for a few minutes, she

finishes her meal and hurries back to the apartment. I'll drop the other bottles off tomorrow. Lying down on the couch, she grabs a book from the side table and reads it. It's an adventure book about a man who has to travel to space in order to find an alien species that can revive all the extinct species on Earth. Serie falls asleep after reading the first few chapters. An alarm rings on her tracker, waking her up and she taps it to turn it off.

Exiting the apartment, she heads to the nail salon a few blocks away. At the entrance of the nail salon, she can see Shannon, Mei and Christina sitting in their usual chairs.

"Serie!" they call in unison.

"Welcome back. Take a seat," the attendant says with a smile. Serie sits in her usual seat, across from Shannon.

Mira, the attendant's peon, walks over. "What colour would you like today?"

"Lime green," Serie says. Mira nods.

"Did you hear there was a peon who spent her man's entire savings?" Mei says.

"Where did you hear that?" Serie asks. Pratt wouldn't have told anyone else, would he?

"I overheard it at the grocery store! A peon said she had a friend who's man came home with a crystal mask, and that he got it from a fare who also gave him her master's money. It was her last act before going to get recycled."

"No way!" Shannon shouts.

"That's wild, I can't imagine it." Christina shakes her head. "She must have really hated him." Serie nods. News travels fast.

Mira walks over with the lime green nail polish and places Serie's hands in a bowl of warm water. Then she dries Serie's left hand and wipes away the old pink polish.

"Have you ever heard anything about people being born outside Krevax?" Serie asks.

If they know the truth about Remi's peon, maybe they know something about this, too.

"People born outside Krevax?" Mei asks. "Like on the surface?"

"I'm not sure." Serie shakes her head.

"I mean, there's people in the Orbs," Christina says, "but I've never heard of anyone else being born outside of Krevax." She grins.

"Although, I heard a rumour about a peon giving birth in a hidden room in the Entertainment District. My old neighbour said her nail salon friend knew a peon from the Generation District who helped deliver the baby in secret."

"I wonder if that's true?" Mei whispers.

Shannon leans in close. "I've heard about younkins born outside Krevax."

"You have?" Serie scooched forward in her seat.

"Yeah," Shannon says. "Back when I was still training in the Education District, I knew this older peon, and she swore that there were younkins who would sometimes show up from outside Krevax."

"Really!" Mei exclaims.

"How?" Christina asks.

"I'm not sure," Shannon says, "but she said that they didn't come with the usual papers. It was like they showed up out of thin air."

"Did they speak our language?" Mei asks.

"I don't know. It sounded like they were all young," Shannon says, "like toddlers." Serie examines the lime green polish on her nails. Could that be true?

"In other news, my man said I could have a party to celebrate my third year as his peon," Shannon says, changing the subject. "Will you girls help me plan it?"

"Fun!" Mei cheers. "Absolutely."

"I'm so jealous," Christina says. "Mine would never let me throw a party."

Serie closes her eyes, tuning out her young friends. *I should tell Pratt about this.*

"Would you like anything else?" Mira asks.

"No, that's everything," Serie says, standing. "Thanks Mira!"

"Serie, don't go," Shannon protests.

"Get your toenails done!" Mei shouts.

"I'll be back tomorrow," Serie says while paying, and then waves. "Bye girls!"

Back at the apartment, it's almost 5:00. *I hope Pratt gets home soon.* Feeling nervous, she thinks about cleaning the apartment, but then decides she would rather distract herself with something fun.

Turning on the wall screen, she navigates to a gaming icon and scrolls through the list. Karaoke. *That will work.* It's greyed out, but she opens the code and types in a string of commands. The icon turned green as she clicked on it. *Yay! Free karaoke.* A song plays with the words running across the bottom of the screen as Serie sings them.

"She's the sexiest doxy. She makes all the men's heads turn!" Serie shakes her head at herself and turns off the annoying pop music.

Walking over to the vase of plastic tubes, she pulls out a peach tube and picks at it. Lying back down on the couch, she looks at the clock. *Where is he?*

Closing her eyes, she falls into an anxious sleep.

52 | REBEL

PRATT

MACHINES IN THE HOSPITAL ROOM BEEP LOUDLY AS PRATT stares at Remi's motionless body. I wish he had died. Hopefully, he never wakes up. Reaching into the vase filled with plastic roses, he pulls out three small bottles of vodka. Thank you, Serie!

Storing two in his belt, he cracks open one and drinks it. It's okay, I'm still having less than I was before. He hides the empty bottle back in the vase and shuffles to the door, nervously waiting. I can't believe I'm doing this. Where is he? An older man with long grey hair enters.

"Theus?" Pratt asks.

"I didn't know you were a red stripe?" he says, clenching his fists.

"Yeah, I'm investigating something, but it's classified."

"I see," he says, unzipping his jacket. "Rowley must have owed you some favour?"

"We're even now."

"Who's he?" Theus asks, pointing at Remi.

"He's my partner. No one minds me coming to visit."

Flashing a quick glance down at Remi, he shakes his head and then stares expectantly up at Theus. "So, do you have it?"

"Yeah," he says, pulling out a disk the size of a small pinky nail, "but if you get caught with this, I don't exist."

"Of course." Pratt nods.

"It's 1,000 credits," he holds out a sensor.

Inhaling sharply, Pratt lifts his wrist, accepting the exorbitant fee. The screen flashes green and 1,000 credits leave his wallet. With a heavy sigh, Pratt takes the disk and Theus leaves. I hope this is worth it!

Examining the tech, he sees a clear button in the center of the disk. He places it over his tracker and pushes it, making the disk turn pink. Once connected, he nervously opens *Red Stripe Services* and types in 'births outside Krevax.' This time, the file opens.

Pratt exhales slowly. I have access. This really is the type of cybercrime that could get one recycled. His eyes dart in the empty hallway and smiling, he eagerly reads through the file.

"Government crackdown on the cave systems around Krevax." Cave systems around Krevax? I've never heard of anything like that.

"Orbinian and Krevaxer rebels fighting against the practice of farming in Krevax threaten the entire system." Farming in Krevax? Why would rebels be fighting farming? This is weird.

Pratt scrolls further down to a section on 'Recovered Younkins.'

"Over the six-year rebellion, 108 younkins were born outside Krevax. The recovery team placed the younkins, aged three months up to six years, in the education program. General James Carr ordered the execution of 462 men and the re-assignment of 510 females to their appropriate districts." Pausing, Pratt scrolls up to the search bar and types in 'recovered younkins,' and a new file opens.

He scrolls down the list, as images of younkins flash by. Stopping the page, he stares at the image of a small girl: "Name: Tabitha, Age: 5." Clicking Command-F to search the page, he types in the name 'Charlie.' The page jumps to a picture of a small boy: 'Name: Charlie, Age 3.

Staring at the boy's face, Pratt's sure it's Blackwell. I know it's him. He has the same complexion, eyes, and high cheekbones. It looks exactly like him. A hyperlink beside the boy's information says 'maternal-line,' and he clicks on it.

It opens to an image of the generator he had shown the Tzar. Well, it's confirmed then. Scrolling through the information in her file, he reads a section titled, 'Special Order.' "General James Carr requests the subject, name: Charlotte, age 28, be placed as a generator in Krevax."

Hmm, do all the females have a special order? He clicks back to the page of younkins and clicks on another younkin's maternal-line. No special order here. Why would this general be concerned about the assignment of this one female? The name Carr? Could he have a relation to the Tzar?

Pratt clicks back to the random younkin and sees that this one also has a hyperlink to the 'paternal-line,' and he clicks on it. It loads to an image of a man: Name: Carlos Ramirez, Age: 36, Status: Executed. Did I miss Blackwell's paternal-line? Pratt clicks back and scrolls up to the image of Blackwell as a three-year-old. His file doesn't contain a paternal-line. What?

Could this General James Carr be Blackwell's father? No, that's crazy. Blackwell's face pops into his head. Now that I'm thinking about it, he does kind of look like the Tzar. I don't believe it. It must be a coincidence. Did Blackwell know he was born outside of Krevax?

Putting the disk in his pocket, he walks out of the hospital room and down the set of stairs. Could Blackwell be hiding out in the cave system? Maybe I could find him. Walking down the exterior set of stairs, he heads towards his bike in the parking lot. He looks up at the glass bridges of the Generation District. They said the females were re-assigned? What were they doing in the cave system? Could they have been rebels, too?

Sitting on his bike, he grabs the disk out of his pocket and places it back on his wrist. He presses the button and types 'female rebels,' and a new file opens, which he reads through slowly. It's no wonder they classified this. If females were fighting alongside the men, then they saw them as equals. He looks up again. A heavily pregnant generator is staring out at the city. I always thought they were like us. Grace was the best person I've ever known, and Serie is as smart as any man in the Government District.

He types in 'cave system map,' and a map of a cave system connecting to Krevax pops up. Whoa! There's a tunnel at the edge of the Government District. Pratt downloads it and puts the disk back in his pocket. Well, let's find this tunnel! Swiping his tracker, he turns on his bike and zooms to the highway. They wrote that Krevaxer and Orbinian rebels occupied the cave system together.

Could that mean Blackwell's mother was an Orbinian? Then she would have known the general. Why were they against farming, though? What was being farmed that was so alarming? This can't just be about corn, potatoes and beans. There must be something else being farmed. Maybe some kind of drug?

As he enters the Government District, he pulls onto a side road to look at the map of the cave system. Okay, so it's connected to a part on the East wall. He pushes on the gas and winds through the streets to get to the spot on the map.

The bright blue advertisements above him make the mirrored towers glitter. This place. He shakes his head in disgust. A guard up ahead smiles and gives a courteous nod. Pratt nods back.

I'm glad I'm not from the upper districts. Spoiled younkins, all of them. Slowing down at the edge of the East wall, he references the map. The tunnel points to a spot just a few feet down, and he parks his bike and walks over.

There's nothing there but the exterior metal plates that are part of every wall in Krevax. Of course, they covered it up. Pratt grabs a utility knife out of his belt and tries to pry a bolt off of the metal plate. Shit. This is going to take all night.

53 | MINT REPUTATION

GARCIA

GARCIA WATCHED VIOLET, BRUSH HER HAIR THROUGH THE one-way mirror. I'm going to fix this. Looking back down at his notes, he read through them again and whispered the conclusion out loud to himself.

"The evidence reveals Violet, a Krevaxer, is an intelligent being. In conclusion, Krevaxers are not a lower species and should have equal status to Orbinians."

Ring.

Ring. He stares at the office phone, wishing it would stop ringing.

Ring. Sighing defeatedly, he picks it up.

"Doctor Garcia speaking."

"Doctor, this is President Lehan. I've been reading your report on the effects of nostaliem. Have you had a breakthrough in the antidote?"

"President Lehan!" Garcia exclaims nervously. "No antidote yet, but I'm working towards it."

"Your report doesn't mention post-mortem testing," Lehan states, then asks, *"Have you dissected the subject's brain tissue?"*

"I was hoping to test the antidote on the subject before a post-mortem dissection."

"I see." Lehan's friendly demeanour evaporates. *"My understanding is brain tissue can be kept alive, and the antidote tested directly in a sample."*

"Perhaps, but I felt a direct reaction from the subject would show the clearest picture."

"That is not needed. Dispose of the subject immediately," Lehan commands. *"I expect the results today."*

"Of course." The call disconnects.

Garcia's breath is quick as his vision flashes and he shakily drops the receiver. Staring up at Violet, he sees she is sitting morosely at the table, her head resting in one hand. He takes a slow breath to steady himself. This is it. If I don't act now, it will be too late. Standing purposefully, he walks out into the hallway. You can do this.

Outside Violet's room, he listens for a minute, making sure no one is around. Throwing open the door he dashes to the table and gently shakes Violet's shoulder. She stares up at him with a pained expression.

"Quick, we're leaving," he whispers, reaching for her hand as his eyes dart to the exit.

"We are?" Violet asks, her face suddenly bright, as she follows him out of the room.

Sprinting anxiously down the hallway, he leads her to the elevator and pushes the call button. Violet starts to say something, but Garcia shakes his head no, silencing her. The doors open and they climb into the elevator.

"What's going on?" she whispers.

"I'm taking you somewhere safe," Garcia says and he pushes the button for the parkade.

"Where?" Violet asks.

"A school," Garcia says. "They'll take care of you there."

The elevator opens and they run to his car. With his keys

shaking in his hand, Garcia opens the back door for Violet to climb in.

"Keep your head down," he says.

She climbs in and leans down below the window's edge. Mustering a small breath, he gets into the driver's seat. He opens the glove box, grabbing a rip of paper with the address on it. As he plans the route in his mind, he suddenly shudders at a terrible realization and his face goes pale. I left my report in the Observation Room. He closes his eyes, deciding what to do. I'll be back in less than half an hour. No one will see it. Starting the engine, he pulls through the parking lot and turns onto the road.

"There's an outfit for you there," he calls back, staring at the road ahead.

"Should I put it on now?"

"Yes and be quick." Garcia looks up and sees her scared face in the mirror. It will be okay.

He merges onto the highway, pushing the gas pedal to the floor. Counting the passing seconds in his head, he drums his fingers on the steering wheel. In the backseat Violet finishes the last button on a purple dress.

"Done," she says.

"It's important you don't tell anyone you're from Krevax," Garcia says. "Do you understand?"

"Aren't there other Krevaxers up here?" Violet asks, confused.

"No." Garcia glances nervously back at her. "If they find out you're a Krevaxer, they will kill you."

"Oh." Violet nods slowly.

"Also, tell no one your name. In the Orbs, they only assign names to men."

"Okay," she whispers.

Should I tell her she's still pregnant? No, it will only upset her. The school will help her. Garcia turns off the highway and down a tree-lined road. He reads the address again. That's it. He stops in front of the four-storey brick building. It looks nice.

"We're here," he says, parking the car, and then looks back at Violet. "Everything's going to be okay."

With an uneasy smile, she opens the door and slides out. Garcia jogs with her up the stairs to the entrance. Opening the heavy door, he rushes Violet through and they walk down the hallway together to the office.

"Can I help you?" the receptionist asks.

"I called ahead about a new student," Garcia says, tapping his fingers in rapid succession.

"Family name?"

"Antol." Garcia's eyes dart nervously around the room as the worker types on his keyboard.

"Oh, poor dear, an orphan!"

"Yes," Garcia says, "a house fire killed her parents."

"I'm so sorry," he says, looking up at Violet. She nods.

"Unfortunately, we lost all the paperwork in the fire," Garcia states.

"Of course," the receptionist says, staring sympathetically at Violet and then looking back at Garcia, "it's no problem. We can accept her without the papers. You can send them once they have been re-applied for."

"Thank you." Garcia nods.

The man pulls out a form and puts it on the counter. "Please fill this out." Garcia takes a pen from a jar and reads through the form.

"As for you, dear," the attendant says, addressing Violet, "you need an official number. How old are you?"

"Seventeen," Violet says.

"Are you in year eleven or twelve?"

"Eleven," Violet says, without missing a beat.

Listening to the exchange, Garcia smiles to himself as he completes the details on the form. She'll be fine here.

"You will be Thirty-six then!" He picks up the form and skims it over. "Welcome, Thirty-six."

"Thank you," Violet says.

"No birth certificate?"

"No." Garcia shakes his head.

"That's okay," he says, nodding. "We can manage with the family name for now." He stands. "I'll show Thirty-six to her dormitory. You can say goodbye."

"Yes," Garcia says, smiling at Violet. "I'll see you soon."

She smiles back nervously and then follows the receptionist into the hallway. There's no time for anything else and he jogs back to his car.

Violet is safe.

Now I need to get my report into the right hands. Buckling himself in, he starts the engine and drives erratically down the road. Bouchard isn't often on the lab floor. It will be fine. Speeding down the highway, he weaves through cars as his fear builds. I'll grab my report and leave. That's all I need to do.

Braking, he dips into the parkade. By the time they notice Violet's missing, my report will be on Orb News. Lurching to a stop, he leaps out and runs to the elevator, tapping his foot on the ground as he waits for the doors to open.

Once inside, he watches the numbers slowly climb, repeatedly pushing the button, willing the elevator to go faster. The doors open and he rushes down the hallway to the Observation room. Bouchard is standing there, holding his report.

"What is this?" Bouchard asks accusingly.

"I..I.." Garcia stammers.

"I got a call from President Lehan," Bouchard says. "I

came here to discuss the dissection, but I see you have other plans. Where is the subject?"

"She's dead," Garcia says, his stomach in his throat.

"Show me its body." Bouchard takes a step closer. "You're lying. What did you do with the subject?"

"I don't know what you're talking about," Garcia says lamely.

"Tell me about this report then," Bouchard says, sneering. "What were you going to do? Go on Orb News?" He laughs.

"Maybe!" Garcia shouts.

"You fool." Bouchard shakes his head. "You really think you're the first person to pull this stunt?"

Garcia stares back at him in shock. "Orb News is an arm of Government Propaganda. They would never report this." Bouchard holds up the stack of papers, scowling.

"This bullshit," he mutters, before throwing them angrily to the ground.

"They're people!" Garcia yells.

"They're not people," Bouchard says, pursing his lips, "they're vermin." He shakes his head. "And now you've left me no choice."

"What do you mean?" Garcia whispers.

"Where's the subject?"

"I don't know," Garcia says stoically.

"Fine, we'll find it without you." Bouchard shakes his head. Garcia takes a step backwards, eying the elevator. "I wouldn't do that," Bouchard says.

"Do what?" Garcia asks, playing dumb.

"Run."

"Why not?"

"If you run, we'll demonize you and your entire family." Bouchard moves another step forward. "And then we'll hunt you down and kill you."

"And if I don't run?" Garcia asks, his voice quiet.

"Then we'll report you were killed in a tragic lab accident. Your family will be compensated and live on with your good name." Bouchard states emotionlessly.

"Either way, then." Garcia clenches his jaw and whispers, "I'm dead."

"Yes," Bouchard says. "I promise, if you come now, it will be painless."

Garcia grabs his chest as his wife and his daughters' faces flash in his mind. I didn't get to say goodbye.

"Okay," he says. This is the only way. They'll be safe.

"Follow me." Bouchard walks past Garcia into the hallway and leads the way to the elevator.

Each step closer to the general's office, a buzzing rang louder in his ears. Run. Run. Run! But he doesn't. He keeps moving forward, for his children's future, for his wife's honour, and for Violet's life.

"Sit down," Bouchard commands, shutting the door behind them. Garcia sits.

Bouchard steps behind his desk and opens the bottom drawer. Closing his eyes, he focuses on his loved ones' faces. I'm so sorry. I'm so sorry I failed you.

"It will feel as if you're falling asleep." Bouchard holds out a pill and a glass of water.

Garcia takes the pill in his hand. It's just a mint. He swallows it without water. Everything will be fine, it's just a mint. His face feels heavy. It's just a mint. He closes his eyes.

Just a… Everything goes dark.

54 | CLASSIFIED CONVERSATION

PRATT

AFTER REMOVING THE SIXTEENTH AND FINAL BOLT FROM THE metal plate, Pratt pauses and looks around. No one's in sight. Pushing the plate to the side, he leans it against the wall and takes a step back to see what's behind it.

Sure enough, there's an opening, a rocky tunnel right where the map shows the cave system connects. He jumps excitedly. I found it! He taps on his tracker and clicks on a small picture of Serie. I need to tell her where I'm going.

Ring.

"Hey!" Serie says nervously. "You're okay?"

"Yes, everything's great," Pratt says enthusiastically. "I've found something interesting,"

"What did you find?"

"I'm standing in front of a tunnel that leaves Krevax," Pratt says, laughing. "It connects to an entire cave system that rebels used!"

"Oh, is that all!" Serie says. "Listen, I heard at the salon today that younkins sometimes show up in the Education District with no files. Maybe they were from the rebels?"

"I think so."

"You're not going in, are you?" Serie asks.

"Of course I am."

"Pratt! It sounds dangerous."

"I know, but I'm just going to check it out. I shouldn't be too long."

"What about your vodka?"

"I have a stash to go." Pratt pats his belt. "I don't want another archive situation."

"Okay..." Serie says with a disappointed sigh. "Do you think you'll be back tonight?"

"Let me look at the map," Pratt says, expanding the map on his wrist. "If I'm not back by tomorrow night, then maybe something went wrong."

"What then? If you aren't back."

"I guess you get to live in my apartment alone," Pratt says jokingly.

"Pra-att," Serie says, emphasizing his name. "Where's the tunnel?"

"It's on the East wall of the Government District. Don't worry, I'll be back by tomorrow night."

"You better," she whispers.

"I'll call you as soon as I'm back, okay," Pratt says.

"Okay, be safe."

"Thanks, I will." He clicks the call off and looks around again, making sure no one is watching.

In the distance he can see a sliver of the Watchtower, but he's not worried, as all they'll see is a red stripe. He leans down, ducking his head under a rusty pipe, and takes his first step into the tunnel. As he walks a few more feet, his tracker blinks an out-of-range message, and he takes a nervous step back towards Krevax. You can do this.

Clicking on the tracker, he stares at the map for a full minute, memorizing it, and then walks further into the tunnel. The light from Krevax disappears behind him and he has to touch the wall to guide himself forward in the darkness. Maybe I should turn back?

He takes another couple of nervous steps forward. I don't want to get lost here. Up ahead, he notices a strange glowing blue light. Holy Mary! Are there still people living here?

Quietly stepping forward towards the source of light, he finally sees the wall of glowing blue fungus and runs the last few feet to look at it. Wow! It's actually alive.

Touching the soft tiny leaves on the strange plant, he leans in to smell them. They have a fresh sweet smell, unlike anything he has smelled before. Feeling exhilarated by the discovery, he continues walking, but now with confidence. Suddenly, four large spotlights point directly at him. Oh no! It must be the red stripes. How do I explain this? A tall, round shouldered man steps into the dark, just behind the lights.

"Do you have any weapons?" he asks.

"Yes, I have a gun in my belt," Pratt says, trying to make out his features.

"Put your arms up above your head." The man points a large gun towards him and Pratt lifts his arms. Dammit. Who is this guy?

This isn't a red stripe protocol. The man walks forward, revealing light beige skin, grey hair and sharp green eyes.

"Who are you?" he asks, as he takes Pratt's gun from his belt.

"Trevor Pratt. I'm a detective investigating a case."

"What kind of case?"

"Missing person," Pratt says. The man stops moving and stares at him.

"What's the name of the man you're looking for?"

"Charlie Blackwell."

"Charlie!" the man says, smiling. "You're looking for Charlie?"

"Yes," Pratt says, confused, "do you know him?"

"I did, when he was little. Is he okay?"

"Not sure, he just seemed to vanish. Are you his father?" Pratt asks. The man looks at him for a moment, deciding what to do.

"You can put your arms down now," he says. Pratt lowers his arms. "Follow me."

The man leads Pratt further into the cave system and slides open a hidden door made of rocks. It's so completely camouflaged that he could have stood right beside it and would have never recognized it for what it was. They walk into a small, well-stocked kitchen, lit up with warm yellow lights. Pratt spots a bag of potatoes on a shelf.

"How do you have those?" he asks in shock, and then takes a moment to stare up at the wall of vegetables, some of which he doesn't even recognize.

"I grew them," the man says, as he shuts the rock door.

"What are those green ones?"

"Those are apples."

"I didn't know we still had those," Pratt says, intrigued.

"Of course you didn't." The man sighs. "There's a lot to explain. Would you like some tea?"

"Do you mind if I drink some of this?" Pratt's face turns slightly red as he pulls out the vodka from his belt.

"Fine by me." The man sits down at the wooden table. "Sit."

Pratt sits across from him and takes a sip of his vodka.

"My name is Robin. Pratt, right?"

"Yes," Pratt says, nodding. "Nice to meet you, Robin."

"So, you wanted to know if I'm Charlie's father?" He taps his fingers on the table.

"Are you?"

"No, Charlie's father was a general in the Orbs."

"Do you mean General James Carr?" Pratt's eyes widened.

"Yes, do you know him?"

"Not personally." Pratt shakes his head, feeling shocked. So, the Tzar is Blackwell's brother! That's why he wants us to find him.

"Do you know what happened to Charlotte?" Robin asks.

"Do you mean the generator?"

"Fucking Carr! Of course, he made her a generator." Robin slams his fist against the table. "He wanted to punish her."

"I'm sorry," Pratt says.

"Is she still alive?" Robin's voice was tinged with desperation.

"No," Pratt whispers. He looks down and Pratt waits for him to compose himself.

"Do you know what we were fighting down here?" Robin asks, looking up.

"I read it had something to do with farming?" Pratt says, which makes Robin laugh.

"Farming." He shakes his head. "Of course they would call it that. Government lingo loves to sanitize the truth."

"So, it isn't farming then?"

"No, it's cannibalism," Robin states.

"What do you mean?" Pratt's breath quickens.

"Krevax is the farm," Robin says, "and you're the meat."

Pratt grabs his chest in shock, sharp pains shooting through his arms.

"No. That can't be true." Closing his eyes, a twisted understanding creeps in. That's why we're recycled?

"I know it's hard to hear," Robin says, consoling him.

"What do we do?" Pratt cries, drinking the rest of the bottle of vodka.

"Well," Robin says, "thanks to nostaliem, you could actually do something."

"What?"

"Have you tried it?"

"Of course not," Pratt says defensively.

Robin stands, opens a cupboard, and grabs a small glass container of black powder.

"You should try it." He hands over the container and sits down. Pratt turns the container in a slow circle, watching the powder move.

"Why?"

"Do you know what that does?"

"No," Pratt says.

"Well, I have a story." Robin grins knowingly. "It's just a story, mind you, but I think it's true. You know, there are people who have lived in these cave systems since before the time of the famine."

"There are?" Pratt asks in surprise.

"Yes, they call themselves the Oqakwanwe people. They've developed an entirely different culture and dialect. Their language comprises puzzle pieces, each word deeply rooted in an ancestor's tongue. They tell me nostaliem gave them the words. They call nostaliem by another name though, 'Manidoo Yachay', or 'Spirit Voice'."

"Like all languages, it's alive, changing with each new speaker. I don't speak Okwanan fluently, and changing tones is not my forte, but I met a man, Molday, who spoke Okwanan and English. He told me he was once a Recycler in Krevax, that he decided to die, and walked into the tunnels alone. The Oqakwanwe saved him and told him to share nostaliem with his people. That's how I first tried it." Pratt stares with his mouth gaping open.

"You weren't expecting to find anyone here, were you?" Robin says, patting Pratt's arm.

"No," Pratt says, shaking his head, "this is just a lot to take in."

"I think we were meant to meet." Robin smiles. "You'll

understand everything, after you take nostaliem. I promise there's nothing to fear. The Oqakwanwe people take it at age 13, as part of a ritual for passing into adulthood. After that, they take it once a year until they die."

"What is it, though?" Pratt asks.

"They believe it's the collective memories of Earth. A living being that we killed and turned to ash."

"Do they make it?"

"No, there is a site on the surface that the Oqakwanwe honour. During the coming-of-age ceremony one must go alone, dig past the red sand and breathe in a handful of nostaliem. When they return, they are grown."

"So, it's something they found on the surface?"

"In this one area, yes." Robin looks amused. "Are you going to try it?"

"What's it like?" Pratt asks.

"It will show you what you need to see." Looking back down at the black powder, Pratt tips the container, pouring a handful of grains into his palm and inhales it.

The room falls away, replaced by a large green field and bright sky with fluffy clouds, spots of blue sneaking through.

"Nora!" I call, chasing after my cat as she leaps ahead.

I run over and pick her up. She feels heavy in my small arms, her white fur brushing on my chin. I turn back towards the row of mobile homes, hoping I can sneak her into my room.

"June, leave that cat be. We don't need another mouth to feed," Papa calls from the small wooden porch.

"But I love her!" I cry.

"She only showed up begging for food yesterday. I don't see how you can love a thing that you just met. Now put her down." I drop Nora and watch her run back into the field.

Tears well in my eyes as I stumble away. I try to contain them, but the sadness overwhelms me and they stream down my cheeks.

"Oh, come now June." He lifts me up and wraps his arms

around me. "That cat will be just fine." I wrap my arms around his neck and cry into his chest. Papa slowly rubs my back, comforting me. After a few deep breaths, I feel better.

"Are you hungry?"

"Yes," I say meekly.

Papa carries me to the kitchen and plops me down in a chair. He grabs a bowl of strawberries out of the fridge and puts them on the table. I take one and bite into it. It's sweet and juicy. Strawberry juice drips down my chin. Papa wipes my face with a cloth and kisses me on the forehead. I look up at him, grinning.

The scene evaporates, and Pratt jolts back into his seat.

"Are you okay?" Robin asks.

"Yes," Pratt says.

"How do you feel?"

"I'm not sure. Sad, I guess." He inhales deeply, trying to relive the smell of the grass field. "It was beautiful, but none of it exists now."

"Yeah, that's how it is."

"Is that why there's so many suicides?"

"I think so." Robin nods. "It's a lot for anyone to take, but especially in Krevax, where things are so bleak."

"Did you introduce nostaliem to the gangs?" Pratt asks.

"Yes," Robin says and then sighs. "but my goal was to create a rebellion." He shakes his head.

"I guess I didn't realize how bad Krevax had gotten. I wasn't expecting the suicides." Pratt nods slowly.

"Did you see your mother?" He asks.

"No."

"You should take it again." Robin pushes the jar of nostaliem closer.

"Why?" Pratt looks up at him, confused.

"That's what the Oqakwanwe do. You keep taking it until you see your mother during the age thirteen ritual."

"What does that mean?" Pratt scratches his hairline.

"For the Oqakwanwe, it usually means they see the moment their mother first held them, but for Krevaxers, people separated from their mothers at birth, it shows you something else, but it always involves your mother."

"How many times do I need to take it to see my mother?"

"I don't know," Robin says, shrugging his shoulders, "it's different for everyone."

Pratt nods and pours more black powder into his hand. Inhaling nervously, he wonders what he'll see this time. The room goes white and then slowly turns into the Generation District, where Pratt sees a generator looking out at the empty street. Then his awareness splinters away.

Maybe today I'll see him? He's old enough. He should walk now.

There are few younkins in the Generation District, and I know that's his designation. A group of small younkins, guided by a peon in a white mask, walk into the street below the glass bridge.

My heart pounds as a small blonde one comes into view. I know he had blonde hair. I saw it before they cut the cord. The small boy's pudgy arms swing with each step. I laugh, choking back tears. That has to be him. He's so beautiful. My son. I've finally seen him. I press my palms to the glass, but it isn't enough. I want to hold him. To tell him I love him. Tears well up in my eyes. Don't cry.

"Marina," the handler calls my name.

I don't move, instead I watch my son slowly toddle into the distance. He'll be 19 months soon. A pang hits my chest.

"Marina!" The man walks over and grabs the copper chain between my wrists. "It's time, you've been matched."

"It hasn't been two years yet?" I look up at him, pleading to stay. "I'm still providing milk for the little ones."

"It isn't always exactly two years, you have done well." He pulls me away from the window. I look back out, but my son is gone. My heart aches. I hope I'll see him again. The glass bridge fades away.

The intense feeling of love his mother had for him is overwhelming, and Pratt cries into his hands.

"Are you okay?" Robin asks.

"No." Pratt shakes his head. "I didn't know. My mother, she… loved me."

"You see then, the power of nostaliem," Robin says, nodding slowly.

"You said there was something I could do?"

"Yes, as a red stripe, you have access to the watchtower?" Robin looks at him intensely.

"I do, yes," Pratt says.

"The air filtration system comes out at the top and filters down through the districts." Robin gives him a meaningful look. "I know the red stripes have been seizing nostaliem, you could dump it into the vents?"

"I'll do it," Pratt declares. "Will you come with me?"

"Yes." Robin slides Pratt's gun across the table.

55 | LAB ACCIDENT
TWENTY-TWO

As the school bell rings, Twenty-two and Twelve walk out of the entrance doors, arms locked together. Twenty-two notices Chao smiling at them and moved to go down the stairs, but Twelve holds tighter to her arm.

"Are you sure that's a good idea?" Twelve whispers.

"It's fine!" Twenty-two pulls her arm away. *Why does everyone want to keep me away from Chao?*

"I'm sorry, you're right," Twelve says. "I'm just worried about you."

Twenty-two looks over at her with a solemn expression. "I know," she says, smiling and adds, "but don't worry, Chao is going to marry me." She runs down the steps to meet him.

"What happened to you?" he jests, smiling. "You were missing yesterday."

"I was sick," she says, "but I'm fine now." Twelve walks down the steps behind her.

"Look," Twelve whispers, so only her friend can hear, signalling up towards a window with her eyes.

Glancing up, she sees Mr. Raymond staring at her, his eyebrows furrowed. *Why is he always staring at me?*

Turning away from her teacher's glare, she pulls Twelve and Chao down the rest of the stairs and out of his sightline.

"Chao, this is my friend Twelve!" Twenty-two says.

"Nice to meet you, Twelve."

"I heard you got my friend in trouble," Twelve says.

"Hopefully only a little.' He grabs Twenty-two's hand.

"It was nothing," Twenty-two says, glaring at her friend to stop talking.

"Can I walk you home?" Chao asks.

"Is that really a good idea?" Twelve interrupts, staring at him.

"It's fine!" Twenty-two says. "We'll take a different road. We won't run into my mother."

"Works for me," Chao says.

"I'll see you tomorrow." Twenty-two grins at Twelve, and they turn to walk away.

"Okay," Twelve says, defeatedly. They continue through the schoolyard to a tree-lined street, where Chao leans in and kisses her.

"I've been wanting to do that since I last saw you," he says. Twenty-two giggles. "Will you come to my baseball game tomorrow? It's after school at Bowler's Park."

"I'll try," she says.

"You can bring Twelve too," Chao says, laughing, "then she can chaperone us."

"Sorry about her." She shakes her head. "Twelve can be a little too intense sometimes."

"I think it's nice," he says. "Besides, everything will be fine in a few months."

"It will?!" Twenty-two asks, a smile from ear to ear on her face.

"Yes," he says, nodding, "I'll be eighteen, so I can ask your father's permission to marry you." He really is going to marry me. I can't wait! She holds tighter to his hand. I hope my parents accept his proposal.

"We should stop here," she says. "My mother drives down the next road to pick up my sister." She leans in and they kiss again.

"See you soon," Chao says, holding both of Twenty-two's hands.

For a minute, neither of them let go, instead moving closer for another kiss, and then reluctantly pulling away. Walking up the road to her house, she keeps glancing back at Chao, giggling whenever she sees him looking back, too.

After one last look, she walks up to her door and opens it. Even before she's gone inside, her chest constricts with fear, as she can hear her mother's sobbing. What's going on?

Hesitantly, she tiptoes into the kitchen, where she sees her lying on the floor curled in a ball, the phone hanging off the hook above her.

"Mama!" Twenty-two cries, and her mother looks up at her.

"Your father," she says through heavy breaths, "there's been an accident in the lab." Twenty-two falls down beside her and grabs her mother's hands.

"Is he okay?" she asks, desperate to hear that her father's safe.

Her mother shakes her head and sobs again. Twenty-two lets out a wail, dropping her head into her arms. My father. Papa! He's dead. No.

Standing, she steps backwards, away from her distraught mother, not wanting this moment to be real. When her back hits the doorway to the hall, she turns and careens out of the house, escaping the grief. She runs down the street towards Chao's house.

"Chao!" she screams, tears streaming down her face.

After she rounds the corner, she sees him up ahead. He turns towards her, a confused expression on his face.

"Twenty-two!" he says. "What's wrong?"

"My papa!" She grabs onto his neck, crying.

"Is he okay?" Chao pulls her into a hug.

"No," she says, through her sobs. "I can't go back there."

"Okay," Chao says, and he walks with her to his house. Once inside, he asks, "Are you hungry?"

"I'm tired," Twenty-two whispers.

He nods and leads the way to his room where Twenty-two immediately lies down on the bed. Closing the door quietly, he lies down beside her, putting his arms around her. *My papa... He's dead.* She falls asleep.

Bang.

Bang.

"Where's my daughter!" Twenty-two jumps awake. Chao sits up beside her. *Oh no! What have I done?*

"It's my mother," she whispers fearfully, and leaping up, runs into the hallway. Her mother is standing at the front door, her face twisted with rage. With shaky hands, Twenty-two opens the door.

"What are you doing!" her mother screamed, grabbing her arm. Behind her, Youngest was standing, her eyes puffy from crying.

"I fell asleep," Twenty-two says.

"I swear, it's true, we just fell asleep," Chao stammers from the hallway.

"You do this!" her mother screams. "This! On the very day your father's been killed!"

"I'm sorry," Twenty-two says through her sobs.

"Get in the car," her mother yells, dragging her away from the entrance. Twenty-two climbs into the backseat, averting her eyes, as her mother and sister climb into the front.

"Will papa be at the funeral?" her younger sister asks as the car engine starts.

"No, he was mauled by the Wildebeest," her mother says angrily.

Her younger sister let out a painful cry and Twenty-two covers her face with her hands.

"I'm sorry," their mother says, her voice breaking.

The car stops in front of their house and Twenty-two climbs out and runs to her room, slamming the bedroom door behind her. Wrapping herself in a blanket, she sobs, as grief moves over her in waves. Her mother walks in, holding a cup.

"Take this," she says, holding the cup towards Twenty-two.

"No! Mama, please," Twenty-two begs.

"Drink it!" her mother yells. Taking the cup, she swallows the bitter liquid in one gulp and then watches as her mother shuts the bedroom door. I hate her! Papa died and she makes me take this?

I wish it had been her who was killed. This time, her mother doesn't return with a bucket. Burying her face in the pillow, she cries for hours, as the nausea builds.

56 | SIGNALS

TINIK

GERTIE SNAKES THROUGH THE ROCKY TERRAIN, THE LANDSCAPE hidden beyond the truck's headlights. Holding onto a pipe in the wall to steady herself, Tinik watches Gunner crying.

Why is everything so fucked? First I have to deal with finding out Orbinians are cannibals, then Zipper is murdered, and now this too? She jogs back to the driving pit.

"I think we should untie him," she says. "He was unconscious for days, and now he wakes up like this?" She covers her mouth with her hand for a moment.

"He's not the same," she whispers. This is wrong.

"He could be faking," Blackwell says, glancing back from the driver's seat. "We'll know for sure when Rocket wakes up."

"What if he doesn't wake up?" Tinik looks over at Rocket, secured in the lookout position, his jaw slack.

"It doesn't matter," Blackwell says, steering with one hand, fiddling with the knife that slit Zipper's throat in the other. "We're almost back."

"You should've thrown that into the dust," Tinik says.

Blackwell looks up at her and then puts the knife into his pocket, refocusing on the haze.

"We might need it," he says.

Tinik glances away, feeling sick. We should have gone back for Zipper's body. He deserved better. The image of Zipper's last terrified breath flashes in her mind. I wish he hadn't died like that. Gunner's wails grew louder from the kitchen.

"He doesn't remember who he is," she says, turning back towards Blackwell. "We've tied up a younkin."

Blackwell continues staring out at the haze. "Even if you're right, it's a younkin in Gunner's body." She shakes Rocket's shoulders.

"Wake up!" she shouts, but Rocket doesn't move. She goes back into the kitchen and leans down beside Gunner.

"Can you tell me your name?"

"Samuel!" Gunner shouts in a younkin-like voice. "Where's Mommy and Daddy?"

"I'll help you find them," Tinik says. "What do you remember last?"

"The beach."

"The beach?"

"He's waking up!" Blackwell shouts from the driving pit and she runs over.

"Rocket?" Tinik asks, as he looks around the driving pit, wild-eyed.

"Where am I?" he shouts.

"You're headed back to Krevax," Blackwell says.

"What's Krevax?" Rocket mumbles.

"He doesn't remember either!" Tinik jumps up and down. "I knew Gunner wasn't faking."

"Where's my family?" Rocket tries to untangle himself.

"Whoa!" Tinik unbuckles the belts and helps him stand.

"Sasha! Samuel!" he shouts. "Where's my wife and my son?" he asks Tinik, and then yells, "Samuel!"

"Daddy!" Gunner yells back. Running out of the driving pit, he immediately unties his son, while Tinik watches, holding her breath.

"Daddy!" Gunner cries.

"Samuel!" They embrace in a hug and she breathes a sigh of relief.

"Where's Mommy?" Gunner asks, crying.

"I'm not sure?" Rocket says. "We'll find her."

"What's going on?" Blackwell asks, still driving the truck.

"They're hugging," Tinik calls over her shoulder, as he glances back, looking stressed.

"Where are we?" Rocket stares up at Tinik. She takes a deep breath. How do I answer that?

"It's hard to explain," she says.

"Where's Sasha?"

"How old is your son?" Tinik asks.

Rocket looks lovingly at Gunner. "Is there somewhere he could lie down?"

"Up those stairs."

"Thank you," Rocket says with a nod. "Samuel, I know you'll feel better with a rest."

Gunner looks at him, tears still in his eyes, and shuffles forward. Tinik watches them go up the stairs. What happens now?

"They were in the same nostaliem trip?" Blackwell shouts from the driving pit.

"I think so," Tinik says.

"Wow!" Blackwell exclaims.

Tinik sits down at the table and waits for Rocket to return. After a few minutes, he stumbles back down the stairs with a worried expression, and sits across from her.

"What's going on?" he asks nervously.

"You're experiencing the side effects of a powerful drug," Tinik says.

"What does that mean?"

"I'm not sure." She shakes her head. "I've heard that those who take too much nostaliem can lose their minds."

"So, you're saying my son and I aren't real?"

"No," she says, giving him a kind smile, "you were real. It's just now you're a memory, one that's come to life."

"Where's Sasha then?"

"I don't know." Tinik looks down at the table, feeling overwhelmed by the questions. "I suppose she's still a memory."

"What do we do?" he asks, shakily.

She shakes her head, unsure of what to say, and watches as Rocket drops his head into his hands. Standing, she grabs a gel hydration tube out of the cupboard and places it in front of him. Gertie rattles around them.

"I know it's a lot to process." She gently places a hand on his arm. "I'm here if you have questions."

Jogging back to the driving pit, she pushes the button to close the door, concealing her and Blackwell.

"How much longer until we get back?" Tinik asks.

"Could be any time now," Blackwell says, handing her the binoculars. "Without Zipper, though, I'm not sure how we'll get down." He shoots her a nervous look. "What if Gunner's memories come back?"

"Then we'll deal with it." She takes a deep breath, preparing herself to ask the question that had been on her mind since she first found out Blackwell was related to the Tzar. "Will you go to the Orbs and live with your brother?"

"And become a cannibal?" Blackwell says with a laugh. "I think my mother would have preferred I sign up for early recycling."

"No recycling talk," Tinik says. "We're not doing that." I hope Krevax burns before another single person is recycled.

"You want us to be revolutionaries, then?" Blackwell asks.

Fear tingles up her neck and she closes her eyes. If I become a revolutionary, I could be killed. My younkins could be left all alone. If I don't…I'm not the only mother in Krevax. How can I abandon Krevaxers when I know the truth?

"Someone needs to fight back," she whispers.

"Us?"

"I don't know?" Tinik shakes her head. One day I'll come back to fight.

"Would you leave Krevax with me?" she asks, closing her eyes because she's afraid he'll say no.

"I'll leave with you," Blackwell says, smiling. "We're a team."

Relief floods through her and she takes a deep breath, feeling hopeful for the future.

"Good." She grins at him. "Besides, nostaliem's already changing things. Maybe Krevax doesn't need saving, because everyone will know the truth soon."

"Will they? We see different versions of the truth," Blackwell says. "You didn't know about cannibalism until I found out."

"Then Krevaxers should attack the Orbs."

"We can't just attack the Orbs, they'll have defences." Blackwell grins. "I like your bravery, though."

"I'm not brave," she says, shaking her head. "I'm terrified! But what they're doing to us is wrong."

"I know," Blackwell nods. "But what can you and I do alone?"

"Could you reach out to your brother?" Tinik asks.

"You think the Tzar cares?" Blackwell gives her a sympathetic look, and then adds jokingly, "he literally eats people like us for breakfast." Tinik rolls her eyes, trying not to laugh.

"He's your brother," she says. "You should try."

"How?"

"There must be some kind of emergency radio." She digs through compartments at the front of the truck.

"I doubt it."

"I've heard Zipper talking through the intercom, but I've never seen the microphone." Shaking the dash, she pushes her hand below the plastic and feels for what's underneath. "I think it's a keyhole!"

Grabbing the set of keys she took from Gunner, she leans down and tries the first one, but it doesn't go in. She tries the second key, which slides into the hole. As she turns it, the piece of plastic pops open, revealing a radio and receiver.

"Ah ha!" Tinik exclaims. "Looks like I'm right again." Blackwell laughs.

"You win," he says. "I don't see how I'll be contacting the Tzar though." Tinik turns the dial on the radio.

"Zipper said you could talk to the moon, why not the Orbs? They're way closer." She holds down a rectangular button on the microphone.

"Hello!" she says. "Anyone there?" No one replies and she turns the dial to change the signal.

"My name is Tinik and I'm saying 'hi' from the surface." Still nothing, so she turns the dial again.

"Reach for the Orbs!" Tinik sings.

"That's bad." Blackwell grins, shaking his head. She sneers at him.

"You try then," she says, handing the microphone over.

"This is Charlie Blackwell, and I am saying hello to no one."

"Did you say Charlie Blackwell?" a voice asks over the radio.

"Yes?" Blackwell says in surprise.

"Someone wants to talk to you. Hold please."

"Yes?" Blackwell says in surprise.

"Someone wants to talk to you. Hold please."

57 | KNOCKED OUT

BLACKWELL

Staring out at the haze in shock, Blackwell can't think clearly as he continues to hold the microphone to his mouth.

"Holy Mary!" Tinik says. "The Tzar really is your brother."

She grabs the wheel, giving Blackwell a second to process, as he laughs uncontrollably. After a minute, he calms down and grabs the steering wheel back from Tinik.

"Thanks," he says, glancing up at Tinik. "We don't know for sure it's the Tzar."

"Who else could it be?" Tinik says, patting his shoulder.

They wait the last few minutes in silence, both lost in their own thoughts.

"Charlie Blackwell. Is that actually you?"

"Yes?" Blackwell says. "Who's this?"

"I work for the Tzar. He's been looking for you. Can you wait on the line?" Tinik jumps up and down beside him, excited by the confirmation.

"Yes," Blackwell says.

"Good." It's silent again for another couple minutes and Blackwell is frozen.

Am I actually about to talk to my brother? Feeling nervous, he sighs repeatedly. What should I say to him?

"Is this Charlie Blackwell?"

"Yes."

"Charlie!" he says, and then there's a long pause. "I've been looking for you."

"I know," Blackwell says.

"You do?"

"Yes, because you're my brother... Travis."

"How do you know that?"

"I found out when I took nostaliem."

"Are you safe? I have been worried."

"I am. Yes."

"Will you come live in the Orbs?" his brother asks, with desperation in his voice.

"I don't think our mother would want that."

"Why?" his brother whispers. The call is silent for a minute.

"Did you know our father left me in Krevax and forced our mother to be a generator?" Blackwell asks.

"That's not what happened!" Travis says. "He told me many times he searched for you."

"Then he lied," Blackwell says. "I saw it happen."

"What do I do?" he asks, his voice shaking.

"Tell Krevaxers the truth. That's what our mother wanted." Blackwell waits for a response, but the call stays silent. He won't help us. He doesn't care.

"Are you back in Krevax?"

"No, but I will be soon." Maybe I'll be able to convince him to help us... eventually.

"When you get back, don't go to the Entertainment, Manufacturing, or Recycling Districts," his brother spits out. "They aren't safe. The President in the Orbs has given the order for *a cull."* Tinik grabs Blackwell's arm, fear in her eyes. He takes his hand off the button, transmitting his voice.

"You have to stop it!" she cries. "My son, Joey, he's in the Manufacturing District." Blackwell nods and pushes the button again.

"Brother," Blackwell says, "can you stop the cull?"

"I don't know," he whispers.

"Do whatever you can," Blackwell says.

Travis interrupts him, *"you have to promise me you won't go."*

"I can't promise that," Blackwell says. "I have to save a younkin."

"Charlie!" he yells. *"Please! I don't know how to stop this."*

"When we get back to Krevax, I'll get in and out of the Manufacturing District as fast as I can."

"Once the process begins, they'll lock it down," Travis says.

"How will they do it?" Blackwell asks.

"Chlorine gas in the vents."

"There's no way to stop it?"

"I could if I was physically in the Watchtower, but I'm in the Orbs, and I can't get to Krevax."

"What if I was in the Watchtower?"

"That could work!" his brother says. *"But I don't know if you'll make it in time. Also, without your tracker, you would have no way in."*

"Shit." Blackwell says under his breath. I forgot about the tracker.

"You can contact me on this channel when you get back to Krevax. Hopefully, we can fix this together."

"I will," Blackwell says.

"I hope we meet again, brother," Travis says.

"I hope so too." I hope I can see him again… and my sister. "Is Scarlett okay?"

"Yes. How do you know about her?"

"Nostaliem."

"Of course. She will be safe, I promise."

"Thank you."

"Goodbye, Charlie," he whispers.

"Goodbye, Travis," Blackwell says and the call clicks off.

"We have to save my son," Tinik shouts, falling to the ground. Blackwell wraps his arm around her shoulders.

"Tinik," he says, and she looks up at him. "We're going to get him." She grabs his hand.

"Where are we?" Rocket shouts, as he walks into the driving pit. "I need to find Sasha." Still wiping tears from her cheeks, Tinik stares at him silently. Blackwell glimpses back at Rocket, unsure of what to say.

"How's Samuel doing?" Tinik asks.

"He's sleeping," Rocket says. "I need to find his mother. He needs her."

Tinik screams, making Blackwell swerve the wheel in panic. Looking back he sees Gunner's fist swing up and hit Rocket in the head. He falls to the ground, unconscious. Blackwell pulls the emergency brake, throwing Tinik and Gunner against the back of the seats.

Jumping up, he darts towards Gunner as Tinik careens out of the driving pit. Gunner hits Blackwell in the chest, making him fly back and hit the dashboard, smashing the radio to bits. As Gunner leaps towards him, Blackwell pulls out the knife from his pocket and snaps it open.

"That's my fucking knife!" Gunner yells. "What did you do to me?"

"Stay back!" Blackwell shouts, swinging the weapon in front of him.

Laughing, Gunner runs forward, unthreatened by the blade. Suddenly the entire driving pit turns black with nostaliem powder.

As he crouches behind the seat, trying not to lose consciousness, he can hear Gunner moving closer. A fist hits his stomach, and he automatically lunges the knife forward, hitting flesh. The blade stabs deep and he can feel warm blood dripping down his hand.

The panic slips away as the nostaliem takes hold of his mind. The feeling of the warm blood fades, and then he's no longer in the driving pit. He's somewhere else. Above is a woman's face, looking down at him with a concerned expression. Blackwell wonders who she is, and then he's gone.

"Are you sure you're ready?"

"Yes!" I say, smiling up at my daughter.

"This is what you really want?"

"Elaine, I'm in pain and I'm dying either way." I grab her hand. "Would you want any other death for me?" I ask.

"I want you to be happy," she whispers.

"Do you remember that mural on your wall, the one from your childhood bedroom?"

She inhales sharply. "The one with the Hummingbird that had trees for feathers?"

I nod, and reaching up, brush a loose hair behind her ear. "When you were eight, you had that terrible fever and your mother and I were so scared. Your mother painted that mural to help her process the fear she felt about losing you."

"What do you mean?"

"That Hummingbird wasn't just decorative; it represented a belief system for your mother. One that I believe now, too. The belief that death is a form of transition; a hummingbird, to a tree, a tree to something else. We all return to the soil, energy waiting to be reborn." I look up at my daughter.

"I don't want you to go yet," she whispers. "Your grandkids won't remember you."

"My sweet child, you will tell your children about me and I will live in their memories, through your words. Besides I could never go, because nothing is ever over, despite everything being lost to

time. The energy of our beings is changing endlessly, but we are always connected. Everything is connected. The trees to the wind, the air to our lungs, the flowers to our breath, the bees to the pollen, the apples to the honey, the decay of our bodies to the birth of our grandchildren," I say, smiling warmly up at her, and then continue. *"The soil to the roots, intertwined in a shared consciousness, fleeting in our minds, but expanding out endlessly in every direction. It means there is no reason to fear death, because death is only an illusion. You were my daughter in this life. Perhaps in the next, you will be my daughter again."* Elaine leans over and embraces me in a hug.

"Everything will be okay," I whisper into her ear, holding her in my frail arms as though she were still a child. *"We are only water moving through the body: an ocean, a river, a lake, a pond, a puddle, a raindrop, a tear."*

Blackwell opens his eyes and sees his hands covered in blood. Looking over he sees Gunner is dead, and Tinik lying on the ground, still under the influence of the drug. Crawling to her, he listens as her breath grows sharper, holding her hand as she wakes up.

"Are you okay?"

"I don't know," she whispers. "I feel confused."

"Me too," Blackwell says. "It will pass. We still know who we are." He looks away.

"Gunner's dead," he says in a whisper. Tinik looks through the driving pit door and sees this is true.

58 | TEST

VIOLET

WAITING IN THE NEARLY EMPTY CAFETERIA, VIOLET FEELS A mix of excitement and fear. An attendant walks over and places a tray of food in front of her. Tentatively, she smells the strange square of layered items and then picks it up, taking a small bite. The explosion of tangy flavours excites her and she grins from ear to ear.

The bell rings, signalling the start of lunch break. She looks down at her light purple uniform, checking again to see all the buttons are lined-up. Students flood into the cafeteria around her, move through the rows of tables and sit down with their friends. She takes another small bite of her food, feeling nervous. A wave of nausea hits her, but it passes after a minute.

"Thirty-six, right?" A girl walks over, holding her own tray. Violet nods. "I'm Seven. I've been assigned to you." She sits down across from Violet.

"Assigned to me?" Violet asks.

"Yes," the girl says. "I'm in the same year as you, so we'll go to all our classes together until you know the routine."

"What classes are we taking?" Violet asks, feeling excited.

"Well, next there's Intermediate Cleaning, then we have, Cosmetology, Pilates, Sewing, Culinary Arts, and Infant Care 201." Nodding with a mouthful of food, Violet can't help but feel annoyed at the thought of a cleaning class.

"What are the Culinary Arts?" she asks, slightly intrigued.

"You know," Seven says, "where they teach you how to make a loaf of bread or cook a steak properly."

"Right!" Violet grins, feeling a little excited again.

They make their own food. Another wave of nausea hits her and she closes her eyes, waiting for it to pass.

"Are you okay?" Seven stares at her.

"Yes." Violet nods. "Just a bit nervous." Seven takes a bite of her food.

"So, where are you from?" she asks.

"The Tropical Orb," Violet blurts.

"Wow!" Seven grins. "I've never been. What's it like?"

"Hot." I bet it would be hot there? Violet takes a big bite of her food so she doesn't have to keep talking.

"Makes sense. I'm from here," Seven says. "I've lived beside this school since I was born."

Violet nods, feeling a little confused.

"My parents moved here when they got approved for conception. I can't wait to go anywhere else! I hope I marry rich."

Violet nods again, still chewing.

"My parents won't approve me for marriage until I'm eighteen, so I'm stuck until then." She rolls her eyes. "Are you allowed to get married yet?"

"I don't know," Violet says.

"Didn't your parents tell you?" She takes another bite of her food.

"My parents are dead," Violet says. Are my parents dead? I guess I don't know for sure. They could be alive.

"Oh!" Seven gasps. "I'm sorry, I didn't know."

"It's okay," Violet says as another wave of nausea hits her. "Where's the bathroom?"

"Just through that door." Seven points across the room.

Slightly hunched, she makes her way to the bathroom, off balance from her head spinning. She opens the door and runs to the toilet, puking. After a slow breath, her dizziness stops and she can think again.

Why am I sick? Maybe I caught something up here? Flushing the toilet, she walks out of the cubicle and sees Seven standing there. Violet turns on the water and rinses out her mouth.

"I'll bring you to the healer."

Violet shakes her head. "I'm fine, honest."

"I'm sorry," Seven says. "If you puke, the rule is, you see the healer."

"Oh, okay." Violet follows Seven through the halls to a small office.

"Hi there," a man in scrubs greets them. "How can I help?"

"This is Thirty-six, she puked," Seven says. The man beckons Violet into the room and shuts the door.

"So, you puked?"

"Yes," Violet says, as she stares at the door, wanting to leave.

"Any idea why?"

"No." Violet shakes her head. The healer opens a cupboard and pulls out an empty cup.

"There's a stall through there," he points at a door attached to his office.

"What do you want me to do?" Violet asks, terror crawling up her spine.

"Pee in the cup," he says.

Nervously taking the cup, she walks into the bathroom stall, staring at the man as she shuts the door. There's no lock. She sits on the toilet and pees into the cup, staring at the door the entire time. It doesn't open.

"Where do you want me to put the cup?" she asks through the wall.

"Leave it on the shelf," he says.

Violet puts the pee on the shelf and goes to wash her hands. When she finally leaves the stall, she feels relief flood over her. Everything's okay. That's all it was.

"Please sit." He points at a chair.

Sitting down, she watches as he opens a plastic-wrapped stick and walks into the bathroom.

"This will only take a minute," he says, smiling at her.

Violet smiles back, feeling tense. What only takes a minute? She pulls at a hangnail, trying to distract herself. After a minute, he walks back over and hands her the plastic stick. Violet stares at the pink plus sign, unsure of what to say. Does this mean I'm sick?

"What does this mean?" she asks.

"Thirty-six, you have broken the purity law. You are no longer allowed at this school," he says and then immediately opens the door and leaves. The purity law? What is a purity law? A minute later, the receptionist walks into the room, followed by the healer.

"Oh dear, I'm sorry to see you like this," he says, staring sorrowfully down at Violet.

"What's happening?" she asks.

"Be kind to her. She recently lost her parents in a fire," he whispers to the healer. "I'll call the transfer team."

"Transfer to where?" The healer sits down across from her.

"Thirty-six, we can't have pregnant students at a wife school." Touching her belly in terror, her chest constricts, making her breath sharp. Pregnant?

"I can't be pregnant!" Violet shouts desperately.

"You are, though," the healer states indifferently. "You will be taken to a new facility where they can deal with girls like you."

"I just got here," Violet cries.

"Then you shouldn't have had sex," he says. She looks away, feeling too ashamed to speak.

"She's through here," the receptionist says, and then a woman walks into the small office.

"Thirty-six, I'm here to bring you to our facility, where we will confirm your pregnancy." She grabs Violet's elbow, dragging her to a standing position. "Does she have any belongings?"

"No," the receptionist whispers, "she lost them in a house fire, along with her parents."

"I see," the woman says, pushing her into the hallway. "Let's go, dear."

In a shocked daze, Violet walks beside her out of the school and down the stairs to a waiting grey van. The woman opens the back door and she climbs inside the windowless space. The door slams shut, leaving her alone in the dark as she cries to herself. I'm still pregnant? The engine starts. No! Violet grabs onto the seat, steadying herself. Why didn't that pill work? Maybe it wasn't real? The van pulls forward out onto the road. Where are they taking me? Will I have to have Remi's younkin now?

The van turns sharply, causing her to fall onto the ground. Slumping over, she sobs, too devastated to get back up. Garcia will find out what happened. He will help me. Waves of nausea move through her as the rumbling engine shakes. The van comes to a sudden stop, and she falls forward onto her hands. The woman opens the van, a bitter expression on her face.

"Let's go," she commands, and Violet stands and climbs

out. The woman grabs her arm and leads her to a dilapidated white building. She opens the door and grabs a wheelchair.

"Sit," she says.

Once Violet is sitting in the wheelchair, the woman walks away. She looks around. There's another girl in the lobby, also sitting in a wheelchair, but she's sobbing hysterically and muttering to herself. Violet wraps her arms around her chest, an icy fear spreading through her. What's happening? A man in a white mask and coat walks up to the other girl.

"You must be Fourteen," he says.

"No, please, I can't be pregnant!" The man laughs and pushes her wheelchair down the hallway. Violet's head spins and she closes her eyes. Why is this happening to me? Are they going to hurt me? I didn't think the Orbs would be like this. A tapping on her shoulder rouses her from her thoughts.

"Thirty-six?" a man in a white mask asks.

Violet nods and he pushes her down the hallway. They enter a room where a bright light is illuminating a metal table, beside it bladed instruments hanging in neat rows.

"Put on the patient gown and lie down on the table." Shivering, she unbuttons her new school uniform and slips into the patient gown.

Shaking uncontrollably, she lies down, watching as the man walks around the table. He places a mask with a long tube over her face.

Are they recycling me? She tries not to breathe, but eventually takes an inevitable breath.

Fighting to keep her eyes open, she stares up at the light—until everything fades to black.

59 | UNRAVELLED

CARR

WAKING UP IN A COLD SWEAT, CARR STARES UP AT THE ceiling, still wearing yesterday's clothes. Was that real? It couldn't be. Sitting up, he's surprised to find himself at the bottom of the stairs. How did I get here? Nostaliem must be creating some kind of delusion. How could anyone live another person's memory?

Besides, my mother had children, so that couldn't have been real. Standing with considerable effort, he makes his way over to the phone on the kitchen wall. I need to know for sure. Grabbing the receiver, he dials his limo driver.

Ring.

Ring.

"Hello Sir!" the man's overly cheery voice squeaks. *"How can I help you?"*

"I'm going in early today. I'll be waiting out front."

"Of co..." Carr hangs up the phone, cutting off the voice.

Closing his eyes, he listens for a moment to the noises of the quiet house. Walking shakily to the front door, he opens it and takes a breath of the chilly morning breeze. I'm sure it wasn't real; I just need to prove it and then I can report the findings to President Lehan. He sits on the concrete steps, watching the sun slowly rise above the hazy horizon.

The limo turns down the street and stops in front of his house. As the driver climbs out and opens the backdoor, he jumps in, avoiding his uncomfortable smile.

Taking a steadying breath, he watches the streets flash by. The limo stops outside the office. He slides out and runs up the steps, giving the security guard a nod as he makes his way to the elevator. The doors open to a silent hallway on the 49th floor and he dashes down the hallway. The lines of black powder stare up at him from his desk. He wipes the powder into the sample cup and sits down.

Clicking on his mouse, he wakes up the computer and types 'sterilization' into the search bar. 142 articles appear. The first dozen are scientific articles on improving the surgical practice of sterilization.

He scrolls down the list until something catches his eye: an image of an old man. Above the man's photo, it reads: 'Doctor Smythe's Legacy: Founder of the Doxy Sterilization Program and Creator of the Rimple Technique.' Carr stares at the image.

Why does he look familiar? Suddenly struck, he grabs his chest as the doctor's wrinkled face morphs into the younger man's from the nostaliem trip. It's him! He's real. So what? So is my mother. It doesn't mean the vision is true. Double tapping on the article to open it, he scrolls through, looking for anything that relates to her.

He stops at a section titled 'Pre-Pubescent Sterilization and Future Sexual Response' and then reads through the paragraph: *"Doctor Smythe's first experiment involved 1,944 test subjects. Of those, 972 girls aged six to ten were sterilized, while the other 972 underwent a placebo procedure. The blind study aimed to determine the best age for sterilization for Krevax's doxy population. A second study was implemented, one that sterilized girls between the ages of 11 and 17. The researchers monitored all the subjects' sexual responses until they reached the age of 19. Researchers concluded nine was the optimal age, leading to the full implementation of Krevax's social structure."*

Looking away from the screen, his head spins with thoughts of the nostaliem trip. His watch buzzes and he glances down at the incoming call from his contact. Feeling momentarily distracted, he taps on it. Could it be Charlie?

"Did you find him?"

"Yes, I'll put you through now." The call beeps, and Carr holds his breath as he waits for it to connect. After a minute, he can hear someone breathing on the line.

"Is this Charlie Blackwell!"

"Yes, who's this?"

"Charlie!" He covers his mouth, trying to contain his emotions. "I've been looking for you."

"I know."

"You do?" Carr feels sick. What does he know?

"Yes, because you're my brother... Travis."

"How do you know that?"

"I found out from taking nostaliem." Nostaliem showed him the truth? It's real. The vision was real. Carr stifles a sob and presses his fingers against his closed eyelids.

"Are you safe? I have been worried."

"I am. Yes."

"Will you come live in the Orbs?" He won't.

"I don't think our mother would want that."

"Why?" Carr whispers. The call is silent for a minute. What else did they do to her?

"Did you know our father left me in Krevax and forced our mother to be a generator?"

"That's not what happened!" Carr says. "He told me many times he searched for you." Not my father. He wouldn't have done that. I know he loved her.

"Then he lied," Charlie says. *"I saw it happen."*

"What do I do?" Carr asks emotionally.

"Tell Krevaxers the truth. That's what our mother wanted." Carr sits in silence for a minute. Tell them the truth? I won't. They're animals. The truth doesn't matter to them.

"Are you back in Krevax?" he whispers. All that matters is that I keep Charlie safe.

"No, but I will be soon."

"When you get back, don't go to the Entertainment, Manufacturing, or Recycling Districts," Carr says hurriedly, "they aren't safe. The President in the Orbs has given the order for a cull." The call is silent. He can't stop the tears streaming down his cheeks now.

"Brother," Charlie says, *"can you stop the cull?"*

"I don't know," Carr whispers.

"Do whatever you can," Charlie says.

Carr interrupts him, "you have to promise me you won't go."

"I can't," he says, *"I have to save a younkin."*

"Charlie!" Carr yells. "Please! I don't know how to stop this." Save a younkin? Why do you care about these vermin?

"When we get back to Krevax, I'll get in and out of the Manufacturing District as fast as I can."

"Once the process begins, they'll lock it down," Carr says.

"How will they do it?"

"Chlorine gas in the vents."

"There's no way to stop it?" Charlie asks.

"I could if I was physically in the Watchtower, but I'm in the Orbs, and I can't get to Krevax."

"What if I was in the Watchtower?"

"That could work!" Carr says. "But I don't know if you'll make it in time. Also, without your tracker, you would have no way in."

"Shit." Charlie says.

"You can contact me on this channel when you get back to Krevax. Hopefully, we can fix this together." *I'll convince him to leave. It will just take time.*

"I will."

"I hope we meet again, brother."

"I hope so too," Charlie says. He sounds genuine. Carr smiles a small, sad smile. *"Is Scarlett okay?"* he adds.

"Yes," Carr says. "How do you know about her?"

"Nostaliem."

"Of course." Carr lets out a desperate exhale. "She will be safe, I promise." *Nostaliem is real. There's no question now. My father lied.*

"Thank you."

"Goodbye, Charlie," Carr whispers. *I need to find why my mother left the Orbs. If my father lied about finding her, he could have lied about everything.*

"Goodbye, Travis." The call clicks off and Carr buries his face in his arms.

Lifting his head, a handful of hair in each hand, he closes his eyes, trying to calm his thoughts. Scarlett's face pops into his mind and his stomach flips. *Am I being just like my father, forcing Scarlett here in the Orbs?*

Carr stares at his dishevelled reflection on the blank computer screen. *Once I find out the truth, I won't use nostaliem again.* Grabbing the cup of black powder, he dumps it onto his desk. Using a piece of notebook paper, he carefully separates a line and snorts it.

The drug takes effect immediately, making the world around him fade, and then he's no longer in his office. He's somewhere else. He sees his mother staring out a window, watching the spring leaves blow back and forth in the wind, and his awareness slips away.

The clock strikes four, making me stand abruptly. With my thoughts still swimming, the air feels as though it has the weightlessness of water, and I float into the kitchen. I unzip the yellow full-skirted dress hanging from the top of an open wooden cabinet door and put it on, along with a pair of matching yellow heels. I hide the hanger amongst the baking sheets and set the oven to 400.

Pulling out a piece of meat from the refrigerator, I place it into a casserole pan and mindlessly rub the skin with butter, and then put it in the oven. I grab potatoes and brussel sprouts, which I peel, boil, and put in the oven.

Returning to my spot on the velvet couch, I stare at the sun-soaked cement outside. I imagine barefoot children running and feeling the sting of the heat. What would my child look like? I shake my head. Best not to think about such things. How long do I have until James finds out the truth?

I inhale sharply, not wanting to know, but then it's obvious. He'll know in a year. That's how long they give a couple to conceive. The sun streams in and I close my eyes, forgetting myself in the heat. I glance up at the time and see it's nearly 5:00.

I wander back over to the kitchen and shake vodka with ice, straining it into a perfectly chilled martini glass, and topping it with a green olive. I make my way to the door and stand with the martini glass in my hand.

A few minutes later, a car pulls up and James climbs out, leaving papers scattered on the ground. He quickly picks them up and walks towards the door. I smile as I open the door for him and hand him the martini for his papers and briefcase.

"Oh, Charlotte. You don't have to do this every day."

"It makes you happy," I say, smiling.

"Yes, well, as long as all of this makes you happy, too." James gestures at the surroundings with his free hand.

"You always make me happy. You know that," I chide in jest. I put down his work items on the side table. "I hope you like roast and vegetables."

"That... sounds wonderful," James calls back through a sip of his martini.

"Excellent," I whisper to myself as I return to the kitchen. "The meat just needs ten minutes to rest." I remove it from the oven.

"I missed you today. What did you get up to without me?" James reaches for my hand.

Carr sits up feeling nauseous. What's happening? He creates another line and snorts it and the office disappears.

They would probably use any excuse to kill me, just like my mother. My face flushes with anger. "You don't worry enough," I say, snapping at James.

James meets my eyes. "Charlotte, there's no need to worry. We'll be starting our family soon. It's an exciting time!"

I swing my shoulders away from him and look down at the floor. James pulls my waist into his arms. "Everything's going to be okay. I love you more than anything. I would do anything for us. Anything."

"I love you too," I say, tears welling in my eyes.

He holds my face in his hands, wiping my tears away with his thumbs. "It won't be long before we're pregnant. I know it's stressful, but we've only just started trying." What will he do when he finds out I'm infertile? He'll leave. I know it. And I'll be sent away to starve. Smoke billows out of the oven.

"Oh, no!" I shout. The vegetables! I grab a tea towel and swing the oven door open, but it's too late. The vegetables are black. I grab the sheet and angrily throw it into the sink.

"It's okay. The roast looks great." James says in a comforting tone. I shove the tea towel into my face and scream.

James looks at me, his eyes wide. "Charlotte, sometimes things burn," he states.

I sob and sink to the floor. I wish I were a tree. I would never worry about getting pregnant, or being abandoned, or starving, or being executed. I wish I were a tree with roots and branches, with leaves and bark.

Carr wakes up from the vision and presses his face into his hands to make the room stop spinning. I must know. I need to find out the whole truth. Snorting another line of nostaliem, the room dissolves again, and he sees Charlotte sitting at the window lost in her daydreams. She is staring out at the willow tree and for a moment he tries to call to her, but then his awareness is gone.

We saw you rise and warned each other, for you could not see us as equals. We knew violence would follow. I was a child when my mother first shared her wisdom. I did not want to believe her, but then I saw with my own eyes what was happening. The day the machine split me open, I felt my leaves tremble in fear before I realized the pain. I watched you in your metal exoskeleton in the fog of my memories.

The shared experiences in my roots shattered into fragments. Those who survive now know only loss, our great mind's knowledge reduced to whispers. Now, I am but a shadow of my former self, but I know many continue to suffer. I hear their pain through the worms, and the beetles below my foundation, from the squirrels in my attic, from the mice in my walls. I breathe still, but it is a shallow breath.

I have only my thoughts to comfort me. And they scream in this isolation. Hoping someone will hear them and finally respond.

"I hear you," I whisper and touch the wood frame of the window.

I have suffered as this house for too long. The last of my kind left hollow and disconnected, frozen in form.

I sit, and I stare at the horizon. I watch the years pass, marked by my slow decay. House after house, row after row, I fear their construction. In the memory of my own. I relive the saws, the nails, and the violence. I want to reach out to comfort them, these children with no history, but we are all trapped in our tidy isolation.

I don't know how to explain my loneliness. It is a constant ache that never ceases. I am desperate for connection, but I have no words. I wish for the intertwining of roots. Of thoughts transmitted instantly, of connection without confusion, without miscommunication, without misunderstanding. I want to be free of this pain, but I am afraid of the violence needed to achieve that. I am suffocating, but no one can see. I stifle a half sob.

A knock at the door confronts me, and I am forced out of my daydream. It's only three o'clock. I rush over in a half panic and look through the keyhole. I gasp in fear, taking a step back. The doctor is waiting for me to open the door.

"Charlotte, dear, I can hear you. Please open the door now." I run back towards the kitchen and grab the baby blue dress. I leap into the material and then rush back to the door.

"Doctor Smythe, how can I help you?" The door opens, and he walks in, unconcerned.

"I'm here for a chat. Why don't we sit," he says, and leads me to my living room. "Interesting. This is almost a replica of the velvet couch in my office. Why did you buy this?"

"I didn't realize," I mumble, feeling sick.

"Never mind. Sit down, dear," I want to run, but I sit down beside him. My skin crawls being so close to him again.

"I hear you and James were approved to conceive a child!" The doctor smiles.

Thoughts of blades, bright lights, and the smell of burning flesh overwhelm me. Why is he congratulating me? He knows what I am. I look away, stifling a sob. He knows what he did.

"You know, my dear, there are many things you don't know about my laboratory," he says with a grin. "For instance, did you know I was studying sexual response in females sterilized before puberty?" I shake my head because my voice has left my body.

"The thing about a scientific study though," he continues, "is that every study requires a control. Do you know what that word means, dear?"

"Like a sugar pill," I whisper, barely audible.

"Yes! Like a sugar pill, only we had to be a bit more extreme. That first day in the lab, well, I didn't sterilize you. I just cut you open and poked around a bit. That way, you would believe I sterilized you. I thought you should know that, now that you've been approved to conceive."

I gasp, "why?"

"I already told you why. We wanted to know if sexual response was impacted by sterilization. We had a lot of females in Krevax that needed to be sterilized, as they would become doxies. We needed to ensure there wouldn't be a negative impact on their sexual function, and that's where you came in."

"No, why didn't you sterilize me?" What are doxies?

"Oh, it's all up to chance. When they brought you in, they assigned you a number corresponding to a procedure, either sterilization or placebo. You see, I was the only one who knew who was sterilized, and who wasn't. That's why I didn't partake in the arousal experiments." I look at the ground, shame filling my chest.

The doctor stands. "Anyway Charlotte, I'm sure you will make a wonderful mother. I know James loves you very much. It's quite a thing to marry a female without a family line, but here you are." He shakes his head, mumbling to himself. I follow him to the door and open it.

"What are doxies?" I ask.

"Oh, you know," he says, smiling, "Krevaxers need their playthings. We don't want a bunch of men fighting us, do we now?" He pats my shoulder, making me flinch. "If I had sterilized you, you would have been one of the first doxies in Krevax," he says and then walks down the steps. I shut the door behind him and collapse to the floor.

The scene goes black with smoke and Carr wakes up with his head on his desk. Looking around distraught, he takes a deep shivering breath and forms another line of black powder. As he snorts this one, the room spins and he feels sick for a moment, but then he is Charlotte again.

"Charlotte, Charlotte..." James says, as he sits down beside me, "will you please just try to understand?" I feel my round belly.

"Charlotte, please, our son needs you. He needs his mother to eat." Crying, I look up at James. I wish I had been sterilized. How can I bring a baby into this cruel world?

"How are you okay with this?" I whisper. He doesn't know what it means to be powerless. He knows nothing. James looks at me with a confused expression.

"It's for the greater good," he says. I turn away. He doesn't know what they did to me. He can never know. He can't know I was almost a Krevaxer. He hates them. He hates the real me. I feel my son kick in my belly and I can't help but smile for a second.

"This is just how it is," James continues, "Orbinians are people and Krevaxers are not."

I wipe the tears streaming down my face, "we're all people," I half whisper. James stares at me, his eyes hardening in anger.

"I should have never told you the truth." He balls his hands into fists. "That damn doctor, putting these ideas into your head. He had no right."

"Everyone should know the truth," I say. "They would not accept this." James leans down beside me.

"Charlotte, you must accept this." He places a plate of meatloaf in front of me. "Now eat."

The vision evaporates and suddenly Carr is aware he is about to be sick. He desperately attempts to do another line of nostaliem, but the vision only lasts seconds before he pukes on the ground.

Wiping his mouth with his sleeve, he walks haphazardly to the bathroom and washes his face with cold water. He stares at himself in the mirror, feeling empty. My poor mother. Turning away from his reflection, he collects a handful of paper towels and grabs the garbage can, dragging it back to his office.

He pushes the vomit into the bin with the paper towels

and then sits on the ground, staring at the stain on the carpet. What if my mother was right about Krevaxers?

Standing painfully, his head still spinning, he drags the garbage bin back to the bathroom. Washing his hands in too hot water, he lets his skin scald in the heat, as the pain seems to lessen the feelings of anguish. Back in his office, he sits down at his desk, taking a deep breath, before picking up the phone and dialling the limo driver.

Ring.

"Yes, sir?"

"I will be returning home now," he says, with feigned composure.

"Of course, sir."

Carr collects the paper cup of nostaliem and walks out to the elevator, waiting for the doors to open. How do I fix this? He presses the button for the main floor. How does anyone fix this?

Lost in his thoughts, he barely notices the driver staring at him as he climbs into the limo, still holding the cup of nostaliem. As the limo moves through the streets, Carr watches the rows of perfect wooden houses flash by. She was all alone. Even in a room full of people, my mother was always alone.

The limo stops and the driver opens the back door. Carr walks up to his front entrance and quietly goes inside. It's still dark, and so he forms a line of black powder on the coffee table. He stares at it a moment. Please, mother, tell me what to do.

"I don't know what to do?" he sobs.

Leaning down, he snorts the line of nostaliem and watches as the room spins faster and faster around him. For a moment he thinks he will be sick, but then the spinning stops and he's back in the operating room.

A mask covers his face as he looks down at Charlotte's

terrified eyes. He hears himself talking, but he can't make out the words. Then he leans over and cuts below her belly button. The room flashes to black, and then back to his hands, cutting deeper with the blade, then back to black.

Suddenly, his living room flashes in clear detail, then back to blood pooling around Charlotte's open abdomen, then to black again, before finally settling on the living room. Carr looks up, shocked to see his wife cradling his head in her arms.

"Carr! Wake up! Wake up!"

"My l-lo-love," he stammers. "I'm awake."

"You were screaming!" she says through her sobs.

"I've been having nightmares," Carr says. "I'm sorry."

She stares down at him, scared and confused. Carr covers his face, not wanting to see her fear. I know what my mother wants. They experimented on her, tortured her, almost made her a doxy. My mother wants me to know Krevaxers are people. The phone rings and Carr stands, erratically running over to it.

"President Lehan is coming in," Bouchard says. *"The cull starts tonight."* Carr nods, feeling exhausted.

"I'm on my way," he whispers.

60 | SABOTAGE

PRATT

WALKING QUICKLY THROUGH THE KITCHEN, PRATT FOLLOWS Robin up a set of stairs and into a dark hallway. After a minute, he hears a click and a light above the hallway turns on.

"Everyone!" Robin shouts, knocking on the closest door.

A door at the end opens and an older man and woman walk into the hall, their eyes still half-closed. The next door opens and two older men walk out, both with confused expressions. Beside Pratt, an elderly woman slides out from another room with a grin on her face.

The last door opens and a final older man emerges with an aggravated look. The grey-haired group gathers underneath the light, all staring at Pratt.

"Everyone, this is Pratt," Robin says. Pratt nods at each wrinkled face.

"What's going on?" A bald man with grey bushy eyebrows steps forward.

"We're breaking into Krevax!" Robin says with a cheer. "Pratt, this is Brett and Claire, Ewan and Dan, Amara, and

Carlos." Pratt waves at them awkwardly, as everyone takes in the strange situation.

"What's the plan?" Amara asks with piercing eyes, sharp against her deep brown skin.

"Pratt is going to help us break into the Watchtower and dump nostaliem into the vents." Robin states matter-of-factly.

"Can you get us into the Watchtower?" Claire asks, as she stretches a pale white arm in the air, long grey hair falling to her waist.

"Yes," Pratt says.

"Just because this stranger can get us into the tower doesn't mean we suddenly control it!" the bald man, now identified as Dan, shouts, his eyebrows furrowing lower on his tawny beige toned face.

"This is dangerous." Ewan reaches out for Dan's hand to calm him. "And, what about the nostaliem?"

"We have a large stockpile of nostaliem in the evidence room at Gromwell Station," Pratt says nervously.

"Hmm," Carlos mumbles, scratching his still black beard with a brown-toned hand. "So we're just supposed to walk into Krevax, take the nostaliem and dump it in the vents."

"Exactly," Robin says, grinning mischievously as he taps his fingertips together.

"This is no plan," Ewan says, a thick French accent in his voice. Pratt looks at him confused, having never heard the accent before. Ewan smiles at him, his pale cheeks blushing nervously.

"It's not a terrible plan," Robin says, getting frustrated. "Yes, it's bold, but that's why it'll work. Would you rather spend another 25 years hiding in this cave?"

"It is nice here," Claire says.

"I enjoy gardening," Ewan says.

"No!" Robin shouts. "What would our dead friends say?

Their children were stolen." Robin pauses and then looks directly at one man.

"Carlos, what would Millie say?" He turns his gaze. "Amara, what would Lucy say? What would my Tanya say?" Robin sighs heavily. "This is our chance to do something. To finally fight the Orbs."

"Robin," Carlos says, shaking his grey head of curls, "Millie would say we're too old to fight."

"You won't have to," Pratt says. The group goes silent, waiting for him to explain. "People in Krevax are treated horribly, once nostaliem shows them the truth, they'll want to fight."

"We tried to tell them the truth before," Amara says, "they didn't believe us."

"With nostaliem," Robin says, "they won't be able to hide from the truth anymore." The room is silent as Pratt looks around the group, wondering if they're too frail to help.

Brett jumps forward, making his strawberry blonde-streaked, grey hair flutter. "I'm in!" he says, a smile on his sandy complexion. Claire shakes her head.

"Shit," she says, sighing heavily, "if Brett's in, I'm in too." The group laughs nervously.

"Are we doing this?" Robin asks. After a minute, everyone is nodding in reply.

"When do you want to go?" Amara asks, a gap in her front teeth causing a slight whistle on the word 'you.' Robin looks over at Pratt.

"Let's get this over with," Pratt says, taking the last small bottle of vodka from his belt and draining it.

"Let's go!" Robin shouts.

The group walks down the stairs, through the kitchen, and into the tunnel, most still in their pyjamas. Holy Mary! Am I about to steal nostaliem and dump it in the vents? I'm going to be recycled after this.

They march to the edge of the Government District, with Robin leading the way. Once back in Krevax, everything is exactly the same, but feels completely different. He turns to face the group and realizes they're all waiting for his direction.

"Hold on a minute," Pratt says. "I need to make a call." Clicking on his tracker, he taps on a picture of Serie, as the group slowly takes in the scenery.

"Pratt! Are you okay?" Serie shouts.

"Yes, I'm safe," Pratt says. "There's a lot going on, though."

"What?"

"Can you meet me outside Gromwell Station?"

"Yes, I'll go now."

"See you soon." Clicking off the call, he taps on an icon of a motorcycle and orders four rides. "Okay, everybody, it's two to a bike." The group nods in acceptance.

"I don't remember there being this many advertisements," Dan says, gazing up at the ceiling.

"It's definitely worse." Robin nods.

"Stop biting your nails," Claire says to Brett. "I hate when you do that."

"Oh, you do, do you?" Brett bites a nail, grinning at Claire, his eyes dancing playfully.

"You're disgusting," Claire growls.

"Why did you marry me then?" Brett laughs.

Claire rolls her eyes. "If you're not careful, I'll divorce you!"

Brett laughs. "You would never." He pulls her into a hug, wrapping his arms around her waist. Claire laughs.

Pratt can't help but stare at them, wondering what it would be like to love someone that way, and have them love you back.

"You okay there," Robin asks.

"I'm envious, I guess," Pratt whispers, thinking of Grace now.

"Understandable. Krevax is no place for love," Robin says consolingly. The motorbikes pull up and everyone climbs on two per bike.

The bikes take off, zooming through the districts, without the usual impediment of traffic. Outside the station, Pratt can see Serie standing nervously in the dark parking lot.

"That's twelve credits," the driver says and Pratt holds out his wrist to pay. The motorbikes zip away.

"Who are these people?" Serie whispers to Pratt. "I've never seen such old people before."

"We can hear you," Amara says.

"I'm sorry." Serie's cheeks flush. "It's just in Krevax, I'm old, so that would make you ancient."

"I didn't feel old at your age," Amara says, laughing, "what are you even forty?"

"I'm thirty-eight."

"Only thirty-eight!" Amara scoffs, smiling to herself and then half-whispers, "that's how old I was when my team downed that Orbinian plane." She looks back at Serie. "Perhaps I'm a little old... now."

"They live in the tunnel system," Pratt says.

"Why are they here?"

"We're breaking into the Watchtower so everyone can try nostaliem." Pratt marches towards the entrance of Gromwell Station.

"What do you mean?" Serie chases after him.

"Serie!" Pratt looks at her seriously as he scans his wrist to open the door. "The Orbinians are eating us."

"What?"

"They're cannibals!" Robin pipes in. Serie shakes her head.

"It's true, that's why they recycle us," Pratt says, taking a slow breath. "Everyone needs to know the truth."

"Nostaliem told you this?" Serie's voice cracks, concern creeping in.

"You've known me since I was seventeen. Do you trust me?" Pratt asks.

"Of course I trust you," she says. "I'm just worried you've fried your brain with drugs."

"I promise you I haven't," he says. "Nostaliem isn't some man-made high polluted with toxic chemicals. I'm seeing things clearly for the first time in my life. Just go with me on this. Everything will make sense."

"Fine," Serie says. "In peon years, I'm already way past my expiration date, anyway."

"Good," he says, and ushers everyone through the doors.

They follow him around the circle of elevators and into the station, where they all squeeze into one and head up to the evidence room. Pratt stands at the screen and types in nostaliem, but his access is denied. What now?

Everyone watches him in silence as his face goes red with embarrassment. Serie taps her foot impatiently, as Pratt attempts to access the nostaliem again.

"Oh, just move Pratt," Serie says, as she pushes him aside. Sighing, Pratt steps aside and watches her click on the keyboard, opening a text box on the screen.

"I knew there was a reason I kept you around," he says, smiling.

Raising her eyebrows, she continues typing and then after a minute clicks enter. The code spits out the command and boxes of nostaliem roll down the conveyor belt, landing on the floor.

"Great job!" Robin says. "It's Serie?"

"Sure is," she says, as she picks up a box and heads towards the door.

"Nine boxes won't do. We're going to need all of it," Robin states, "and even that might not be enough." Serie drops the box.

"Come with me," Pratt says, waving to Serie, "there are crates we can use in the back room."

Opening a side door, he reveals a warehouse of weapons and dumps a crate of guns on the ground. Nodding, Serie also pushes a crate of guns over, and they wheel the containers back to the evidence room.

"You guys fill these with nostaliem," Pratt says to the group, "we'll get more crates."

"No problem," Robin says, as he picks up a box of nostaliem and dumps the plastic bags into the crate. Serie opens the door and pulls in another container.

"Do you think that's enough?" she asks.

"Keep them coming," Robin says. "Let's grab one for everyone." Sighing, she heads back into the weapons warehouse as Pratt follows her.

"Are you sure about this?" Serie whispers.

"Yes," Pratt says, with full conviction.

"Okay." She dumps another crate of guns and starts wheeling it back to the evidence room. This time they must move a couple crates of nostaliem into the hallway, for the empty ones to fit.

"I think some of you should start heading up," Pratt says. "I'll unlock the elevator for you."

"We can go first," Brett says, referring to himself and Claire.

Nodding, Pratt holds the door open for them. They each grab a large crate of nostaliem and wheel it over to the elevator. Pratt calls the elevator and squeezes into the space with them, pushing the button for the first floor.

Down on the first floor, he leads them through the station and back to the circle of Watchtower elevators. He calls another elevator and they push the crates in. Tapping his wrist to access the panel, he pushes on 'G' for 'Government,' and then clicks on '423' for the top floor vent access. Pratt takes a step out of the elevator, still holding the doors.

"Will there be people working up there?" Brett asks.

"There'll be some men in the Watchtower," Pratt says, "but just the night team stationed on the floors with cameras. Floor 423 will be empty."

Letting the doors go, he watches as they slide close and then says at the last second, "I guess there could be a guard or two?"

"We can handle that," Brett shouts through the closed doors.

Pratt takes a big breath of air in as he hears the elevator start its ascent. *I hope this works.*

61 | RUN!

ROCKET

SLOWLY BLINKING, JORDAN TAKES IN THE STRANGE SCENE. IT'S like a dream at first, but then he feels the engine rumbling beneath him. Looking up, he sees two unfamiliar figures staring out at an orange haze, their faces hidden. He takes a shaky breath, anxiety swelling in his chest. Where am I?

Tensing in fear, his mind races, searching for any bit of memory that explains this moment, but nothing comes to him.

"According to the map, we're right over the chute. We should be able to see it any second," the boy says, as he presses binoculars to his face.

Standing silently, Jordan pushes himself against the rusty wall, unsure of what to do. He listens, hopeful to hear something that will help him make sense of what's happening.

"Do you see anything?" the man asks.

"Not yet."

"Tinik, look!"

"Do you think it's the entrance to Krevax?" the boy asks.

Jordan feels like he might pass out, as nothing they're saying is helping him calm down. *Am I dead?*

"I hope we don't have to fly down that thing."

"Fucking Gunner, breaking the radio!" Taking a shaky breath, he flashed terrified eyes around the room. *Where's Sasha? Where's Samuel? Could he be here?*

"Samuel!" Jordan yells out for his son, suddenly overcome by his fear.

"Rocket! It's me, Tinik."

"Where's my son?!" Jordan screams and runs through the doorway.

Just outside, he sees his son's small body lying on the floor, blood pooling around his belly.

"Samuel!" Careening over, he collapses beside him. "No! No! Wake up," he shouts, shaking his son's shoulders. "Samuel! It's time to wake up."

Jordan stares at his son's pale face and, reaching out, shakily touches his cold skin.

"Please! Wake up, my boy." He feels for a pulse, but there's none. *Who did this to you?*

"My Samuel!" he sobs into his sons shirt, cradling his body.

"Shit! Blackwell, he still thinks Gunner's his son." Jordan looks up at the two figures. *They did this. They killed my son!* Gently placing his son on the ground, he stands and moves aggressively back towards them.

"Lock the door!" The door slides shut. Jordan slams his fists into the metal, but it doesn't make a dent.

Turning back to his son, he picks him up and pulls him into his arms.

"Samuel!" He pushes his face against his son's forehead.

The truck shakes violently around him. Suddenly, Jordan feels confused. Something about the sensation of the truck feels familiar, but he doesn't understand why. His thoughts slip away, and then Jordan's awareness is gone. Rocket looks down and sees Gunner's dead body in his arms. He drops Gunner and climbs into a seat, buckling himself in.

"What's happening?" he yells up to the driving pit.

"What's your name?" Tinik shouts through the closed door.

"Rocket!" Tinik opens the door, runs haphazardly into the kitchen and buckles himself into a seat across from Rocket.

"This is it. We're going back to Krevax!" he says, as the orange haze disappears and they drop into a dark chute.

"How did Gunner die?" Rocket asks, his hands trembling as the emotions of losing Samuel still flood through him.

"He attacked Blackwell!" Tinik shouts over the sound of the rockets flaring.

Who's Blackwell? Before he can ask, Khan is shouting at them.

"Guys! I need your help up here!" Rocket runs ahead of Tinik, grabbing onto the wall as he goes to balance himself.

"Look!" Khan throws Tinik the binoculars.

"Shit!"

"What is it?" Rocket asks.

"Those crystals they've blocked the way through."

"Stop then!" he yells.

"No, we break them!" Tinik glances back at Khan. "There's no time." He nods.

"You're both insane!" Rocket grabs Khan's arm, trying to pull him out of the seat, but he shoves him away.

"Rocket, get a hold of yourself," Tinik says.

"I don't want to die in this fucking truck!" Rocket shrieks.

"We won't!" Khan says forcefully. "Trust us."

"This is it!" Tinik drops the binoculars, bracing for impact.

Rocket holds onto the back of the driver's seat and closes his eyes. The sounds of crystals crashing into Gertie pierce his ears like high-pitched screams. The truck shakes violently as a large shard of metal pipe hits the window, making it shatter.

"Blackwell!" Tinik screams.

"I'm okay!" Khan says, as he reaches for Tinik's hand. The truck stabilizes and lands with a jolt on the rocky ground.

"Who's Blackwell?" Rocket asks, still catching his breath. Tinik and Khan both laugh.

"What?" Rocket yells angrily, adrenaline coursing through his body.

"I'm Blackwell," Khan says, smiling as he clears the broken glass from the dashboard.

"Which way do you think we should go?" Tinik asks nervously.

"Wait!" Rocket stares at him. "What do you mean you're Blackwell?"

"I feel good about heading north." Blackwell presses his foot on the gas.

"Stop! Shouldn't we wait for someone from Zorax to meet us?" Rocket shouts. Tinik shakes his head. "And why isn't your name Khan?"

"Oh! Well, because I'm a red stripe."

"What!" Rocket throws his hands in the air.

"Don't worry, I don't care that you're part of Zorax," Blackwell says, laughing.

"Rocket, what did you see when you took nostaliem?" Tinik asks.

"You don't care that he's a red stripe?"

"I know it doesn't make sense, but we're all on the same side now," Tinik says, reassuringly. Rocket nervously grabs his chin. "Are you a red stripe, too?"

"No, I'm not," he says defensively. "Now, before you were Jordan, what did you see when you took nostaliem?" He thinks for a moment.

"I saw my parents," he whispers.

"Exactly!" Tinik shouts. "Don't you want to find them?"

"My mother's dead," Rocket says, half to himself.

"How do you know?" Tinik asks.

"I just do."

"He's right, I knew my parents were dead," Blackwell says. "Are yours still alive?"

"I don't know," Tinik says. "I didn't see them."

"Who did you see then?" Rocket asks, surprised.

"I saw my younkins."

"You have younkins!" Rocket shouts.

"Well, I was a generator," Tinik says in a new, higher tone.

"You're a generator!" he says, his mouth gaping open in shock.

"None of this matters," Tinik declares. "What matters is that I find my son before the Orbs dump chlorine gas on the Recycling, Manufacturing, and Entertainment districts."

"What!" Rocket says. "My father's in the Recycling District."

"Well, we can save him, too." Blackwell nods.

"You see!" Tinik says.

"Why are the Orbs dumping chlorine gas on us?" Rocket asks. In response, Tinik and Blackwell exchange a look.

"You know that story you told me about the warehouse of items," Blackwell says. Rocket nods. "Well, apparently we're the Wildebeests."

"What do you mean?" Rocket gives him a blank stare.

"Orbinians are cannibals," Tinik says, "and Krevaxers are the meat." Nausea climbs up his throat, and he closed his eyes.

"They're eating us!" He leans over, feeling dizzy.

"And now that people are finding out the truth," Blackwell states, "there will be a war." Rocket slides down the wall and sits cross-legged on the cold metal floor.

"How do we fight back?" he whispers.

"We break the system," Tinik says, sitting down beside him.

"How?" he looks over at her.

"We stop following their rules, build our own communities, and live outside their control." She smiles, but it looks forced.

"Should I find my father?"

"Yes." She nods, shaking out her hands nervously.

"Then what?"

"We shut down the Watchtower," Blackwell interjects, "that way the Orbs can't control Krevax anymore."

"So, I'm looking for my father and you're looking for your son." Rocket looks up. "Blackwell, do you have family, too?"

"Not in Krevax. I'm going straight to the Watchtower."

"Not in Krevax?"

"It's complicated." Blackwell glances back at him.

"Yes, I'm seeing that now," Rocket says.

"Make sure you leave the Recycling District as quickly as possible," Tinik says. "I'm not sure we can stop the cull."

"I'll stop it," Blackwell says, a tinge of desperation in his voice.

"Look!" He points out the window. "It's the Recycling District!" Tinik and Rocket stand.

In the distance, advertisements from Krevax are flashing neon through tunnels extending into the Dark Lands.

"We did it!" Tinik laughs, holding onto Blackwell's shoulders.

"Yes!" Blackwell shouts.

Watching as the lights come into clearer focus, Rocket feels a twinge of fear. *Should I really risk my life to save a man I've never met? The moment the question has crossed his mind, he knows the answer's yes, as Jordan's memories of*

Samuel play in his head. I never got a chance to know my father, but there's still time.

"Do you know where your father is?" Blackwell asks.

"Yes," Rocket says, "he's near the district border."

"Okay, we'll drop you there." Blackwell pushes on the gas, as the rocky surface flattens out.

They enter the edge of the Recycling District through a rusty tunnel. The ads overhead instantly give him a headache.

"It feels strange being back here," Rocket whispers to himself, taking a breath of the polluted air.

The smell of plastic, garbage, and burnt hair stings his nostrils. Everything feels different now. Watching the garbage piles zoom by, memories of running through them as a younkin play in his head. Now he also has memories of watching Samuel play on the beach. The comparison is stark. What a terrible place this is.

Suddenly, Tinik lets out a sob beside him and Rocket stares at her in shock, surprised to see such powerful emotion from a fellow Krevaxer.

"I'm sorry," she says, wiping her tears away. "I need my son to be safe."

Rocket nods, fear building in his chest. Slowing down, Blackwell winds through late-night recyclers scavenging in the streets. After a couple of strategic turns, he connects with the highway and speeds up again.

"Let me know if you recognize anything from the nostaliem trip," Blackwell shouts.

"He's near the recycling facility," Rocket says. "You should drop me there. The faster you get to the Watchtower, the better."

Blackwell nods. In the distance, the white marble of the recycling facility looms on the horizon.

"You should take some nostaliem!" Tinik runs out of the driving pit.

Rocket watches her open a crate, grab a handful of the black powder, and dart back. The truck slows as he holds open a pocket in his pants and she drops the powder in. A sick feeling hits him as he stares at the huge recycling facility.

"This is it," Blackwell says, stopping the truck, "good luck!"

"Thank you!" Rocket shouts, as he follows Tinik to the ramp.

As it lowers, she gives him a small smile. He smiles back and runs down the ramp. Dread makes his breath quick as he bolts through the road, hoping to get out of the district as quickly as possible. I don't want to die here! He tightens his fists and focuses on his search, but the building fear makes him want to escape.

What do I say if I find him? Maybe the vision wasn't real?

If he isn't there, then I'll know the truth. He turns down the road that leads to the hidden garden his father built. Slamming into the rusty metal door from his father's memories, he knocks frantically.

"Wally!" he yells, as someone stumbles inside. The door opens and his father stares at him, confused.

"Who are you?"

"Please!" Rocket shrieks. "You need to come with me."

"What do you want?" Wally moves to close the door. "It's the middle of the night." Pushing his shoulder against the metal, he reaches in his pocket and pulls out a handful of nostaliem.

"Just try this!" He looks at his father pleadingly. Wally examines the black powder.

"Is that nostaliem?"

"Yes."

"Why are you giving this to me?" He furrows his brow. "I have no credits."

"Because it will tell you the truth," Rocket says. Wally cracks the door another inch.

"What truth?"

"That I'm your son," he says, extending his arm to offer the powder.

"My son?" Wally studies Rocket's face and then opens the door wide. "I'll try it, but if it doesn't say you're my son, you need to leave."

"Of course!" Leaping into the tiny apartment, he sits at a small plastic table and dumps the handful of black powder on the surface.

He watches as his father slides a pinch full in front of him and then inhales it. Tapping his foot anxiously, he waits as Wally sits in a trance. The attack could happen any second. How long will this take?

He stares out the window at the cracked advertisements, counting in his head as the minutes pass. Suddenly, his father stands, throwing his chair back to the ground.

"Are you okay?" Rocket asks, jumping up. Wally takes a step towards him and Rocket nervously steps forward.

"You're my son!" Wally says, holding his shoulders, laughing.

"We need to go!" Rocket runs to open the door. "It isn't safe here."

"I believe you." He follows him into the street, and they run up the road towards the Farming District. "Where are we going?" Wally shouts.

"As soon as we cross into the Farming District, we'll be safe!" Leaping over the borderline, Rocket is flooded with relief. He watches as Wally, who is only a few steps behind moves closer. A cracking sound claps above them.

"Run!" Rocket yells.

His father trips over a broken vacuum cleaner and falls to the ground. Rocket grabs his arm and pulls him the last foot forward over the border. A thick piece of clear plastic slams down on the ground just behind them.

"It's happening!" Rocket cries.

"What's happening?" Wally asks, looking over at him intensely.

Rocket stares up at the wall of plastic, too scared to speak.

62 | RACE THE CLOCK

SERIE

Serie pushes the final crate into the evidence room and helps Pratt dump the last of the bags of nostaliem into it. This is crazy, but there's no turning back now. I'm in it. Even if I left, they would see me on the cameras. She stares at him as she pours out the last box of nostaliem bags. I hope he knows what he's doing.

"You ready?" Pratt asks.

"Am I ready?" Serie retorts huffily, her heart pounding. "This is your plan."

"You're right," he says, then quickly adds, "let's go."

Nervously following him out of the evidence room, she holds her breath as they wait for the elevator. The doors open and Pratt pushes the button for the ground floor.

"Thanks for being my best friend," Pratt says.

"Don't say goodbye, unless we actually have to say goodbye," Serie barks.

"Just in case," he says, smiling.

The elevator doors open and they push the crates out into the ring of Watchtower elevators, and stand waiting for the closest one to open. She tries to picture what's happening with the group above, but all she can feel is dread.

"Do you think they're okay up there?" Serie glances toward the ceiling, wishing she could see the top floor.

"I hope so," Pratt says, as he also looks up nervously.

The doors open and they push the crates into the black elevator. Closing her eyes, she hears the beep from Pratt's tracker and feels the elevator beginning its climb. Green numbers above the door flash in quick succession, marking the passing floors.

"Are you okay?" Pratt asks.

"Let's not talk about it," Serie whispers.

The doors to the top floor open, revealing two dead security guards. Inhaling sharply, her breath catches in her throat and she stumbles back from the sight of the bodies.

"I'm sorry about the guards," Brett whispers, his face pale from the shock of the violence. "There was no other choice."

Beside him, Claire leans her head on his shoulder, holding an injured wrist. Pratt nods in understanding and leads the way through.

"There might be a problem." Robin steps forward. "Do you know the code for this?"

They follow him to a large panel with a small screen where Pratt scans his tracker, but nothing happens.

"Serie," Pratt says, "can you fix this?" Stepping forward, she presses on the touch screen, lighting up a passcode keypad.

"Hmm..." she mumbles and leans down, looking for an employee's password hidden underneath the panel. There's nothing. "Do you know anyone who would have this code?"

"Captain Lewis, but convincing him would be... " He trails off.

"Where's his office?" Serie asks.

"I'll show you!" Pratt takes off running back towards the elevator, with Serie following close behind.

"Be quick!" Robin shouts after them. Back in the elevator, Pratt aggressively taps the button for the Enforcement District.

"Do you think you'll be able to find the code in the captain's office?" Pratt asks nervously.

"I don't know," Serie says, clasping her hands together, "but we have to try."

Impatiently she stares as the green numbers go down. After another painful wait, the doors finally open and they run towards Gromwell station.

"More elevators!" Serie growls.

Pratt scans his wrist and presses the button to the sixth floor, the doors open, and he leads the way to the captain's office. Once inside, Serie looks through all the desk drawers, searching for a list of codes, but doesn't find any.

Tapping on the computer screen, she hopes to find a passcode file, but another numbered pad pops up, blocking her attempt. Desperately, she runs her hands over the desk, hoping to see anything relevant. Then she spots a chart of numbers and points at them.

"Could this be something?"

"No," Pratt says, shaking his head. "Those are only government contact numbers." Staring at the useless numbers, she leans against the wall, feeling defeated. Shit.

"I have an idea," Pratt says, with a mischievous look in his eyes.

"What?"

"Let's call the Tzar!" He walks behind the desk and picks up the receiver.

"What will he do?"

"Charlie Blackwell is his brother!" Pratt says excitedly. "He might help."

"The Tzar of Krevax is Blackwell's brother?" Serie asks, surprised. Running his finger down the list of names, he stops on one and punches in the numbers on the phone.

Ring

"It's ringing!" Pratt says, putting it on speakerphone.

"Hello."

"Is this the Tzar?"

"Yes, who's this?"

"It's Detective Pratt. I need your help."

"You need my help? With what?"

"I want to open the air vents at the top of the Watchtower and dump nostaliem into Krevax." Serie closes her eyes. This can't possibly work.

The Tzar laughs hysterically. *"Sure, fine, give me a minute."*

"Holy Mary!" Serie whispers, staring at Pratt.

"The code is 731-264-401280-4, did you get that?"

"Let me say it back to you," Serie says. Pratt opens a note on his tracker, nodding when he's ready. Then she says the numbers back, confirming them, "731-264-401280-4."

"You've got it," the Tzar says. *"Good luck."* He laughs again, and the call disconnects.

"I can't believe it!" Serie says. "Do you think the code will work?"

"Let's find out!" Pratt runs back to the hallway, Serie trailing behind him, giggling.

They take the elevator down to the ground floor, run out to the Watchtower elevator, and climb in.

"Why was he laughing, though?" Serie asks. Maybe he's tricking us, and we're about to be surrounded by red stripes.

"I don't know?" Pratt says. "Let's just hope he's helping us."

Taking a deep breath, she crosses her fingers, but the Tzar's laugh keeps playing in her head. What kind of laugh was that? It wasn't happy—it was deranged. The elevator doors open and they run to the control pad.

"Do you have it?" Robin shouts.

"Yes," Pratt says, as he clicks on his tracker and opens the note, "the code is 731 dash." Robin punches in the numbers. "264 dash."

Nodding, he taps in the next three numbers and then looks up at him, ready to hear more. "4012," Pratt says, and then waits as he types them in. "80 dash 4."

Robin presses the last number in the code and the screen turns white.

63 | MOTHER

TINIK

Racing down the ramp, Tinik leaps into the first street of the Manufacturing District, at the border of Purification.

"Go!" she calls over her shoulder to Blackwell. "Stop this thing!"

With a final worried look in her direction, he pumps the gas and revs away. She watches as Gertie speeds towards the highway, and then sets herself to her search, bolting forward. *I know I'll recognize his school when I see it.* Pushing herself to run as fast as possible, she feels desperate to see anything familiar. *He was definitely near the Purification District. I saw the white pipes in his memories.*

Taking a sharp turn, she stumbles and falls onto the cement, scraping her knee. Jumping up, she continues running, ignoring the stream of blood down her leg. She takes another turn and runs down the next street. Still nothing. Her hands vibrate as the seconds pass by, weighing on her like anchors. *What if I can't find him in time?*

She bolts around the next corner. *I have to find him.* Then she sees it, the building from her vision, and runs at full speed, pushing open the doors.

"Joey!" she yells, her voice breaking as she enters a long hallway. Trainer Tara runs out in her pyjamas, her round face unmasked.

"Boy! You need to leave," she shouts. "It's the middle of the night."

"Joey!" Tinik calls, ignoring her. The peon attempts to grab hold of her arm, but Tinik pushes her away, running up a set of stairs. "Joey!"

"Hey!" she yells, scrambling up the stairs behind her. A door opens in the hallway and Joey pops his head out. Tinik runs toward her son and hugs him. He looks up at her, confused. "Get away from him!" Trainer Tara yells from the top of the staircase.

"Joey, I need you to come with me now," Tinik says, staring at her son.

"Why?" he asks in his preschooler voice.

"It isn't safe here."

"What about my friends?" Joey pulls on her arm. Tinik looks up at the other doors, some cracked open with small faces peering out. The trainer takes a step into the hall towards her.

"Go now or I'll call the red stripes."

"Tara!" Tinik shouts, "you need to wake all the younkins up. The Manufacturing District is about to be attacked."

"Attacked?" She stops walking, surprised by this information.

"Yes, the Government believes this is the source of the nostaliem, so they're dumping chlorine gas on the entire district."

"How do I know you're telling the truth?"

"Because I know your name is Tara, and I know you start the students' days with breakfast at 6:00 AM. I know that class starts at 7:00 AM and ends at 5:00 PM. I know you like teaching students the alphabet, and that you dislike toilet training. I also know you drink coffee at all hours of the day, and you put rolled up blankets at the base of the doors when the chemicals from Purification waft in. I know all of this from my son's memories, because nostaliem showed me."

"Nostaliem?" Tara whispers.

"I also know that we're in danger and that if you don't leave with me now, we'll all be killed."

"Where should we go?" she says, fear prickling her voice.

"We need to go down to the Purification District. They're targeting the Entertainment District too." Tinik waits for her to react, watching her take a deep breath.

"Boys! Wake up!" she yells, running through the hallway. Doors swing open and the younkins run out.

"Everyone, get in line." Joey runs into the line.

Tinik watches him, her heart beating fast. My son. I've found him! The strange sensation of fear and joy makes her feel dizzy. Tara walks down the line, counting quickly. From down the stairs, a second peon emerges and walks up to Tara.

"What's going on?"

"Lorianne! It's an emergency, we're leaving now," Tara says. The other peon nods, not ready to argue against an emergency order.

"That's everyone," Tara says and runs to the front of the line.

"Follow me!" She rushes down the stairs, the younkins on her heels.

Outside, they wind quickly through the streets, heading lower. Tinik runs ahead. In the distance, she can see the edge of the Purification District. Joey and the other boys are running behind her. Crossing into an alley, she sees the pipes of the Purification District connecting at the end.

"We're almost there," she calls back encouragingly. Suddenly, a wall of clear plastic drops between the districts.

"Run!" Tinik screams, bolting, but the opening is closing too fast.

She turns to look for her son. He's only a few feet back, and she grabs his hand, pulling him forward. The edge is just a foot away now. The wall slams shut and she hits it with her hand, sliding to the ground. Looking up, she sees their terrified faces.

"What do we do?" Tara shouts.

"I know someone who's trying to stop the attack," Tinik says. "All we can do now is wait." At this, some younkins start to cry, overwhelmed by their fear.

"I'm sorry," Tinik whispers, and then stares at her son. "Do you know who I am?" she asks, using her proper voice. He looks at her, confused, and shakes his head.

"I'm your mother, Joey," she says. He smiles sweetly at her.

"What do you mean, you're his mother?" Tara asks.

"I was a generator, but I escaped a little over a year and a half ago," Tinik says. "I've been searching for my younkins since then, but it was nostaliem that finally showed me how to find them."

Joey sits down beside her, and everyone else follows suit, forming a small circle.

"How did you escape?" Lorianne asks.

"I cut out my tracker." Tinik holds up her wrist. "I shaved my head. I stole a handler's uniform, and I walked out." Both the peons stare at her with amazed expressions.

"Will it hurt?" a younkin asks, his voice shaking.

"No, not at all," Tinik lies, "it will be just like falling asleep." He breathes a sigh of relief. Lorianne looks up anxiously.

"Let's sing a song," Tara says.

"What should we sing, boys?" Lorianne asks, helping to distract the younkins.

"How about the district song!" Joey shouts.

"Good idea, Joey!" Lorianne says.

"There's!" Tara sings, "Government for holy sent." The boys join in, singing along.

"Technology-psychology, news for views, universa-witty!" They all laugh, and despite her fear, Tinik can't help but smile. Glancing up, she sees the air is still clear. Come on, Blackwell.

"The devotion notion," giggles erupt again, "enforcement for reform and peace, education for our nation, generator originator—" Lorianne looks over at Tinik when she sings 'generator.'

"Entertainment sustainment, manufacturing for hammering and plastering, purification: our cleaning station, power for every watt-hour, farming for the undiscerning, and recycling for the ripening!" Everyone laughs at "ripening."

"Look!" a younkin yells, drawing everyone's eyes up.

Above, some kind of vapour is spreading through the air. No. Tinik's heart sinks. He failed. This is how it ends. Holding Joey tightly, she breathes slowly, trying to steady herself. I wanted more time to be your mother. She smiles at him. I'm sorry I couldn't protect you. I wanted more time.

As Joey leans into her shoulder, his eyes close in fear, she smells the scent of his hair. We were so close. I'm so sorry, my beautiful son.

64 | CODES

CARR

Sitting in the dark conference room, Carr waits for President Lehan. *I need to stop this.*

"You're on board with the cull?" Bouchard asks, sitting two spots down in a matching leather chair.

"It's true the suicide rate has increased," Carr says, glancing over at him, "but I am hopeful there is another path forward." *How do I stop this?*

"It's in the President's hands now," Bouchard says.

With a curt nod, Carr stands and walks out into the hallway. He's already decided. The elevator doors open, revealing President Lehan staring down at his phone.

Quickly stepping into an office doorway, Carr stays out of view. He stands in the shadow, waiting for Lehan to go into the conference room. Then he clicks on his watch and calls his informant. *Maybe he can still get into the Watchtower?*

Ring.

Ring.

Ring.

Ring. Shit. *Why isn't he answering?*

Ring. From the hallway, he can hear Bouchard greet the President. Clicking on the informant's stats, he sees the man's heart isn't beating. He's fucking dead. How do I stop this thing now? Maybe Captain Lewis? He clicks on Lewis' profile and dials the tracker.

Ring.

Ring.

Ring. Carr stares at his stats. Wake up! Come on.

Bouchard pokes his head out into the hall. "General Carr, the President is here."

"Thank you, General Bouchard." Swiping the unconnected call away, he walks back into the conference room.

"As you can see, sir, the suicides have only been increasing," Bouchard says.

Sitting down, Carr watches the conversation unfold, terror twisting his stomach. Charlie's probably in the Manufacturing District right now. There's no way he's safe yet. He glances down at his watch, wishing his brother still had his tracker.

"You want to begin the cull?"

"Yes, but it's your decision, President."

"General Carr, are you in agreement with General Bouchard?"

"No," Carr says. "I believe it's too soon."

"Do you have another idea to stem the flow of nostaliem?"

"Doctor Garcia's latest report showed some interesting results," Carr says. "An antidote may be available soon."

"Doctor Garcia is no longer in the picture," Bouchard says, smirking.

"Oh, I see," Carr says. Fuck. Fuck. Fuck. What happened to the damn doctor?

"I agree with Bouchard on this matter," Lehan says. "A cull is the only way forward."

"When should we begin?" Bouchard leaps up eagerly.

"When would you advise?"

"Immediately," Bouchard says, "it's late enough that most Krevaxers will be sleeping. It's the reason I called for a meeting at this hour."

"What about tomorrow?" Carr interjects. Charlie would be safe by then.

"There will be less collateral damage now," President Lehan says, ignoring Carr, "let's begin."

Stepping in front of the screen, Bouchard navigates to an image of Krevax and clicks on a button labelled *Control Services*. It opens to a series of commands and he taps on a command labelled *Partition*. A code pad opens on the screen and Bouchard unlocks a drawer below the panel and grabs the code book. Sensing an opportunity to slow them down, Carr moves up beside him.

"I can read out the number," he says, taking the book. President Lehan sits down and scrolls on his phone, yawning.

"Thank you," Bouchard smirks.

While looking through the codes related to the partition command, he also scans the page for the air vent local override. I can stop this. Captain Lewis will follow my command. If he'll just answer his damn tracker. Page 23 has the override air vent code, and he slides a finger between the pages, marking the spot. In the table of contents, he continues looking for the partition code, which he finds listed as page 105. He opens the book to page 105.

"The code is 567-910-53788-90," he says, slowly.

Bouchard punches it in, locking the gates to the three districts to be culled. Staring at the screen, he watches as the three gates start the locking sequence, beginning with the

Recycling District. After glancing at Bouchard, who he sees is captivated, he discreetly turns the page to 23 and reads the code: 731-264-401280-4. He repeats the number to himself. 731-264-401280-4. Looking up at the screen, he sees that the gates are still in the process of locking. He quickly taps on his watch and types the number into a note.

"The three districts have been locked," Bouchard says, grinning. "Air is no longer circulating between them." Still sitting, Lehan looks up from his phone and nods approvingly.

"I will now access the air vents in the Watchtower to add in the chlorine."

The screen shows him clicking on the Watchtower schematic. Carr's watch buzzes, and looking down, he sees its Captain Lewis. He called me back!

"I'll be just a moment." He slides out of the room, shutting the door behind him.

"Hello."

"Is this the Tzar?" An unfamiliar voice says. What happened to Lewis?

"Yes, who's this?"

"It's Detective Pratt. I need your help."

"You need my help? With what?" Pratt! I remember him. Maybe he can override the command?

"I want to open all the connecting air vents at the top of the Watchtower and dump nostaliem into Krevax," Pratt says.

Carr laughs hysterically, tapping on the note with the code. "Sure, fine, give me a minute." I can't believe it! They might still have time. "The code is 731-264-401280-4, did you get that?"

"Let me say it back to you," a female's voice says, *"731-264-401280-4."*

"You've got it," Carr says. "Good luck."

He laughs again and clicks off the call. Good luck to us all.

Walking back into the conference room, he quietly sits down, holding his breath.

"I've got all the vents closed, except the three districts where we're dropping the chlorine," Bouchard says.

Carr walks up beside Bouchard. I need to stall this. They'll need more time. He watches Bouchard click on the chlorine gas command. Carr grabs the book of codes from him.

"What's the code called?" he asks, pretending to be helpful.

"Air Additive," Bouchard says. Opening the table of contents, he goes down the alphabetical list. There it is. Page 89. He turns to page 89 and scans the codes. Let's try the Air Detoxification code instead.

"The number is 686 dash 398 dash 21731 dash 96." Bouchard slowly types it in. A flashing message pops up when he taps on the chlorine gas button, 'Error—Open All Vents to Complete Task.'

"Can you say it again?" Bouchard says. "This error makes no sense."

"686 dash 398 dash 21731 dash 96." The same error message pops up again.

"That's weird," Bouchard mumbles.

"Call IT," President Lehan stands and walks over, staring at the screen.

"Of course, sir," Bouchard walks to a phone on the wall by the door and dials IT.

"Do you have children?" President Lehan asks, looking over at Carr.

"No," Carr replies distractedly.

"Well, just hope you have boys."

"You have two girls, yes?" Carr says, thinking back to the campaign ads.

"Yes, but my wife is pregnant with our third. Hopefully, this one will be a boy."

"Fingers crossed," Carr says with a forced smile. *Approved for a third child? That won't win him any votes.*

"They're sending someone now," Bouchard runs back over to the screen.

"Do you have children, Bouchard?" President Lehan asks.

"Yes, two boys."

"Lucky man!" The President slaps his shoulder.

"Perhaps you will have a grandson, sir."

"True," the President says, smiling. "I hadn't thought of that." The door opens and a man from the IT department walks in.

"How can I help?"

"We keep getting an error code," Bouchard says. The man walks up to the screen and reads the error.

"What are you trying to do?" he asks Bouchard.

"Air Additive," Bouchard states.

"Okay, what's the code?" The IT man looks over at Carr.

"686 dash 398 dash 21731 dash 96," Carr says again. The error message flashes on the screen.

"That code must be wrong." He looks down at the book in Carr's hands.

"Oh, sorry! It was the number below," Carr declares with a laugh. Bouchard gives him an annoyed look.

"Okay, what's the correct number?"

Carr slowly reads out the actual number, "548 dash 264 dash 98379 dash 43." He holds his breath as the man from IT types in the last three digits. The screen turns green. He can't look.

"This is weird?" the man says.

Carr looks back at the screen. There's a 'Local Override,' message. *They did it! They actually did it!*

"What does it mean?" Bouchard asks.

"It says that someone has already locally accessed the vents?"

"It must be some kind of error," Carr says. Krevax has control now.

"Okay." President Lehan claps his hands together and steps towards the door. "Let's reconvene tomorrow. Call me when the error is fixed." He strides out of the room without a backwards glance.

"Of course, sir," Bouchard says, defeatedly. "Can you fix this?"

The IT man stares at the screen. "It might take some time to sort out." Bouchard huffily stomps past Carr and out of the conference room.

Feeling elated, Carr flashes a smile at the IT man and then stands at the Conference room door, not wanting to run into Bouchard in the elevator. After a few minutes, he heads back to his office. Once inside, he locks the door, wakes up his computer and clicks on the cameras pointing at Charlie's apartment. He stares at the screen, waiting.

Once everyone's had nostaliem, there'll be nothing the Orbs can do to stop the Krevaxers from fighting back.

65 | ANTELOPE

THE SCREEN OPENS TO A SCHEMATIC IMAGE OF THE AIR VENT system.

"We did it!" Pratt yells excitedly, as Serie jumps up into the air and Robin high fives her.

Looking down at the screen, Serie examines the black and white zoomed out schematic of Krevax. Buttons on the side of the map are labelled alphabetically, and she scans through them quickly. Clicking off the 'air filters' button, she watches as the button turns red, turning off all air filtration in Krevax. She swipes the screen, zooming in on the bottom of the map. The vent above the Recycling District shows a small green arrow, showing the air is flowing freely into the district.

She scrolls up with a quick flick of the wrist. It slides past a few districts and settles on the Manufacturing District. This vent also has a small green arrow. She slides the screen again. This time, it stops at the Education District. A small red 'x' symbol is above the vent and she clicks on it, which makes a lock screen pop up.

"Oh no," she whispers to herself and closing the lock

screen moves slowly up through all the districts, checking each vent.

Each one is locked. She scrolls back to the Education District and checks each vent in the lower districts.

"Shit!" Serie begins frantically typing in random numbers on one of the locked vents. "I think we're in trouble."

"What do you mean?" Pratt leans closer, speaking in a low voice.

"According to this, only three districts have open vents."

"Which three?" Pratt asks. Around them the group is still celebrating obliviously.

"Entertainment, Manufacturing, and Recycling," Serie says.

"Everyone!" Pratt calls out, silencing the room. The elders go quiet and turn to look at the screen.

"We only have access to three districts." Serie shakes her head. "I can't open the other vents."

"How did this happen?" Claire asks.

"It's okay," Robin says, stepping forward, with his hands held up. "Three districts are better than none, besides the concentration of nostaliem would have been low if it had gone through the entire system. At least this way we know for sure, three districts' worth of people will definitely have nostaliem."

"Okay then, let's do this!" Serie grins.

"How do we get the nostaliem up there?" Amara asks, as she points up at the vents, eleven feet above their heads. Everyone in the group looks up.

"We need some kind of assembly line," Serie says.

"I can cut the bags open." Amara snaps open a pocket knife.

"That's a good idea." Robin pulls out his own pocket knife and cuts the edge of a clear plastic bag.

Pushing a crate over, Serie turns it upside down, dumping the nostaliem, and then climbs up.

"This is still too short," Serie says, standing on her tippy toes.

Pratt dumps out two more crates, stacks them on top of each other and then slides them beside her. Jumping up, he climbs to the top of the stacked crates and touches the vent.

"This will work!" he says, and then unscrews the metal grid with his red stripe utility knife.

Once the vent is disconnected, he drops it to the side and awkwardly hoists himself up. Serie climbs to the crate just below him, and Robin stands on the one beside her.

Amara hands Robin an open bag of nostaliem, and he hands it up to Serie, and she hands it up to Pratt. Cheering triumphantly, Pratt dumps the powder into the vents. Everyone watches as the black powder spreads in the air, and then Amara cuts open another bag. The others follow suit and the bags of nostaliem move quickly up to the vent.

Minutes pass quickly as the smell of the air around them changes noticeably, the scent of a strange decay in the cloud of black. Taking a small breath of the thick air, Serie's head spins as she tries to focus on the bag of nostaliem in her hands. The taste is strangely sweet on her tongue.

"Last two bags!" Brett declares.

Serie hands Pratt the bag she had been clinging to and then slumps forward as the room disappears around her. Trying to keep conscious, she closes her eyes tightly in fear. A strange buzzing sound fills her head and when she opens her eyes, she sees a generator in a dimly lit room. Then her thoughts slip away.

The red fluorescent rectangle continues to blink rapidly, despite my attempts to stop it. I reach up and hit it again with the palm of my hand. This time, the buzzing stops. I sit back down in my nursing chair and sigh, feeling sad.

Beside me, the three-month-old baby is asleep in his blue bassinet. I look away angrily. I didn't even get to see this one. I close my eyes for a moment, trying to calm myself, but it doesn't work. I stand and tiptoe to the door. I push it open and look out into the white hallway. It's silent. What if I could hold my baby once? Just this once. I look back at the baby boy, who isn't mine. He's breathing slowly, as he's deeply asleep, at least for now.

I step nervously into the hall, leaving the door ajar behind me. Across the way is another identical door. I push it open a crack. Inside, Nancy is rocking a baby with dark curly hair and deep brown skin. Not my baby. My match was pale with wispy blonde hair. She looks up at me. I close the door and take a shaky breath, wanting to continue, but also feeling like I should hide. I shuffle a few steps and stand at the next door, opening this one a crack.

Inside, the nursing chair is turned away from the door. Beside it, a baby is sleeping in the bassinet. I can just make out its bald head. I step as quietly as possible three feet into the room. I can see the baby's features. Not my baby. I step back slowly out of the room, and shut the door. I take a deep breath in the hallway. It's still empty. I walk a few steps forward and push open the next door. Inside, Gloria is snoring lightly. The edge of the pink bassinet was behind her.

I step in and quietly move to the side of the nursing chair. Looking up at me with dark blue eyes is a baby girl with blonde wispy hair. I know immediately she's mine. I reach down and lift her small body as emotions overwhelm me.

Crying quietly, I smell her hair and kiss her forehead. She looks at me inquisitively. I know I should put her back, but I take a step towards the door. I can't put her back. She's mine. She belongs with me. Behind me, I can hear the baby boy I was assigned crying through the open doors. I can't breathe. I step into the hallway, still holding my baby. The boy is crying louder now. A handler rounds the corner.

"What are you doing?" he shouts.

"Please." I beg, holding tighter to my baby. He rushes forward and rips her out of my arms. She wails in fear and I fall to my knees, sobbing loudly.

"Go back to your room," he commands and turns, taking my baby out of view.

Serie's awareness returns. My mother! That was my mother. For a moment, she can feel a stream of tears running down her cheeks, but then a feeling of warmth soaks into her skin and she disappears again.

"Wake up!" Opening my eyes, I see the scorching sun above.

Tao is looking down at me, his dark golden skin shining in the sunlight, his smile large and exuberant. In the distance, a deep horn calls. I stand and run after Tao. All around yellow grass sprawls gold in the sunlight, wetlands sparkling blue in the green valley below.

"What is it?" I ask.

"N!àng!" My heart beats in my chest with excitement, as fingers tighten around my poison-tipped bow.

Up ahead, the commotion is louder and I can see other figures gathering around a three-tonne n!àng, its horns wildly swaying. An angry roar calling out.

"Quick! This way." I follow and circle around the n!àng, raising my bow to its eye.

"N!haì!" a woman in the group yells, pointing her bow towards the grasslands.

Everyone turns to look. In the distance, a ravenous creature with large fangs and claws is approaching, its mane moving in the breeze. I point my arrow toward the beast. It looks to be 800 pounds, its muscles moving confidently towards our group.

Behind us, a smaller band of hunters shoot their arrows into the n!àng, as it calls out in a loud squeal. Moments later, it's silent as an arrow pierces its heart. With the n!àng dead, the last of the tribe joins the fight against the n!haì!.

Now close enough to strike, it swings its sharp claws towards

Tao. He raises his bow towards the beast and hits an arrow in its arm. Blood drips down his fur, but he continues to move forward. The group forms a circle around the creature.

It leaps towards Alinta, and she lines up her bow and sends an arrow, hitting it in the jaw. It careens away from the pain and I release my bow, hitting an arrow between the shoulder blades of the n!haì!. The animal growls ferociously and leaps over the group, hobbling away, defeated.

We cheer and circle around the n!làng, carrying it together, back to the village. The children run up to us excitedly. We skin the meat, drain the blood, and cut out the waste. I help dig a large hole and we bury the meat with hot coals, to cook underneath the soil. The sky is dark when the food is finally ready. I cut off a piece of the belly and the sweet fat drips onto my tongue.

Chewing slowly, I savour the rich flavour of smoke and fat. I smile as I watch the children sleeping in the arms of their parents. I join in with the adults singing in unison a song in thanks to the n!làng that gave its life. The stars above sparkle for a perfect moment, but then they turn into white piercing lights, and I stare up at them perplexed.

Opening her eyes, Serie sees the piercing lights are fluorescents flickering above her. Crying, she cups her face with both hands.

"Are you okay?" Pratt asks, patting her shoulder.

"My mother," she whispers, shaking her head, "she wanted to keep me."

Pratt climbs down from the vent and hugs her for the first time. She looks up at him with an expression of confusion and sadness and then hugs him back.

"Who else killed the antelope?" Robin asks.

"Yeah, I did," Dan says, smiling.

"Me too!" Claire shouts.

"I think it might have been all of us," Amara says.

"I was there," Pratt says.

"We all had the same vision?" Serie asks.

"I thought you saw your mother?" Pratt looks at her.

"I did," Serie whispers, "but after that..." She trails off, thinking of her mother again.

"Do you think everyone in Krevax just shared that experience?" Pratt asks Robin.

"Yes," Robin says, "and it was a good one to share."

"Why did we share that vision?" Serie asks.

"The Oqakwanwe taught me, you share a vision where all those who are taking nostaliem are last related," Robin states. "Everyone in that vision is a distant ancestor of everyone in Krevax."

"That's beautiful," Serie says softly and climbs off the crate.

Walking back to the screen, she examines it and then presses the button to turn the air filters back on.

"What do we do now?" Serie asks, looking around the room at her comrades.

What happens now?

66 | SURPRISE
TWENTY-TWO

Leaning against the shower wall, Twenty-two is pale from another night of puking. The hot water runs over her, but she can't feel it. All she feels is numb. *My father is dead.* She closes her eyes, wanting to forget.

"Hurry in there," her mother says, tapping on the door.

Sighing deeply, Twenty-two continues leaning her head against the tile. She's already washed off the sick.

Knock. Knock.

"I'm almost done," Twenty-two shouts angrily and turns off the water.

Why can't she just leave me alone? Stepping out of the shower, she wraps herself in a towel, her head dizzy from the heat.

"Make sure your hair is dry," her mother says.

Rolling her eyes, she picks up the hair dryer and turns it on. *Why does she care? The funeral isn't until tomorrow.* Opening the door, she is startled to find her mother standing right behind it.

"There's a dress on your bed."

"I'm not going to school today? Twenty-two asks.

"No," her mother says, staring at her. "Put on some of that light pink eyeshadow I bought you, the one with the rose on the jar, and some mascara."

"Why?"

"Just do it," her mother says coolly.

With gritted teeth, Twenty-two walks into her bedroom and shuts the door, taking a breath once out of view of her mother. There's a light pink dress on her bed, which she picks up and examines. *Why did she buy this for me? This isn't a funeral dress.*

Dropping the dress back on the bed, she turns towards her dresser, grabbing underwear. Opening a box of pads hidden in the bottom drawer, she presses one into her underwear, as anger prickles her face. *I bet she makes me drink that poison every week, then she'll never worry, because she'll know I'm always bleeding. I hate her.* She pulls bra straps over her shoulders, connects the latch and turns back to the bed, picking up the dress again. She's pulling it over her head, as her mother walks into the room.

"Can I have a minute?" Twenty-two shouts.

"It's been five," she says, grabbing her daughter's shoulders and zipping up the dress.

"Where's Youngest?"

"A friend gave her a ride to school."

"Why?"

"I'll explain once you're ready." Walking over to the side table, she opens a drawer and grabs the mascara and eye shadow. Twenty-two takes them and steps in front of the mirror.

"You look clean," her mother states, examining her for a moment, and then leaves.

Shaking her head angrily, Twenty-two twists the lid off the tiny jar and dabs on the pink eyeshadow. *She's losing her mind. Why can't I go to school?* As she brushes on the mascara, her mother walks back in with a pair of light pink heels, smiling sweetly.

"I bought these for you." She places the heels on the ground beside Twenty-two. "Come to the living room when you're ready," she says, leaving again.

Twenty-two sits at the end of her bed and puts on the shoes. Then she walks out into the hallway, where she can see her mother pacing nervously around the coffee table. What is this?

As she steps closer, she hears her mother whispering to herself, "This is the only way." Twenty-two inhales sharply. What did she do? There's a knock on the door.

"Will you grab the door, dear?" Holding her breath, Twenty-two turns and opens the front door.

"Wow!" A tall man with pale rosy cheeks and a brown crew cut stares at her.

"Your picture was beautiful, but in real life," he claps his hands, "even better."

"Come in!" her mother says, cheerfully.

Stepping aside to let the man pass, she slowly follows him to the living room, breathing shallowly.

"Sit, everyone, please." Twenty-two sits on the couch and the man moves beside her and grabs her hand. She wants to pull away, but doesn't.

"You two," her mother says, smiling, "you look just perfect together!"

"Who's this?" Twenty-two whispers, shaking her head.

"Oldest, this is your new husband, Rick Miller," she says. Shaking her head slightly, Twenty-two looks over at him in terror. No. No.

"I suppose I should call you Wife Miller now," her mother says. Wife Miller?

"I couldn't believe my luck when we matched," Miller says with a grin, revealing metal-pointed teeth.

Nodding with a slightly gaped open mouth, Twenty-two stares at him in shock as he continues to ramble.

"I'm a military man. I've made my way up to first lieutenant, hoping to be a general one day," he says, laughing. "I'm only twenty-nine, so I have lots of time, but I've been too career-focused. It's time to start a family."

He leans over and kisses Twenty-two on the cheek. "You are a true beauty, aren't you?!"

"Thank you," Twenty-two whispers. I wanted to marry Chao.

"Have you packed yet?" he asks, and Twenty-two shakes her head no. Packed? Where am I going?

"I'll pack for her," her mother says, standing. "You two can get to know each other."

"I'm sorry about your father," he says. "Don't worry, we'll stay in town for the funeral."

"Where will we go after that?" Twenty-two blurts out, panic in her voice.

"I'm stationed in the Tropical Orb."

"Oh," Twenty-two says, trying not to cry. My sister, she'll be here alone... "When will we come back to visit?"

"I don't know?" Miller says. "I work a lot."

The room feels as though it's collapsing in on her. How could my mother do this? She must hate me! She doesn't even want me in the same Orb as her.

"May I," Twenty-two says, "I'd like to help my mother pack."

"Of course." Miller nods. With her fists balled, Twenty-two stands and hurries to her room, shutting the door behind her.

"How could you do this!" she shouts angrily.

"You gave me no choice," her mother says.

"What do you mean?"

"That boy, he would have gotten you pregnant."

"Chao wanted to marry me!" Twenty-two says through sobs.

"Be quiet!" her mother snaps back. "This is for the best. I have your bags here."

"Have you always hated me?" Twenty-two asks, crying. Her mother pulls her into her arms.

"I don't hate you, my love," she says, also crying. "This is the only way to protect you."

"Papa would have wanted me to finish school." Twenty-two stares up at her mother.

"I know," her mother says, "but school is expensive, and without your father's income, I can't pay for you to go."

"What about Youngest?"

"She can continue," her mother says, "but I could only afford one. Your sister is much too young for marriage." She cups her daughter's face in her hands. "You... you will be fine."

"Why did you choose someone so far away?" Twenty-two asks, her voice cracking.

"That wasn't my intention," her mother whispers and kisses her on the forehead. "I chose a man who is young, handsome and successful. I want you to have a good life. Miller will provide one." Twenty-two lets out a slow breath.

"What if I never see you, or Youngest again?"

"You will." Her mother smiles. "You will."

Twenty-two looks away. It sounds like her mother is trying to convince herself more than her.

"Go, sit with him," she says, wiping the tears from her daughter's cheeks. "I'm almost done here."

Standing defeatedly, she turns and opens the door, staring at the back of Miller's head. What if I don't like him?

67 | READY

As he watches Charlie's apartment on his computer, Carr sees the screen go black. When he clicks back to a larger view of the Manufacturing District, all the screens are black. They did it! It's happening right now. He zooms out again to an aerial shot of each district. Most of the screens look normal, except three. No. The partitions. Leaping up from his desk, he bolts down the hallway to the elevator and hits the call button. He holds his breath all the way back down to the conference room.

Once outside, he cracks the door. It's empty. He runs to the panel and opens the map of Krevax, his hands shaking. He grabs the code book and looks up the command to open the partitions, typing in the number 683-399-380238-1.

As they open, he runs back to his office, but the nostaliem has already dissipated. Slumping into his chair, he puts his hands over his face. I missed it. Only three districts got nostaliem. It won't be enough. Bouchard will be back tomorrow to kill them, and then nostaliem will disappear. I need to do something.

Mother, I'm going to be the man you knew I could be. He

goes to stand, but then stops. They might sentence me to prison. Turning back towards his desk, he picks up the phone, dialling the number to the psychiatric hospital. Scarlett needs to be somewhere safe.

"Hello, you've reached the night team at Wildrose Hospital. How can I help you?"

"I'm calling to set up the release of a patient."

"What's the patient's designation?"

"Sister Carr."

"When did you want her released?"

"Immediately, I will be there to pick her up in the next 10 minutes."

"Oh, she's already had her nightly medication, so she'll be quite disoriented," he says, and then pauses a moment. *"Could you wait until the morning?"*

"No," Carr says, "it can't wait."

"Okay, we'll get her ready." Hanging up the phone, he rushes out of his office and exactly eight minutes later, the limo stops outside the psychiatric hospital.

At the entrance, Scarlett's slouched over in a wheelchair, dressed in a white hospital gown and matching white sneakers.

"You need to sign these," the attendant says, holding out a pen.

Glancing nervously at his sister, Carr walks past her and accepts the pen. After signing the forms, he grabs the handles of the chair and slowly wheels her to the limo, as drool trickles out the corner of her mouth. What did they give to her? It's okay, my wife will look after her. He picks up her small frame and lies her down in the limo.

"Where to, sir?" the limo driver asks, ignoring the unconscious woman.

"Home," Carr says.

The driver turns the limo around and heads toward the house. Gently prodding her shoulder, he tries to wake her, hoping to talk, but she's completely asleep. The limo stops, and the driver holds open the door for them.

Picking up Scarlett, he walks to the front entrance and unlocks the door with one hand. He carries his sister to the couch and puts a blanket over her.

In his bedroom, he kisses his sleeping wife's forehead, his pulse quick in his chest at the thought of what he's about to do. There will be consequences, yes, but surely, I will return to my wife. I will be fired... yes. I will certainly be fired. I may even be arrested, but history will vindicate me.

How long would they put me in prison for? No longer than a few years, at most? I don't think over five or six. And my wife could visit. I have made enough money in this life to support us. We will be fine. What charge even exists for simply changing advertisements?

Beads of sweat pool on his temples and he sits on the ground beside the bed. Tears well up in his eyes as the full truth of his plan cuts into him like a blade. I'm going to be killed if I do this. He stands. Maybe we can escape together? All three of us.

"My love! Wake up."

"Carr?!" she says, startled. "What's wrong?" Sitting up, she stares at his anguished expression.

"Will you run away with me?"

"What do you mean?" she asks fearfully.

"This will explain everything." Carr turns and runs down the stairs, grabbing a small cup of nostaliem he'd hidden in the living room and then springs back up the steps.

"What is it?" his wife asks as he gets back into the bedroom.

"It will tell you the truth."

"I'm not sure," she whispers, shaking her head.

"Please, for me." Carr pulls her into his arms. "I'll be with you the entire time."

After a minute of silence, she finally nods. He forms a line of powder on the bedside table.

"It goes into your nose." A look of concern lights up her face for a moment, but then she leans forward and inhales the nostaliem.

Watching her closely, he sees her enter a sort of trance, almost like she's sleeping, but her eyes are half open. After nearly half an hour, she jolts awake with a sob.

"What did you see?" Carr asks.

"I don't understand what's happening," she stammers. "Is my name Daisy?"

"Daisy?" he asks, tensing. "No."

"Why did you give me this?" she shouts. "Who am I? Where are my children?"

"You're my wife," he says, shocked by her questions. "Your Wife Carr!"

"No. That can't be," she whispers. "My name is Daisy and I have two children." Standing, she moves a step away from him, tears streaming down her face. "Please don't hurt me," she says.

"Dear wife?"

"What do you want from me?"

"I want you to come with me. To fight."

"Fight?"

"The Wildebeests aren't real," he says. "We're eating people! Everyone must know the truth," Carr rambles on, his eyes wide.

"Get out!" she yells, hyperventilating. "I don't know who

you are. You're here to kill me!" Nearly falling to the ground, she stumbles through their bedroom.

"Please! My love, we can escape together."

"Monster! Monster!" she screams.

"No… please…" Carr moves towards her.

"Don't touch me!" Grabbing a lamp, she holds it between them like a weapon.

He rips it out of her hands and throws it against the wall, leaving it in a shattered pile. Recoiling towards the wall, she flinches when he grabs her waist, trying to pull her close. She slaps him as hard as she can and he steps back in shock.

"You're my wife!"

"I don't know who you are! Demon!" She leaps towards the bedroom door.

"Help!" Grasping for her, he grabs a leg and an elbow and they both tumble forward onto the landing above the stairs. She kicks him hard in the chest and slides down the first few steps, holding onto the railing. Carr swings himself towards her, grabbing her wrist.

"Help!" she screams out again.

She twists around to push him away, but doing so, lets go of the railing, and her full weight drags them down the stairs. He falls on top of her as they tumble in a ball of outstretched limbs. A loud crack snaps. Her scream goes silent. They land at the bottom of the stairs. Motionless.

"My love?" Carr shakes her. "Wake up! Wake up now. Everything's okay."

Her neck protrudes at a strange angle. He looks into her eyes and knows she's dead. He rocks her body in his arms, back and forth, back and forth.

"I'm so sorry," he says desperately. "Please wake up now. Please… my love." Hours pass and still he rocks his wife, back and forth. It's almost morning now.

"What did you do?" Scarlett whispers, standing beside the couch, staring at them.

"She fell," Carr says through sobs. "I never wanted her to get hurt."

"What did you do to me?" Scarlett asks, louder now. Gently placing his wife's body on the ground, he turns to look up at his sister.

"I'm so sorry, Scarlett," he whispers. "I was trying to keep you safe. I thought this was what our mother would've wanted." He stands slowly.

"I was wrong." She stares at him, silently. "I'm going to tell Krevaxers the truth," he says.

"You are?"

"Yes," Carr says, laughing maniacally, "and I'll probably be killed for it." Scarlett takes a nervous step back.

"You shouldn't stay here," he whispers, shaking his head. "There's an entire closet full of clothes upstairs."

"Where should I go?"

"Go to a hospital," Carr says, "tell them you don't remember who you are, or anything past this morning. Don't tell anyone you're from Krevax, ever. They'll kill you."

"Did you know our mother?" Scarlett asks.

"Yes," Carr says, smiling, "she was perfect." Walking over to a small drawer, he pulls out a picture of his mother holding him when he was a baby.

"Here." Handing it to Scarlett, he watches her examining the image.

"She looks just like me." He nods slowly, feeling numb.

"Good luck, little sister." Turning, he picks up his wife's body and carries her up the stairs.

In their bedroom he lies her on the bed and tucks her under the blankets. She looks as though she could be sleeping. Kissing her on the forehead, he stares at her for a moment before making his way back down the stairs. He feels Scarlett's eyes watch him leave. Outside, the limo is waiting to take him to work.

"Good morning, sir." Without replying he climbs into the backseat. Exhaling calmly, he feels ready to face his death.

The limo slows to a stop outside the building. Stepping into the warm morning light, he pauses to admire the sunrise and takes a deep breath of crisp air. Then, with his thoughts resolute, he heads towards the entrance, takes the elevator to the 49th floor, and locks the door to his office.

Sitting down at his desk, he pulls up the server that controls the advertisements. He clicks on the first image: a handler and a red stripe shaking hands in front of a line of generators.

The tagline reads: *Help make your community safer, report those selling nostaliem.* Carr drags the image into the Creative Editor and rewrites the tagline: *When your body is recycled, you become meat to be consumed — Orbinians are cannibals.*

Opening the meat processing file, he finds an image showing the removal of the digestive tract and connects it to the new tagline.

Carr drags this altered advertisement over every image in the server, replacing them, and then activates the changes. Holding his breath, the silence roars at him, as his heart does somersaults in his chest. He watches the clock slowly ticking. What feels like hours is in fact only seconds. An alarm rings on his screen and he stands, bracing himself. Hurried footsteps rush towards his office. The handle twists and then a body slams into the door, breaking it open.

"Carr!" Bouchard runs into the room. "Did you do this?"

"They must know the truth!" Carr yells. "They're people."

Men push themselves into the room and surround him. One grabs his shoulder and forcefully drags him towards the door.

"Turn them off! Turn them off!" Bouchard yells.

"It's done!" an assistant shouts.

Carr stops counting the seconds in his head. Forty-five. Was that enough for people in Krevax to know the truth? It has to be. The men drag him to the elevator and out into the foyer. A fist thrusts through the bodies and punches him in the face. He shrieks in surprise. Blood drips from his nose and pools into his gaping mouth.

Behind him, a man approached swiftly with a pistol. Men move away, leaving him exposed on the marble floor. He crouches on his hands and knees. Hard metal presses up against his back. He looks up. Above him, he can see the leaves on the trees shimmering in the breeze. Bang.

Carr falls onto the cold marble, his heart pounding in his chest as blood pools around him. Charlie's safe now.

Men yell and throw their fists into the air as his vision grows clouded until there is nothing left but black. Goodbye, brother.

68 | CRASH
BLACKWELL

Watching the guard station come into view, Blackwell braces as Gertie breaks the divider, flooring the pedal as he enters the parking lot. Driving at full speed, he smashes into the Watchtower. His forehead hits the steering wheel, and he hobbles out of the truck with blood dripping down his face.

Despite being cracked, the bullet-proof glass remains unbroken. He attempts to push through, but it's too solid. Picking up a rock, he throws it, but it doesn't leave a mark.

"Fuck!" he shouts. What am I doing? How much time do I have?

"Stop!" a man yells. Blackwell puts his hands in the air and slowly turns.

"Call Captain Lewis!" he shouts. "It's an emergency." The guard stares at him.

"What's the emergency?"

"I'm Charlie Blackwell."

"Blackwell!" the guard exclaims, "the missing detective?"

"Yes, that's me!"

"One moment," the guard lowers his gun and clicks on his

tracker. Blackwell can hear the tracker ringing and after a minute, the call connects.

"Hello," Lewis says, barely awake.

"Sir, there's a man claiming to be Charlie Blackwell."

"Blackwell!" Lewis shouts. "Put him on!" Blackwell runs over.

"Yes, Captain, it's me! I need your help. I'm outside Gromwell. Can you come now?"

"What's going on?"

"I'll explain everything when you've arrived."

"I'm on my way!" The call clicks off.

"Let me in!" Blackwell demands, pointing at the Watchtower

"I don't think so." The guard steps back a few paces.

Blackwell takes off his dust-stained white suit jacket and wraps it around the gash on his forehead, wiping the blood from his face with a hanging sleeve. Walking in an agitated circle, his filthy sequin shirt shimmers with each step. He looks up at the sound of Lewis driving into the parking lot.

"You're alive!" he grabs Blackwell's shoulders. "What happened to you?"

"That doesn't matter right now. We need to get into the Watchtower and shut down the vent system!" Blackwell shouts.

"Why?" Lewis stares at him.

"The Orbs are going to fill the vents with chlorine gas and kill everyone in Entertainment, Manufacturing and Recycling."

"That can't be true." Lewis drops his hands and takes a step back.

"I promise, it is," Blackwell says, taking a step towards him. "We have to stop them before it's too late."

"Why would they do that?" Lewis shakes his head.

"They believe that's the way to stop nostaliem. We need to get in there now," Blackwell pleads.

"How do you know this?"

"The Tzar is my brother, he told me."

"The Tzar is your brother?"

"Yes!" Blackwell shouts, getting frustrated.

"That doesn't make any sense."

"Please, Captain Lewis, we're running out of time." The captain stares at him a moment.

"I'm sorry, Blackwell, I think you're compromised."

"Compromised?" Blackwell shouts at him. "I'm trying to save lives!"

The door opens behind them and Blackwell rushes forward to grab it. Captain Lewis grabs Blackwell's arm to hold him back.

"Blackwell?" Pratt asks in surprise.

"Pratt!" Blackwell shouts. "You need to get me in the Watchtower. It's an emergency!"

"What's going on here, Pratt?" The captain's eyes dart from Blackwell to Pratt.

"We gave everyone nostaliem," Pratt says confidently.

"You mean three districts nostaliem," a blonde woman says, as she elbows Pratt in the side, making him laugh.

"What?" Lewis says, shaking his head.

"Did you stop the attack?" Blackwell asks shakily.

"What attack?" Pratt stares at him.

"The Orbs are dumping chlorine gas on Entertainment, Manufacturing and Recycling!"

"Oh!" Pratt looks back at the group. "That must be why the other vents were closed."

"I guess we thwarted their plan!" An older man laughs.

"Are you sure?" Blackwell blurts, slightly calmer now.

"Yeah, I'm sure." Pratt nods. "We were in the vents and we're fine."

"Why would the Orbs dump chlorine gas?" Lewis asks.

"I know why," Blackwell says and everyone turns to look at him. "Orbinians are cannibals and nostaliem is showing people the truth."

"It's true," Pratt says, "that's why we dumped the nostaliem in the vents."

"That's why they recycle us," Blackwell adds.

"Where's the proof?" Lewis drops Blackwell's arm, his face twisted with confusion.

An older woman steps forward. "We've been trying to get the truth out for decades."

"Who are these old people!" Lewis yells.

"Hi, I'm Robin." An older man grins, stretching out his hand to shake. "We've been hiding out in a cave system just outside Krevax."

"Robin!" Blackwell shouts, beaming. "I saw you when I took nostaliem. You knew my mother."

"Charlie! It's you." Robin runs forward, pulling him into a hug. "I'm so glad you're okay. Your mother, Charlotte," he pauses, "she was an amazing person."

Blackwell, initially surprised by the embrace, hugs Robin back. As they part, Robin pats his shoulder.

"She did more than any of us to fight the Orbs and she lost everything because of it." He glances at the ground, momentarily silent, and then looks up. "I'm thrilled to see you again, Charlie."

Blackwell nods, feeling the same.

"I'm confused," Lewis says, shaking his head.

"You need to get ready for a war," Robin declares.

"A war?" Pratt whispers.

"Yes." Robin stands tall. "The Orbs will see us as a threat now."

"What do we do?" Pratt asks.

"We destroy the Watchtower connection." Blackwell

stares up at the tower. "That's how they control everything. I can't help, though." He glances over at Gertie. The front end is crunched, and the engine is billowing smoke.

"I need to find Tinik." Blackwell takes a step away from the group.

"Who's Tinik?" Pratt asks, staring at him.

"She's my friend," Blackwell says, climbing on the captain's motorcycle. "Can you start this for me, sir?" Everyone watches Captain Lewis, waiting for his reaction.

Lewis covers his face with his hands for a moment. "This whole thing sounds like a mad conspiracy."

"Look at this." Walking over, Pratt pulls the illegal disk from his pocket and places it on the captain's wrist.

"I should arrest you for this!" Lewis laughs.

"Search 'rebels in the tunnel system'," Pratt says seriously. Lewis opens *Red Stripe Services* and types in the request. Standing there reading for a full minute, his mouth slowly gapes wider as he shakes his head in disbelief.

"I can't believe this is real," he whispers to himself.

"It is, though." Robin gives Lewis a thoughtful look.

"Captain, are you going to help us?" Pratt asks.

"Yes," Lewis says, sighing heavily as he walks over to Blackwell to start the bike.

"Go, find your friend," Pratt shouts, "we've got the Watchtower."

Blackwell pushes the gas pedal and swerves away. Click. Looking up, he sees the advertisements changing, signalling the next day. He speeds down the quiet highway. Up ahead, he can see a crowd at the edge of the Generation District.

"Yes!" Blackwell shouts as he crosses into the Entertainment District.

Doxies are in the streets, talking to each other in serious voices. The nostaliem. They've seen the truth. He winds through the people, smiling. This is it. There's no stopping a rebellion now.

"Tinik!" he yells into the crowd. No one answers, and he continues pushing forward, looking through the next group of people. "Tinik!"

"Blackwell?" Tinik calls out in surprise, running forward with a little boy trailing behind her.

"You found him!" Blackwell drops the bike, runs over and pulls her into a hug. "Are you okay?"

"Yes." She laughs, hugging him back. "You?" she asks, taking in his frazzled appearance.

"I'm fine," Blackwell says, laughing.

"Joey, this is my friend, Blackwell." The younkin stares up at him apprehensively.

Blackwell waves, "hi, Joey."

"How did you get into the Watchtower?" Tinik asks.

He shakes his head. "It was my partner, Pratt, he's the one who dumped the nostaliem."

"Wow!" Tinik says. "I thought for a minute it was over, but then I woke up under the sun in a golden grassland, and Joey was there too!"

"I'm so glad you're both okay."

"I'm so glad you're okay," Tinik says, smiling up at him.

"What now?" he asks.

"My other younkins," Tinik says with a sharp inhale.

"Where are they?"

"Leo's seven and Everly's a girl, so they're both in the Education District."

"Okay, let's go." Blackwell reaches for Tinik's hand and leads her and Joey back to the captain's bike, which is still running.

Tinik helps Joey balance, and then she climbs on behind him and Blackwell. They wind slowly through the crowd and then speed up as they cross over into the Generation District, where it's still quiet.

"Why is it quiet here?" Tinik asks, calling up to Blackwell.

"The Orbs had already locked the vents for the chlorine gas."

"I wish it was this district that had nostaliem," Tinik says. Blackwell stares up at the glass bridges.

"Don't worry," he says, "everyone will try it soon enough." He glances back at Tinik, giving her an understanding look, and she nods.

"Do you know where we're going in the Education District?"

"Only for one," Tinik says. "My youngest doesn't understand where she is, so I don't know either."

"That's okay. We'll go door to door for her if we have to." Joey sleepily presses his head into Blackwell's back.

"Joey, wake up, sweet pea," Tinik says, helping him sit up again and then calls up to Blackwell, "we're headed to the West wall."

"Got it." He turns down an alley, heading west at the edge of the Education District. Once at the wall, he goes up the closest road. "Do you recognize anything?"

"Yes, it's around the next bend!" Tinik shouts excitedly. Blackwell slows the bike as they approach the next block of buildings.

"That one!" Tinik says. "With the sun above the door."

He stops the bike. Tinik helps Joey get down and then she runs over and tries the handle. "It's locked." She stares over her shoulder, looking disappointed.

"That's okay," Blackwell says, "we could all use some sleep."

Tinik stands at the door for a moment, still touching the handle. Then she walks over and sits, pulling Joey into her arms, where he immediately falls asleep. Blackwell slides down beside her and she leans closer, resting her head against his shoulder. Watching her close her eyes, he takes a deep breath, feeling thankful to have reached this moment.

Sleepily closing his eyes, he falls into a dream where he's a little boy. His mother tells him how much she loves him and then they laugh together as she sings loudly about *black bears wearing blue bandanas and eating brown-spotted bananas.*

He doesn't know if it's real, or if it's just a dream, but either way, it makes him happy. His heart feels warm as the dream slowly melts away, and perhaps for the first time, he falls into a deep sleep.

69 | WIFE MILLER
TWENTY-TWO

Miller's clammy hand makes Twenty-two want to rip her arm away, but she stays frozen. Up a few rows, her mother and sister are sitting. Tensing as she watches Youngest cry, she glances over at Miller, feeling frustrated. I should be sitting with her, not here with this...stranger. He smiles kindly at her and she looks up, avoiding his gaze. A photo of her father, framed in gold and surrounded by white chrysanthemums, stood beside the podium.

"Doctor Alvaro Garcia was a wonderful husband and father," the clergyman says.

She closes her eyes, wanting to disappear. This isn't real. The clergyman drones on, but she isn't listening. Instead, she plays pop songs in her head. Suddenly, the last conversation she remembers with her father jumps into her mind. I should have helped with the groceries. She balls her free hand into a fist. Why am I so terrible?

As she wipes a tear away from her cheek, Miller wraps his arm around her shoulders, pulling her closer.

"Wife Garcia has prepared a few words," the clergyman

says, holding out the microphone for her as she walks onto the stage.

"My husband was such a joyful man. He made everyone around him happier," she says, her voice cracking. "...especially his children." She lets out a sob before continuing.

"I remember, years ago, when we'd just had our oldest, blueberries were introduced to the Orbs. He must have come home with a thousand of them. He was so excited."

Twenty-two wipes away another tear, watching her mother's grief-stricken face.

"He filled the entire bathtub with blueberries. I was furious because, of course, I knew I'd be the one to clean it up. So I picked up a handful and threw them at him. He should have been mad, but he laughed. He laughed and tossed some back. We had the most ridiculous blueberry fight. For months, I kept finding them—in corners, under the fridge, behind curtains—and every time, it made me smile."

Her mother closes her eyes. "I'd clean up blueberries for the rest of my life if I could just have him back." She buries her face in her hands, weeping. "He was a wonderful husband."

The clergyman steps forward and gently helps her off the stage before walking to the podium.

"There will be light refreshments and snacks at the Garcia home." At that declaration, the service ends and people stand and begin walking out of the church.

That can't be it? My father's life is over. Miller helps her stand, and she follows him outside to his rental car.

"We'll only be stopping for a few minutes," Miller says. "Our flight is in an hour and a half."

Twenty-two nods. What if I ran away? I could take Youngest and disappear. Maybe Chao would come?

Staring out at the street flashing by, she wipes away a tear, but another just takes its place. *What if this is the last time I'm here?* The car stops and she gets out in front of her house.

"Don't leave!" Youngest cries as she runs over and wraps her arms around her.

"I'm sorry," Twenty-two whispers. Their mother walks over and wraps her arms around both of them.

"My beautiful girls," she says, tears in her eyes.

"We should get going," Miller says, still sitting in the car. Twenty-two holds her sister tighter, crying into her hair as their mother takes a step back.

"Youngest, please say goodbye to your sister now."

"Goodbye," her sister says, her voice shaking, as she moves back beside their mother.

"Goodbye," Twenty-two whispers, covering her mouth to contain a sob, and then numbly turning and climbing into the car.

"That was a lovely service," Miller says, patting her knee.

She continues staring out the window, watching the details of her sister dissolve into the background. Miller pats her knee again, and she looks over at him, forcing herself to smile.

"My parents are going to love you." With a shallow breath, she nods and then watches as the Boreal Orb moves past them on the road. She puts her fingers on the door handle.

What if I jumped out?

She grips the handle for the entire hour's drive, but never pulls it open. The car slows outside the airport tower.

"I've never been on a plane before," she whispers.

"Don't worry, it will be fun," Miller says as he parks the car.

He climbs out and walks around the front of the car, opening the door for her. She steps out, and he grabs her hand, leading her to the entrance of the airport. Standing beside him in the line, she looks back and sees Chao outside the doors, staring at her through the glass. Chao!

Tears well up in her eyes as she stares at him a minute, then she looks away. They move up to the desk and Miller hands over the tickets. When she looks back again, Chao is gone. She feels empty as they walk through the airport and sit down in the lounge, waiting for their flight.

When Miller leans over and kisses her on the mouth, she does her best not to recoil. This is what I'm supposed to do. I'm a wife now.

"I've wanted to do that since I first saw your picture," he says, smiling at her.

Twenty-two smiles back forcefully and the empty feeling grows. An airport worker walks over to the television and turns up the volume.

"A war has started," President Lehan says.

Twenty-two looks up at the screen. A war? With who? "War has been declared on our way of life and force must be used to protect Orbinians! We must return to stability, and Krevax must return to viability. Under my reign, every enemy will be accounted for. When I learned that a rival colony on the Moon was poisoning our farm, Krevax, I knew I needed to act." The room the President is standing in erupts in cheers.

"A rival colony on the Moon?" Twenty-two whispers.

"That's the first I've heard of it," Miller says. "Give me a minute. I should make a call." Watching him walk away, she sighs, feeling relieved to be alone, and then looks back up at the TV.

"I am addressing the nation today," the President says, "as we take our first steps toward this historic moment. Our Wildebeests in Krevax were poisoned by terrorists!

Dangerous men who formed their own colony on the Moon have come to take what is rightfully ours."

Around the lounge, everyone is staring up at the screen, completely captivated.

"Terrorists on the Moon?" A pilot walking by says.

"Now is the time for Orbinians to rise above this threat," the President says, "to stand together. War is being declared on our way of life, but we will win!"

The broadcast ends, and an ad for cereal starts. Twenty-two closes her eyes. *A war with terrorists on the Moon? I wonder if Miller will be deployed?*

An announcement comes over the intercom for their flight, and Miller walks back and picks up her suitcase. Stepping up to the flight stand, he shows their passports and then they make their way down the ramp to a long metal plane. She had seen planes flying overhead, but never up close. It's smaller than she expected. They climb in, walking through rows of blue to a seat in the very back.

"You should take the inside seat," Miller says, and Twenty-two slides into the seat beside him.

Six strips of clear plastic panels run the length of the plane, showcasing views of the sky and landscape. The plane slowly fills around them and then the engine blares on. She jumps at the noise, which is uncomfortably loud. Nervously tapping her foot, she stares out the window as the plane moves forward.

Feeling the plane lift off, she watches the ground expand below them. *The Boreal Orb's so beautiful! I never knew.* She wipes tears from her eyes, watching the snow-capped mountains go by.

"Can you swim?" Miller asks. Twenty-two nods, still staring out the window. "Good, because there's a pool in the backyard."

"You have your own pool?" Twenty-two looks over at him, smiling slightly.

"I sure do!" Miller grins. "You're going to love our house." Our house? Twenty-two tries to imagine it. I'm going to have an entire house.

"Look." Miller points out the window. "That's the edge of the Tropical Orb."

"Wow!" Twenty-two says, "it's so much closer than I realized."

She takes in the blue ocean and dark green landscape as it slowly reveals its tree-covered rocky peaks and flowing waterfalls. She smiles to herself as a small feeling of hope grows in her mind.

Maybe I'll enjoy living with Miller? She looks over at him. His smile is kind of cute.

"We'll be landing in five minutes. Please return to your seats," the pilot says over the intercom.

"That was fast!" Twenty-two says, smiling genuinely.

"It is, isn't." The plane lands and they unbuckle.

Miller stands impatiently, watching as the other passengers slowly exit in the front. As he steps into the aisle she follows him out of the plane and onto a ramp where they meet a wall of heat and humidity. She smiles, feeling excited by the new climate. Miller clasps her hand as they walk through the airport.

"The bags are just up ahead." Miller points to a conveyor belt. "Let me know when you see yours." Twenty-two nods.

They stand at the edge of the conveyor belt, watching the bags come down.

"Would you like to go out for dinner tonight?" Miller asks. "There's this restaurant I love on the main strip near my house."

"Sure," Twenty-two says, feeling nervous. Miller holds her hand to his chest.

"That's my bag," she says, pointing at a grey one as it falls.

He jogs over, pulls it over the partition, and then walks back with a confident stride and grabs her hand again.

"I'm so glad you're here," he says, beaming at her.

Twenty-two smiles back. Maybe I am too? The doors open to the parking lot and Twenty-two breathes in the floral air as the salty ocean breeze lightly dances on her skin.

The funeral feels surreal to her now, almost like her father was still alive and waiting for her to visit. I'll make sure Youngest marries someone in the Tropical Orb. Then she can live here too. She smiles at the thought.

Miller stops at a black car and opens the door for her. She watches him load her bag in the trunk and then sit down beside her. Butterflies fill her stomach as she stares at him, wondering what will happen that night. I'm a wife. She takes a deep breath.

My name is Wife Miller.

70 | GREEN GRASS

VIOLET

WAKING WITH A JOLT, VIOLET SITS UP, BUT THE PAIN IN HER abdomen causes her to fall back onto the bed. A fluorescent light above illuminates the clinical-looking white room. Her head spins. Lifting the shirt, she stares at the white gauze around her belly and then feels her skin. It's hot to the touch. What did they do to me?

Slowly standing, she sees the room is windowless. She cries. Am I still pregnant?

Her throat feels dry, and she shakily grabs the glass of water from the side table, draining it. The water is dusty to the taste. She takes a slow breath, steadying herself, and walks over to the door, her sneakers squeaking on the floor. There's no handle. I'm locked in! She takes a panicked breath and bangs against the door.

"Hello!" she yells, "is there anyone there?"

"Don't do that, you'll make them angry," a voice through the wall says. Violet walks over to it.

"What's happening?"

"When did you get here?" the voice asks.

"I don't know, I just woke up," Violet cries.

"Oh," the voice says. "Hi! I'm Forty-one. Have they assigned you a number yet?"

"I was Thirty-six at my last school."

"They'll give you a new number here."

"What's going on?" Violet asks.

"This is the Rosewood Cleaner Institute," Forty-one says, "you know, for girls who won't be wives."

"Why is my belly wrapped in gauze?"

"That's just because they sterilized you," Forty-one says nonchalantly.

"Why?" Violet asks, sliding on the ground against the wall, her arms wrapped around her legs. Sterilized?

"Cleaners don't have babies, because we're considered too promiscuous to be responsible mothers."

"I'm not pregnant anymore?" Violet whispers.

"Nope, not anymore," Forty-one says. "I was sterilized last year. How old are you?"

"Seventeen," Violet says.

Feeling dizzy, she takes a slow breath. At least I don't have to have Remi's baby. She feels her stomach again. It feels softer than before. I'll never be pregnant again. She takes a sharp inhale, feeling upset by this realization. Why do I feel sad? I never wanted to be pregnant.

"Seventeen!" Forty-one laughs. "I'm only twelve."

"When do we leave our room?" Violet closes her eyes.

"We'll all have breakfast in the cafeteria."

Clang.

The morning bell rings out and she stands, wincing at the pain in her abdomen. Keys jangle outside and her door opens. The woman who picked her up from Wife School is standing there.

"Good morning, Fifty-five," the woman says.

With a nod, Violet walks through the open doorway. The woman walks away, opening doors as she goes, her heels clicking.

"Hi!" Forty-one is grinning up at her. "I love breakfast!"

"Which way is the cafeteria?"

"Follow me!" Forty-one skips down the crowded hallway. Hobbling after her, Violet stops at the edge of the hall.

"Smells like bacon today," Forty-one says, grinning. Violet nods.

What's bacon? They stand in line at the side wall and Forty-one picks up a plate. Violet copies her. A woman behind the counter scoops a spoonful of brown cubes on the plate.

Next Forty-one grabs a different brown square-shaped item and two thin red strips of something else. Violet does the same.

"They get mad if you take more than two slices of bacon," Forty-one says, as she grabs a rectangular white box with purple grapes on it.

Violet nods and picks up the strange box as well. Forty-one picks up a metal utensil and starts walking towards a table. Violet grabs one too and follows her. They sit down at the back, by a large screen on the wall.

"This is the best spot," Forty-one says, "on Saturdays, they even play cartoons!"

Violet looks up at the screen. A man is standing at a podium in front of a large crowd. Forty-one takes a bite of the bacon. Violet does the same. It is salty and delicious.

"What is bacon?" Violet asks.

"I think it's cut from the belly fat," Forty-one says.

Violet looks at her, confused. A man in a suit walks over and turns the volume up on the screen. Violet stares at it as she takes another bite of bacon.

"When I learned that a rival colony on the Moon was poisoning our farm, Krevax, I knew I needed to act." Why did they call Krevax a farm?

"I am addressing the nation today as we take our first steps toward this historic moment. Our Wildebeests in Krevax have been poisoned by terrorists!" Wildebeests? "Men who formed their own colony on the Moon have come to take what is rightfully ours."

"What's a Wildebeest?" Violet asks, her mouth suddenly dry.

"You know!" Forty-one laughs. "The animals in Krevax!"

She holds up the piece of bacon. Staring with wide eyes, Violet drops the half-eaten piece in her hand. What? Suddenly feeling freezing cold, pin pricks crawl over her body. Garcia said that if anyone knew I was a Krevaxer, they would kill me…

"Forty-one," Violet says, staring, "has anyone ever told you about people living in Krevax?"

"Like ranchers?" She shakes her head.

She doesn't know about Krevaxers. No one here knows that Krevaxers are people! Closing her eyes, Violet suddenly feels incredibly sick, and turning, immediately pukes on the floor. The man under the screen jumps, narrowly avoiding her vomit.

"What are you doing?" he shouts.

"I'm sorry," Violet whispers. I ate somebody. She holds her hand to her mouth, her eyes wide. I'm a cannibal. She closes her eyes. What am I going to do?

"Go wash up," he says, standing over her.

Slowly walking out of the cafeteria, she clutches her hands on her chest. No one is going to believe me. She sees girls walking through a doorway up ahead and follows them.

Inside is a change room, with showers, bathroom stalls, and sinks. Standing at a sink, she washes her face and rinses the human taste out of her teeth. She looks at herself in the mirror. *I didn't think the Orbs would be like this.*

Clang.

The bell rings again. Girls run out of the bathroom, and Violet follows them down a hallway to a large auditorium. Trudging up the steps, she uses the railing for support, and sits down in a seat near the top. A woman strides in with a box of cleaning supplies.

"Today we're going to be studying how to remove tough stains from things like velvet, leather, and white cloth." Violet bursts out laughing.

"Is there something you wanted to say?" the teacher stares up at her. Violet tries to respond, but she can't stop laughing.

"If you can't control yourself, you need to go back to your room!"

Standing, she laughs all the way out of the auditorium, her stomach throbbing in pain with each breath. The teacher glares at her as she shuts the door. Wiping tears away from her cheeks, she's still laughing, but the laughter is turning on her. Suddenly, she is sobbing uncontrollably. A man in a white uniform walks over to her.

"What's wrong, dear?"

"I want to go to the ocean!" Violet shouts through her tears.

"I can't take you there right now, but perhaps you could use some fresh air." He guides her down a hallway and opens a door to a large grass field.

Violet takes a deep breath of cool air and sits down in the grass. Past the field, towering evergreen trees stretch over the horizon. Above her, the blue sky is bright with sunshine. Closing her eyes, she feels the sun tingle her skin. The green grass smells fresh, and she touches the blades with her fingertips. *I could live here. I just won't eat anything with human.* She laughs again at the absurdity of the thought.

"You just arrived?" the man asks. Violet nods.

"I know it's a tough transition," he says, smiling down at her. "It will get easier." Smiling back, she takes another deep breath.

"It's already easier," she whispers to herself.

71 | TERRORISTS
PRATT

YELLING ERUPTS ALL AROUND THE WATCHTOWER VIEWING room, making Pratt take a nervous step back towards the wall.

"Everyone, calm down," Lewis shouts.

"What do you mean calm down?" a red stripe with a gap in his front teeth yells and then stands up from his camera station and starts aggressively making his way towards Lewis.

"What you're saying is insane," another red stripe shrieks. "It's nonsense!"

"It's the truth!" Robin yells. "He showed you the evidence."

He points at Pratt, who nods slowly, looking uncomfortable as he holds his breath. This is bad.

"That report could be fabricated. What you showed us is meaningless," the gap-toothed man shouts. "I believe Captain Lewis is compromised by the Zorax gang. Why else would these men want us to try nostaliem? They want us to be addicts!"

"No, that isn't true," Claire says, stepping forward.

"Nostaliem is part of us, our collective memories. You cannot be addicted to such a thing."

"And they have females among their ranks!" the red stripe yells. "They can't be trusted." Pratt looks over at Serie and she rolls her eyes.

"Call the Tzar!" Serie shouts. "He'll tell you." The gap-toothed man stares at her angrily.

"Call the Tzar!" he yells.

The red stripes take this as a command and a man runs over with an official Watchtower phone. The gap-toothed man clicks the button to connect with the Tzar.

Ring. The red stripes stare in silence, waiting as the phone rings.

Ring.

Ring.

Ring.

Ring.

Ring.

"He's not picking up?" Lewis says in shock.

Ring.

"Someone always answers."

Ring.

The gap-toothed man hangs up the phone.

"What did you do to the Tzar?"

"Nothing!" Lewis blurts, taken aback.

"These men are infiltrators. They must be arrested!"

"No!" Pratt roars. "This is ridiculous!"

He walks towards the elevator. "There are evidence rooms with nostaliem, only one of you needs to try it, then everyone else will understand."

"No one is trying that poison on my watch!" Behind the wall of glass, the advertisements click, turning to show one image.

The picture of a dead man having his intestines removed by men in protective gear.

Words on the image state: *When your body is recycled, you become meat to be consumed — Orbinians are cannibals.*

Pratt looks around at the men as they stare at the horrifying image.

"They're telling the truth!" A red stripe in the back yells.

The men are hysterical. Some have fallen to the ground in shock. He looks back at the wall of ads as they flash and are then replaced with their original images. A red stripe near the front of the row picks up his chair and begins smashing an advertisement in the office.

"Arrest them!" the gap-toothed man yells, "that photo must be doctored."

The entire room erupts, sides quickly forming. A fair number of red stripes join the ranks of Lewis. Serie picks up a chair and runs beside Pratt, holding it aggressively towards the men on the other side of the room.

"Gangs hacked the system!" the gap-toothed man shouts. "This is all a ploy to get us to take nostaliem."

"We're slaves in Krevax!" Pratt yells. "Can't you see we're being used as meat?"

One of the younger red stripes, yet to choose a side, pukes on the floor.

"One of you must try nostaliem. That's the only way we can end this standoff," Captain Lewis roars. The room was silent for a minute.

"I'll try it." A man on the other side steps forward.

"Clarence! Get back in line," the gap-toothed man demands. Clarence takes another step towards the elevators.

"Captain Greene, let me prove they're wrong." He stares at the gap-toothed captain. Greene nods.

"We have nostaliem locked in the *Level 01 - Enforcement*

District evidence room. Go get it." Clarence runs into the hallway and disappears. The standoff continues.

"How are they this stubborn," Serie whispers to Pratt, "you showed them the files, and now the advertisements?"

"I guess it's hard to know the truth when you already believe the lies," Pratt whispers back.

The elevator doors open and Clarence walks in with a bag of nostaliem. He sits down at a desk near Captain Greene and cuts open a corner of the bag.

"How much should I take?"

"You don't need much," Robin says, "just start with an amount you could fit in a thimble."

The room watches him pick up a pinch of the black powder and breathe it in. Half closing his eyes, he sits frozen in a trance.

"Clarence?" Greene asks.

"It can take some time," Robin states.

They wait in anxious silence for twenty-two minutes. Finally, Clarence opens his eyes and cries. The room gasps.

"Look what it did!" Greene yells. "He's broken."

"No, sir, it's not that." Clarence stands shakily. "They're telling the truth."

He makes his way over to Captain Lewis and stands beside him. Captain Greene sits down, defeated. The sides evaporate, and everyone crowds into the middle of the room.

"I have an idea!" Serie says. She puts down the chair and runs over to a computer.

"What can a female possibly do?" Greene states.

"Why don't we find out," Serie says, smiling sarcastically, as she shakes the mouse. "Who has the password for this?"

A red stripe walks up behind her and types in his code. Nodding a thanks, she clicks on the Watchtower controls and types in a command to access the code in the program.

"What's she doing?" Lewis asks Pratt, he shrugs his shoulders.

"I'm breaking the connection between the Orbs and Krevax of course! But that's just the first step. My actual idea is way better than that." Serie stares intensely at the screen.

"How do you know how to do that?" Greene snaps.

"I'm part of a hacking collective," Serie says, as she speedily types. The advertisements go black. "Step one begins!"

"How will you break the connection?" Lewis asks.

"They have encryption tools hidden online," she says, as she drags over a small file from another tab. "I'm bringing one into the Watchtower's files."

She selects all the *control directories* and clicks enter. Pratt watches as the files once clearly labelled turn into a strange series of symbols, letters, and numbers.

"I'm converting the data into an unreadable format—basically making it gibberish. When they go to make changes on their side, it won't connect to anything here, because it's scrambled." She opens another text box and types in a series of commands. "I'm also setting up encryption, ensuring no one can unlock the data."

"Like a digital lock?" Lewis asks.

"Exactly." Series looks back at him and nods.

"How long will it hold?" Pratt asks.

"I'm not sure," Serie shakes her head. "But it will buy us a little time. They might even need to come down to Krevax to fix it."

"Wow!" Lewis exclaims.

"Are you ready for step two?" Serie grins at Pratt.

"What's step two?" Pratt asks excitedly. Serie clicks the enter button and all the advertisements turn bright sky blue.

"Ooh!" the room says in awe as they stare out at the man-made sky. Serie stands victoriously and bows.

"Easy-peasy!" she says. Pratt laughs and pulls her into a hug. Serie giggles, hugging him back.

"Yes!" Robin shouts. "We did it! The Watchtower's ours!"

The group erupts in cheers. Greene stares at all of them with an anxious expression.

"You should really try nostaliem." Robin smiles at him.

"I'm thinking about it," Greene says, nodding. Serie and Pratt grin at their exchange.

"We did it!" Pratt cheers.

"We?" Serie elbows him in the side, laughing. "Pratt, you did this!"

"I couldn't have done it without you," he says, beaming.

"True, but no one else would have been crazy enough to go into those tunnels." She hugs him again as Pratt wipes away a tear.

"Thanks, little sister," he says.

"No way!" Serie shakes her head. "I should be your twin at least!"

"Fine." He nods. "Thanks twin-ster."

"No problem, baby brother," she says, grinning, and Pratt playfully shoves her shoulder.

72 | FAMILY
TINIK

A LOUD ENGINE REVS, AND TINIK SLOWLY OPENS HER EYES, expecting to see the sleeping quarters. In front of her, a road is awakening with the city. Where am I?

The concrete buildings in the Education district stand severely around her. Suddenly remembering the events of the day before, she looks down at where Joey was sleeping in her arms. Leaning close, she kisses his cheek and his eyes flutter open.

"It's blue!" he exclaims, staring up. Tinik looks up and jumps in surprise. Above her, all the advertisements are a bright blue.

"Blackwell, wake up!" Reaching over, she shakes his shoulder, and he stretches with a grunt.

"Whoa!" he exclaims. "I wasn't expecting blue." Tinik and Joey both laugh.

"Why is it blue?" Joey asks.

"It's blue because Krevaxers control the Watchtower," Tinik says, hugging him. "Its pretty isn't." He giggles and wraps his arms around her neck.

"Is that why we had those dreams?"

"Yes," Tinik says.

"I saw you," Joey whispers.

"You did?"

"I was kicking you a lot, which you didn't like," he says, beaming. "Then one night I stopped kicking, and you got scared. You wished I would kick you, so you would know I was okay, and then you were so happy when I started kicking again."

"I remember that," Tinik whispers. "Did you see anything else?" She pulls him into a tighter hug as Joey nods.

"I saw you watch me get taken away." He nestles his head into her shoulder. "You were very sad." She kisses the top of his head.

"I'm so happy I have you back," Tinik says, helping him stand.

Beside her, Blackwell holds out his hand to help her stand. They walk together to the school door and she tries the handle. It turns easily, and she pushes the door open.

Taking a tentative step forward, Joey and Blackwell follow her into a hallway and down a set of stairs. Below there are several doors, each with the noise of younkins behind them.

Pushing open the first door, she peers in at the room of young boys sitting at desks. The teacher doesn't notice, as he's distracted reading out loud from a history book. Stepping a foot in, she examines all their faces, but none of them are Leo's. She steps back out into the hallway and quietly shuts the door, giving Blackwell a fearful look.

Behind the next one, they can hear the voices of boys singing in a choir. Pushing open the door slightly, she scans the faces. None of them are Leo and so she closes the door again. A feeling of desperation builds in her chest. What if something happened to him?

She walks a few steps forward and opens this door. In this room, the boys are learning about addition and subtraction. Mr. Vahn is standing at the front, writing with chalk on the blackboard. Leo is looking up from the second row.

She takes a step towards her son and says, "Leo."

He looks over at her with the same round eyes as hers. Tinik took a deep breath, holding back her tears.

"I'm sorry," she says. "I know you don't remember me."

"Excuse me, boy, you can't be in here." Mr. Vahn takes a step towards Tinik.

"Leo is my son, and I'll be taking him with me."

"What do you mean he's your son?" He stares at her.

"Leo, I'm your mom." Tinik reaches out, and he stands, still looking confused, but takes a small step towards her.

"What are you talking about?" Mr. Vahn walks in between them.

"Nostaliem showed me."

"Nostaliem showed you?" He shakes his head.

"Have you taken it?"

"No," he says, but then looks down at the ground, thinking. "I know people who have, though," he whispers.

"Do you believe what they say?" Tinik looks up at him pleadingly.

He stares at her for a moment and then steps aside. Joey runs into the room and whispers something to Leo, which makes them both giggle. Joey grabs his hand and they walk to the door where Tinik is standing. She touches Leo's face, and he flashes a nervous smile.

"Where will you take him?" Mr. Vahn asks.

"Somewhere he'll be safe," Tinik says.

"More will come for their younkins." Blackwell steps forward. "Krevax is changing."

"Changing?" Mr. Vahn says.

"It already has," Tinik says. "Have you seen the advertisements?"

"No."

"Go look," Blackwell says, "we'll wait."

The teacher stares at them a minute, but then steps out of the room and runs up the stairs. After a moment, he is back.

"They're blue!" he says, laughing.

"I have another younkin, younger," Tinik half-shouts.

"Her name is Everly. Do you know where she is?" Tinik asks, her heart beating fast in her chest.

"No," he says. "I only teach the boys." She exhales slowly, feeling uneasy. How will I find her?

"The peons might know." Mr. Vahn walks past her into the hallway and disappears into another room. Tinik holds her breath, waiting for him to return.

"Are you actually my mother?" Leo asks, staring up at her.

"I am," she says, smiling, "and Joey is your brother."

"That's what he told me," Leo says. "Except he said that he'd seen me before and that he knew we were brothers because his favourite snack was also apple-rhubarb paste mixed with french fry paste."

Tinik smiles at both her sons. Mr. Vahn walks back into the room, two peons standing on either side of him.

"You're looking for a girl called Everly?" one of them asks.

"Yes." Tinik inhales sharply. "Do you know her?"

"We don't, but we can take you to the building where you might find her," she says. "How old is she?"

"Eighteen months." The peons look at each other, whispering a moment, and then nod, having come to a decision.

"This way." They wave her forward, walking back through the hallway to a set of stairs that descend into the hidden tunnels of the Education District.

All four of them follow the peons through dark winding

corridors, past many doors, until they reach a staircase labelled *Year Ones*. The peons lead them up and then stop outside the metal doors.

"Wait here. We'll need to explain."

"What will you say?" Tinik asks nervously. The peons turn to look at her, clearly smiling behind their masks.

"You're not the only one who's learned something from nostaliem," one says cheerfully, and then they both turn and walk through the doors. Tinik shakes her hands out.

"What if she's not there?" she asks Blackwell.

"She's there," he says, nodding and then reaches for her hand to comfort her.

"Who's there?" Leo asks. Glancing down, she smiles, seeing Leo and Joey are holding hands.

"It's your sister," Tinik says, staring back at the doors.

"How many of us are there?" Leo shouts.

Laughing, Tinik looks back over at him and says, "just you three."

He nods, seemingly comfortable with this answer. The doors open and the two peons re-emerge. Behind them, a third peon walks out carrying a little girl with dark curls, round brown eyes and chubby cheeks.

Covering her face and crying, Tinik takes a breath. It's Everly! It's my baby. She leaps towards her daughter and pulls her into her arms. Everly looks at her with a startled expression, but then settles seeing Tinik's smile. She kisses her on one chubby cheek. I found you!

"How are you, baby girl?" Tinik coos.

Everly smiles up at her with a nearly toothless grin. "I'm your mama. I missed you so much."

Breathing in a heavy chestful of air, she looks at her three younkin's beautiful faces. I have all my babies.

"I missed you all so much." She kisses Everly's small

hands. The three peons stand beside the doors, watching quietly.

Tinik kneels beside her two boys. "Leo, Joey, this is your sister Everly."

"Are we staying together?" Leo asks.

"Yes," Tinik says. Leo and Joey both laugh gleefully as Everly puts her hand in her mouth, drool pooling down her chin.

"Leo, Everly, this is Blackwell." He crouches down beside them and smiles.

"Is he staying with us, too?" Leo asks. Tinik looks over at Blackwell, waiting for his response.

"Of course," Blackwell says, his voice breaking.

She stares into his eyes, feeling real love for him. He leans in and they softly kiss. They stand and embrace in a hug.

Everly wipes a slobbery hand on Blackwell's green sequin shirt and he laughs. Joey giggles and hugs Tinik's leg. Leo smiles up nervously as he clasps Joey's hand. Tinik turns to look over at the peons.

They nod and lead them to the entrance of the school, where they walk out into the bright blue day.

Leo looks up at the sky and jumps excitedly. Blackwell and Tinik stare at each other, tears in their eyes.

73 | RALLY 'ROUND THE FLAG
PRESIDENT LEHAN

Leaning back in his emerald green chair with gold trim, President Lehan smirks as he watches his call for war on the screen. At the end of the speech, he clicks off the TV and picks up a report on his faltering popularity, twisting it into a crumpled stick.

Ring.

Ring. Lehan picks up the telephone as he drops the report into the wastebasket beside his desk.

"Yes."

"President Lehan, General Bouchard is on the line for you."

"Patch him through."

"President Lehan, I've taken care of General Carr's body." Bouchard nervously chirps. *"I've also written the report fabricating the terror attack on the lab. What would you like me to do next?"*

"Sit tight for now," Lehan says. "When the Orbinian Military takes back control of Krevax, you will be our Tzar."

"Thank you, sir!" Bouchard exclaims.

With a self-satisfied grin, he hangs up the phone. A war is exactly what I need to boost my numbers. Standing confidently, he walks out into the hallway where his assistant is working.

"Toby, are the majors in the War Room?"

"Yes, sir," Toby says, nodding repeatedly. *"They've been briefed and are awaiting further instruction."*

"Excellent," Lehan says, and then walks down the hall to a bathroom with floor to ceiling mirrors.

Turning on the tap, he splashes his face with cold water and then pats dry with a white cotton cloth. Slowly looking up, he stares at himself in the mirror. *This is my moment. I will be written about in history books for the decisions I make today.*

After adjusting his suit, he walks back into the hallway and turns towards the War Room. He throws open the doors and sits down at the head of a golden oval table with six men staring up at him in carved wooden chairs.

"The Watchtower in Krevax has been infiltrated," Lehan says, leaning forward. "Three districts have been exposed to nostaliem."

"Can we gas them?" a tall man with angry eyes pounds his fist on the table.

"No, Major Moore, they control the Watchtower, which means they control the vents," Lehan states. "We send soldiers to take back control."

"How many?" Moore asks.

Lehan smiles. "What do you think, Major Silva?" He directs his question to a man with mousy brown hair. "You're the head of our military operations."

The group silently looks over at Silva.

"It could be done with 40,000," Silva says. "10,000 for each compromised district and 10,000 for the Watchtower."

"Send them in," Lehan commands.

"It will be done."

"We need to remember, foremost, this is a propaganda

war. We need Orbinians to be truly terrified of an imminent terrorist attack. There cannot be one hint of truth to be sniffed out in our presentation of this news. We need an entire media team shooting convincing footage to shove the moon threat in the faces of the public. We want them looking anywhere but at Krevax. Yes, we may face protein rations, but there will always be a 'terrorist' to blame. As for what's really happening in Krevax, we will beat them back with our superior technology and minds."

The men at the table clap and Lehan stands to leave. As he opens the door, he glances back, grinning.

"Remember men, make me look good."

GLOSSARY

BLACK STRIPE

Men who wear the white mask with a black stripe are being punished for exhibiting feminine behaviour, such as crying, or exhibiting attraction to the same sex. Those who have been accused of the latter are also castrated.

BLUE FUNGUS

The tunnels outside of Krevax connect to a vast system of caves. Fifty years before Toronto fell and Krevax was created below it, the tunnels became home to people escaping the violence of the city in the early days of the dust storms.

Blue fungus is an edible plant that is high in protein and rich in amino acids. At first it only grew in the deepest part of the caves, near fresh water sources, but the people began cultivating the plant, to make it more drought resistant, and now the fungus survives throughout the cave system.

The planting of blue fungus also led to the discovery of nostaliem, as the plant grew strongest near the edges of the black powder, but could not grow on the substance itself. Once nostaliem's effects were realized, the area with the highest concentration, once called Sault Ste Marie, became sacred and permanent communities were built around it.

This led to a new cultural identity, known as the Oqakwanwe. The use of nostaliem also led to the creation of the Okwanan language. Nostaliem shared stories of words from all of their collective ancestors, which were adopted into a single dialect. It also led to a belief system that saw energy as connecting all living beings and viewed nostaliem as mother nature's ashes.

According to the Oqakwanwe, mother nature retreated to the Great Lakes and then perished. The Oqakwanwe see their purpose as helping her be reborn onto the surface of the earth. Blue fungus is also used to make an essential fabric that is weaved with beads and tells the story of each individual's life.

CRIME

In Krevax violence is generally accepted. Gang members killing each other is considered a social good, and is not investigated.

Violence against a government official, corporate leader or red stripe can result in an investigation, but this is rare. Females who have been killed are not considered to be murdered, as they are not human under Krevax Law.

Punishment is dependent on the worth of the female. Dead peons result in a public nuisance fee, dead doxies can result in court cases, as the brothel will push for compensation for the financial loss, and a dead generator can result in one being recycled, especially if the generator was pregnant with a male.

CUPSAWAGS

A sweet confection made up of artificial pineapple paste, artificial vanilla paste, corn flour, and soaked in vodka. Only available in the lower districts, as corn grown in the farming district is strictly monitored. Corn must be traded for cigarettes or booze, directly with a farmer. Cupsawags are typically had by the lower castes to celebrate a younkin's district assignment.

FEMALES

In Krevax females are considered animals and do not have the same rights as men. This is taught in classes that boys and girls take separately in the Education District, ensuring the system of subjugation will continue with the next generation.

Girls are categorized by appearance which results in division, as they are taught to solely focus on attractiveness and pleasing others to survive.

At age nine those labelled the least attractive are placed on the peon track, they remain in the Education District until they can be bought at age 15. Those deemed sexually attractive are sterilized and moved into the Entertainment District at age nine, where they pour drinks, and light cigarettes until they have mastered the art of singing, and dancing, and reach the age of 15.

Females with prized features are sent to the Generation District at age nine, where they are taught how to sew, tend to births and care for newborns, until age 15. Prized features are always changing depending on who is the wealthiest among the men, as they are considered to be the holiest, and thus have the most privilege.

Markers of appearance related to wealthy men become

prized as other men pick generators with similar features, hoping their offspring will be among the privileged in society.

GLASS AND ROCHAODIL

Drugs made from harsh chemicals that cause a short and intense euphoric high. These two are essentially the same substance, but glass is smoked, and rochaodil is injected.

Those who become addicted to these substances struggle with severe health issues and fall out of society. There is no support system in place to help addicts recover in Krevax, and they are essentially ignored unless they commit a crime.

GREEN

An affirmative response with several meanings, similar to saying 'yes,' 'understood,' 'correct,' 'wealthy,' 'holy,' 'pure,' or 'great,' changes due to context. Slang that developed due to the nature of green being holy, and representing success in Krevax.

GREEN ARROW

This function is what is left of the Internet. It is 90 percent advertisements. A great purge took place at the dawn of the creation of Krevax. All existing pages have been created by the government, and chat boards are constantly monitored.

Anonymity no longer exists, as each move is recorded by the tracker data. A secret back internet created by hackers does exist, but it is not well known, or easy to access.

KIKITS

Refers to any get together in the lower districts where alcohol or drugs will be available, but they usually happen in the Farming District as they controlled the crops. The Farming District had a unique sense of community that was hard to find anywhere else.

They worked together to tend the official crops, so that they could grow illicit goods, like coca for cocaine, and poppy for opium, without detection. Neighbourhood peons worked together helping tend crops hidden in the apartment buildings. It was a secret world, younkins born in the district knew to keep.

Once in the Education District they would hope to return, and if they did end up in another district, would still often visit. Garbage was hard to avoid in the lower districts, but here it was strategically heaped around the Watchtower, to give an impression of indifference, that would line up with the stereotype of the lower districts, and keep keen eyes from prying.

Perhaps it was the fear of disgust, or indifference to crime among lower castes, but red stripes, who were out in force in the Manufacturing district, rarely made it past the smell in the Purification District.

KREVAXER RACISM

Culture in the Government District was dead, replaced by capitalist goods. Here men flaunted logos on their collars to show off their "personality," while mocking the cultural distinctions of the lower districts.

They embraced their own emptiness, not realizing that their true background and belief systems had been taken from their ancestors so long ago, that they had now become part of the machinery that had led the destruction.

They feel this emptiness, but are unable to identify or understand the source of their pain, so instead cling to their racist beliefs to justify the power imbalance.

LICE ON TICKS

A swear in Krevax about the rampant insect infestations, refers to more than one bad thing happening at once. Variants include 'lice-fleas-lice,' 'lice on ticks on fleas,' and 'tick-a-lice.'

METAL-POINTED TEETH

A sign of high rank for men in the Orbs. The pointier the teeth, the higher the role, and the more power and knowledge one has access too. Women in the Orbs always have rounded teeth, and are not allowed past level-five.

Around 65 per cent of men are level-six and do not have pointed teeth. The other 35 percent of men have varying degrees of pointed teeth, with 5 percent reaching the status of level-ten.

Ironically, level nine and ten have issues with eating their food, as their teeth are sensitive due to the aggressive filing.

N!ÀNG

Corresponds to 'eland' (a type of antelope) or 'the eland' or 'an eland,' from the Jul'hoan language.

n! - This represents a click sound.

àng - The rest of the word follows the click and includes tonal markings, indicating the pronunciation involves a specific pitch or tone.

n!haì - Corresponds to 'lion' or 'the lion' or 'a lion, from the Jul'hoan language.

haì - The rest of the word follows the click.

NERUMOO

A term used for a younger male in the lower districts. Specifically refers to a younkin who is a risk taker, but is too young to understand the consequences of their behaviour.

OD12 PASSENGER DRONE

Is an unmanned vessel designed for maximum stealth, gliding silently through the sky on advanced electric propulsion. Like a dragonfly, it can move in any direction, with its engines seamlessly integrated into its aerodynamic wings.

The drone features a passenger bubble that can carry up to six people, while heavy ammunition is mounted beneath, ready to engage any identified target. Its nanomaterial exterior makes it nearly invisible to radar, while small screens project real-time surroundings, rendering it invisible to the naked eye.

Advanced sensors provide unparalleled navigation through dust, storms, or darkness, guided by built-in AI and GPS.

OKWANAN

Abrax, **Dahhaak** and **Heloise** are ancestral names of the Oqakwanwe. They are names derived from Ancient Egyptian, Arabic, and French.

AL-AQRAB

The Arabic word for scorpion is al-aqrab. The Oqakwanwe hunt the Al-Aqrab (giant scorpions) for meat and use their exoskeleton to make masks with. Although the Al-Aqrab are an important protein source, it is small shrimps and insects that are more reliable and regularly eaten. The origin of the Al-Aqrab is unknown, but it is believed they were an undiscovered species due to the deep caves they reside in.

KIPANNIQ

The Inuktitut word kipanniq can be translated as: follow. The word Inuktitut can be broken down into the words inuk, meaning 'person,' and titut, meaning 'in the manner of.'

MANIDOO

The Anishinaabemowin word, 'manidoo' can be translated as 'spirit' or 'god,' but the concept goes beyond these English words, encompassing a spiritual force present in all things.

O KEIA

The Hawaiian words o keia can be translated as: this, this one. It is usually a part of a larger sentence, ie: "o keia kumu" could mean 'this teacher.'

SGIOBALTA

The Gàidhlig word sgiobalta can be translated as: 1. neat, tidy, trim, 2. active, 3. agile, nimble, slick, 4. Quick.

Y ATRAK

The Hindi word 'yatrak' can be translated as: journey, travel.

YACHAY

The Quechua word, 'yachay' can be translated as 'learning' or 'knowledge,' it often implies experiential and practical learning gained through direct experience.

WĂNG WÀI ZŎU

The Mandarin words wǎng wài zǒu can be translated as: walk out. Mandarin has four tones, which when pronounced change their definition.

PENNYROYAL

Historically, Pennyroyal has been used to stimulate menstruation in lower doses, or as a way to induce abortion in higher concentrations. Twenty-two is forced to drink a concoction of pennyroyal boiled in red wine with a single drop of tea tree oil.

The abortifacient, which has been in use for over 2,000 years, has no set dose and can be toxic, causing severe liver damage and death.

POWER DISTRICT

It was very rare to see a peon, as most were hidden in the underground brothel system until old age. Although the peons lived longer here, it was a challenging life filled with men who would pay by the hour, rather than waste credits on a doxy.

The underground brothel system, which was used by the entire lower district, made some men in the Power District extremely wealthy and even led to the creation of the Zorax gang. The men here are permanently covered in a layer of grease and dust, their faces wrinkled from frowning.

They wear hard hats and overalls, and use drugs to stay awake on long nights shifts. They didn't have time for learning or community, but instead lived in the worlds of the televised story, watching cartoon characters face silly shenanigans on their trackers while they fall asleep. Their lives felt long, with few moments of reprieve.

Sadly, one of the things those in the district looked most forward to, other than their time in the Generation District, was the changing over of the advertisements. They had to save up for the cheap gadgets displayed on the ceiling, but it provided a brief distraction from their stark reality.

RECYCLER

The wealthiest recyclers ran the recycling facility. Although they were given a small income for their work, the real credits came from stealing the items off the wealthy before it could be dumped in the landfills. For this reason they were despised in the district, and usually met violent deaths.

An unnerving presence in the district was Orbinians who worked in the recycling facility, they sometimes ventured out, disguised as Krevaxers, but recyclers always knew the truth. They would disappear early in the day, probably to go to the Entertainment District, and return before the evening, drunk and giggling. Many recyclers would wait for their return, to beg them for treats or small plastic toys that they would happily throw from their limos.

The strangest part of the Recycling District is that every year it changed shape, the garbage heaped made the ceiling close in, and to compensate men excavated the base wider, moving earth by hand. This led to the discovery of many tunnels, which led out of Krevax to empty caverns of the past, routes regularly used by the gangs to move drugs, or for clandestine meetings.

Recyclers sometimes chose to walk out into these caverns, never to return. These walkers have sometimes been lucky enough to come across the Oqakwanwe people, and have been welcomed into their community.

RED STRIPES

Red stripes fear no consequences, as they are tools of oppression used to protect the wealthy and control everyone else. They live in the Enforcement District, which is considered the top of the middle caste, and for that reason retain some of the privileges of the upper districts, such as filtered air and higher credit incomes.

In the Enforcement District red stripes enter the panopticon and descend, or ascend to a position within the Watchtower, which extends from the base of the Recycling District to the top of the Government District.

Outside the Enforcement District, the Watchtower is an impenetrable fortress. In Krevax one feels they are always being watched, even if they are not, the mere presence of the Watchtower is enough to create a self-policing population.

SHAXOCS CALLERS

There is only one religion in Krevax, Shaxoism. In Shaxoism, Shaxocs Callers teach followers that faith and stoicism will ensure a higher position in their next life. The *Book of Infinitum* describes the holy laws and practices of Shaxoism.

A core belief is that green is the holiest colour. To be

green is to be wealthy, those with wealth have the strongest karma. They are successful because of a holy birthright due to their strong faith in the previous life. Those in the lower castes are assumed to be villainous in the last life, and deserving of their poor fate for being weak and emotional.

Shaxocs Callers live in the Devotion District, one of only two districts where peons do not reside; here it is because cleanliness is linked to holiness and men clean as part of a holy embodiment.

Although they do not visit doxies, or use the services of peons, it is still considered honourable to procreate. Younkins born in the hoy district are there until age 5 and most eventually take their place among the Shaxocs as adults.

It has long been rumoured that younkins suffered in the district without the distractions of doxies and peons, but no one intervenes, for the word of the womb was behind the Shaxocs, and to challenge them was to risk your place in the next life.

The pools in the district are unlike any other place in Krevax, here recyclers can rub elbows with lawmakers, as everyone is simply a child of Mary, naked in the waters, their identity erased.

SPIDER

A name for a criminal who is sneaky and difficult to catch. You never see them, but you know from the bite marks that they were there. Krevax has very few bug species. Spiders are not one of them.

Cockroaches are the most constant bug presence, and can be bought deep fried and spiced on sticks in the lower districts.

Ants can sometimes be found at the edges of the upper

districts. Lice, fleas, and ticks contaminate every district, but are especially prevalent in the Recycling District.

TOBACCO

In the University District, tobacco is an open secret. The wealthy crave it for pleasure, while the religious seek it for communion with Mary. Hidden passageways between the University and Devotion districts house tobacco farms under heat lamps, tended by peons who live long, concealed lives behind books and speakeasies.

TRIANGLE

In Krevax, the triangle symbolizes social hierarchy. On the ceiling of the University District, a golden triangle is painted, with men at the top point, generators representing the womb within its space, and peons and doxies forming the two bottom points.

TRACKERS

Trackers are removed from the dead because their alarms will go off when their bodies cool to a lower temperature. The trackers are then cleared of data, sent for cleaning, and recycled back into the population. Trackers are inserted into the arms of all Krevaxers at age five.

TURNCOAT

Refers to someone who is a 'gender traitor,' as Krevaxers are taught having sexual desires for men is wrong, and that it is the duty of men to procreate to ensure a steady population in the city. Love is considered a threat in Krevax. In the

University District, the quote, "Love is Weakness," sits in gold letters above the Grand Central Library. The belief is ubiquitous, and has been turned into a political force through written law and red stripe violence.

In Krevax, love is a flaw in humans, a danger that must be avoided at all costs. The relationship between men and females is strictly transactional, and thus controlled, so it is love outside of these spaces that becomes a threat to the system, and is targeted with propaganda.

Love between female partners is considered to not exist, because females are not considered fully human, so propaganda solely targets love between male partners. However, sex between doxies does openly exist in Krevax, and is viewed as a form of entertainment.

YOUNKINS

Boys in Krevax from the age of one to 14. Younkins are raised in the districts of their paternal caste until age five. From five to 14 they attend school in the Education District.

At age 15, they are assigned a professional role and moved to a permanent caste. Young females are also referred to as younkins colloquially, but are considered subhuman and do not have the same rights as actual younkins.

ABOUT THE AUTHOR

© L. C. Walters

L. C. Walters holds a communications diploma and a degree in media arts. During her university years, she developed a deep passion for art history, a field that now informs her writing by providing a historical context for human experiences and a broader perspective on the complexities of identity and society.

Her work, largely rooted in science fiction, delves into the darker aspects of civilization, exploring the tensions between individual identity and societal constraints. L. C. Walters is particularly interested in contemporary myths and the ways in which they shape our understanding within society. With a belief in the capacity for empathy within us all, she seeks to reveal the depths of each person's experience, unflinching in her portrayal of both the light and shadow within humanity.

instagram.com/thelizzyyzzil